SHE'S MINE

J.M. ROBINSON

She's Mine
Copyright © 2015 by J.M. Robinson. All rights reserved.
First Print Edition: January 2016

Editor: Donna
Cover and Formatting: Streetlight Graphics

ISBN- 13: 978-1523302567
ISBN- 10: 1523302569

ACKNOWLEDGEMENTS

I would like to thank the following people for all of the support given to me in writing this book. First of all, I want to thank Donna for all of her help with editing, suggestions and overall support. Donna, you have missed your calling. You should have been a publishing agent. Everything you have suggested I do was spot on! I would also like to thank two of my dearest friends Marci and Susie. I really appreciated your advice and your very good constructive criticisms. Marci, it made me feel very good when you told me you could see this book becoming a movie. Susie, you have listened to me for hours over the past 8 months discussing my book characters and have been extremely supportive. Without your friendships and support, I might not have finished my book. I would also like to thank my friends Jolene and Kenny, David and Mary, Robert, Beatrice and my sister-in-law Pam for all the support and wisdom into some of my characters. A special thank you goes to Streetlight Graphics for the amazing book cover and formatting of this book. Your company came highly recommended and your expertise has made the final aspects of publishing much easier for me. I want to give a big thank you to my husband, Danny, for his encouragement in writing my book and to my children. I love you all!

CHAPTER 1

ANNIE

July 3rd

"HELP! SOMEONE PLEASE, HELP ME!" Annie screamed. She was running as fast as her legs would carry her. "Help, please, someone help! He's going to kill me! Please, help!" she screamed. She stopped long enough to catch her breath. Beads of sweat were rolling off of her face. Her breathing was rapid and her heart felt like it was going to pound out of her chest. She was extremely parched. She looked all around, but she didn't see anyone. "Oh my God! Where am I?" she cried in fear. She looked all around trying to find something that looked familiar.

Suddenly, cold chills ran down her arms. She knew that feeling all too well. Someone was watching her. She heard footsteps running towards her. She looked frantically all around, but saw no one. Annie screamed, "Who are you? Why are you stalking me? Leave me alone! Help, someone, please!" She started running again. The footsteps were sounding faster and they were getting closer! She stopped to look around again. There in the distance, she saw a dark-figured silhouette running towards her. She finally realized where she was. She was standing in the parking lot of her apartment complex. She ran into her apartment building, unlocked her door, ran inside and quickly secured the deadbolt and chain just as the dark-figured silhouette opened the door to her apartment building. Just as she reached for her cell phone to call 911, her radio alarm sounded.

Annie sat straight up in her bed. Her heart was pounding rapidly in her chest. She felt drained and her body felt clammy. After looking all around in her room, she realized she was safe in her bed in her apartment. She shook her head. "God in Heaven! What a nightmare!"

Annie jumped out of bed. "That's odd," she thought to herself. "Why is my bedroom door shut? I don't remember shutting my door." She yawned. She had decided she needed to make some coffee... a whole pot of coffee!

After opening the living room window curtains, she walked into her kitchen to make a pot of coffee and noticed the coffee can was not in the cabinet over top of the coffee pot where she kept it. She had purchased a brand new can yesterday evening.

"Where in the world did I put it?" she thought as she started looking in all of the cabinets. "This is not like me to put something away in a different place. Am I losing my mind? I know that is where I put it last night!"

"I really do need some coffee, but there is no way I will go to the Campus Coffee House!" she stated out loud. She knew their coffee really sucked and besides, she couldn't stand the owner, David Morgan. Her thoughts took her back to a time when she went out on a date with him. He was in his third year of college at Columbus Music Academy and was one of the cutest guys around. She was just in her first year. Then something happened and she hasn't wanted to think of him since. David had tried to rape her while on their second date and she thinks he has been stalking her for the past six years. Suddenly, she got a cold chill and rubbed her arms.

"Maybe I forgot to purchase the coffee yesterday. I wonder what I did with my grocery receipt," she said out loud, trying to get thoughts of David Morgan out of her head. She was thirsty, so before she hunted for the receipt, she went to the refrigerator to get some juice. She opened the refrigerator and there in front of her was the can of coffee that she had purchased. She gasped, "This just doesn't make sense to me. I have never put coffee in my refrigerator!"

She took the can of coffee over to the coffee

pot and placed it on the counter. She removed the lid and immediately let out another gasp! The can was open! Another horrible chill went through her body. "Has someone been in my apartment?" she thought as she looked around in her kitchen, living room combination. She tried to get that thought out of her mind. "Stop it, Annie," she said out loud. "Maybe I bought it like that at the grocery store."

She decided to check the coffee filter in the coffee pot. She always threw away the used filter of coffee and rinsed the filter holder out right after making a fresh pot. It was a habit her mother had taught her. Why she always did that, she didn't know, but she had picked up many of her mother's cleaning habits. Her fingers trembled as she raised the lid to the reservoir. She jumped back and let out another gasp. Someone has been in my apartment! She looked in the sink where a lone cup sat that had not been there last night when she went to bed. "OH, MY GOD!"

Scared out of her mind, she quickly looked everywhere in her apartment for anything else that may have been out of place... or God forbid, someone in her apartment. Then she noticed the entrance door to her apartment. The door was unlocked and the chain was not attached. She was positive she had locked the door and hooked the chain before going to bed. Her only conclusion was that someone had to have been in her apartment when she had come home last evening from grocery shopping and must have hidden when she came in the door.

"God, what do I do? I need to think a minute!" She started pacing the floor back and forth. Just then her cell phone rang.

CHAPTER 2

QUINN

IT WAS 7:15 A.M. WHEN Quinn's cell phone rang, waking him up from a deep sleep. He had just fallen asleep an hour earlier, even though he had gone to bed around 2 a.m. Quinn hadn't had a decent night's sleep in 11 years. Either he couldn't fall asleep, or his nights were very restless, dreaming about war zones or the woman he still loved that dumped him 11 years ago. He picked up his phone after three rings to see who it was. It was Kevin Thompson, owner of Thompson Construction in Atlanta, Georgia. Quinn had hired Kevin to build another La Seals nightclub located next to another one of Quinn's "Taylor Suites Hotels."

He thought about letting it go to voicemail, but decided against it. He needed for the construction to remain on schedule as much as possible.

"Damn it, Kevin, don't you know what time it is? For heaven's sake, birds aren't up this early!"

Quinn complained as he was sitting up on the edge of his bed. "Yes, Kevin, I'm awake. What's going on that you have to call me so damn early?"

Quinn listened to what Kevin was telling him. "Okay," Quinn replied, "here is what I want you to do. I want you to call that S.O.B. and tell him I do not want substandard materials used in this club. I don't care what it costs him. I made it very clear that he had to use the best materials before he made his bid. I will not mess around when it comes to electrical needs. A contract is a contract. He will honor it or I will see to it that no one hires him again. You tell him I said that! I DO NOT want corners cut just to save him money. This building must be built to my exact specifications. If you have any trouble with him, call me back and I will set him straight! You got that, Kevin?"

Quinn hung up his cell phone and tossed it onto his bed. He stretched his arms upwards and yawned. He grabbed a remote, pressed a button, and the window curtains began opening. The Columbus skyline was beautiful. There wasn't a cloud anywhere. Off in the background in the western sky, he saw a jet airliner starting to slow its descent heading for the airport. The city was just waking up. He saw traffic moving on the streets below, and some of the cars were turning into the garage at Taylor Suites. A convention, plus two different wedding receptions, had been booked at his hotel. There were no vacancies, as all of the rooms had been reserved. Columbus was hosting "Red, White and Boom" that weekend in honor of Independence Day, so he knew that the next few days would be very busy and hopefully very profitable.

Quinn headed for the bathroom. After taking care of his bathroom needs, he slipped on his running clothes and placed a small towel in the waistband of his shorts. After exiting the hotel, he stretched his legs and took off jogging, then into an easy run, steadying his pace. He liked to run a total of five miles.

It was nearly 9:30 a.m. when he returned. He was very hot and sweaty. Quinn walked into the hotel kitchen and grabbed a bottle of water from one of the refrigerated walk-ins. The cold air felt wonderful.

He heard his head chef, Eula Stewart, yelling at him to get out of her walk-in, spouting something about "catching a cold." He respected her a great deal.

Eula was hired as a sous chef when the hotel first opened many years ago and had worked herself up to head chef. During that time she had prepared many dishes for Quinn and his family. She was an amazing chef and Quinn knew it would not be long before she retired.

He walked over and gave her a big sweaty hug. She pushed herself away from him. Several female employees were standing around watching him as he flexed his arms and chest muscles on purpose in front of Eula. Quinn knew the ladies were swooning and he knew it pissed off Eula.

She grabbed the towel hanging from his shorts and flipped him with it and yelled, "Get out of my kitchen! Go on! Get! You man whore! My girls ain't gonna be worth two cents now after looking at you and those sweaty muscles! Go on! Get!" she laughed as she swatted him with the towel again.

Quinn grabbed the towel back from her and blew her a kiss. "Bye, Eula," he said laughingly as he passed her female employees. "You know you love me, Eula!" She was the only employee he could not intimidate. She wasn't afraid of him and he liked that about her.

As soon as Quinn arrived back into his penthouse suite, he headed out onto the rooftop to a private terrace. The terrace had a lap-style swimming pool.

He took his tank top off, then his socks and shoes and dove into the pool and immediately started swimming. He liked to swim at least 50 laps every morning after he ran, all before breakfast. He was all muscle. Quinn attributed his strong muscle mass to his strenuous workout ethics he developed as a Seal. A couple of times a week, he liked to lift weights. At six-foot-six inches tall and 255 pounds, he looked like one lean, mean fighting machine.

After his swim, he heard his cell phone ping,

indicating he had two messages. He quickly toweled off and picked up his cell phone to read his texts. The first message was from Kevin, letting him know the electrical problem had been solved. The second message was from Dr. Carver's office at the VA, reminding him of his appointment at 2 p.m. today. He rolled his eyes. "Shit, I hate those appointments!"

Mrs. Davis, his private housekeeper had prepared breakfast. On the table sat a plate of scrambled eggs, bacon and buttered toast. A carafe of coffee, a small glass of orange juice and the local newspaper were sitting next to his plate. He poured himself a cup of coffee and added some creamer.

After he had eaten his breakfast, he picked up the newspaper. On the front page of the newspaper were photographs of six women who had been raped over the past year and a half. The authorities had not been able to catch this man. The police put the article in the newspaper to warn all women to travel in groups or in pairs. The article read that this rapist could be very dangerous. Even though the rapist had not killed any of the women, their fear was that it is just a matter of time.

As Quinn looked at the photographs of each woman, he noticed they all looked alike. They each had very long dark hair and light blue eyes. As he read on, the article mentioned that all six women were of college age, around five-foot-two inches tall and weighed approximately 110 pounds.

Quinn put the newspaper down and finished drinking his coffee. He wondered what made any man want to treat a woman in such a manner. "I hope they catch that son of a bitch!" he blurted out.

After he had finished eating his breakfast, Quinn jumped into the shower. He dressed in khaki dress pants and a white, button-down shirt. He had an appointment to get his oil changed in his Lexus at 12:30. Afterwards he would go to Dr. Carver's office.

Quinn had visited Dr. Carver's office twice a month for the past year for PTSD. The doctor had given him enough anti-depressants, anti-psychotics, and sleeping pills to last a lifetime; but Quinn refused to take them. He didn't like to take any kind of medication that "messed with the mind."

The old doctor was well educated in the effects of war and what it could do to our service men and women. He was very easy to talk with and Quinn didn't mind opening up to him on what he had seen as a Navy Seal. He had confided in him about all of the atrocities of U.S. military personel being killed, and the friends he had lost while serving. He didn't even mind talking about some of the enemy soldiers he had to kill. The doctor knew he had bad dreams, but Quinn refused to discuss them.

"Quinn," Dr. Carver asked. "Are you still having bad dreams?"

Quinn ran his hands through his hair. "Yes," he responded.

"Would you tell me about them?" asked the doctor.

Quinn got up from his chair and walked over to the window. He didn't look at anything in particular. "I don't think I am ready to talk about it yet," said Quinn as he put both hands into his pockets and stared out of the window.

The dreams that haunted Quinn were related to a "Dear John" letter he had received about a year into his enlistment in the Navy. He drank whiskey every night before going to bed, hoping it would help him sleep. Most nights he became very restless and moaned as he tossed and turned. His dreams were of Kayla holding a gun with a big bullet. The bullet was engraved. It read, "For Quinn." Then she aimed the gun at him and shot it into his heart. He couldn't get this dream out of his mind.

He had been engaged to Kayla McKinney for about two months when he had enlisted. He wanted to marry her before he left, but she was in no hurry. She said she wanted to graduate from college and med school before they married. He did not like it, but he accepted her answer. He knew she wanted to be a pediatrician and had years of schooling ahead of her. He loved her more than life itself, and there wasn't anything he wouldn't do for her. If he had to wait, then he would wait.

Quinn thought she was the most beautiful woman in the world. She was quite tall with a very curvaceous body, long blonde hair, perfect skin and brown eyes. However, she was a flirt. Quinn didn't mind what he thought was "harmless flirting" because he knew she really loved him, so he thought.

When he received the "Dear John" letter, he was crushed beyond words. He wanted to die. He was so angry and became consumed with hatred. He hated that he awakened everyday. He hated that every time a fellow comrade died from enemy fire that it wasn't him. He began hating and distrusting all women. And more importantly, he hated himself for being born. How could he have been so stupid to think Kayla truly loved him? After Kayla had dumped him, he felt like he didn't have anything to live for.

Truth be told, the "Dear John" letter had more of an impact on him than any atrocity of war. Losing Kayla may have turned him into the mean, fighting Navy Seal he became. When she dumped him, he lost his reason to love, so women became inconsequential to him except for one purpose and one purpose only. He wasn't ready to talk about it to Dr. Carver. The old doctor would have a field day with that.

Luckily, Dr. Carver's watch let out a ping indicating Quinn's time was up. He was glad his hour-long session was over. He left feeling no better, but definitely feeling no worse for keeping his appointment.

Quinn decided he was going to La Seals to talk with his friend and co-owner, Joe Turner. He had planned on spending the evening at "Dom's Emporium." Dom's was the place to go to have clean sex with a woman without all the hassles of a relationship. For some reason, he didn't feel in the mood to go anymore.

He parked his car in his parking spot at the hotel and went straight to the hotel dining room. He hadn't eaten since breakfast and he knew if he didn't eat before going to La Seals, alcohol would become his dinner. Alcohol with no food makes for a bad hangover.

CHAPTER 3

ANNIE

"HELLO, RILEY. HOW ARE YOU?" Annie said. "I'm fine," not wanting Riley to know she feared someone had been in her apartment. She paused to listen to what Riley was telling her. "Oh, that sounds like fun. Sure, what time do I need to be there? Okay, I will be there around 7:15 p.m. You know I have never been there before. What do I wear?" she asked. "Okay, something sexy and tight it is, that is if I have something like that in my closet," and she gave a nervous giggle as she was looking around her apartment. "Why don't you want me to drive?" she asked, then paused to listen. "No, you don't have to pick me up. I'll just take a cab. La Seals isn't that far from my place anyway." She paused. "Okay, I'll see you tonight. Bye."

She walked over and put the chain back on the door, but felt very nervous. "I wonder if Tony is home. Maybe he can come over and help me check all of the closets and under the bed." Her mind was running 90 miles a minute. She started to panic. "What if the intruder is still in my apartment?" All of a sudden, that weird feeling that she had often felt over the past several years made her shiver. She had never had this feeling inside her apartment—only when she was away from here. She felt like someone was watching her. It was creeping her out.

Tony O'Hara was her best friend and he lived just across the hall from her. Actually, he had been her only true friend over the past two years. He understood the problems that she had to endure, and even understood there wasn't much she could do about it as long as she wanted to attend Columbus Music Academy. He had, in a sense, become somewhat of a protector. She knew she would hate to lose Tony as a neighbor and friend when he returned home to Ireland in September.

Tony came to America to study music two years earlier. He was very talented with many musical instruments, but he favored the bagpipes. He was quite tall and was very handsome, and looked exceptionally cute when he dressed in his Irish kilt outfit. Irish men don't typically wear kilts, but for some reason, Americans like to see any person, male or female, dressed in a kilt when they played the bagpipes.

The ladies loved him, especially when he upped his charm and turned on a very heavy Irish brogue.

He usually worked a couple of nights a week at an Irish Pub located on the east side of Columbus, but liked to keep his weekends free. He made very good money playing his bagpipes at weddings, funerals, and parties.

When Tony opened his door, she explained to him her fears. He immediately came into her apartment and started looking around. She felt so much better when they determined that no one was in there, but she still could not shake the feeling that someone was watching her.

She offered Tony a cup of coffee. He liked her coffee so much better than the Campus Coffee House that he frequently went to daily. He often complained that CCH's coffee was "strong enough to grow hair on me chest and made a man out of ye!" Within a half an hour, Tony left. He had a few errands to run and he had to get ready for a wedding in the afternoon.

He hadn't been gone long when he knocked on her door. He handed her a spare key to his apartment and told her if she ever felt something was wrong to go into his apartment, lock the door behind her, and call 911. That was so sweet of him. She immediately put it on her key ring.

She fixed herself some cereal, but really didn't feel like eating so she threw it out after only eating half. The apartment wasn't messy as she had cleaned it fairly well the night before, but she did go in and make her bed. She didn't have to start getting ready to go to La Seals for at least another six hours.

She poured herself another cup of coffee and decided to read a book. She liked the real feel of a book, but lately she had been using a reading app on her tablet. She would like to go to the library to check out some books, but felt very uncomfortable when she left her apartment. She only went out when it was absolutely necessary. She feared her paranoia was making her a prisoner in her own place. She really didn't like that feeling.

She liked reading. Sometimes, she read way into the night because they were just too damn good to put down. Sometimes the books were sappy and way too steamy. Annie was a virgin and she dreamed that someday she would find a guy that would truly sweep her off her feet like some of the guys in the books she had read.

Four hours later, she had finished her book. She decided to prepare herself something to eat. She fixed herself a bowl of soup, a tuna sandwich, and a glass of iced tea. She ate it rather quickly admitting she was hungrier than she thought. She cleaned up the tiny little mess she had made then walked to her bedroom to choose the clothes she wanted to wear that evening.

She decided on a black sleeveless tight-fitting dress with a V-neck and a thin belt. It had a little bit of bling, but otherwise was very plain, but dressy enough to go clubbing. She found a matching purse and some black strappy heels to wear. She wished she had some stiletto heels instead, but resigned to herself that she probably couldn't walk in them anyway.

She hopped into the shower. Even though she knew no one was in her apartment, she still felt like someone was watching her. She thought to herself, "Maybe I should have called the police this morning and reported what I think is a break-in, but they would only laugh at me. After all, what would I tell them? Someone broke in and made a pot of coffee? It sounded silly even to me. Maybe I am just being paranoid. Anyway, going out with my cousins tonight would be a welcomed distraction."

Not being able to shake that awful feeling, she showered and toweled off quickly and slipped on a lightweight robe. After she applied her make up, she dried and fixed her hair into a knotted bun on the lower back of her head. Once she discarded her robe, she quickly put on her underwear. It was a sexy little bra and thong, as if anyone would see them, let alone take them off. "Hmm," she thought to herself, "I may as well wear granny panties the way my life has been going. I think I am destined to be an old maid." Slipping on her little black dress, she kept her jewelry to a minimum with fake diamond stud earrings and matching necklace. Looking at herself in the mirror, she lightly sprayed herself with some soft fragranced perfume, a birthday gift from her mother. This should do. Then she called the cab company. She was ready a few minutes earlier, and wanted to leave as soon as possible.

CHAPTER 4

QUINN

"HEY, BUDDY, I THOUGHT YOU were taking the night off to do something relaxing," said Joe.

"Well, you know I don't have a life, so this is as good as it gets," said Quinn with a smirk.

"Did you see Dr. Carver today?" Joe inquired.

"Yeah, but I don't think I'm going back. The doc says the same old shit over and over," said Quinn with a frown on his face.

"Really now. Let me just guess what he said. Hmm, that you are an idiot because you can't seem to move on?" said Joe, giving him a very irritated look. "Careful Joe, I'm not in the mood for your lip!"

It wasn't quite time for the club to open, so Joe sat two bottles of beers down at the end of the bar so they could talk a little more seriously.

Each took a long swig of their beers and sat

the bottles back down on the bar. "QT," asked Joe, "have you ever told your doctor about Kayla?"

After a long pause, Quinn looked at Joe and frowned. "No, I don't feel like talking about her to him."

"And why not?"

"What good would it do? He would probably just tell me the same shit that you keep preaching," Quinn said as he took another drink of his beer.

"Look Quinn," Joe said with a little more understanding. "I know what she did to you, and I know the pain you have felt all these years. Maybe you should talk to your doctor about her. He might be able to help you. I wish she had loved you just half as much as you loved her, then maybe you would not be going through all of this pain!"

Quinn stared down at his beer bottle, and he became very quiet. He knew Joe was right. He knew he should tell his doctor, but he couldn't make himself do it. Quinn felt like a failure when it came to relationships. He didn't know what he did wrong for Kayla to leave him. Admitting failure was not in the Taylor gene pool.

"Look Quinn," Joe continued, "you have got to find a way to move on. Eleven years is long enough to pine over the likes of her. You just need to start looking for a woman and settle down!"

"Damn it, Joe, do you think I haven't been looking?" he said as he slammed his beer bottle down on the bar. "I have dated several women over the years, but they are not right for me!"

Joe handed him another beer.

"Do you honestly think I like being alone? Going to parties with family and friends and me being the only single person there? Do you think I like the fact that I don't have any children of my own? I'm not getting any younger you know! Don't you think I would like to get married someday and start a family? I just haven't met anyone like"... and Quinn stopped talking, realizing what he had just said.

Joe looked at his old friend and took another drink of his beer, then slammed the bottle down on the bar and spoke rather harshly, "That's just what I thought. You have lowered your standards by looking for someone like Kayla. You have been comparing all women to the likes of her, haven't you? No wonder you are so miserable! Well, you need to understand something Quinn. There are better women out there than Kayla! But if you keep looking long enough and hard enough, I am sure you will find someone just like her and she will dump your sorry ass, too!"

Quinn looked at Joe with a sad look on his face. "Look, Joe, I know you mean well, but I just haven't met the right woman yet. I know most of the women that come in here and all they see me for is my money. I want someone who is going to want me for me, not my bank account. I want someone who can challenge me in ways I have never been challenged. I want a woman who can experience everything good in life that life has to give. She just isn't out there!"

"I hear you man, but you know, Quinn, you have got to quit comparing all women to her! Don't you understand she is consuming your life and messing with your head! Look my old friend, what has it been, 11 years since she sent you that damn "Dear John" letter? It's time you get over her. I just want you to have a wonderful life with someone you can love. You know, meeting my Cindy and falling in love with her was the best thing to have happened to me in my life. She has been my saving grace. I just want that for you, too, but you have to want that for yourself. Don't you see that?"

Quinn took another drink of his beer. He lowered his head and ran his right hand through his dark hair.

"You still going to Dom's?" Joe asked. Quinn nodded his head yes, and looked up at Joe. "Maybe you should quit going to those places. I doubt you'll find what you are looking for there." Joe looked at his watch. It was almost 7 p.m. "Duty calls," said Joe. "Time to go to work." He picked up the empty beer bottles and tossed them into the garbage can and yelled back at Quinn, "Maybe you need to work on your charming skills and get rid of that crummy dominant, controlling attitude you have!"

CHAPTER 5

ANNIE

THE CAB ARRIVED AT 7 p.m. Annie opened the curtains and turned on the small lamp setting in the middle of the large picture window in her living room. She didn't want to return to a dark apartment. She checked to make sure everything else was turned off. Grabbing her purse and keys, she locked the door behind her.

She arrived at the club at 7:15 p.m. and paid the driver. There was a very long line of people waiting to get in. She hadn't been out on an evening celebration in at least six years. Her cousins Riley and Emma wanted to take her out to celebrate getting her PhD in music education. Several other family members had graduated from college, but Annie was the first in the family to receive two masters degrees and a PhD. She was looking forward to having a good time tonight.

As she stood in line waiting to go into the club, she noticed that all of the women waiting to be granted entrance wore very swanky attire. Most were wearing very short skirts or dresses with a lot of bling while others wore dressy slacks with low cut blouses and stiletto heels. All of the men had on dress slacks and shirts while some wore blazers with their outfits. No one wore jeans.

She thought she looked pretty good at her apartment, but now after seeing all of these beautiful ladies, she suddenly felt like she should be on Columbus's Worst Dressed list. If Riley and Emma weren't already inside, she believed she would turn around and go home.

She was greeted at the entrance of La Seals by what appeared to be three club bouncers. All three bouncers were dressed in white pants and royal blue shirts with a La Seals logo on the upper left side of their shirts. They were very neat in their appearance and each man sported a crew cut.

One of the bouncers looked at her with a smile and asked to see her ID. She gave him her driver's license. He kept looking first at her ID and then would look back at her several times. "Is there a problem, sir?" Annie asked. He said no one under 21 was permitted inside and he didn't believe she was 24 years old according to her license. Annie then showed him her student ID card and a picture of herself receiving her PhD, assuring him of her age. He conferred with the other two bouncers. They decided to let her through. Annie smiled a smile that did not reach her eyes as he handed her back her ID's and she entered the club.

She stopped to look around and could not believe her eyes. Everything was done in blues and whites with boating memorabilia, neon lighting in soft blues and greens. Sailor ropes, anchors, and 3-D sailboats were hanging on the walls everywhere, along with palm trees. There was a very long bar to her left, and a long bar on the other side of the room to accommodate the large crowds.

The clubroom was huge. The areas for seating were about ten feet down from the bars and had roughly 100 medium-size round tables that had six seats per table. The area for dancing was located another ten feet down from the seating area. In front of the dance floor was a stage where a band could easily set up, but it was empty. To the right of the stage was a platform that housed the DJ and all of his equipment. "Captain DJ" was the DJ on duty tonight. This place was awesome!

The place was starting to fill up and she was having trouble locating her cousins. She decided to send Riley a text to find out where they were sitting. Riley responded and told her they were sitting at the end of the bar to her left and that they had saved her a seat.

They greeted each other with hugs and kisses. "Thanks for inviting me this evening," she said. "This place is great! I can't believe how big it is!"

Emma looked at Annie and smiled and said,

"We want you to have a good time tonight. What has it been, five or six years since you have been out?"

Annie looked at Emma and smiled rather sadly. "Well," Emma said, "college is over and it is time for you to have some fun!" Emma let out a big ole giggle!

Riley laughed, "Maybe you'll met a guy tonight—you know, it's time to lose your innocence!"

"Riley, that's enough! Beside, how do you know I haven't already lost it?" Annie yelled back.

Emma blurted out, "Well, you know it takes two to tango and you haven't been on a date since you were 18 years old! That would be kind of hard to do, if you know what I mean!"

"Oh girls, please tell me you haven't tried to fix me up tonight," Annie pled and they all started giggling.

Annie walked over to her seat and placed her purse on the bar. She realized the bar stools were very tall as she tried to sit down. "Well shit," she thought. "How am I going to get onto this chair?" Emma and Riley were talking and did not notice the trouble she was having. She hated to ask for help because she had always been the brunt of short jokes in her family. "I wish I had some stilettoes after all. Maybe, if I just raise my dress up a little farther on my hips I'll be able to stretch up just far enough to reach the seat in order to sit down."

She looked around and saw there was a hallway

leading to the public restrooms and to some offices, and an exit door leading to a patio of sorts. No one was in sight. So she raised her already too short dress another three inches and leaned over trying to get onto the stool.

As she bent over to scoot onto the stool, she noticed Riley was looking past her with her mouth open in surprise. Then Annie heard a man's voice.

"Uh, excuse me, ma'am. Do you need some help getting onto the stool? I'm about to see your umm…"

"Oh shit!" She said as she lowered her feet to the floor and quickly grabbed the hem of her dress and yanked it back down her legs. "I didn't think anyone was back there!"

He asked again if he could help her get onto the barstool. Her pride was wounded. Why did God make her so short! Actually five-foot-2 inches really wasn't that bad, especially with two-inch heels, but she couldn't help it if the chairs were just too dang tall for her. Her cousins were of no help to her and besides that, they were giggling uncontrollably.

Annie knew she had a stupid-ass grin on her face when she looked over at this man.

He sat down at the end of the bar where he had been sitting before she had arrived. He had a grin on his face and one could tell he was trying not to laugh, but the cousins were not much help in preventing his laughter. So, with an annoyed look she asked, "Are you laughing at me?"

"Oh no, ma'am. I would never do that," and he covered his mouth with his hands to keep from laughing.

The cousins were still laughing as she started to tap her fingers on the bar looking very irritated.

"You know," he said, "I really can help you get on the chair. It's not a problem for me."

"And just how would you help me get on the chair? Is there a step stool somewhere that you could get for me to use, or perhaps a shorter bar stool?"

"No ma'am. No step stools and no shorter bar stools. I will have to pick you up. You know, you really don't want to stand up all evening long."

Emma looked at her with a smile. "You know Annie, it wouldn't hurt you to let him help you."

"Ok, Ok, Ok" Annie smirked at Emma. She turned to the man and said, "if you don't mind, kind sir, would you help me into my chair, please?" and she fluttered her eyelashes. For some reason, his breathing hitched.

"Well," he said, "I don't know if I can or not."

Annie threw her arms up in the air and looked at her cousins and smirked, "I don't believe this!"

"Now, don't get your panties in a twist. I just need to ask you a question before I help you," the man said.

"Oh, and what question would that be?" Annie smarted back.

"I just need to know if you have a boyfriend or significant other." He was attracted to her beauty and he was hoping she didn't have a boyfriend.

"And why would you need to know that? You are just helping me get into a chair!"

"Well, I don't want your boyfriend coming over here and punching my lights out just because I am helping you out."

"Oh," Emma blurted out, "She doesn't have a boyfriend and hasn't really dated in six years!" and immediately covered her mouth with her hands and apologized for saying it.

Annie's face turned red with embarrassment! She just wanted to crawl into a hole! "Thanks, Emma!" she said as she gave Emma the evil eye.

"Good!" he said with a wide smile and immediately stood from his chair to help her. Geez, he thought, she hasn't dated in six years? Is there something wrong with her? God, I hope not!

"Are you ready?" he asked. Annie noticed how tall he was. She also noticed he had slightly long dark hair, deep blue eyes and a body that women would drool over. He looked older than her, but only by a few years. "My God, he is drop-dead gorgeous!" she thought to herself.

He bent down and scooped her up into his arms. There was something about him. For some reason she felt a spark of electricity when he picked her up. She couldn't explain it, but being in his arms felt right. She felt very safe. "Oh," she thought, "I have never felt like this before. What is going on?"

"You're very light," he said, but didn't immediately place her on to the chair. "My name is Quinn. Quinn Taylor." He looked at her up and down, and then he smiled a huge smile.

He had two of the sexiest dimples on each side of his mouth that she had ever seen and he smelled wonderful! It made her feel warm all over. Oh wow! Calm down, her protective instincts told her. This evening could be very interesting, to say the least. She smiled.

Quinn finally sat her down onto the barstool. Unbeknownst to Annie, her cousin Riley had taken the barstool and scooted it closer to Quinn and turned the stool so that it would be facing him! When Annie realized what Riley had done, she turned her head back towards her, rolled her eyes and mouthed the words "What are you doing?"

Some equally handsome male bartender came over to where they were sitting. "What can I get for you ladies?"

Quinn spoke up and said "Joe, get them whatever they want and put it on my tab."

"No, thank you" Annie said. "I will pay for my own drink."

"Annie, it won't hurt you to let the nice man buy you a drink!" stated Emma.

"I'm sorry, Emma, I don't know this nice man well enough to let him buy me a drink just yet."

Annie looked at Quinn. "I apologize," she said, "but I really would prefer to pay for my own drinks tonight."

When I looked at him, his brow had squinted a little and he had a frown. I don't know if it was a look of confusion or hurt that I refused his generosity.

"You know," he said "I can afford it."

"I'm not questioning your generosity, sir. It is just the way I am. Please, I would rather pay for my own drinks."

He drew in a deep breath, just as Joe, the bartender, looked at him and winked. I have no clue what that meant.

I ordered a diet drink and gave my cousins a raised eyebrow daring them to say a word for not ordering an alcoholic drink.

No one said anything for a couple of minutes. I was starting to feel like I really didn't belong there; then our drinks arrived. Emma and Riley thanked Quinn for their drinks as I quietly handed Joe, the bartender, some money.

Quinn finally broke the icy feel of no one speaking. "So, I am assuming your name is Annie, since that is what these beautiful ladies have called you. What is your last name?" he asked.

Annie took a sip of her diet cola and stated,

"Marshall, Anna Marie Marshall, but my friends call me Annie."

"May I call you Annie, too?" He asked with a big ole grin.

"Yes," she said, "I would like that," and gave him a big smile.

He offered his hand over for her to shake. "Glad to meet you, Annie," he said.

His hand was so warm and I felt a spark of electricity. He had the biggest hands I had ever seen.

I started feeling very comfortable around him. We danced several dances during the evening. We probably looked like "Mutt and Jeff" on the dance floor, with me being so short and him being so tall, but I really didn't care. I was having a good time.

Around 9:30 p.m. I finally ordered a Long Island Iced Tea. It tasted very good. Riley got a phone call from her babysitter and had to leave. Emma went with her. Quinn assured the cousins, he would make sure I got home safely. I really couldn't believe I agreed to stay.

CHAPTER 6

ANNIE

A S THE EVENING PROGRESSED, I found myself having a great deal of fun with Quinn. He was so funny and so sweet. I felt very relaxed with him.

He asked me to dance a slow dance. I wondered who taught him to be such a smooth dancer. We both laughed when he dipped me at the end of the dance.

We danced several more times during the evening. Several ladies had asked him to dance and he politely declined. It was like he only wanted to dance with me. He had made me feel like a princess that evening and I don't think any guy had ever made me feel that special. But then, I have never really dated very much. I think I like him… a lot!

When our dance ended, Quinn grabbed my hand and started walking towards the back exit located near our seats.

"I have something I want you to see."

We walked out onto a huge patio. The floor to the patio had a beautiful brick pattern befitting of La Seals. There was a large wrought iron gate as an exit route at each corner of the building with a decorative La Seals logo within a circle on the gate. A concrete wall with matching bricks extended from the gates in a wavy like design, much like an ocean wave, all the way down to the riverbank.

There were beautiful marble tables with matching chairs all around, and at least five round fire pits. Beautiful flowers and shrubs were everywhere. Wrought iron benches placed in concrete were just beyond the steps that lead down to the river where there were five fountains that changed into red, white, and blue colors and shapes. It was breathtakingly beautiful!

When we stopped at the top of the steps to look at the fountains in the river, I said, "I think I could stay out here all night. Listening to the water droplets hitting the river is like listening to a nice summer rain. This is very relaxing," and I closed my eyes.

When I opened my eyes, Quinn was standing one step down and facing me. He stared me straight in the eyes and said, "You are the most beautiful woman I have ever laid my eyes on," and he leaned forward and pressed his lips to mine. His lips were so soft and luscious; I wanted him to kiss me again. He took one hand and gently moved one of my hair tendrils behind my ear. He then took both hands and placed them on the sides of my head. One of his thumbs pulled down on my bottom lip causing my mouth to open and then he kissed me again, inserting his tongue into my mouth.

Next thing I knew, one hand was on the back of my head holding me in place, while his other arm was around my waist pulling me closer into him. I could feel him growing and I felt like I was melting into him. I couldn't remember ever being kissed like that. Wow, I knew I had never been kissed like that! All I knew was that I wanted him, and that it was time for me to become a woman. Suddenly I felt very nervous. What should I do? What if he asks me to go home with him? Should I tell him I am a virgin?

No, I can't tell him that, I thought. He will just change his mind! After all, he is around thirtyish and very experienced and I'm, well, I haven't experienced the first thing about sex. I decided to just go with the flow... after all, he might never ask me.

Then he stopped kissing me. While looking me in the eyes, he took both of his hands and gently removed the pins from my hair. He parted my hair in the back with his fingers and gently brought my hair to the front over each shoulder, letting my very long hair hang down past each breast. His breathing hitched. His hands were still entangled in my hair.

"Annie," he says, "I know we just met this evening, but will you spend the night with me?"

I know my heart skipped a beat just then, maybe two beats. Then he kissed me again very softly and whispered in my ear.

"Please say yes. I promise to make this night one you will never forget."

Oh my God, my mind was saying yes, but I couldn't seem to get my voice to speak. What was wrong with me? If I could speak, I know my voice would probably sound very strained or squeaky, so I smiled and shook my head yes.

QUINN

Quinn couldn't believe she said yes! There was something about her that was driving him crazy. He hadn't been this relaxed or mesmerized with a woman in years! Those feelings were totally foreign to him. He wondered, "What is she doing to me?"

Quinn gave her another kiss on the lips. He grabbed her hand and together they walked back inside the club to get her purse. Joe had put it in back of the bar for safe keeping while they were on the dance floor. He went behind the bar to retrieve it while Annie waited near the bar for him. The music was very loud so he leaned into Joe's ear and told him they were leaving.

"Where are you taking her?" Joe asked in a very clipped voice. He knew every woman Quinn had ever picked up always spent the night with him at his hotel across the street. "We are going to my home in Indian Creek, if it is any of your business."

"Your home?" Joe asked looking very surprised. "Wait… Quinn…" Joe said. "I've been watching you two all evening. You've been acting like a schoolboy with raging hormones. Be careful man and watch what you are doing. She seems like a really nice girl!"

"What is your problem, Joe? You're the one that keeps telling me I need to move on. Well, I'm trying to do just that, so, mind your own fucking business!"

"I can see what you're doing!" said Joe.

"What do you think I'm doing?" asked Quinn, with some irritation to his voice.

"You're trying to reel her into your lair. I just don't want to see you get hurt if something goes wrong man," said Joe. "If she breaks your heart, I am coming after her! I don't think I could stand to see you go down that road again! If you end up breaking her heart, it will just prove you are still consumed with Kayla and that you are a sorry-ass bastard!"

"Watch your mouth, Joe!" said Quinn with a growl as he pointed his index finger towards Joe's face. "You are the only one who can talk to me like that and only because I know you mean well! Remember, there is only so much lip I'll take from you!" and with that said, Quinn walked out from behind the bar.

He took Annie's hand and they walked across the street towards the hotel. When they stepped onto the sidewalk, she stopped walking, jerking Quinn to a stop.

"Why are we going into the hotel?" she asked.

He could feel her petite little hand shaking in his. "Annie, do you have a problem going into a hotel with me?"

"Well," she said. "I can't spend the night with you if this is where you are taking me."

His heart almost stopped beating. "And why is that?" he asked.

Her hand was still shaking in mine. Maybe she wasn't very experienced or maybe she had a bad experience at a hotel. I don't want to think about that. I just don't want to think about her being with another man, even if it was before me.

She lowered her head and spoke very softly when she answered my question.

"I think going to a man's hotel room would make me feel like a hooker whore or something. I can't do that."

Her answer just about floored him and wasn't what he had expected.

We stood there for a minute and I knew I was

looking perplexed. I knew I was more dominant, but she had all the power. How should I handle this?

I had to think. I gave her a hug and a kiss on top of her head. "Annie, it's okay. My car is in the parking garage. I wanted to take you to my home in Indian Creek if that would be okay with you?"

Annie smiled as we walked hand in hand towards the parking garage. She seemed a little apprehensive. I was wondering if she was having second thoughts about going with me. Surely she wasn't a virgin. I am usually very astute with reading people. It was one of the best skills I had while a Seal in the Navy. Learning to read faces of the enemy had helped me on many missions. However, Annie was not the enemy. How old is she, 24 or 25?

How many 24 or 25 year olds are still virgins, especially when they look as beautiful as she?

I helped her into my sporty black Lexus and watched her as she buckled her seat belt, then walked over to the driver's side and climbed in. I started the engine, turned on some soft music, and proceeded out of the parking garage.

She looked so sexy sitting in the passenger seat of my car. As I looked at her seat belt, I began thinking about all the ways I would love to tie her up and have my way with her. She looked so beautiful and so sweet. I grabbed her hand and noticed she was still trembling. I wanted to ask her why, but I didn't want to embarrass her.

"Why do you live at the hotel if you have a home just 20 minutes away?" she asked.

"Well," I said. "I moved back home to the hotel when I was discharged from the military. My Dad gave me this hotel. In fact, he gave me all of his business holdings in the United States. He still owns several across the world.

Anyway, I purchased the land across the street from the hotel and started building La Seals. It just seemed like the right place to be. After La Seals opened, I hired the same construction company to build me a new home. It is a beautiful place, but I must say I don't have it completely furnished. I will tell you this, other than my housekeeper, Mrs. Davis, you will be the first woman to step into my home. I really hope you like it."

"Hmm" she said as she smiled and turned her head to look at me. "I rather like the sound of me being the first."

We turned into my long, gated driveway and I think her jaw dropped to her knees. "This is your house?" she asked. "This isn't a house, this is a mansion!"

I parked the car in front of my rather large estate instead of pulling into the garage around back. I helped her out of the car and took her hand as we walked to the door. We climbed three steps and I unlocked it. Instead of letting her walk through the door on her own, I surprised her and picked her up to carry her over the threshold. She let out a little scream and giggled, "Why are you doing this? Carrying a lady over the threshold is just for married couples!"

"Well", Quinn stated in fun, while raising his eyebrows, "I'll have you know, it is very proper to carry the first woman to step into my home over the threshold!"

I gently placed Annie down on her feet. She immediately started turning her head to look around, but did not move. I placed my keys on the small table by the door in the entry hall, locked the door and entered the security alarm code into the keypad. She seemed to be impressed by the double staircase at the end of the entry hall.

"Come," as I grabbed her hand, "I'll show you around a little."

We went through a large living room, very large dining room and then into the kitchen. I poured us each a glass of white Zinfindel, hoping the wine would relax her.

She was very nervous. "I don't know about this, Quinn. I don't think I'm in your league," she said as she took a drink of her wine.

"What do you mean, my league?" I asked, shocked at the insinuation.

"You know. You must be very wealthy with a good head on your shoulders for business. I am just a poor girl from humble beginnings, just trying to make a place in this world for myself. What could we even have in common?" she asked.

I wasn't expecting her to say anything like that. I found her very intriguing. "Annie, why would you even say anything like that? We all come into the world the same way and leave the same way. The way I see it, you are a woman, a very beautiful woman at that. I, on the other hand, am an average looking man. I think we like each other. At least I think we have had a very nice time together tonight, haven't we? Can we just forget the fact that I have money and just continue to have a good time?"

I wanted to know everything there was about this woman. She was exquisite and I found her mesmerizing, to say the least. After she drank her wine, I picked her up and placed her on the counter top. I walked to the refrigerator to get some strawberries. I don't think she realized I was watching her because she was looking all around my kitchen. She had crossed her legs and was leaning back on her hands. She started licking her lips and as she did, her lower lip went into her mouth like she was sucking her own lip and then pushed her lip out of her mouth.

I don't think she realized what her actions were doing to me as I pulled my shirt out of my pants. This petite little woman oozed with sensuality and sexuality more than any woman I had ever seen. I don't think she even knew it. I felt like I was getting harder by the minute. I must have her soon.

I placed the bowl of strawberries next to her and poured some more wine. I fed her one of the strawberries and then I ate one. She took a drink and giggled. She put another strawberry halfway into her mouth and leaned forward for me to take a bite from her. That did it! We each ate our half of the strawberry. We kissed long and hard and very passionately! I put the bowl of strawberries back into the refrigerator, turned off the kitchen light, and picked her up from the counter top into my arms, taking her up the stairs to my bedroom. She would not take her eyes off me while I climbed the stairs. She was still shaking a bit.

I sat her feet down gently on the floor and unbuckled the belt to her dress. I moved around to her back and slowly unzipped her. Slowly, I removed her dress from her shoulders, letting it fall to the floor.

I kissed her gently on her shoulders and instructed her to step out of her dress. I unsnapped her bra and let it fall loose from her arms. I picked the dress and bra up from the floor and placed them neatly in a chair.

She still had her shoes on. When I turned back around to look at her, she was smiling. She was a picture of beauty, an absolute goddess! I honestly didn't think Michelangelo himself could capture all of her beauty! She was flawless! My God, what was this petite little woman doing to me? I wanted to kiss this woman all over her body.

I stood before her and instructed her to undress me. She squatted down and removed my shoes and socks and placed them by the chair where I had laid her dress. She unbuckled my belt and unsnapped/unzipped my pants and helped me out of them. She started to unbutton my shirt, but she found she was having too much trouble with her nails being long so she grabbed the front of my shirt and ripped the shirt open, popping all the buttons off. She looked up at me, smiled and said, "Sorry, I have always dreamed about doing that someday." I should have known she was inexperienced right then, but honestly, that was one hot move! She helped me take off my T-shirt.

I got down on my knees and removed her heels and tossed them, not really seeing where they landed. I helped her out of her thong and threw it over my head. She smelled wonderful. I began kissing and sucking on each breast, tweaking her nipples into hard little beads, then kissed her stomach all the way down to the top of her pubic hair. She took a deep breath and placed her hands on top of my head.

Her knees were weakening. I knew I needed to lay her down on the bed. "Relax, Annie, and breathe," I said softly.

I placed Annie on the bed and hovered over top of her giving her deep throat kisses. She had the sweetest tasting mouth I had ever kissed. I proceeded as before, tweaking and caressing her breast then kissing down her stomach. Her body was responding to me in a very sensual way. I began sucking on her clit and licking into her entrance. The sound of her purrs and her body writhing was doing me in. I knew she was close to an orgasm. I put one finger into her entrance and noticed how tight she was. So, I put another finger in. Oh shit! She must be a virgin! How is this possible? She was 25 years old!

"Annie, honey, you are so tight!" I said.

"Will you be gentle with me?" she asked.

"Annie, are you a virgin?" She didn't say anything.

"Oh baby, why didn't you tell me?" I sat up on the side of the bed, putting my elbows on my knees with my face in my hands. Well shit, what should I do now? I had never been with a virgin before. I had always had rough sex, never gentle!

"Quinn?" she said, but I did not respond to her. She got up from the bed, removed my hands from my face and climbed onto my lap. "Look at me, Quinn," she said in a whisper. "I'm sorry, did I do something wrong? Please look at me."

When I looked into her eyes, I saw the darkest, ice blue colored eyes I had ever seen. They were beautiful. The more I looked into her eyes; I knew she was the woman I had been looking for all of my life. I knew right then I was falling deeply in love with her.

I must have had a look on my face that scared her, because the next thing I heard was her crying, bolting off my lap, and quickly moving about the room putting her thong, bra, and dress back on as fast as she could. She was spouting off something about feeling so humiliated. She found one shoe, but could not find the other and started running down the stairs to leave.

"Annie," I yelled, "it's not like that, please don't leave! Annie!" I ran down the stairs to stop her, but she was faster than me. She threw the only shoe she had at me, barely escaping my head. She stopped, looked back at me and grabbed my car keys.

"Sorry, you can pick your car up at your hotel," she yelled and out the door she flew causing the door alarms to start sounding and leaving the door opened.

Being naked, I could not go out of my house. I watched as she got into my car, started the engine, and drove like a bat out of hell down my driveway. Oh, fuck, she has been drinking and she should not be driving in her frame of mind! She'll surely kill herself! I can't believe she stole my car!

I reset the house alarm, and quickly ran upstairs to dress, throwing on my t-shirt, undershorts, pants, and shoes without socks. I grabbed my wallet, her shoes, and went into my home office to grab an extra set of house keys and a set of keys to my Porsche that was in the garage. It was a faster car, so maybe I could catch up with her. I grabbed her purse she had left in the kitchen, turned the lights off, and keyed in the security alarm.

CHAPTER 7

ANNIE

"OH MY GOD!" I SAID out loud as I was driving Quinn's car on I-270 towards his hotel. "I am so humiliated! I don't think I can ever face him again! What was I thinking! I could have saved myself from all of that embarrassment if only I had either told him the truth or just told him I didn't want to go home with him! Oh shit, this could have been one of the most beautiful nights of my life. Well, he most definitely kept his promise! He made this a night I will definitely never forget! Shit, I royally fucked up! Damn it anyway! Here I am nearly 25 years old and I hate this virginity albatross hanging around my neck!"

After I parked the car in the hotel parking garage, I gave the car keys to the attendant with instructions to contact Quinn. The attendant could see that I had been crying. He politely looked at me and told me not to worry, that he would take care of it. I walked out of the garage.

———◆———

"What the fuck do you want, Joe? You have never called me this late before," Quinn said in a very hateful tone.

"What's going on, Quinn? Are you all right?" asked Joe.

"Yeah, I'm okay," said Quinn.

"We have an intruder at the club," said Joe.

"Is it Annie? Did she break inside or what?"

"No, Quinn, she is outside on the back patio."

"What is she doing?"

"She's sitting on the bench facing the river. Her elbows are on her knees and her face is in her hands. Quinn, she looks like she's crying. What's going on?" replied Joe. "Cindy is getting dressed to go out and talk to her to see if she is okay."

"No!" yelled Quinn into his cell phone. "Tell Cindy to leave her alone. I'm almost there. I'll talk to her. Turn the water fountains back on, too. That will help calm her down."

Quinn pulled into the parking area at La Seals, climbed out of his car, grabbing Annie's shoes and purse. He quietly walked to the back of the club and found Annie crying. His heart felt like it was breaking into a million pieces. He couldn't stand to see her cry. Why did she run away so fast?

Quinn quietly spoke her name so as not to scare

her, and squatted down in front of her. He wiped the bottoms of each of her feet with his hands and slipped her shoes back on her feet. He grabbed both of her hands and gently kissed them. "Annie, look at me baby. Please look at me."

"Go away," Annie said tearfully.

"Come on, Annie, please look at me," begged Quinn, "You have this all wrong. I want to explain to you." It took a few minutes, but Annie raised her head and he immediately saw big watery tears in her eyes.

"Oh, Annie, I am so sorry. Please don't cry." He leaned in, took his thumbs and rubbed the tears away and gently kissed each eye. He placed a kiss on her lips and picked her up and placed her on his lap. He tucked her head gently into his neck and held her tightly into his body. Just then, the water fountains came back to life.

He sat there for about 15 minutes saying nothing, hoping the sound of the water droplets from the fountain hitting the river would help calm her down. When he felt like she had calmed, he began to speak.

"Annie, you need to know something about me. I think that is the only way you might understand why I reacted the way I did tonight. If you aren't satisfied, then I will walk away and you will never see me again. I really hope you don't let me walk away, because I really do like you. Will you listen?"

Annie stared into his face trying to decide what to do.

"Please, Annie, what have you got to lose by listening?"

"Okay," she said, "I'll listen."

Quinn took a deep breath. "About fourteen years ago, I fell in love with my high school sweetheart. At least I thought I was in love. She was beautiful, full of life, and very intelligent. We had attended a couple of years of college together when I proposed marriage and she had accepted. Not one time did we ever make love! Don't get me wrong, Annie. We had sex… a lot of sex and quite often, too. When we did, we went at it like animals. We were always well satisfied."

"My major in college was business administration. Dad had taught me so much about running a hotel empire and other businesses that I felt I didn't need anymore education. After giving it much consideration, I decided to drop out of college and I joined the Navy, at the end of my second year. Kayla was not happy with me at all."

"Roughly a year into my enlistment, my heart was shattered into a million pieces. I got a "Dear John letter." She dumped my ass big time. I haven't had a girlfriend since her. She has been at the front of my mind all those years until last night when I met you."

"Joe had been telling me for years to forget about her and move on, but I couldn't do it. After meeting you last night, something changed for me."

By now, Annie had moved onto the bench next to him, listening very intently.

"Okay, so what does this all have to do with what happened tonight?" asked Annie.

He looked deep into her eyes and had a frown on his face. "Up until yesterday, Annie, I believed I never ever needed a woman. When I wanted sex, all I had to do was go to a BDSM club and have all the sex I wanted. They don't make love there. If nothing else, it's usually very intense. That way, you don't have the emotional attachments of getting hurt. I've always told myself if I was ever lucky enough to find the right woman I would know it as soon as I met her."

"Well, Annie... I never believed that God would ever smile down on me like that, but He did and it shook me to my core. I knew when I took you back to my house that you were really special. I still can't believe you came with me, but tonight, when you asked me to look into your eyes... do you remember asking me that?"

"Yes," Annie said.

"Well, when I looked into those beautiful eyes of yours, I saw love. I could tell you were falling in love with me and I knew right then and there I was falling in love with you, too. It scared me! I knew you deserved to be made love to, not rode hard. I've never had a virgin before, and, well frankly, it shocked me, Annie! I had to think. Look at me, a big ole Navy Seal more afraid of this than any mission I have ever gone on. You deserve better than me."

Quinn got up off the bench and dropped to his knees in front of her. "I know, Annie, I am declaring my feelings to you rather soon and I am sorry for that, too. I don't know how else to say any of this except truthfully. Please, Annie, I am so sorry for my actions. Can you find it in your heart to forgive me?"

ANNIE

I ran my hands through my hair as I looked into his beautiful blue eyes. I wanted to forgive him. The feelings I have for him were scaring me on some level, too. He said if I didn't want to forgive him, then he would leave me alone and I would never see him again. Was that what I really wanted? I had never really had a boyfriend before. What if Quinn was really genuine? What if I let him walk away and I realized I shouldn't have let him? What if he was the one man that was meant for me? Oh, what was it Annie with all of these what if's?

"Annie?" Quinn said, as he looked me dead in the eyes.

His eyes had turned a sapphire blue and even looked a little watery. His eyes looked so sad and I felt he was being sincere. What the hell, I'm

55

hurting now over what happened this evening. I knew if he left for good, I would just hurt more, but why was that? I had just met him! So, why not forgive him and see where this took us. If it didn't work out, well, it didn't work out. I was a firm believer that what will be, will be. I really did like him a lot and I knew I didn't want to lose him. Maybe he was right. Maybe I was in love with him. So I put my arms around his neck and said, "Yes, I forgive you, but only if you forgive me for running. I'm sorry, too, Quinn."

Quinn pulled Annie into him and gave her a sweet, seductive kiss.

"So, where do we go from here, Quinn?"

He stroked the side of her face with his fingers. "I don't know. Would you like to see where this goes?" he asked.

"Yes, I think I would," and she licked her lips.

"So, let me get this straight, because I really want to make sure I understand this," Quinn said. "You're okay with being my girlfriend?"

"Well," Annie said with a soft smile on her face. "Yeah, I'm okay with that as long as you let me pay for my drinks," and she let out a cute little giggle.

"Hmm, I don't know if I can do that, after all I do make more money than you," said Quinn in his dominate, husky voice.

Annie studied his face for a few moments. "We are just going to have to work on that!" she said softly.

Quinn was studying her face, too. He made a

little curve of a smile with his lips and said, "Now, can we go back to my place? We really do have some unfinished business if you know what I mean."

Annie had to laugh to herself. Here he was 30 something and he sounded like a high school boy trying to get laid after the prom!

"Are you sure, Quinn?"

"Hell, yes, I'm sure! I'm going to make love to you like no one has ever been made love to before. You are going to have to beg me to stop!"

CHAPTER 8

I T WAS NEARLY 4:30 A.M. when they had returned to Indian Creek. It had been a long day for them both. Annie had fallen asleep in the car. Quinn did not have the heart to wake her. He wanted to make wonderful love to her when he got her back to his place, but she just looked so exhausted. He told himself he would wait. He wanted her awake, and he wanted her to experience just how wonderful he would make her body feel. Just thinking about her lying next to him made his whole body tingle all the way to his core!

Kayla, his ex-girlfriend, with whom he was engaged to eleven years ago, entered his mind. I don't think I was ever in love with her. It must have been total infatuation. With my hormones raging at that age, I must have been thinking with my dick and not my head, he thought. The feelings I have for this gorgeous, exquisite, petite beauty sitting in my car asleep surpasses anything I had ever felt for anyone. Looking back now, I am very grateful to Kayla for dumping my ass. The only thing I regretted was that it took 11 years for someone like Annie to enter my life. Wow, someone like Annie! Not Kayla! I felt like a dark cloud had lifted. Annie was definitely nothing like Kayla!

I had always told Joe I would know who the right woman was the day she entered my life, even though I really didn't believe in love at first sight. I never thought it would happen to me.

Note to self... call Joe and tell him Kayla was officially out of my mind for good... He will be thrilled.

Quinn gently picked her up and carried her upstairs to his bed. He removed her clothing and slipped one of his t-shirts on her. The wine must have done her in, along with the Long Island Iced Tea and the Miami Vice she drank at the club. Second note to self... no more than two drinks, especially if one of them is a Long Island Iced Tea.

After ever so gently putting her to bed, he covered her up with his blanket. Quinn went back downstairs and pulled the Porsche into the garage. He went into the kitchen and grabbed a bottle of water from the refrigerator. He set the security alarm and drank his water. Afterwards, he went back to his bedroom, stripped down to his shorts and laid down next to Annie.

He watched her sleep. The soft contours of her face, the way her chest moved with each breath she took, and the soft sounding purrs she made as she exhaled her breathing, made his heart soar. He felt almost at peace. Quinn spoke out a soft prayer. *"Dear God in heaven, please make her mine. Amen."* He positioned his body next to Annie, kissed her softly, and wrapped his arm around her. Then he fell asleep quickly for the first time in 11 years.

It was about noontime when Annie woke up with a sudden urge to go to the bathroom. Quinn's right arm and leg were wrapped around her body. She managed to move easily from underneath him being careful not to disturb his sleep and went to the bathroom.

She washed her hands and noticed his toothbrush. "I wonder if he has an extra toothbrush?" she said to herself. She looked in all the vanity drawers and in the bathroom cabinets, but could not find any extras. She smiled to herself and decided she would use his toothbrush anyway. After all, just thinking about his tongue in her mouth sent delicious shivers throughout her body; so using his toothbrush shouldn't matter. Besides, he had asked her to be his girlfriend.

She found a clean washcloth, washed her face and then brushed her teeth. There weren't any hairbrushes anywhere in the bathroom. She knew a comb would not work as her hair was too long and would take all day to comb out the tangles. She took her fingers and tried to run them through her hair to make herself halfway presentable. "What a mess!" she thought as she looked into the mirror.

She had to take her birth control pill so she decided she would go downstairs to the kitchen. Her stomach started to growl. Maybe I can fix breakfast for the both of us, she thought. She put on Quinn's socks, since the only shoes she had were heels. The thought of cooking in heels did not appeal to her already aching feet. She grabbed his long sleeved shirt that she had ripped the buttons from and slipped it on. The air-conditioning was a little cool, so his shirt would keep her warmer since it would hang a little longer on her legs. She took the belt to her dress and secured it around her waist to keep it together. She didn't think Quinn would mind.

The sleeves hung way past her hands, down to her knees. She let out a snicker, but covered her mouth quickly thinking her little laugh would awaken Quinn. When he didn't stir, she took the shirt off, rolled up the sleeves and put it back on. She knew if Quinn saw her wearing his shirt like this, he would surely laugh. She walked downstairs to the kitchen.

"Yes, I think I will fix him some breakfast and serve it to him in bed. Just think of the possibilities after we eat!"

She figured Quinn would be waking up soon, so she started looking in the pantry and then in the refrigerator to see what food items were available. "Hmm, French toast, bacon, orange juice, coffee, and strawberries too!" And her mind slipped back to the night before, when Quinn fed her strawberries, while looking at the spot on the countertop where he had placed her. She smiled.

She grabbed the thick bread from the pantry, and turned on the stove to get the built-in griddle hot. She opened the cabinet and took out a small mixing bowl and two plates. She grabbed three forks and two spoons from the silverware drawer and put a pot of coffee on so that it could be brewing while she prepared breakfast. She got two coffee cups and some creamer. She didn't think she saw Quinn using sugar in his coffee last night when he drank some at the club.

The griddle seemed hot enough now, so she got some eggs, bacon, milk and butter from the refrigerator. She went back to the pantry for some maple syrup and looked in the cabinet for some cinnamon and vanilla. She hoped he was not allergic to cinnamon. She started frying four strips of bacon on the far side of the griddle, and then mixed the milk, eggs, vanilla, and cinnamon together. She dipped the bread into the mixture and began cooking. She poured some orange juice, placed some strawberries in some small soufflé cups, served the French toast on the plates, buttered it and put some syrup on it, added the bacon and poured two cups of coffee. Breakfast was ready.

"Hmm, something smells good!" Quinn said as he was leaning against the door to the kitchen.

"How long have you been standing there?" she asked with a smile.

"Oh, about three or four minutes. You look like you know your way around a kitchen," he said as he walked towards the kitchen island to look at the food she had prepared. He took some placemats and some napkins from a drawer in the kitchen island and placed them on a small table next to a window. He walked back to Annie and gave her a hug and a kiss, then helped her take the plates of food and coffee and juice to the table.

"You know, Quinn, I was going to serve this to you in bed," she said softly.

"Well, wench, maybe you can serve me some desert instead," as he pulled her down on his lap and started tickling her.

Annie screamed with laughter, but was able to escape from his endearing clutches and sat herself in a chair next to him. She smiled.

They sat there in silence as they started to eat. "Hmm, this is really good, Annie," he said as he took a bite of the French toast, dripping some of the syrup onto the side of his mouth. Quinn grabbed his napkin, wiped his mouth and took another bite of the delicious food, dripping more syrup on his lips and down his chin. He laughed.

"I think you are doing that on purpose," Annie said with a giggle.

"Maybe you should feed me," said Quinn with a sheepish grin as he spilled more syrup on his lips, forcing some of it onto one side of his cheek again.

Annie got up from her chair with her napkin. She sat down on his lap, straddling him and said, "Maybe I should feed you," and Annie then leaned over and licked the syrup from the side of his cheek and lip with her tongue. "Hmm, you taste delicious!" said Annie.

Quinn smiled really big. He opened his mouth for Annie to feed him another bite of the French toast, purposely forcing some of the syrup onto his bottom lip. Once more, Annie licked the syrup from his lower lip. "Hmm, more please," said Quinn. Never had he experienced anything so hot!

For a virgin, she was sizzling! How did she know to do such things? I really didn't think I would last through breakfast.

"We need to go upstairs now, baby. I don't want your first time to be on the floor in the kitchen!"

Annie jumped off his lap. "Wait a minute, I have to take my pill first," she said.

"Good girl," he said as he watched Annie walk over to the counter where she had left her purse. He wondered why was she on the pill being a virgin? He'll have to ask her. Just as she was pulling the birth control pill container from her purse, her cell phone rang. I walked to the refrigerator to get her some water.

"Hello, Tony? What's going on? You never call my cell. Is there something wrong? Are you okay?" She paused to listen. "Yes, I'm fine," she said. "I promise you I am okay. Yes, Tony, I spent the night with a friend. Tell me what is going on!"

All of a sudden, the color drained from her face and she turned white as a ghost. She started breathing rapidly and her voice went up an octave.

"My apartment? Someone has broken into my apartment?" She listened for a few seconds longer and said, "We're on our way."

CHAPTER 3

QUINN

I WATCHED HER AS SHE DISCONNECTED the call and started scrolling her recent phone call list and messages. Then she looked up at me with scared little eyes. I handed her the bottle of water and instructed her to take her pill. She looked like she was going to faint. I shook her shoulders a little and made her look at me.

"Annie, it's going to be all right. I will keep you safe. Take your pill baby and let's go get changed." She took her pill, put the pill container and her cell back into her purse and up the stairs we ran.

We were both silent as we dressed. I knew she was scared. What if she had gone back to her apartment last night? What if the intruder had been there? What if she had been hurt or killed? I don't want to think about it.

I grabbed my cell phone and her purse, set the security alarm, and we ran to the garage for my

Porsche and sped out of my long drive toward her apartment.

"Annie, what else did your friend tell you?"

"Tony said when he got home last night the door to my apartment was open and all the lights were on. He said he yelled for me, but when I didn't answer, he went to the laundry room downstairs thinking that maybe I was staying up late doing laundry. When he didn't find me, he checked his apartment for me and then went outside to see if maybe I had taken the trash out. He said he had been calling me since 3 a.m., but when I didn't answer my phone, he said he called the police. He thought that maybe I had been kidnapped or something. He said the police came and checked my place out, but said there really wasn't much they could do for at least 48 hours. He said he locked my place up after the police left."

We turned onto N. College Avenue and I recognized the apartment building right away. It wasn't a big apartment building like some of the apartment complexes in and around Columbus. This one has 11 apartments... three in the basement with a utility room for laundry, and four apartments on each of the other two floors.

"Is this where you live, Annie?" I asked.

"Yes," she replied.

"Really, I think I own this building. I think Dad bought it about six years ago," Quinn said with a questioning sound in his voice. Annie looked at me with an odd look. The one thing I noticed right away was all of the trees and shrubs. They were everywhere and blocking most of the lampposts and streetlights. This is most definitely not a safe place for anyone to walk, especially a female. I parked my car. We both got out of the car rather quickly and I took Annie's hand feeling like I should protect her. My instincts as a Seal kicked in as if I were on a covert mission. Something did not feel right.

I noticed Annie's hands were trembling and all of a sudden, she stopped walking. She started looking all around the area.

"Annie, what's wrong?"

"I feel like someone is watching us," she replied in a scared voice.

It was broad daylight and I immediately started looking around for any signs of people and any signs of street cameras.

"I am so glad you are with me," she said. "I don't know what I would do if you weren't here."

I didn't see anyone lurking around, nor did I see any of the typical street cameras used by various police departments and businesses. What I did notice was a reflection of light shining off of something hidden in some of the trees.

There was something in a tree facing the side of her building entrance, one near the parking lot, and one in a tree located near the front of a second-floor apartment window. I just bet that apartment was her apartment. It would not surprise me that there could be something on the other end of the building, too. With my suspicions, I would say there were at least four surveillance video feeds out here. If there were four out here, just how many were there inside her building or even in her apartment. She was not going to live here anymore!

I did not have the heart to tell her that I had the same suspicions as she had.

"Annie, I need for you to trust me now," I said sternly. I grabbed Annie's hand and turned toward my car. I leaned down to her as we walked and said in a whisper, "Annie, don't say a word. We need to get into my car for a minute. Just put your arm around my waist and smile. Just trust me baby, okay?" I asked with a smile. "I will explain in a few minutes."

"Okay," she said with a fake smile.

We walked arm in arm around each other's waist, back to the car. I kissed her on her forehead, then opened the car door for her and instructed her to put her seat belt on.

I jumped into the car, started the engine, pulled away from the parking spot and turned back onto the main road. I drove about four blocks to be sure I was completely out of range of any kind of surveillance cameras and equipment that could easily be activated and parked the car.

"What are you doing, Quinn?"

"Annie, I think someone has a surveillance camera on your apartment and possibly on you. There may even be audio with it."

"That may explain the odd feeling like someone is watching me all of the time," she said, rubbing her arms.

"How long have you been feeling this?" I asked.

"I don't know. Maybe about six years, but I had only felt it when I was outside. I have always watched my surroundings and I have never seen anyone. I figured I was just being paranoid." She paused. "Yesterday, I felt like that in my apartment and it freaked me out," she said anxiously.

I let out a hissing sound. "There's more," she said. "I think someone spent the night in my apartment Thursday night."

"Why do you think that?" I asked.

"I know it sounds silly, but someone made a pot of coffee and left their empty cup in the sink and stored the can of coffee in my frig."

"Are you sure you never made the coffee?"

She gave me an annoyed look. "Just asking, hon. I have to be sure of all my facts. Is there anything else?" I asked.

She continued speaking. "I just purchased a new can of coffee when I went to the store Thursday evening. I had not opened it and I know I put it in the cabinet over top of my coffee pot. I never store my coffee grounds in the refrigerator. When I found the can in my refrigerator, I thought, well maybe I accidentally put it in there. Quinn, when I lifted the lid from the top of the can, I found it was already opened. Don't you see? I didn't make any coffee the night before! Oh God!" Annie cried. I grabbed her hand. Shit, she was really shaking. Then she proceeded to speak some more.

"My apartment door was unlocked and my chain was unhooked. I know for a fact that I locked my door and put my chain up; it is a ritual for me and is always the last thing I do before I go to bed." She was still trembling and looked very scared. "Quinn? What do I do now?" she asked with tears starting to roll down her cheeks.

I leaned over the gearshift and pulled her as close to me as I could and gave her a gentle hug and kiss on her forehead. "Don't worry, babe, I'm here and I'm going to protect you." I tried to be very reassuring, but I don't think I was as convincing as I had hoped to be.

I pulled out my cell phone and called Joe and explained to him that Annie's apartment had been broken into.

"Joe, would you and Jax run over to her apartment and see if you can pick up any kind of video/audio feeds? Yeah, it's the first apartment building you come to on N. College Avenue right off Campus Row. Yeah, that's the one by The Campus Bar and Grill. Go quickly. Something isn't right here, man. I think she could be in danger. Call me back asap." He hung up his cell phone.

Quinn started the engine to his car and pulled into traffic.

"Where are we going, Quinn?" Annie asked.

"We are going to La Seals and wait for Joe's call. I don't want you anywhere near your apartment until we figure out what is going on."

About an hour later, Joe called Quinn telling him they were at the far end of the parking lot on N. College Avenue where Annie lived.

He informed Quinn they have detected some video buzz. With the small amount of intel that Jax had detected on the outside of the apartment building, he was reasonably sure he would find surveillance bugs in Annie's apartment and probably in the hallways as well.

Quinn told Joe not to do anything yet. He said he was going to order some pizza and then go through a drive-thru and pick up some beer. If the rat bastard was watching her apartment, he wanted everything to look normal like we didn't suspect anything.

He told Joe not to acknowledge them when they arrived. He wanted to start making out with Annie to show whoever had bugged her place, that she belonged to him. Quinn wanted to send a strong message. "SHE'S MINE!" Once they had been inside about ten minutes, Jax was to scramble the feeds. When the feeds had been disengaged, then Jax could come in and make a sweep of her place to see where the bugs were located.

CHAPTER 10

JAX WAS SHORT FOR JACKSON Andrew Xavier.
Jax was his call sign as a Navy Seal. He was
just a couple of years older then Quinn and
Joe, and had been a Seal longer than they had been.
When Quinn made the offer to build La Seals
clubs all over the country, Jax decided it was time
to quit the Navy. He had served his country very
well for at least 12 years and his body was starting
to feel all the wear and tear. He had decided he
would like to live in Atlanta, Georgia. Quinn
was currently building a new La Seals for him in
Atlanta. Jax had agreed to stay at the Columbus
location for training until the new La Seals had
been completed.

Jax was 35 years old, with golden blonde hair
and big green eyes. He was 6-foot-6 inches tall and
weighed around 245 pounds. He was solid muscle.
He could usually be found working out in a gym,
usually four hours a day, plus he ran a minimum of
five miles per day. He had been accused of working
out to impress the ladies, often flexing his muscles
to see their reactions. He was such a character.

He seemed to get his fair share of women, too. Since his scare with a woman claiming he got her pregnant, he was a little more cautious now. He had no intentions of ever getting married. He stated he was having way too much fun for that nonsense.

QT really liked his Seal brother. He was one of the bravest of men he had ever known, always volunteering for missions before anyone else. Jax, like the rest of his Seal brothers, was a good man to have around. He felt that family and friends were the most important gifts in life next to God. His motto was to "treat your women like royalty; and your family and friends like you could never live without them."

Jax had some pretty high-tech surveillance equipment not available to the public. He knew exactly how to use it to its fullest capabilities. With the use of a few codes, Jax could spy, and record the perpetrator without the perp's knowledge. The sad thing was, he could not pin point the exact location of the perpetrator, only the general location. Finding the exact location would take some good old fashion legwork.

When Quinn and Annie walked into her apartment, Quinn immediately placed the pizza box and the beers on the coffee table while Annie opened the living room curtains. "That's odd," she said, "I could have sworn that I left my curtains open when I left my apartment last night."

With the curtains opened now, Jax was able to detect a bug inside the room. He was able to access both a video and audio feed of the two of them. They were kissing each other in between bites of pizza. As planned, QT started unzipping Annie's dress. That was the signal to scramble both the video and audio feeds. QT did not take her dress off. Instead, they continued kissing until they heard a text come through on his cell phone. Jax had locked the scrambling feed in place and was headed inside.

Joe was trained in the surveillance equipment as well, but had agreed to stay in the van basically for security reasons. By the time Jax had knocked on Annie's apartment door, QT had zipped up her dress.

Jax did a sweep of the room and found a video camera in her bedroom, bathroom, two in her living room and one in her kitchen. He also detected audio bugs in several locations of the apartment. Bugs were detected at each entrance to the building, one in the laundry room and one in front of both Annie's door and at Tony's door. Quinn was absolutely livid!

He looked at Annie, who was trembling all over. She was desperately trying to be strong, trying her best not to cry. He knew she was scared out of her mind.

"Annie," stated Quinn, "You are not staying here

tonight or any night until we catch this person. You are going home with me."

"But Quinn, I can't do that and I won't have you put your life and your friends lives at risk for me!" said Annie.

"So what do you think you are going to do?" yelled Quinn in a slightly raised voice.

"I don't know... I'll call the police and let them know what you found... then maybe I'll get a hotel room somewhere," said Annie as she walked the floor. She was very afraid.

"Anna Marie Marshall! You listen to me!" Quinn said with gritted teeth as he stood in front of her, putting his hands on her shoulders.

"Don't you understand someone is after you? Someone is watching you getting undressed, watching you dress, watching you take your showers, watching you sleep, hell he is watching everything you do!"

Annie started shaking and then started to cry. "I don't understand why. I haven't done anything to anyone!" Then she buried her face into Quinn's chest and sobbed.

Quinn put his arms around her and held her tight kissing her on the top of her head.

"Annie, I need for you to cooperate with me. I promise I will protect you. We are trained Navy Seals and we know what to do. Will you trust me?"

"Ms. Marshall?" Jax said to Annie. She looked at him with tear-filled eyes.

"Ms. Marshall, where I come from, no one messes with your woman. And with us Seals, you better believe no one messes with any of our women. We are here to serve and protect. That is what a good man does. You need to trust QT." He said as he handed her a tissue.

She stepped away from Quinn and started wiping the tears from her eyes. "I'm sorry for being such a wreck," Annie said. "I'll do whatever you tell me."

"You promise?" said Quinn. "Because I'm sure you may not like some of the things I will need for you to do."

"Like what?"

"Well for starters, you will need to let me buy you some new clothes, shoes and toiletry items," he said.

"AND WHY DO I NEED TO DO THAT?" she asked with a raised voice.

"For one thing, we are going to have to leave soon and you really don't have time to pack. I just don't want whoever this monster is to suspect we are on to him. I don't want him to think you have moved out. We need to catch this son-of-a bitch and we need to catch him as soon as possible!" Quinn argued back at her.

Tony peeked his head into the opened door of the apartment.

"Annie?" said Tony.

"Oh, Tony!" Annie said and walked over to hug him.

"I am so glad to see that you are okay!" said Tony as he hugged her very tightly.

Quinn did not like him hugging her at all and growled.

Annie heard the growl and looked over at Quinn with a disapproving look. Now was not the time for that kind of behavior, she thought. "Quinn, I want to introduce you to my very best friend, Tony O'Hara. Tony this is my boyfriend Quinn Taylor."

"As you can tell by his accent, Tony is not from the USA. He's from Ireland."

The two men sized each other up first and then each stuck out a hand to shake. Quinn spoke up and said, "Thank you for looking after Annie."

"No problem," said Tony.

"Annie, you never told me you had a boyfriend. When did that happen?" Tony inquired as he looked questioningly at Annie.

"Well, recently actually," she said with a half smile.

Quinn's Seal training kicked up a notch. He noticed Tony's hair was black and he had very dark brown colored eyes. He had a summer tan, dressed like a college student would dress with cargo shorts, and t-shirt, and athletic shoes without socks. He noticed his body structure... how he stood, the way he walked, his hands, if he had dimples, how he smiled and whether he had tattoos or birthmarks. He put all of this into his memory.

Quinn had a great eye for detail, especially when he was on a mission and lives were at stake. After all, his instincts told him Annie's life was in danger. He sensed something about Tony, but he couldn't put his finger on it. He didn't like Tony.

What if he wasn't really who he said he was? What if he was the monster that was bugging Annie's apartment. He decided he was going to check him out.

"Tony, would you meet us at La Seals in about an hour? I would like to bring you up to date on our findings," stated Quinn. You know the old saying... keep your friends close and your enemies closer.

"Sure, I can do that," replied Tony.

"We are going to have to leave in a few minutes. I want things to look as normal as possible." He handed Jax and Tony some pizza and told them to eat up. Annie said there was no way her stomach could eat anything. He asked Tony if he would go back into his apartment and stay there for at least 20 minutes. He asked him not to say anything to anyone regarding this.

Tony gave Annie a questioning look.

"It's okay, Tony. I will see you at the club. I promise."

When Tony had left, Annie ran to her bedroom and changed quickly into a pair of jeans and a t-shirt. She grabbed a much bigger purse, more suitable to pack smaller pieces of clothing. "Quinn may make me move from my apartment for a few days, but I'd be damn sure if I'd let him pay for my clothes or personal needs!" she thought to herself. She quickly grabbed a couple of bras and thongs along with a couple pair of shorts and short-sleeved tops. Then she went to the bathroom and grabbed her hairbrush and toothbrush.

Jax had left a few minutes earlier with instructions to resume the video and audio feeds in five minutes.

Quinn had suspected the live feed came back on just as Annie had sat down and was putting on a pair of tennis shoes. When she was finished, he pulled Annie back farther on the sofa and started kissing her.

After a few minutes had passed, Quinn asked Annie if she would like to drive to Buckeye Lake and take a walk. Annie knew they weren't really going to the lake, but she stood up and walked over to the picture window and turned on the small table lamp. She grabbed her purse and keys. Quinn opened the door, turned off the overhead lights and they left, locking the door behind them.

They walked with their arms around each other's waist rather slowly towards the car. Quinn opened the door for her, then walked to the other side and climbed in. It would only take about 15 minute to get to La Seals.

CHAPTER 11

LA SEALS WOULD BE OPENING for business in a few hours. Some employees had already arrived and were getting the club ready for the night. Quinn and Annie were the first to arrive, next came Tony, and then a short time later came Joe and Jax. They all went into Quinn's office and shut the door.

Jax sat down at Quinn's desk and fired up his laptop. With the codes he had used, he would be able to see what this creep looked like when he came on line. The monster had not yet turned on his computer, so Jax programmed his computer to ping when he did.

They all sat there in silence for a few minutes. Quinn had been pacing the floor, running his hands through his hair. Finally, he spoke up and told Tony of his findings. Tony yelled out, "That bastard! I'll kill him if I get my hands on him!"

Quinn immediately walked over to him and yelled, "Who is it, Tony? You know who it is don't you!"

"No man, I really don't know who it is! Truly I don't!"

"Tony?" Quinn said in a long drawn out tone. "If you are lying to me, there will be hell to pay!"

Tony looked over at Annie. It was a look that told Quinn they both knew something. Quinn wanted to bury his fist into the wall.

Just then, the computer made a pinging noise. Within as few moments, Jax could see this monster. It most definitely was a man, but he had put on a facemask that covered everything, but his eyes. He had very dark eyes that didn't quite look right to Quinn. The monster was evidently watching the recording of Quinn and Annie kissing on the sofa. He let out a long list of expletives and even pounded his fist on his desk. "NO!" He kept yelling.

Quinn was clinching his fists over and over and his neck muscles were tightening up. He finally asked Annie to look at the video. Annie looked, but she didn't recognize him.

Quinn kept studying the picture. Something wasn't right. There was a hint of blue on the outer edge of one eye, which would suggest he was wearing colored contacts. He noticed the man had on a short sleeved shirt. He had reddish or blonde hair on his arms and freckles. Very few men have brown eyes and freckles. Quinn was sure this man had light colored hair and blue eyes. He asked Annie and Tony to look at the computer again and think of anyone that they would know that would fit that description.

Annie let out a gasp and put her hands over her mouth. Tony had a look of surprise on his face. "Surely it can't be him!" he said. Annie started to shake.

Quinn walked Annie over to the sofa in his office and they sat down together.

"Annie, who is Tony talking about?" She could not speak. It was like she was going into shock. Quinn pulled her tightly towards him.

He tried to reassure her as he turned and gave Tony a look and said, "Tell me what you know, now!"

Tony gave Quinn a very concerned look. He knew everyone wanted answers. "His name is David Morgan. Rumor has it that dear ole daddy paid for a couple of girls to transfer to different colleges to keep David out of trouble for knocking those girls up. I heard it was not consensual sex."

"Are you saying they were raped?" Joe asked.

Tony sat down next to Annie on the sofa. He took one of her hands in his.

"Annie, you need to tell them the rest."

Annie looked at Tony and then at Quinn with very scared eyes. She hated reliving that whole experience, but she knew she needed to tell him and everyone else in the room. After all, they were trying to help her.

Tears started rolling down her cheek. She hung her head down. Her words came out of her mouth slowly.

"He tried... to rape me when... when I was in my first year of college." And she took a deep breath.

"Rape you?" said Quinn, and he immediately thought of the newspaper article he had read yesterday as he turned and looked at Annie.

Annie had the same features as the women mentioned in the newspaper article. Long dark curly hair, light blue eyes, just over five feet tall and even though he really did not know how much she weighed, she had felt like she only weighed 100 pounds when he picked her up in his arms.

"Fuck!" he said as he looked at Joe running his right hand through his hair.

The room became very quiet as they were all trying to absorb what Annie had just said. Finally, she broke the eerie silence.

"It was near the end of September, my freshman year. He sat down next to me at the college library and introduced himself to me. David was in his third year of college. He was one of the most popular guys on campus and all of the girls wanted to go out with him. He kept asking me to go out on a date with him, but I always told him no. He was nice enough, but I really didn't want anything to do with him. My roommate said I was playing hard to get, but I didn't think so. I finally agreed to go. He really was cute and seemed harmless enough. I was so excited. No one that popular in high school had ever asked me out, so I kind of felt special. We went to a football game, then to dinner. It really was the perfect date. All we did was hold hands. He didn't even kiss me goodnight."

"The next day, he called me up and asked me if I would go on another date with him the following Saturday. I told him I would. This time he wanted me to meet him at the Campus Bar & Grill just around the corner from my apartment. I agreed to meet him at 7:30 p.m."

"When I arrived, David had already been there for several hours and he was absolutely drunk out of his mind. His breath smelled of cigarettes and liquor and it was such a turn off to me. I turned my head as he tried to kiss me on my lips, forcing him to kiss my cheek instead. He was not very happy about that."

"I remember a slow song was playing. He grabbed my hand and tried to pull me out onto the dance floor. I didn't want to go. He could barely walk. He finally managed to drag me out there. The dance started out okay, but then he started groping me. I told him to stop. He said he was sorry. Then he grabbed one of my breasts. I slapped him really hard and pushed him down. I ran out of the bar, past some guys."

Annie's eyes were filling with tears and her body started to tremble. Quinn held her tightly. Annie continued talking.

"He came running after me. I started screaming as loud as I could. He caught up with me. I'll never forget what he said. His words were slurring and he growled, "Oh baby, I like my women feisty!" Then he grabbed my blouse and bra and ripped them off of me."

"I was so scared. I don't know how I managed it, but I kicked him in his balls as hard as I could and pushed him down again. By that time, the guys who had been standing outside in front of the bar, ran up to me. One of them took off his shirt and put it on me and even buttoned the shirt up. They couldn't believe David would do something like that."

"One of them asked me if I wanted to call the police. I should have, but I said no. I told them to take him back to his dorm and let him sleep it off with instructions to tell him that I never wanted to see him again, ever!"

"The next day, he came over to my dorm asking to see me. I did not want to see him, but he was very insistent. I finally agreed, but I had my roommate, Lisa, go with me."

"David apologized for his behavior and he seemed sincere. I accepted his apology. He wanted to know if I would go on another date with him. I told him no and he became furious. He hit the wall with his fist and yelled out, "If I can't have you, nobody can have you!" I remember how he gritted his teeth at me when he spoke, "YOU BELONG TO ME, DO YOU HEAR ME? YOU BELONG TO ME!" That look he gave me totally scared me to death. I vowed right then and there to stay completely away from him."

"Not long after that, all female students, especially in my dorm were treating me funny. They didn't want to talk to me and within two weeks, my roommate moved out. Then most of the guys quit talking to me. I couldn't understand what was going on. I hadn't done anything. Then I heard a rumor that everyone thought I was gay and had some kind of herpes or Aids or something."

"That is when I went to see the Dean. I told him about the situation and asked if I could move off campus and still keep my scholarship. He told me no. So I went to the President of the Academy, Dr. Charles Gilmore and explained everything to him. I even asked him if they would do an investigation because the rumors were not true. Again, I asked if I could move off campus and keep my scholarship. He refused to let me move and he did not want to do an investigation either. He said David's father donated to the school and he would not jeopardize that. I couldn't believe he wanted his money more than he wanted to help his students. That was when I threatened him with a lawsuit if anything were to happen to me, knowing the academy would not help. I could tell he was not happy with me. He kept studying me. Then he said, "you are dismissed, Miss Marshall!""

"The following weekend, I went home to see my parents and I ran into my high school music teacher. He asked me how I was enjoying college life. I started crying and told him what had happened. I told him that I might have to quit if the president didn't let me move to my own place and still let me keep my scholarship. Mr. Johnson told me not to worry. He said he had connections and he would see what he could do. He also told me if I had any problems with David Morgan, he would be only too happy to take care of that problem as well."

"Anyway, about a week later, I got a letter from Dr. Gilmore, the President of the Academy. It said to stop by his office to pick up a key to my new apartment. He didn't seem very happy with me. When he gave me the key, he said I must have some very powerful friends to have pulled this off. I didn't know what he was talking about, but I figured Mr. Johnson had something to do with it. He kept looking at me and licking his lips."

"He told me I had to be on my best behavior because if he heard just one rumor about me, he would kick me out of school. He also made it very clear that I could not make anything less than a 3.5 GPA in all of my classes or he would see to it that I would lose my scholarship. I did not like him, but I showed him. I ended up with a 4.0 GPA."

"After I had moved off campus, I still felt like someone was watching me. That was when I chose to keep to myself. I devoted all of my time to my studies, my music, and even took on other classes outside of the academy. Then Tony moved in across the hall from me. We just seemed to hit it off. He became my best friend."

"Tony, I don't know what I would have done without you these past two years!" and she looked at Tony with such sad eyes.

"Then yesterday," as she continued, " I felt like someone was watching me in my apartment. I actually thought I was being paranoid. I never dreamed my place was bugged. Quinn, why is he doing this? What am I supposed to do now?"

Quinn hated seeing her like this. She seemed so weak and vulnerable to the point of exhaustion. He knew in that exact moment what he wanted to do, when Annie said that David Morgan tried to rape her. He wanted to find Morgan and beat the living shit out of him, but he knew he couldn't, at least not yet.

Quinn looked at Jax and then Joe and asked what their thoughts were.

"I think we have a psycho on our hands," said Jax.

"I agree," said Joe, "We need to proceed with extreme caution."

Quinn knew his friends were right and he knew they needed to strategize very carefully what they needed to do.

"Tony," Quinn stated, "I think now would be a good time for you to fly back to Ireland."

"Why should I go back to Ireland? As far as I

can tell, he is not after me. Besides I need to stay here and help you all protect Annie," said Tony.

"That is where you're wrong, Tony. You are a threat to him, too, just like I am a threat. That is why he has a bug facing your apartment. You saw how upset he was with me when he saw me kissing Annie. If he thinks there is anything going on between the two of you, I am afraid he might try to kill you," said Quinn.

"Oh, Tony," Annie said. "He's right, you should go!"

"But, I don't have all the money saved up for my trip. I wasn't planning on going back until September," said Tony as he ran his hands through his hair.

"Not to worry man. I have a jet. I will have my pilot take you. Can you be ready to leave in an hour?"

"I don't know, Quinn," said Tony shaking his head. "What about my car, and getting my deposit back on my apartment? And then I need to close my bank accounts plus pack everything."

"Do you have a clear title to your car?" asks Quinn.

"Yes," replied Tony.

"How much is it worth?"

"About seven thousand dollars."

"Where is your car parked?"

"About a block away," replied Tony, "why?"

"Jax, would you take your surveillance equipment and—"

"I'm on it, QT."

Just then they heard a loud explosion. They all ran outside to see what had happened. Jax ran down the street towards the explosion and saw a car burning. He ran back to La Seals.

"Tony, what kind of car do you own?" asked Jax.

"A black Trailblazer." Jax looked at Quinn, then Joe. They knew Annie was in danger, now Tony was in danger too.

"Fuck!" said Tony as he turned around looking so pissed.

"Come on, we've got to get out of here. We are sitting ducks here in the open!" yelled Quinn. And they all ran back inside La Seals.

"Tony, give me your cell phone, you, too, Annie, now!" demanded Quinn.

Annie and Tony did as he asked. Quinn and Jax opened up the cell phones and noticed they had been bugged, and each phone had a small explosive device enough to blow someone's head off. Jax grabbed the phones and quickly ran outside and threw both phones into the river, first Annie's phone and then Tony's. As soon as each phone hit the water, they exploded.

Quinn immediately pulled his cell phone out and called his pilot. "We'll be there in 30 minutes. Be ready to go," and he hung up.

Just then, Joe appeared with three HK416's and enough ammunition to go to war.

"Good thinking" said Quinn as he and Jax grabbed a weapon.

They each very quickly disassembled their rifles and put them into a tote bag. If the Columbus Police Department saw them carrying loaded rifles across High Street, they would all be arrested.

Annie's eyes were as big as saucers and her senses were high on alert. She didn't know whether to cry or scream. Quinn put his arms around her.

"Don't worry Annie, I won't let anything happen to you," and he kissed her gently on her lips. "Joe, we need some passports."

Joe unlocked the safe and took out six passports. Quinn, Jax, Joe and Cindy had legal passports. Next, he grabbed two fake passports, one for Tony and one for Annie. Tony remembered his passport number and Joe was able to put it on the fake passport. Everything looked good.

"Joe, I think we should close down La Seals for the next few nights—just to keep everyone safe."

"I'm in agreement Quinn, but you know tonight is one of our biggest nights of the year."

"I realize that, but I would rather err on the side of caution than put anyone's life at risk," responded Quinn.

Joe walked out to the floor and gathered all the employees. Without telling everyone what was going on, he gave everyone the evening off plus the next two days with pay.

"Just make sure everything is turned off that should be turned off and everything is locked up tight before you leave! Don't pussy foot around. I want you all to leave NOW. Champ, I need to talk to you in private." Joe was in his Seal mode now. You could hear the seriousness in his voice. Champ knew something big was up. You didn't cross the CO when he barked out orders like that.

Champ's real name was Cane Curtis. He was a former seal. He got his "Champ" call sign because he liked to box. He was a huge man at six-foot-five-inches tall, weighing in at 230 pounds and he was all muscle. Champ worked at La Seals as one of the bouncers until a new La Seals could be built for him in another city.

Champ walked over to Joe, "What's going on CO?"

Joe took Champ aside and told him he needed for him, Jason and Danny to run surveillance on La Seals while they were gone. Joe filled Champ in on what was going on with Quinn, Annie and Tony.

"Quinn may be in danger and this club may be in danger too. If you think you need extra help, call in any Seal you need. You know the drill. If you think the police needs called, then call them. Here is my new cell number. Keep in touch." Joe handed Champ the keys to lock up the place.

"One more thing, Champ. Call the radio stations and have them announce we will be closed through Monday. Tell them we had a death in the family. Put a sign on the door with the same information, too."

"Okay, let's go," Quinn grabbed Annie's hand, Joe took Cindy's and Tony and Jax were right behind them. They ran across the street to the parking garage of the hotel and took the service elevator to the top floor. They took the stairs to the rooftop. Waiting for them was a sleek, top-of-the-line new passenger helicopter with enough room to seat eight passengers plus a pilot and co-pilot.

Rocko Jergensen, the pilot, was standing outside the helicopter. "Good evening, sir." "Good evening, Rocko." Quinn said as they shook hands. "We are in a bit of a hurry. Did you receive clearance?"

"Yes sir, I did."

"Very good," Quinn said. "We need to go now."

"Yes, sir," and Rocko climbed into the pilots seat.

Everyone had their seat belts on and was putting their headphones on over their ears. Quinn closed the door and started buckling himself in. The pilot started the engine to the helicopter and was heard talking to the airport for final clearance in taking off. Quinn noticed Annie's hands were shaking as the rotor blades began to turn, so he pulled her as close to him as possible and then kissed her gently on the lips. Annie smiled, but said nothing. He could tell she was feeling very overwhelmed.

Five minutes into the flight, Annie started relaxing and was looking out of the window. Quinn pointed out the airport and a few other notable spots of Columbus, such as the big "Horseshoe" at Ohio State University and the Easton Mall. There weren't as many landmarks going towards eastern Columbus as there were in Central and Western Columbus. Another ten minutes and they would arrive at their destination. They arrived at Taylor hanger where two pilots were on standby, waiting on Quinn and his passengers.

Quinn walked behind Annie up the stairs and into the jet. There was a table on each side of the jet with four seats, two seats facing each other. The tables were made of a black material almost like onyx and all of the seats were made of soft white leather. The walls were white, as was the floor except in the center of the floor was a mosaic design of Taylor Suites Hotels. The jet was very elegant looking. Annie noticed there were two doors in the back of the jet. One was a restroom and the other, she could only imagine, was possibly a bedroom for long trips or for "whatever." She didn't want to think about that. There was a kitchen galley near the cockpit and a place for the stewardess to sit.

Quinn instructed Annie to sit next to the window. He had been on numerous flights over his years, especially as a Seal, so sitting next to a window to see the sights was not on his list of priorities. Annie, on the other hand, had never flown anywhere, so he wanted her to experience the beauty below from the air.

After seeing that Annie had securely attached her seat belt, Quinn introduced Captain Henley and Captain White. He talked with the stewardess for a moment, and gave her some instructions and headed back to his seat.

ANNIE

The stewardess introduced herself. She said her name was Kathy White and that she was the wife of one of the pilots. She was the typical looking stewardess in that she was very beautiful with short blonde hair and long slim legs. "I wish I had some of her long legs," Annie thought.

I listened to what the stewardess had to say should there be an emergency event, though I knew Quinn would be there for me and would help if there was an emergency, if he could. She announced that she would be serving food and drinks once the jet has taken off, and she told us we could move around in the jet freely after the pilot turned off the "Fasten Your Seat Belt" sign.

After making sure we were all securely buckled in, she phoned the pilot telling him we were set. She sat down in her spot by the galley and buckled herself in. The jet started moving toward the runway.

I was feeling very nervous and could feel my hands shaking. Quinn put one arm around my shoulders and grabbed my hand. His hands were so warm and I still felt that electrical pull. I felt more comfortable around him than I had ever felt around any man. I felt strangely at ease. Instead of looking out of the window, I laid my head on his shoulder and closed my eyes. That was where I belonged, at least for now. I silently wished we could fly off somewhere permanently and forget about all the madness in Columbus, Ohio.

Within a few minutes, the jet leveled off and the pilot announced we were flying at 35,000 feet. The sign indicating we could unbuckle our seat belts came on. Kathy started serving us Chinese take out from a Chinese restaurant. The food really smelled good, but I didn't have much of an appetite. To be this thoughtful in supplying all of us with food, was just amazing. Quinn must have been one hell of a Seal. He just seemed to know what needed to be done and he did it. I was in awe of him. I started picking at my food.

"Baby," Quinn said, "You really should try to eat something. We will be flying at least 10 hours. Would you please eat a little for me?"

I looked at his gorgeous deep blue eyes and thought how could I deny this man anything. He looked so worried and I knew he was only trying to take care of me.

"Okay, I'll try," I said. I took a few bites of some pork-fried rice and ate some wonton soup. I even managed to eat a vegetable egg roll and drank some diet cola. Even though I wasn't that hungry, it really did taste good. I would say I was feeling much better since I had eaten something.

About two hours into the flight, Quinn got up from his seat and went into the galley. He had made us both a mixed drink and had informed Kathy to make everyone else something to drink as well.

"This is very good. Did you make it?"

"Only if you count opening up a package and squeezing it into a glass," Quinn said with a smile. "A lot of the alcohol on my jet consists of premixed package drinks so that I don't have to worry about glass breakage."

"Hmm, well, this really tastes good. What is it called?"

"It's a Frozen Margarita," Quinn said. "I take it you have never had one before?"

"No, I haven't, but then I have never been much of a drinker. "Umm, I think I may want another one of these." Annie smiled at Quinn. She was feeling very relaxed.

"Well, finish what you have first and then we will see about fixing you another," Quinn said with a laugh.

CHAPTER 12

QUINN

QUINN WAS HOPING THAT ONE drink would relax Annie enough to the point of going to sleep. He wanted her to lay on his bed in his private quarters so he could strategize with Joe and Jax on what to do about David Morgan. It didn't look like that was going to happen. Annie was wide-awake. So, he decided to include Annie in the strategy session.

"Have you all looked at the local newspaper lately or the television newscast regarding the rapist?" asked Quinn. Everyone acknowledged they had.

"Did you see the pictures of the rape victims?" He paused. "Did you see anything particularly familiar about the ladies?" asked Quinn.

"Other than they all looked very much alike," Tony replied. "Quinn, what are you getting at?"

Quinn reached into his pants pocket and pulled out a newspaper clipping of the article with the pictures of all the girls and passed it around.

He asked Annie to take her hair down from her ponytail and instructed her to move her hair to the front so that it hung over each shoulder.

"Now,"Quinn said,"Look at the photographs and then look at Annie. Do you see any resemblance?"

"Let me see that picture!" Annie demanded.

Quinn handed the newspaper article to Annie. "Oh my God! As if I didn't have enough to worry about!" Annie dropped the newspaper article to the table, put her elbows on the table and placed her face into her hands.

"I saw this article in the newspaper and watched it on TV yesterday morning. I didn't get the connection until Annie said David Morgan tried to rape her. What I am wondering is this. Is David Morgan the rapist of all six girls and then found a new victim with Annie, since she looked like the others or, are the other six girls a manifestation of Annie in his mind because Annie didn't want anything to do with him?"

Annie immediately dropped her hands from her face. She looked at Quinn with a confused, distasteful look.

She yelled, "You mean to tell me, he searches for girls and rapes and tortures them, all because they look like me? Oh my God, Oh my God, Oh my God!" Annie screamed! "Could this day get any worse?"

Quinn grabbed Annie's arms and pulled her from the chair and walked her into his private quarters. He shut the door and locked it. Then he pulled Annie into his arms. Annie was sobbing into his chest. He held her for a very long time.

"I'm sorry Annie. We'll catch this bastard. I won't let him get near you, I promise."

"Are the other girls okay?"

"I don't know, but when we get back home, we can go to the police and tell them of our suspicions. All right?"

"Quinn, I am so scared. I promise you I have never done anything to encourage him in any way."

"I know, baby, you can't help it if you are the most beautiful woman in the world."

"Oh, Quinn, stop saying that because it is just not true."

"It is to me, Annie," and he hugged her tightly against his chest.

Quinn knew better than to suggest they hop into bed at that moment. He knew he would only feel guilty at the mere suggestion of making love to her while she felt so vulnerable. He just wanted to help her forget everything, even if only for a little while.

"Are you ready to go back out with the others?"

"Yes," as she dried her eyes with a tissue. "I'm okay now."

Quinn unlocked the door and they proceeded to take their seats. Quinn instructed Kathy to make Annie and Cindy another frozen Margarita and beers for everyone else.

Quinn looked at the other passengers. "What are your thoughts on this?" he asked.

"As I said before, I think this guy is most definitely a psycho!" said Joe.

"I think we are a little out of our league on this one guys," replied Jax.

"Why do you think that?" responded Quinn.

"Well, for one thing, we are the best damn Seals on earth. We can go in and fight the enemy and can just about guess what their next move will be. This, on the other hand, is something different. We don't know what his next move will be because he is fucking crazy. He is not thinking with a rational head, you know?" Jax stated.

Joe chimed in. "I think Jax is right Quinn. I think Tony needs more protection than just moving back to Ireland, but I also think he is the least of Morgan's worries. I do think he will definitely come after Annie and you, too. I don't think it will matter where in the world you go because he has the money and the resources to follow you."

"I have done some checking up on Morgan and his father. His father is Paul T. Morgan from Morgan House Pharmaceuticals. He is into major bucks, probably as wealthy if not more so than your dad. He also has some shipping lines and other investments. He is a very shrewd businessman."

"Daddy was upset with David because he didn't want to follow in his footsteps. David doesn't want anything to do with the business. Looks like daddy may have given him an ultimatum. He gave David three years to get his shit together or he would give all he had to charity when he dies. He has another year left of the three, but the best he has done is purchase the coffee shop. Makes you wonder if he is doing this purposely to piss off dear old daddy, or if he wants to stay around girls like Annie. I'm sorry Annie, I mean no offense to you."

"None taken, Joe," replied Annie.

"Quinn, you are a damn good Seal, but you need an arsenal of men around you and Annie right now. I think that is the only way that will keep you both safe from this lunatic."

"Oh, Quinn," Annie pleaded as she grabbed his hand. "Just take me back to Ohio and leave me. I'll go to the police and ask for their protection; that way you can be safe. Please Quinn, do this for me. I don't want anything to happen to you. I can even move back home with my parents."

Quinn took Annie's hands with both of his hands and looked her dead in the eyes.

"I love you, Annie and I won't let you go. I have looked for you for the last ten years and there is no way I will ever let you go! Do you understand that! You are mine now! You will always belong to me. You will never belong to that son of a bitch. I would rather die squeezing the last bit of breath out of him. No, Annie, I'm not going anywhere and neither are you."

"Quinn, why are you doing all of this?" she whispered. "I haven't really declared my love for you, yet. We are so new together. You can't put yourself in danger for me!"

"You don't have to, I saw it in your eyes, remember? The eyes don't lie," Quinn said as he put two fingers under her chin and lifted her face to his.

Annie's eyes filled with big tears. "Oh, Quinn, I am so tired of crying like a baby. I don't know what I ever did to deserve you, but I am falling in love with you," and she reached up and kissed him on his lips.

Quinn smiled from ear to ear and looked at Joe, "Are you happy now, Joe?"

Joe couldn't help but laugh and shook hands with Quinn.

"Welcome to the club man. I just hope this changes your shitty disposition. Did you know Quinn has a shitty disposition, Annie?" Joe cracked a big smile.

Annie smiled while wiping her tears. "Yeah, I just bet he has."

Everyone applauded when Quinn and Annie declared their love for each other.

"So," Jax said, "When's the big day?"

"What big day?" asked Quinn.

"You know, when you get married?"

"Wait a minute guys, we've only known each other for two minutes!" said Annie laughing.

"Hey Joe, what was that Marine's name that went home with your friend Kenny and met his niece, went out with her that night only to leave the next day, came back two weeks later and went out with her again, left the next day and then came back on the third time and married her? What were their names? Do you remember?"

"Yeah Jax, I do remember that story. Their names were Larry... Larry," he said as he was struggling to remember their names. "Larry and Susie. Does that sound right?"

"Are they still married?" asked Tony.

"Yeah, Tony they are. They have been married around eight years or so, I think. I ran into them not too long ago. They were in Columbus shopping one day when I ran into them at the mall. I think they even have a couple of kids, too. They looked like they were still in love. They were holding hands as they were walking through the mall.

"So, Quinn, what are you waiting on?" asked Tony. "You both have already declared your love to each other. Sounds to me like if two people who have never met each other before can marry only after two dates, then happily ever after can happen to anybody, at anytime."

Quinn looked over at Annie and smiled. "You know, Tony's right. I have already declared my love for you."

Annie rolled her eyes at him and pursed her lips together as she shook her head "no."

"WWWhat?"

"We can get married in England and honeymoon anywhere you want in Europe," said Quinn with a smile.

"That Quinn was probably the most unromantic proposal I have ever heard! You will have to do better than that!" Annie said as she shook her finger at him.

"God, Quinn," said Cindy, "You sure are stupid for a smart man!"

"Honey, we are all stupid when it comes to women," said Joe with a laugh.

"Better than that, huh," said Quinn scratching his chin. "Hmm."

They had been inflight for approximately five hours and the mood in the cabin had changed considerably. It was nearly 11 p.m. The high altitude was starting to tire everyone. Annie had fallen asleep with her head on Quinn's shoulder.

"Tony," Quinn said, "how much was your deposit on your apartment?"

"Six hundred dollars," replied Tony.

"Have you already paid this month's rent?"

Tony nodded his head indicating that he had already paid his rent.

"I have made reservations for all of us to stay at dad's hotel. When we get there, I want to give you some money for your car and for the apartment."

"Why would you do that, Quinn?"

"I think I own your apartment building. Your safety was compromised and you deserve a refund," said Quinn. "And your car blew up so I want to give you money to replace your car. I can't help but feel it was partly my fault. I want to give you $8500 for your car and your rent deposit refund."

"That's very generous of you, Quinn."

"Plus, when this is over, I'll fly you back to the states so that you can get the rest of your money from your bank account, the rest of your belongings from your apartment, and I will fly you back to Ireland."

"Why would you do all of that?"

"You have been a good friend to Annie. I think she would really like me to do that."

"You really do love her, don't you?"

Quinn looked down at Annie and kissed her softly on top of her head, then looked back at Tony. "I have waited my whole life for a love like this. I'm never letting go of her. I will be 100% devoted to her and only her until the day I die."

"Promise me you will always take care of her, Quinn. You know she is really special to me, too."

"It's pretty obvious you're in love with her, too, aren't you?" said Quinn. "What happened that it didn't work out for the both of you?"

"Is it really that obvious?"

Quinn shook his head yes. "So what happened?"

"I met her on the first day of classes when I came barreling out of the apartment building. She had dropped an armload of books and had stooped down to pick them up. I wasn't watching where I was going and almost fell on top of her. I started helping her pick up her books. When she looked up at me with those eyes, well, I think it was right then when I fell for her."

"Yeah, I know what you mean," said Quinn.

"I wanted to go out with her so badly. I know I asked her everyday for a year if she would go for coffee with me to the Campus Coffee House. She refused every time I asked her. Finally I quit asking her out, and we became close friends. About six months ago, she told me why she wouldn't go out with me. She said she couldn't stand the owner of the coffee shop, David Morgan. By that time, there was no way she could think of me as anything more than a close friend."

He continued, "I had heard rumors about a year ago that he had tried to rape her when she was a first-year student, but I wasn't going to ask her if it was true. I think she knew that I had heard the rumors. That was when I decided to start looking out for her. She saw me as more of a protector and friend, like a big brother, than anything else. I really didn't know for certain that she was almost raped until today when she actually admitted it. I hated to take stock in rumors, you know. So in a way, I have as much reason to hate David Morgan as you do."

Quinn looked at Tony and had a better understanding of him now. It was very ironic how David Morgan kept Tony from having a relationship with Annie, yet David was one of the reasons why Quinn and Annie were together now. It must have been fate. Annie and I were just meant to be together, he thought.

Just then, Annie woke up, "What were you two talking about?"

Quinn looked at her with a little smile on his face, "Oh, only about my favorite subject."

"Well, let me up. Your favorite subject needs to go to the bathroom; and, when I return, my favorite subject needs to shut up so everyone can sleep."

Quinn got up from his chair to let Annie out, but instead he took her hand and walked her into his quarters, shutting the door behind him and locking it. "You can use the bathroom facility in here, then you are going to lie down on the bed to sleep. And don't argue!"

"Quinn, that's not fair to everyone else. They don't have a bed to sleep in."

"I said not to argue with me. I'll lie down beside you."

Annie knew arguing with Quinn would be futile, so when she finished taking care of her bathroom needs, she laid down beside him.

CHAPTER 13

AN ALARM SOUNDED ON QUINN'S watch letting him know they would be landing in Ireland in about an hour. Annie was sound asleep and he hated to wake her. She looked so beautiful. He reached over and gently placed a kiss on her soft lips, but she didn't respond. So he kissed her again. That time her eyes opened. She fluttered her eyelids trying to focus. "Good morning, baby. Did you sleep well?"

"What time is it?"

"Time to get up. We'll be landing soon."

"Hmm. Thank you, Quinn."

"For what?"

"For being a gentleman; for being there for me."

"I love you, Annie," Quinn stated as he moved her hair behind her ear. "I'm always going to be here for you," and he kissed her more intensely. He smacked her on her bottom and said, "Come on, we need to wake the others, too."

A coffee fragrance could be smelled through out the cabin as they walked in and took their seats. Kathy had already awakened the other passengers and served them coffee. She brought two cups of hot steaming coffee with creamer packets to them.

They barely had enough time to drink their coffee when the "Fasten Your Seat Belt" sign came on. Quinn was pleased Annie had tolerated the flight as well as she had since it was her first time.

As soon as they got off the jet, Quinn checked his cell phone for any messages and called his dad telling him they had arrived in Ireland safely. A limousine was waiting for them. It didn't take long for them to arrive at the Dublin location of Taylor Suites Hotel.

Reginald Taylor had reserved four suites per Quinn's instructions. Quinn looked at Tony and the desk clerk. "You should have an envelope in the safe for me from my father. Could you get it for me, please?"

"Right away, sir."

Within a few minutes, the desk clerk returned with an envelope and handed it to Quinn. He opened it up, smiled, and gave the envelope to Tony.

"Quinn, this is way too much!"

"No it isn't. There is enough in there to order a new set of bagpipes, since you didn't have time to get them from your apartment. I know you are going to need them to further your career until you can get back to the states."

"Thanks," and they shook hands.

Annie smiled at Quinn. "That was very nice of

you to do that for him." Quinn was her hero. He tried to act all big and bad, but he really did have a heart. She knew she had fallen in love with an amazing man.

"Come, everyone, let's go get something to eat for breakfast. I'm starved!"

They ate in the hotel dining room and discussed staying in Ireland for a few days. Before they left to go to their rooms, Quinn had made arrangements for everyone to fly to England at 9 a.m. on Monday morning. He had also made arrangements for a driver to take Tony to his hometown.

"Annie, I am really exhausted!" Quinn said as they walked into their hotel room. "For your own safety, promise me you won't leave this room while I sleep."

"Do you think he is here already?"

"No, but I have to know you are safe at all times until he is caught."

"Okay, I promise. I'll just lie down beside you."

He gently kissed her on the lips and gave her a hug. She could feel him getting hard as he pulled her close to him. He let go of her and ran both hands through his hair. He started taking his clothes off, except for his boxers, and climbed into bed.

What is going on here? She thought as she stripped down to her camisole and thong and climbed into bed next to him. He doesn't want sex? He must really be tired or maybe he has lost interest in me. Next thing she knew, he had pulled her back very close to his front and wrapped his arms around her. "I love you, Annie," he said softly, kissing her on the back of her neck. And the next thing she heard was a gentle sound of a soft snore. Annie smiled to herself. He really was exhausted.

Eight hours later, Annie woke up finding Quinn was no longer in bed with her. She walked out into the living room quarters of their suite and found Quinn already dressed in a pair of navy blue dress trousers and a white dress shirt. He was talking on his cell phone, but interrupted his call when he saw Annie. "I'll call you back in a minute."

"Good afternoon, my love," he said as he walked over and hugged her.

"What's going on?"

"Oh, just making some plans for us for tonight."

"Yeah, like what?"

"Well, Tony has made reservations for all of us to eat at this really nice Irish Pub. He said the pub belongs to his uncle. He swears they have the best food in all of Ireland and guarantees the music is perfect."

"Well, Quinn, I don't think I have anything with me that would even be appropriate to wear. All I have with me are a few pair of shorts."

"Honey, you would look great in anything you wear. I took the liberty of purchasing you a new dress." He walked over to the sofa, retrieved a box, and handed it to her.

"Oh Quinn, you shouldn't have!" She opened the box. In the box was a beautiful white sleeveless dress with layers of lace on the skirt. The skirt to the dress was rather full and hung longer on each side. Each layer of lace had very tiny pale blue flowers, four inches apart around the edging.

"I hope you like it. I told her to get something with a little blue in it to match your eyes."

"Her who? And how did you know what size to get?"

"Do you remember the desk clerk when we checked in this morning?"

"Yes."

"She looked like she was your size, so I asked her if she would have time to go shopping for me. She said her sister worked at a small boutique nearby. So, she called her up, told her what I wanted, and here you are. Do you like it?"

Annie held it up in front of her and looked in a long wall mirror. "It's beautiful! How much was it? I'll pay you back."

"Well, I don't really know. I'll just have to wait and see what the charges are when I get the bill in the mail," Quinn said knowing he had put the receipt in his wallet.

"Quinn, why do I get the feeling that you are lying to me?"

"Busted," he said with a smile. "Because I

don't want you paying me back. Please, can you just accept it as a gift? I have something exciting planned for tonight and I just want everything to be perfect. Pleeeease?" and he smiled very seductively at her. "I replaced your cell phone, too. It's already activated, but you will have to program in your contact numbers."

"How did you know what cell number to use?"

"Tony gave it to me. I replaced his, too."

"Quinn, what am I going to do with you?" she said, giving into his charms.

"Just love me!"

"You are making it very hard to not love you!" and she kissed him. "Thank you!"

"Now, go take your shower. We are going to meet everyone downstairs in an hour."

Annie took the box of clothing to their bedroom and placed it on the bed. She put the dress on a hanger so it would not wrinkle. Then she noticed there were several other pieces of clothing. In the box were five pairs of matching underwear, a sundress with spaghetti straps, three pairs of jeans, three pull-over tops, one pair of white heels, a very sexy nighty, and a pair of soft leather casual shoes.

"What am I going to do with this man? He had spent a small fortune! He has got to stop spending money on me like this!"

Annie quickly got into the shower. The hot water really felt good on her body. She wondered what he had planned for the evening? It was nice not feeling like someone was watching her. She quickly washed her body, shampooed, and rinsed her hair. She turned the water off and wrapped a towel around her hair. Next she toweled herself off. She dried her hair, and decided to leave her hair down for the evening and applied her make-up. Next, she slipped on her thong and put on her bra. She put the dress on and sat down on the bed, slipping on her strappy heels. When she stood up and looked into the mirror, she couldn't believe how beautiful the dress looked. "Hmm, I just wish I had a little necklace to go with this dress," she said softly.

As soon as she walked into the living quarters, Quinn stood up with a smile, holding a smaller box in his hands.

"You look gorgeous and it looks like a perfect fit, too!" He lifted her hand in the air twirling her around causing her to do a pirouette. When he stopped turning her around, he opened the small box in front of her.

"I wanted you to have a little bit of jewelry to go with your dress."

Quinn opened the box in front of her. Inside the box was a delicate white-gold chain with a matching white-gold locket shaped in a heart with a blue sapphire in the middle and a pair of blue sapphire earrings.

She let out a gasp, "You shouldn't have!"

"Do you like it?" Quinn asked as he was taking

the necklace out of the box. He turned Annie around and fastened the necklace around her neck, then kissed her neck softly. She felt little shivers go all over her body.

"It's beautiful, Quinn, but why are you doing all of this? We haven't known each other that long."

"I have missed out on so much these last ten years not being with a woman I could love. Now that I have found you, I want to give you the world. It just makes me feel really good."

"Quinn, I don't need gifts. I just need you, only you. I wouldn't care if you didn't have a dime." Annie said with tears filling her eyes.

Quinn knew he had a keeper. "Why did it take so long for you to enter my life?" asked Quinn as he put his hands on both sides of her face and they kissed each other deeply with their tongues.

"Would you like to go into the bedroom?" Annie asked.

"No," said Quinn with a groan.

"No?" Annie gave Quinn a questioning look.

"No," said Quinn. "We are going to do this right! I am not going to make love to you until you are completely mine," and he smiled at her and kissed her on the tip of her nose. "Besides, it's time for us to leave. Here, I'll let you put your earrings in."

"Quinn," as she looked into his eyes, "thank you for everything."

Annie ran back into the bedroom with the

earrings and fastened them into her ears. She quickly pulled the sides of her hair to the back of her head securing it with a hair clasp. "That looks better."

Annie walked back into the living room and took his proffered hand. Everyone was waiting for them when they got off the elevator. Mac's Pub Tavern wasn't that far away, so they all decided to walk.

Recorded Irish music was playing as they walked into Mac's. A hostess screamed, "Tony," and ran up to him, jumping into his arms, and gave him a big kiss on the lips.

"Patty, how have ye been?" and he kissed her back.

"Where have ye been?" asked Patty.

"I've been in the United States studying for the last two years. How have you been, doll?"

"Fine, now that you're back. This place needs some livening up!"

"Patty, I want you to meet my friends. This is Quinn and Annie, Joe and Cindy, and Jax. We have a reservation for tonight."

"Tony, what name is your reservation under? I don't see your name on the list," she asked with a very girly, seductive smile. "Umm, Quinn Taylor," Tony said as he looked at her backside as she bent over to reach for some menus.

When she straightened herself back up, she smiled and winked at Tony, "Follow me, please."

Patty seated them at a table very close to the stage. "Tony, I think your old band is playing here tonight," and she batted her eyelashes at him. "Not really for sure, but I just saw Mike a short time ago carrying in some music equipment."

"Really? Good, I'll go talk to him in a minute."

"Great, I'll send your server over."

When Joe and Jax thought that Patty was out of earshot, Joe mimicked her and said in a high-pitched girly voice, "What name is your reservation under?"

Then Jax said in the same girly high-pitched voice, "Follow me, please" and batted his eyelashes.

"Hey, what can I say? When you got it, you got it!" smirked Tony sticking his chest out.

Everyone laughed. They all knew Tony did not have the chest circumference that Quinn, Joe and Jax had, but they were not going to say anything. Tony was becoming a new friend to them.

"Is she an ex-girlfriend or something Tony?" asked Annie.

"No, we attended some college classes together here in Dublin. She's been trying to get in me pants for the last six years now."

"So why don't you take her up on it?" asked Joe with a grin.

"Me think she's been in too many pants!" Tony smirked with distaste.

"Sounds like she is right up your alley, Jax!" laughed Quinn.

"And what's so bad about that?" Jax smarted off. "You know what they say about experience!"

"What is this, a sausage fest? Now cut out the male testosterone bullshit, guys!" said Cindy as she poked Joe in the arm with her finger and laughed.

A few seconds later, the server came over to take their drinks and appetizers order.

"Can I make a suggestion before ye order your drinks? Try Mac's beer. They make it downstairs and trust me, it's the best beer you'll ever drink!" suggested Tony.

Everyone agreed, "Tall boys for everyone!"

"Would you like any appetizers?" asked the server.

"Tony, do you have any suggestions?" asked Annie.

"Yeah. Bring us some Irish potato skins and a large onion loaf."

"Thank you, sir," and the server left.

"Irish potato skins?" asked Annie.

"Yes, they're made just like in the States, but they boil the potatoes in a light beer. Me ma makes them all the time. Ummm. Really good."

Just then, the server brought everyone a Mac's tallboy. Quinn looked at Annie and then ordered a large glass of water to go with the beer for her.

"Annie, I'm afraid you will get drunk on me tonight if you drink all that beer. For every drink you take, I want you to take a drink of water, okay?"

"You must think I am such a light weight and

can't hold my drinks," she giggled, "and you're probably right, too!"

Everyone took a drink. "Wow, this is really good," said Annie.

"Okay, Tony, you are going to have to help me keep Annie from getting drunk!" said Quinn as he rolled his eyes.

"Oh, please!" grumbled Annie as she took another drink.

Just then the waitress delivered their appetizers and took their dinner orders.

"Annie, may I borrow you cell phone for a few minutes?" asked Tony. "I left my cell at the hotel."

"Certainly," and Annie handed her cell to him.

Tony excused himself for a few minutes to make a call and returned a couple of minutes later. When he sat down, he handed Annie her cell phone.

As Tony was sitting down, he saw his former band mate, Michael O'Malley, at the bar ordering a beer. "Excuse me. I see an old friend of mine. I'll be back shortly."

When the pleasantries had been exchanged, Tony asked Mike if he could do a favor for him.

"I was wondering if you would bring a young lady up on stage to play a song on your violin."

"Is she good?"

"Only the best musician I have ever heard!"

"Sure, just signal me when she's ready and she'd better be good!"

"Not to worry. I guarantee ye she will get a standing ovation!"

By the time Tony had finished with his visit with Michael, the food had arrived. Tony looked over towards Quinn, smiled and gave him the thumbs up.

"What are you two up to?" asked Annie.

"Oh nothing to worry ye pretty little head over lassie!" said Tony in a very Irish brogue. Everyone started laughing.

Dinner was delicious. The waitress removed their plates. Quinn ordered another round of drinks for everyone, except for Annie. Tony excused himself to go look for his Uncle Mac, while Annie and Cindy excused themselves to go to the ladies restroom.

"Cindy, I think those boys are up to no good. Do you know what they have planned?"

"No, Annie, I don't know," she lied. "But I will say, when these guys get together, you can bet something will most definitely happen!"

The ladies walked back to their table just as the Irish music started playing. It was fun, fast and exciting to listen to. The place was really packed full of people and everyone was clapping in time to the music.

"This is the coolest place I have ever been in," Annie said, as she took hold of Quinn's hand.

Quinn could not believe it when Annie finished

off her beer; and she was feeling pretty good. Just then Tony gave Michael the signal.

"Ladies and Gentlemen, we have a special guest in the house tonight and I'm sure if we give him a big applause, he will join us on stage. Mr. Tony O'Hara."

Everyone applauded. Tony walked up the few steps to the stage and grabbed the portable microphone.

"Thank ye, thank ye, everyone. Thank ye. I have a very nice surprise for all of ye." He stated in a very Irish brogue.

"As some of ye may know, I have been in the United States studying music for the past two years and have met a beautiful young lady." You could hear all the ladies in the audience moaning.

"Now, wait a minute, ladies; unfortunately for me, she is already taken. She is just a very close friend. This lady is the best and most talented musician I have ever heard in my life. It would give me great pleasure if ye would join me in a round of applause to talk her into coming up here to play for ye. Annie Marshall, would ye come up on stage and play something for us?" He held out a violin.

All of a sudden, everyone at her table stood up and started applauding her. Quinn took her hand and helped her stand from her chair, gave a gentle kiss on her lips, smiled and said, "Show them how it's done, baby!"

Tony had walked down the steps and took Annie's hand helping her up to the stage.

"Is there anything you wish for me to play?"

"Danny Boy," yelled someone while another yelled for her to play something American.

Annie looked over at Michael. "Are you sure this is okay? I really don't want to intrude on your wonderful show."

"No, it's fine, lassie."

"Thank you. Would you mind if Tony joined me on the drums?"

"No problem, miss."

Tony smiled from ear to ear. He knew what song she wanted to play.

Michael and the band moved to the side while Tony sat down on the drums. He immediately started pounding out a rhythmic noise that sounded like a train. Annie nervously went to the center of the stage with the violin.

She looked down at Quinn and smiled. She walked over to the microphone and said very playfully, "Ya know, I loooove Ireland! And you know what I love most about Ireland?" She smiled and was now tapping her foot to the sounding beat of a train. "I looove all of you!"

The crowd started applauding.

"I want to ask you a question. Do ya'll like to travel?" And she flicked a couple of strings on the fiddle. The crowd gave her another applause. In a low sultry voice, she asked, "Do ya like trainnns?" and she flicked the strings again.

"Well, I'm gonna play a song for you written in 1938 by the late, great Ervin T. Rouse. It's about a train called the Orange Blossom Special!" and she flicked the strings again.

Tony yelled out, "All aboard!" Quinn noticed her taking a silent 1-2-3 count to herself and she started playing the song. As the music sped up, so did she. She danced and played all over the stage. She was a natural born performer. She was absolutely wonderful. Quinn noticed the crowd getting very excited as she played. She had them eating right out of her hands. They were all clapping to the music as she played. When the song was finished, everyone gave her a standing ovation. Tony and Michael walked out onto the stage, clapping their hands, and gave her a kiss on each cheek. Annie thanked everyone and curtsied to the crowd. Beaming with excitement, she walked back down to her table.

"You were wonderful!" shouted Quinn as he picked her up to hug her and swung her around in a circle. Then he kissed her.

"Whoa! I think I need to sit down, I'm feeling a little dizzy!"

"I think you need to drink some more water right now. You have had a little too much beer and you look a little flushed!" Annie giggled and started fanning herself while she took a drink of water.

Within a few minutes, she was feeling better.

Some of the customers were asking for her autograph. It made her smile.

CHAPTER 14

ALL EVENING LONG QUINN HAD been going over in his mind what Annie had said last night when he had suggested they marry. "You'll have to do better than that!" she had said to him, shaking her finger.

The band was starting to take another break when he asked Annie to walk up on stage with him. She said she was feeling a little woozy and didn't want to go. So he did the only thing he could do. He picked her up and carried her onto the stage.

"May I borrow your microphone for a minute, please?" He said as he put Annie back down on her feet.

"Quinn, what are you doing?" asked Annie.

Tony had already made Michael aware of Quinn's plan, so he gave Quinn the microphone. "Good luck, man."

Quinn started speaking, "Everyone, may I please have your attention?" Everyone became very quiet. Then Quinn turned around to look at his girl.

"Anna Marie Marshall," his voice became very

hoarse and he cleared his throat. "Annie, you are the most beautiful and gorgeous woman I have ever met in my entire life. In the short time that I have known you, I have never felt more alive. You have filled a place in my heart that I never thought could ever be filled. You have filled the piece of my soul that has been empty for years."

Annie's eyes were great big and she covered her mouth with her hands.

"You are smart, talented, and sexy as hell. You have challenged me in more ways than anyone I have ever known. You make me feel special. You make me feel more loved than I have ever known. You have become my whole world. I promise I will always love you, take care of you, protect you, worship, and cherish you for the rest of my life."

Then Quinn got down on one knee, pulled a ring out of his pocket and spoke into the microphone, "Will you please do me the honor of becoming my wife? Will you marry me?"

Annie just kept looking at Quinn with tears streaming down her cheeks, not really knowing what to say.

"Annie?"

All of a sudden, she yelled, "YES" really loud. Quinn slipped a beautiful 3-carat diamond filigree engagement ring on her left ring finger. It looked very much like an antique engagement ring. It was absolutely beautiful. Then she threw her arms around Quinn's neck. They kissed passionately. The crowd roared with hoorahs and applauses.

Joe and Jax had no idea Quinn was going to do that. "Congratulations, man. We can't fucking believe this!"

"Annie, let's get married right now, okay?" Quinn knew there was nothing spontaneous about this planned wedding. Tony had helped him make all of the arrangements this morning. He only hoped that Annie would say "yes." He knew he would be devastated if she said "no."

Annie's brain felt like it was sloshing around in alcohol. She felt a little euphoric, but very happy. Her thoughts took her to his proposal again. She smiled as she looked at the stunning engagement ring on her finger. "Why not, she thought, as she looked into his beautiful blue eyes. After all, she said yes, didn't she! He was such an amazing man! Look at that gorgeous body!" She took a deep breath. She smiled again with another delicious thought. "I am going to become a woman tonight." Her brain felt like it was doing the happy dance. Annie was very inebriated.

Just then, Pastor John Collier approached them. Tony had arranged for the Pastor to be at the restaurant for an impromptu wedding. Most of Ireland is Catholic, but Quinn and Annie weren't. It took some searching, but Tony found a Christian pastor that was willing to marry them in a pub, of all places.

Tony grabbed the microphone and announced there would be a wedding within ten minutes. Again, everyone roared with hoorahs and applauses.

Cindy reached into her large purse and pulled out a wedding veil and a small bouquet of artificial flowers, blue in color to match her jewelry. She placed the veil on Annie's head and handed her the flowers. The pastor walked up to the stage. Quinn followed the pastor, but stood three steps down. Joe and Jax follow as his best men, standing to the right of Quinn. Cindy, the matron of honor, was next and stood to the left of the pastor, three steps down. Tony walked Annie a few tables back so she could have more of a "wedding aisle." He would escort her down the aisle and give her away. It shattered his heart to do that because he loved her as much as Quinn did. He felt Quinn was the better man, and he knew Annie was in love with Quinn.

The band started playing a wedding march as they walked down the aisle. Annie was smiling with tears streaming down her cheeks at the same time. They stopped at the foot of the steps and the pastor started the ceremony. "Who gives this woman away to be married?" asked the pastor.

"Her best friend does," and he leaned down and kissed her softly on her lips. "Be happy Annie; Quinn is a good man. If he ever mistreats ye, ye just let me know. I will always be there for ye." He wiped the tears from her eyes with his thumbs.

"Thank you, Tony. I am happy."

Quinn didn't like that Tony had kissed her on the lips, but he understood why he had. Tony helped her up the steps and placed Annie's hands in Quinn's and walked over to stand with Cindy. The ceremony was short and sweet. After all, Quinn told the pastor to make it a short version since they were in a pub. When the ceremony was over, Pastor Collier introduced the new Mr. and Mrs. Quinnten R. Taylor. Before the pastor left the pub, Quinn and Annie signed their marriage certificate, and Quinn was given a copy.

They celebrated for another hour. Quinn left the table to pay for all of the drinks and food they had consumed during the evening. He gave their waitress a hefty tip.

He gave Michael, the Irish band's leader, a donation for his band. Michael didn't want to take it because it was fun. He had never seen anything like it before. He told Quinn just how much he enjoyed Annie's performance, too.

Before he walked back to his new bride, he made a quick phone call.

Quinn leaned over and whispered in Annie's ear. "Wife of mine, I can't wait to get you home. I need to be inside you," and he nibbled on her ear. "Would you like to leave now?"

Shivers ran all the way down her body as Quinn nibbled on her ear and she let out a little moan.

"I would love to leave now, husband of mine," she said as she gasped for air.

"Ah jeez, get a room!" yelled someone from a nearby table and everyone laughed.

Quinn turned around and faced the table where the remark came from with a big broad grin on his face. "Me thinks that is an excellent idea, sir!" he yelled trying to sound very Irish and he saluted the crowd.

Quinn turned around and looked at his friends, "We're heading back to the hotel. Are you all staying?"

"Cindy and I will walk back with you. What about you, Jax?"

Jax looked at Tony. "Ya want to close this joint down?"

"Sounds like a plan!" and they clinked their glasses together.

Jax winked at Quinn and Joe. "Maybe he'll introduce me to Patty!" said Jax as he raised his eyebrows really fast in a teasing fashion.

Joe knew Jax, in all probability, was not teasing. "I think maybe we should get you married off next brother!"

Before they left, Quinn told his group of friends he had rescheduled the drivers to pick them up at 1500 hours on Monday afternoon. A driver would take Tony back to his hometown; another driver would take them to the airport. The jet was scheduled to take off at 1600 hours.

Annie hugged Tony and Jax goodnight.

Quinn carried her out of the door and the remaining crowd gave them another round of applause. On the way out, Tony's Uncle Mac (and pub owner) walked over to congratulate them and told them he would have some photos for them the next time they came back. He told them one of their pictures would hang on the wall with all of the other famous pictures. After all, how many couples started their marriage in a pub!

They bid everyone good-bye and headed back to their hotel. It was a good thing it was only two blocks away since Quinn had a buzz and he was carrying Annie. She passed out in his arms. He didn't care because he was so very happy. He was happier than he had ever been in his entire life.

———⬥———

They arrived at the hotel within a few minutes. Quinn had awakened Annie and she was able to walk into the elevator on her own. Joe punched the elevator buttons for the 11th floor. Quinn inserted his room key card to access the penthouse floor. When the doors to the 11th floor opened, Joe and Cindy bid Quinn and Annie goodnight. Within a matter of a few seconds, the elevator doors opened to the penthouse floor. There was only one door, twelve feet away from the elevator. Quinn slipped the hotel key card into the door lock and slipped it out quickly. He watched as the little red light went to green and he was able to enter his room. He picked Annie up again to carry her over the threshold, but this time, she put her arms around his neck and wrapped her feet around the back of his waist.

He walked in the door, and put the "Do not disturb" sign on the outside handle. He didn't want housekeeping to walk in on them.

"Hi, Mrs. Quinnten Taylor. I really like the sound of that. Mrs. Quinnten Taylor," and he smiled from ear to ear showing off his double set of dimples that Annie loved so much.

"Hi, yourself, husband of mine. I love the sound of that, too," and she placed her lips on his.

He noticed her eyelids were looking very heavy. Is she even going to make it through our wedding night?

He put her back down on the floor and he helped her undress and laid her down on the bed. He quickly undressed himself and went to the bathroom. When he returned, Annie was sound asleep.

He smiled. "I'm never going to let her live this down," and he turned off the light and climbed into bed, wrapping his arms around her.

It was 9 a.m. when Annie woke up with the urge to empty her bladder. It took her a minute to acclimate herself to her surroundings. Her head was starting to throb when she sat up on the side of the bed. She noticed there were a couple of aspirins on the bedside table with a small glass of juice. As she reached for the aspirins with her left hand, she saw her wedding rings. "OH MY GOD! I REALLY DID GET MARRIED!"

"I need to talk to Quinn," she thought, "but I really do have to pee first." She downed the two aspirins with the juice that Quinn had left for her and quickly ran to the adjoining bathroom.

All she had on was her thong, so she grabbed Quinn's shirt, rolled the sleeves up and put it on, buttoned a few buttons and ran her fingers through her long dark hair. She wanted answers.

She walked to the living room quarters looking for Quinn, but he wasn't there. She heard the sound of a newspaper. She walked through the massive dining room, towards the kitchen area. She froze in her tracks. Standing beside the kitchen island was almost naked Quinn reading the newspaper and drinking some coffee. Her breathing hitched.

He was the most beautiful man she had ever seen. He had a gorgeous body. He was tanned, toned, and tall and on top of that, was the sexiest guy she had ever seen. He was everything she had ever dreamed of in a man. She saw the wedding ring on his left hand. She gasps.

It was coming back to her now. The dress he had bought for her, performing on stage, Mac's beer, and the proposal. It was a beautiful proposal, she thought. Then came the wedding. She was remembering everything now. She had fallen in love with a man and married him in three days, just like Joe's friend Larry.

Her heart was pounding in her chest. She let out a big breath of air. She wondered if his wife, Susie, felt just like she did right now. How could she possibly deny this man anything? He is, well... WOW. She hoped they have a long marriage like Larry and Susie have had. She walked towards him.

Quinn saw her from the corner of his eye. He turned facing her and smiled from ear to ear. "Good morning, Mrs. Taylor," and he picked her up and sat her on the kitchen island cabinet.

"It appears that you, Mrs. Taylor, passed out on our wedding night." He smiled and kissed her lightly on the lips. "How are you feeling this morning?"

"Hungry."

"Oh? What are you hungry for, Mrs. Taylor? Would you like to have some breakfast?"

"No."

"Then what are you hungry for?" giving her a very seductive smile.

"You."

"Me, huh?" he said, "Hmm, you must be a woman of few words in the morning."

"Hmm," she said with a smile.

"Well, you need to eat something first."

"Not hungry for food."

"You need to eat first," he said as he ran his hands over her breast and gently kissed her on her neck. "You need to keep your strength up with what I have planned for you this morning." He looked at her with a very sexy smile.

"Umm, and just what have you got planned for me this morning?"

"Remember when I told you I have never made love to any one before?"

"Yes."

"Well, in a sense, this is like my first time, too," and he started kissing her left ear, down her neck and over to her right ear. "I. Am. Going. To. Rock. You. To. Your. Core!" he said in between each kiss, landing the last kiss on her lips.

He wanted so desperately to take her to the bedroom right then, but he wanted her to eat. He lifted her off the counter and sat her down on a barstool. He walked to the refrigerator and took out two plates of already prepared scrambled eggs with bacon and buttered toast. He put them into the microwave. He poured each of them a cup of coffee. The microwave signal sounded. Breakfast was ready.

Annie climbed onto Quinn's lap. She wanted to feed him like she did at his house. They fed each other until all of their food was gone.

"Finish your coffee, Annie, I don't want you falling asleep," he said with a laugh.

Annie was still on his lap when she finished her coffee and sat the mug down. They smiled at each other.

"Are you ready?" he asked.

Annie immediately shook her head yes. She placed both of her arms around his neck as he stood. As he walked towards the bedroom, she began nibbling and kissing one of his earlobes. He groaned. He walked faster.

As soon as they walked into their bedroom, he laid her down on the bed. Hovering over top of her, he grabbed ahold of his shirt she was wearing and ripped it open, tearing the buttons completely off. He leaned down and kissed her mouth. He feathered kisses down to her breasts. He suckled and kissed on one breast while tweaking and kneading her other one. Then he switched to the other breast. He heard her purr. While sucking on one nipple, he moved his hand to her forbidden zone and inserted first one finger, then a second. Her body writhed and she let out a moan. She was so wet and she was responding to him; just the way he imagined she would.

"Annie, I love you so much, baby. Are you ready for me now?"

"Yes!"

"Say it, baby, tell me what you want, Annie," he demanded as his fingers were moving in and out of her.

"I want you, Quinn!"

"Tell me how you want me, baby!"

"Inside of me, now Quinn, Now!"

"Bend your knees honey and spread your knees open as far as you can," and he placed himself at her entrance.

He leaned down and kissed her on her lips. "This is going to hurt a little, but the hurt will go away." He could feel she was tensing up.

"Keep looking at me baby and breathe. Try to relax for me," and he kissed her again. As he was kissing her, he thrust into her fast and hard one time and stopped, holding himself in place so that she could make herself accustomed to his size.

She let out a moan and breathed in deeply. He saw tears filling her eyes and he started to worry. "Are you okay?"

"Uh-huh," she smiled. "Oh, Quinn, it hurts so good!" He pulled himself out most of the way and slammed back into her and stopped.

"Oh, Annie, you belong to me! I love you so much!" He started moving at a slow pace, then a little faster. Her body was responding and she was moving right along with him thrust for thrust.

"Quinn!" she yelled. She hadn't felt anything like this before and it felt wonderful. He had hit her G-spot and her body was starting to tremble. "Quinn!" she yelled louder.

"Look at me baby, I want to watch you come," he said to her.

She opened her eyes and all of a sudden, she

had her first orgasm. He came at the same time. He screamed her name and laid down on top of her. She wrapped her arms around his neck like she was hanging onto him for dear life. They laid there for a few minutes. He heard her whimper a little cry. He looked at her and saw big tears fill her eyes again. He took his thumbs and gently rubbed the tears away.

"I'm sorry, baby, did I hurt you?"

"No, I don't think I have ever been this happy. You have made my first time so beautiful. I love you, Quinn Taylor!"

Tears fill his eyes and he kissed her like she was the only woman in the world. As far as he was concerned, she was the only woman in the world for him. She was most definitely the woman he had been waiting for all of his life.

"Annie, I have an idea," he said as he kissed her gently on the lips. "I want to take you on a long honeymoon. We can go to the Mediterranean, Paris, Germany, Italy or anywhere you would like to go. We can take a six-month honeymoon or even a year if you like. Would you like to do that?" He was hoping she said yes. It was a way of keeping her safe, at least for a while.

"Hmm," she smiled. "Can we visit Rome and Athens and maybe Hawaii?"

"Anywhere you want, baby!" He smiled from ear to ear.

"Okay. Can we visit my parents first? I would like to tell them we are married?"

He softly kissed her on the lips again. Hallelujah! She had agreed to go. He smiled, "if that's what you want. I'll make all the arrangements when we get back to the States. We can visit your parents before we leave."

He moved over to her side and wrapped her in his arms. "Annie, I love you so much. I will love you till the day I die." He kissed her, probing her mouth with his tongue. "Promise me something, Annie."

"Anything."

"Promise me, we will never spend one night apart from each other. Promise me if I have to travel, that you will go with me and I with you.

I don't ever want to be without you. Can you promise me that?"

"I promise Quinn," and she hugged him as tightly as she could.

Quinn let out a big sigh of relief. His thoughts were of her. He felt like he had been given the most precious gift in life a man could receive. How could one tiny little woman sneak her way into his heart so fast and knock him on his ass so quickly. He closed his eyes and said a little prayer. *"Thank you, God, for answering my prayer. Thank you for making her mine. Now God, please help me protect her from David Morgan and anyone else that may come along. In Jesus name I pray. Amen."*

CHAPTER 15

THEY ARRIVED AT HEATHROW INTERNATIONAL Airport around 5 p.m. and as promised, Reginald Taylor had another limousine waiting to take them to his hotel.

Joe and Cindy were given a room on the eleventh floor, while Quinn and Annie agreed to stay in the hotel penthouse with his parents.

The penthouse had enough room for Joe and Cindy to stay, but they wanted to be on their own. Joe knew Quinn had to discuss some business dealings with his dad, plus he knew he wanted to discuss what had been taking place with the threat on Annie's life. They did not want to intrude on his time spent with his family. Jax also wanted his own room for the same reason.

Quinn introduced his new bride to his father and mother, Reggie and Gloria Taylor. His mother wrapped her arms around her, smiling kindly at her.

"We never thought Quinn would ever marry, honey. Welcome to our family," Gloria kissed her on the cheek, then kissed and hugged her son.

Reggie took Annie's hand and brought it to his lips. "Glad to meet you, Mrs. Taylor," and he gave her a hug.

"Please, Mr. Taylor, call me Annie," she said with a smile.

"I'll call you Annie if you will call me Reggie, okay? Welcome to our family my dear."

Gloria Taylor had a delicious looking meal catered in by the master chef of the hotel. There were barbequed ribs, loaded baked sweet potatoes, fresh green beans, sliced tomatoes, tossed salads, buttered squash, and hot cinnamon rolls. She knew this was Quinn's favorite meal.

"We really hate that we missed your wedding, Quinn. If you had just let us know, we would have flown to Ireland. It really isn't that far away." Gloria scolded her son.

Quinn looked at Annie with a smile, then back at his mother.

"We'll plan another wedding in the states in a couple of months. Her parents weren't there either. That way you won't feel cheated," and he winked at his new wife.

As they sat down at the dining table, Annie started feeling very nervous. She sensed that Gloria was only trying to be nice to her for the sake of her husband and her son. She wondered if Quinn had told them they had only known each other for three days before they married. She feared when they found out what was going on in her life—their lives, back in the States, well, they would hate her. They wouldn't want their son mixed up in danger.

Everyone filled their plates and began eating.

"So, Annie," said Reggie, "Quinn told me that you were a student at Columbus Music Academy. Have you already graduated?"

"Yes sir, I have. I received my BA two years ago and went on to get two Masters Degrees and a PhD in music education during the past two years."

"That's very impressive, my dear," said Gloria.

"What instrument do you play?" asked Reggie.

"All of them."

"All of them?" asked Reggie.

"Yes sir, I can play any musical instrument out there."

"Did you say you started your first year of college six years ago?" asked Reggie as he took another bite of his dinner.

"Yes sir, I did."

"What was your music teacher's name when you attended high school?" asked Reggie.

"Mr. Johnson. Why do ask?" questioned Annie.

"Leo?"

"Why yes, I believe his name is Leo. Do you know him?"

"Where are you going with this, Dad?"

"Well now," Reggie said as he leaned back in his chair, putting his fingertips together like a steeple and patting them together. "This is indeed a small world; a very small world, indeed. You're her aren't you?" he asked with a smile.

Annie looked at her new father-in-law very confused. "Her who?"

"You don't know?"

"Dad, what are you talking about? Obviously Annie is clueless. What gives, Dad?"

"I'm sorry dear, let me explain," replied Reggie.

"You should remember my friend, Leo, son. He had one green eye and one brown eye?"

"Yes I do, now that you said that. I haven't seen him since I was 12 years old!"

He looked at Annie, "Leo was a Navy Seal with me many years ago and he became one of my best friends. He called me up about six years ago and told me he had the most gifted musical student he had ever come across. He asked if I would care to sponsor this student for as long as she wanted to go to college. He told me this student's dream was to attend CMA. He sent me a recording of you playing a beautiful melody that you had written. You were playing it on the violin I had given to Leo when he got his Master's Degree after he left the Navy. It was one of the most beautiful songs I had ever heard on a violin. I called him up and told him I would sponsor you, pay for your education, and all your expenses. He told me you could play any musical instrument by ear, and you played them to perfection. I couldn't believe it."

He smiled, "I am so glad to finally meet you. Here you are, my new daughter-in-law! That is just so incredible! You did good, son!"

"So, what do you plan on doing with all of this education you now have, my dear?" asked Gloria.

"Well, first of all, I want to thank you from the bottom of my heart for sponsoring me. Thank you for believing in me. I honestly never knew who my sponsor was. Leo, that is, Mr. Johnson never told me your name and neither did the Academy."

"So what are your plans?"

"Well, I don't really know yet. I know I can go to any university and teach. I really like writing songs; and, I have even sold a few. I also like to take older rock songs and vamp them up just a little and play them on the violin. I think they really are beautiful."

"Can you sing as well as you play?" asked her husband.

"Well, I can hold my own I guess, but I prefer to play." She looked up at him with a sheepish grin.

Quinn pulled his cell phone out of his pocket. "Annie played the violin last night before we married. I recorded her." He handed his phone to his mother and she and Reggie watched it together. They were very impressed.

"Maybe you will become famous one day and play at Carnegie Hall!" said Reggie. "Nothing would please me more," she said with a smile.

The maid came to clear the dinner dishes from the small dining table only to return a short time later with another one of Quinn's favorite deserts; hot blackberry cobbler with vanilla ice cream.

"Oh my God, this is so delicious! This tastes just like my mother's. I bet I have gained ten pounds since last night!"

"Don't worry baby, we'll exercise it off later," Quinn said as he winked at Annie.

Annie felt her face turning ten shades of red. She was so embarrassed at his little innuendo.

Reggie laughed, "That's my boy!"

Gloria reached across the ends of the table and smacked both Reggie and Quinn on their arms. "Behave yourselves. Don't embarrass her like that! Don't pay any mind to the Taylor men, honey. Sometimes they can be so crude!" Everyone laughed.

"So, how long will you be staying in England, son?" asked his father.

"Probably no more than two days. We have some very serious matters to attend to in Ohio when we return," said Quinn.

"How serious? Is there anything I can do?"

"I'm afraid there is a serial rapist on the loose in Columbus. He is after my Annie."

"What do you mean he is after Annie?" asked Reggie as he sat up taller in his chair with a very concerned look on his face.

Quinn pulled the newspaper article from his

pocket to show his dad. "My goodness, you really do resemble them. Do they have any idea who the rapist is?"

"Well, we think we do, but the police doesn't know yet," Quinn said.

"Who is it and how did you figure it out?" asked his father.

"His name is David Morgan. He owns the Campus Coffee House at the Academy."

"Paul's son?" Reggie asked. "Wait a minute. Annie isn't that the guy that was following you around six years ago?"

"How would you know that?" asked Annie.

"Leo told me," replied Reggie. "I bought the apartment building you live in so that you could move off campus. I told that bastard President of the Columbus Music Academy that you were moving off campus and you were still going to keep your scholarship. He didn't like it because they had some bullshit policy that stated first-year students had to live on campus. If he made exceptions for one, he would have to make exceptions for all out-of-town students."

"I told him, if David Morgan came anywhere near you while you where in school, I would see to it that David would disappear forever. I also told that son of a bitch that I would stop funding his fucking school programs and I would see to it that he was fired if he didn't let you move off campus and keep your scholarship! I should have gotten him fired years ago. He is such a weasel!"

Annie stood up and walked over to the window to look out, but wasn't really looking at anything in particular. She was deep in thought. She didn't know what to say. "Quinn, he must have bugged my apartment right after graduation. He thought Reggie wouldn't do anything to him since I had completed all of my studies."

"All right, son, I think you need to start explaining what is going on."

Quinn walked over and put his arms around his new wife. He could feel her shaking. He walked her back over to the sofa and sat her down, then sat down next to her placing his arm around her shoulder, and pulled her as close to him as he could.

He began telling his parents what they knew. He told about the break-in at her apartment; how David had installed live video and audio feeds; the car explosion; and even the two cell phones that had just enough explosives to blow off some heads. He told his father that he, Joe, and Jax were able to use their own Seal surveillance equipment to see that it was David in disguise. Quinn admitted to his father that he had sent a very strong message to David that Annie was his.

"So, Quinn, if David Morgan has been stalking Annie all of this time, why haven't you stopped him before now? Why did you let this drag on so long before wanting to do something to help her?" questioned his mother.

Annie closed her eyes. Here it comes, she thought. World War III. She will hate me! So much for first impressions!

"Because, Mother," and he took a deep breath, "we just met for the first time last Friday night."

Gloria came up off her seat, angrier than hell. "You mean to tell me that you met this woman last Friday, she put you and the lives of your friends in danger, AND you married her on Monday? How stupid can you be, Quinn? And I bet you didn't even think to have her sign a pre-nuptial agreement."

"Be quiet, woman!" shouted Reggie.

"I will not be quiet! He's my son and someone needs to look out for his welfare! Anyone who marries that fast is nothing but a gold digger in my book!"

Quinn and Annie both stood up from the sofa. "Mother, that's enough! I will not allow you to talk about my wife like that! You need to apologize to Annie!"

"I will not!"

Annie's face felt red as fire and she screamed, "I am not a gold digger! In fact, when I get enough money saved up, I will pay you back every dime for my education!" She picked up her purse and ran for the door.

"Mother, it's no wonder why I don't come home

very often!" Quinn said through gritted teeth. Then he ran after Annie.

He was lucky this time. He caught her just as the doors to the elevator were opening.

"Stay away from me, Quinn!" she ordered.

"You're running again, Annie. Is this the way it's always going to be? When the going gets tough you start running away from me?"

"I didn't say I was leaving you."

"You didn't have to. It's written all over your face!"

Annie started sobbing hard. He pulled her into his chest to try and calm her down.

The elevator doors opened to the first floor. They walked over to the reservation desk. "Are there any more rooms vacant on the eleventh floor?"

"Yes, Mr. Taylor, I believe your two friends are the only guests on that floor at the moment."

"Good, I would like to have a room near them."

"Yes, sir," she typed in some information into her computer and handed him two key cards to the room. "Your room number is 1117. Enjoy your stay, sir."

"Thank you, Ms. Steiner. Would you have the bellboy get our luggage from my father's penthouse please?"

"Yes sir, right away."

———◆———

Within a few short minutes, they were standing in their rooms.

"So, answer me Annie. Are you always going to run?"

She walked over to the window and folded her arms against her body, turning her back to him.

She let out a big breath.

"I'm just so overwhelmed, Quinn. Everything has been happening so fast. It's bad enough I've put your life and the lives of our friends in danger, but now your parents hate me, especially your mother. What's even worse, she thinks I am a gold digger. I just felt like everything was closing in on me, Quinn. I just had to get away to think. That's all."

Quinn turned Annie around to look at him. He placed his hands on both of her cheeks. "I don't care what my parents think. I know you aren't a gold digger. It's not their money anyway. It's our money Annie, OUR MONEY," Quinn stressed. And he pulled her in for a kiss.

Just as they started to kiss, there was a knock at the door. "That must be the bellboy with our luggage."

He looked through the peephole on the door, turned to look at Annie, and hung his head. He opened the door. It was his Father with their luggage.

"Business that bad, Father?"

"Hmm. You only call me Father when you're mad at me," Reggie grumbled. "May I come in?"

Quinn opened the door wider as his Dad handed him their luggage and Reggie entered the room.

"Annie," said Reggie.

Annie looked at him with a blank stare. She didn't want to see him, let alone talk with him.

"I'm sorry for what Gloria said to you. She should have never said those things. Gloria should never have called you a gold digger."

Annie studied him for a moment trying to decide what to say. Gloria's words had cut her to the bone.

"I'm sorry, too, Mr. Taylor, but your apology is empty. Mrs. Taylor is the one who said it, not you; although you were probably thinking it," Annie said in a very harsh tone; and then turned to look out the window again.

"Father, we will be leaving in the morning."

"I see." Reggie placed his hand out in front of him for Quinn to shake. Instead of Quinn shaking his Father's hand, he put his arms around him in a bear hug. "I love you, Dad, but my place is with my wife now. I really do love her."

"I can see that, son. Please be careful and call me when this is all over. You know I will do nothing but worry."

"I will Dad."

"And, if you need anything, don't hesitate to call."

"I'll keep that in mind. Thanks, Dad."

❖

When Reggie had left, Annie walked over to the suitcases and took out some clean underwear and one of Quinn's t-shirts. She went into the bathroom without saying a word and locked the door. Quinn could hear the shower being turned on. Then he heard a muffled cry. It killed him to hear her cry. He wanted so badly to break down the door, climb into the shower with her, and hold her in his arms. In the state her mind was in right now, he knew better than to do that. He would allow her to cry in the comfort of warm water, but he wished he were the water droplets soothing her. He told himself he would hold her when they climbed into bed that night.

It was nearly 9:30 p.m. when Annie came out of the bathroom. Quinn was already in bed. Her eyes looked red and very puffy from crying. She immediately walked over to the bed and climbed in, covering herself with the blankets.

He scooted over beside her and attempted to put his arms around her, but she rejected him.

"Please, Quinn," she said softly. "Please don't. I just need a little space."

"Well fuck," Quinn thought as he rolled himself over to the other side of the bed. He was only going to comfort her. Right now he hated his mother, he hated David Morgan, and he hated everything that was happening to Annie. No, he didn't really hate his mother, but he sure did hate what she said to Annie. *"Dear God, help me to make everything right for Annie. Amen."*

Quinn laid in bed watching Annie sleep until midnight before he finally fell asleep.

It was 3 a.m. when Quinn felt something on his chest. Hair was tickling his nose. He felt something moving around his neck. His eyes were fluttering, trying to open from a deep sleep. He was beginning to think someone was trying to attack him. Then he heard her words. She was gently kissing his neck and talking very softly to him between each kiss. "You. Are. Mine. I. Am. Yours. I. Love. You. So. Much. Quinn. Taylor."

"Annie?" he said as he put his hands on her arms. "Are you okay?"

She raised her head from his neck. He could see tears in her eyes through some filtered light coming from outside the windows.

"I love you," she said softly.

Quinn wrapped his arms around her and turned her onto her back. He moved his hands up to her head and caressed her face. Their lips touched. Tenderly, at first, and then they kissed with such fierce love and passion for each other; like there was no tomorrow. They made love for the next two hours. Their bodies were on fire. The bed sheets were soaking wet from sweat. They were exhausted.

Annie's head laid on Quinn's shoulder as he held her. "No woman has ever made me feel like this before," he thought. How does she know how to make a man's entire body feel like that? I know for a fact that she was a virgin when we made love for the first time. I saw the proof afterwards. Maybe it's because I am in love for the first time in my life. Whatever it is, I don't ever want it to go away. Our bodies were meant to be together. We were destined to be together. We were soul mates.

"Annie, will you marry me again?"

"Honey, I would marry you every day of my life if I had to." She giggled.

"I'm serious, Annie. Would you marry me again when we get back to Ohio?"

"If it is that important to you, yes. Why?"

"I want to make sure we are legally married in Ohio because it is my legal residence. With all of my business holdings, I want to guarantee all of your legal rights to my estate if anything were to happen to me."

CHAPTER 16

THEY ARRIVED AT LaGUARDIA AIRPORT in New York around 7 p.m. on Wednesday evening. The pilot needed to refuel before flying on to Columbus.

They stepped off the jet to get some fresh air while the jet was refueling when Joe checked his cell phone for messages. A text had come across the screen from Champ saying they had re-opened the club for business on Monday evening. There had not been any problems.

There was a voice mail from Champ. "Call me as soon as you get this message. This is urgent."

Joe walked away from the others so they couldn't hear his phone conversation.

"Champ, it's Joe. I just got your message. What's up?"

"There has been another rape. She looks just like the others. This time, the rapist killed her."

"Did they say how he did it?"

"That would be a negative, sir. They aren't giving any details other than she was found dead. Something isn't right about this one."

"What do you mean?"

"You know how they have always reported all the girls were found on a deserted road? Well, they haven't said that. Rumor has it this girl's body was found in a dumpster near CMA. It has the same MO. Don't know if it was a copycat rape or not. The police aren't saying."

"Thanks, Champ. Keep me informed."

"Quinn, I need to speak to you and Jax privately," Joe said, when he returned to where everyone was standing.

Annie looked at Quinn, then at the others and was wondering what was going on. The men had walked out of hearing distance, several yards away, so the ladies could not hear their conversation. Within a few minutes, Quinn looked at Annie and started pacing back and forth. Annie did not like this. She figured they had some news from back home. It couldn't have been good.

Annie's heart started to beat faster. Quinn's body language had changed. Before, he looked somewhat relaxed, but now his body looked tense. He had developed a serious frown on his face and had even closed his eyes. He ran his hand through his hair and turned around. She started running towards them. She wanted answers and she wanted answers now. Cindy followed her.

"What's going on, guys?" she asked with a very serious look on her face.

Joe and Jax looked at each other, then looked at Quinn.

"Oh, nothing to worry your pretty little head over," Quinn said calmly.

"Yeah?" said Annie.

"Yeah," said Quinn, feeling like World War III was about to erupt again.

"If it was nothing, Quinnten Taylor, you would have discussed it in front of Cindy and me. You talk about me running when the going gets tough, well, what about you? When the going gets tough, you want to hide things from me. I want to know what it is now!"

Quinn looked at Joe and Jax for support.

"You're on your own on this one man," said Joe.

Annie spoke, "He's raped again hasn't he?"

Joe walked over to his wife, grabbed her by the elbow and walked away from them. Jax followed.

Quinn put his hands in his pockets and looked down towards his feet.

"Oh, God, he's killed her hasn't he?"

Quinn didn't answer her.

"Hasn't he Quinn?" she asked, very scared. "Answer me, damn it!" she screamed.

He looked at his wife knowing she was going to have a meltdown and slowly started walking towards her.

Annie walked backwards, away from him. "NO!" she screamed, shaking her head. "GOD

NO, PLEASE GOD, DON'T LET IT BE SO!"
she cried as she started to fall to her knees.

Quinn caught her before she landed on the
concrete. He put his arms around his wife. He
held her as tight as he could possibly hold her.
He gently rubbed her back and kissed her softly
about the head, letting her cry. He held her for a
very long time letting her sob hard into his chest.
His heart was breaking into a million pieces.
He couldn't stand to hear her cry. All he could
think about now was protecting the love of his
life. He wanted to take his knife and slice David
Morgan's throat from ear to ear. "Hell, I'd like to
slice something else off!" He thought to himself.
That animal didn't deserve to breathe the same air
as Annie.

She finally stopped crying, but didn't move
from his arms. She looked up at Quinn. Her eyes
were red and puffy, but she had a different look
on her face. Quinn had seen that look before on
many soldiers who were about to lose their cool.
It was a look of sheer determination. A look that
said, "I'm pissed beyond pissed and this is going
to stop now."

She stepped away from him and pointed her
finger. "You," she paused, "you are going to stop
treating me like I am a child, Quinn. I am your
wife now. This whole thing is about me and I have
a right to know everything; even if you don't want
me to hear it!"

She was pissed beyond recognition right now. He started to say something to her. She held her hand up in front of her and spoke, "I don't want to hear it!" She paced back and forth for a few seconds.

"Look Quinn, I know I am in danger; but, you are in danger now, too. So are our friends, all because of me. Do you think I like this? Do you, Quinn?"

"Annie, I promise, everything will be okay. We'll be okay. Our friends will be okay!" Quinn said, trying to convince her.

"No, Quinn. Don't say that! You can't guarantee that. I will tell you this and you'd better listen, because I CAN guarantee this!" she said with gritted teeth. She started shaking a pointed finger at him again. "You start keeping me informed of what is going on or this marriage is over before we can even get it started. Do you hear me, Quinnten Taylor? I mean over! I will not be left in the dark on anything else! Do you understand or do I walk?"

She walked a few feet away from Quinn and stopped. She had her back to him now. She knew she had nowhere to go. She was beyond crying. She was livid, more livid that she had ever been in her life. "I am done with crying," she thought. This shit has got to stop. She took a deep breath.

Quinn walked up to her and stood behind her. He placed a hand on her shoulder. "I'm sorry, Annie, but you're right. You have every right to know everything. I was just trying to protect you. I promise I will keep you informed."

Annie reached up and grabbed his hand and turned herself around to face him. "I'm really glad you are here to protect me, Quinn. I truly am. I really don't know what I would do without you right now; but I think we should postpone our honeymoon. We should go to the police and tell them what we know, too."

"What? NO!" Quinn responded.

"Don't you see, Quinn, it would be like we are running. We can't let this guy keep on raping other women who look like me. It just isn't right."

"I don't think that is a good idea, Annie. It may put you in more danger," he said, shaking his head no.

"I don't care. I'm tired of all this crap and just want it to end. It's the only solution right now." She paused, and took both of his hands in hers. "You accused me of running when the going got tough yesterday. Maybe I was," and she looked into his eyes. "I'm not running anymore. Not for the likes of that bastard!"

Quinn looked at Annie with a frown on his face. He ran his hands through his dark hair, as he began pacing. He knew she was right. It was what he would do, but he needed to keep her safe from all harm. What if something happened to her? What if he failed and Morgan got to her?

What if he killed her? He rubbed his temples. He felt a headache coming on.

"Annie, are you sure that is what you want to do? Because I'm telling you right now, I don't like it one little bit. You are my wife, damn it!"

"No, I don't want to do this, but you know it is the right thing to do." She paused, and then walked over to him. "Hold me, Quinn. I'm just so scared!"

He embraced her with both arms and held her as tight as he could. She was so petite; he didn't want to break any of her delicate bones. "If that is what you want, then I won't make any arrangements for our honeymoon at this time, but only on one condition," he stated.

"Okay, what is your one condition?" she asked.

"You do everything I tell you to the letter regarding your safety. Promise?"

"I promise."

"I mean it, Annie. TO THE LETTER!"

"I promise, Quinn. To the Letter."

"You are one brave woman!"

"Oh, I'm not brave. I'm scared to death."

"Come on. We need to come up with a plan," he said as they walked back towards the others.

Before he boarded his private jet, Quinn telephoned his father and informed him of the latest victim. He told his father that Annie wanted to go to the police. His father had an idea. Quinn listened.

When the "Fasten Your Seat Belt" sign went off, Annie breathed a sigh of relief.

"When we get home, Annie wants to go to the police," Quinn said. "I'm very worried for her safety and I need your help if you are willing."

"Quinn," Joe said, "I'm with you all the way. I think Jax is, too. Just tell us what you want us to do."

He knew his Seal brothers wouldn't let him down. He felt so honored to have served with those men.

"I have a small plan, but I really won't know what we are up against until we go to the police."

He went on. "We should be landing in Port Columbus around 10 p.m. We can rent a couple of cars, then drive to Northern Columbus and stay at the Royal Plaza Suites. I figure, along with Annie's place being bugged, Morgan already has some surveillance on La Seals and my hotel. That way, we can get a good nights sleep. We can meet for breakfast at 9 a.m. I would like for all of us to go to the police station together. Jax, I want you to bring your computer. I think we need to show the police what we have."

"Dad knows the Police Chief. He thinks he should assign a task force to look for Morgan, but Dad thinks the task force should be us and any other Seal we need to add. I don't think that is what I want to do."

"Dad knows I'm going on the hunt for this

S.O.B. He also knows the police don't look very kindly at people who take the law into their own hands. Dad is worried one of us will get shot, especially me."

Anyway, we really don't know what we are up against until we speak to Chief Hansen. I'll call him first thing in the morning and make an appointment for all of us to meet with him tomorrow.

"Jax, after we meet with Chief Hansen tomorrow, could you do a sweep of my penthouse at the hotel, the elevators, and the parking garage? I would like for you to add more surveillance cameras, both video and audio, in the service elevator and the main elevators, in the parking garage, and at all the entrances to the penthouse, even on the roof. We can call a few of the guys in from other teams to help until this is over. I will pay for whatever you need."

Annie looked at her new friends and finally at Quinn. "I have something I want to say," she paused and took a deep breath. "I am truly sorry you are all involved in this. I want you to know, I never did anything to encourage this freak. I appreciate everything you have done. You don't have to help me. I don't want any of you hurt on account of me. Joe, Cindy needs you as much as I need Quinn. Don't feel like you have to do this. The same goes for you, too, Jax."

"Annie," said Joe, "we want to help. There is

nothing we wouldn't do to help Quinn. Now that you are his wife, there is nothing we wouldn't do to help you, too. We are Seals, which means we are brothers. That makes us family. Family helps each other."

"Thank you," she whispered.

Quinn grabbed Annie's hand, as he looked her in the eyes. "I promised we would keep her in the loop on everything, too."

The others could tell Quinn was not happy with his promise, as his jaw muscles were very tight. He did not look at ease.

"Cindy and I have been talking," said Joe. "When we get to the airport, I'm buying her an airline ticket to Denver to see her sister. If you like, you are more than welcome to go with her and stay until we catch this bastard."

"No, thank you. I'm staying right here." Annie stated adamantly.

"Quinn," Joe said, "we are going to stay at one of the hotels at the airport tonight in hopes of getting her an early flight out. Then I'll drive to the Royal to meet you for breakfast."

"Understand," Quinn said as he looked at Annie. "Remind me to call Mrs. Davis in the morning. I'm giving her more time off. I don't want her anywhere near my house or the hotel until this is over."

Annie took a deep breath and placed her head on the headrest. She was not looking forward to the events that could possibly take place over the next few days. She was deep in thought, "Will Morgan kidnap me? Will he succeed in raping me this time? Will he finally kill me?" Suddenly a very cold chill ran through her body and she started to shake. She laid her head on her husband's shoulder.

The jet landed safely at Port Columbus International Airport at 10:05 p.m. As per their plans, Quinn rented two cars at the airport and Joe was able to book a flight to Denver for his wife. She would be flying out at 7:30 a.m. tomorrow.

Quinn gave a set of keys to Joe so that he could meet them in the morning at the Royal for breakfast. Jax would ride to the Royal with Quinn and Annie, then to the police station in the morning. Afterwards, Quinn would take him back to his place to get his van of surveillance equipment.

By the time they had retrieved their luggage from Quinn's personal jet, rented the cars, bought a plane ticket for Cindy and drove to the Royal Plaza Suites, it was nearly 11:30 p.m. They were exhausted. Annie had refused to lie down on the bed to rest on the plane trip back from New York.

Annie walked over to the window to pull the draperies closed. She got one of Quinn's t-shirts out of his suitcase to sleep in. He had his back to her. He had already removed his button – down shirt, and was pulling his t-shirt over his head. He heard Annie let out a slight gasp of approval.

"Umm," he thought. "Let's see where this goes." He started flexing his arms, showing how big his arm muscles were as if he were Mr. Universe. Annie started laughing.

"Well, Mrs. Taylor, what's so funny?" It was good to hear her laugh.

"You."

"Me?"

"Yes, you," and Annie began laughing. She started to walk to the bathroom, but Quinn caught her by the arm as she tried to walk past him. He sat down on the end of the bed and pulled her to his lap.

"Are you going to tell me why you are laughing at me, wife of mine?"

"Well, that depends on why you were showing off, husband of mine," she said with a smile.

"Umm," he started to nibble on her ear. He trailed kisses from her ear down her neck and over to the corner of her lips. "You. Are. An. Amazing. Woman," he stated before he planted a soft, sensual, sexy kiss on her lips that sent shivers throughout her body from the top of her head to the bottoms of her feet. "Now, tell me why you were laughing at me," he said as he held her in his arms.

She took her hand and placed it gently on his cheek. "You absolutely melt my heart. In the mist of all this madness, you have made me smile."

"Come on. We are going to take a bath. We'll soak in a steaming hot tub of water, then, I'll bathe you and take care of you. You will feel so relaxed; then I will let you fall asleep in my arms," and he took her hand. "Would you like for me to wash your hair too?"

Annie smiled at her husband. "No, it's too late to wash my hair. It would take too long to dry it tonight. If you don't mind, you can help me wash it in the morning."

She looked at her husband with love. Quinn was so thoughtful, putting her needs before his own. She couldn't tell him no. What if something happened to him? What if he got hurt or — she didn't want to think about that! "Let's go take that bath," she stated as she took his hand.

The bathroom was really nice. It had a huge walk-in shower, two sinks, and a huge tub. Quinn turned on the water to the right temperature and adjusted the plug. He found some jasmine bubble bath on the ledge by the water faucets, compliments of Royal Plaza Suites Hotel. He poured some into the water and the water started bubbling up immediately. The fragrance smelled divine.

Annie watched as Quinn finished undressing himself. He was very meticulous in folding his pants. He placed them, along with his undershorts and socks, in a neat little pile on top of the sink. He must have learned to be very neat while in the military; or he was trying to be sexy because he knew she was watching. She thought it was a little of both.

This man looked like a god. He had large broad shoulders with huge muscular biceps. His chest was ripped. He looked like he had an eight pack. His waistline was thin and he had long muscular legs. He had a nice golden tan everywhere except on his private area and his nice round butt. He was a beautiful man.

He slowly walked over to her with a tantalizing, seductive smile. She felt a tingle go through her body, especially down there. He started to undress her. First, he dropped to his knees and slipped her sandals off of her feet. Then he slowly slid the zipper down on her jeans. He pushed her jeans down her backside and slowly down her legs and instructed her to raise first her left foot and then her right, as he pulled the jeans off. "Oooh, I am feeling flushed!" she declared. Then he folded her jeans and reached over with his long arms and placed them on top of his clothing.

When he looked back at Annie, he had a sheepish grin on his face, but said nothing. He slipped his thumbs inside the waist of her thong and slid it down to her feet, instructing her to step out of them. He folded her thong as best as he could as there was very little fabric and laid it on top of her jeans.

His seductive look was killing her! Quinn grabbed a hold of the hemline to her shirt and pulled it over her head. He unsnapped her bra with one hand. He folded the bra and her shirt and placed them on top of the rest of the clothes.

"You are so beautiful," he said as he leaned in and kissed her chest.

Quinn stood up quickly and turned the water off. He took her hand, helped her to step into the tub, and he stepped in. "Turn around," he demanded, "that way your back can lean against my stomach."

"No, I don't want to sit that way. I would rather face you instead," she said to him with a smile.

He smiled great big and showed those dimples that she loved so much. He sat down into the tub, but slid his bottom forward so there would be enough room for her legs. She could feel him as soon as she sat down on top of his lap. She placed her hands on his cheeks and looked deep into his eyes. She felt one of his hands slide around her waist while his other hand went to the back of her head. His eyes looked dark navy and carnal. They kissed, opening their mouths wide. Their tongues collided with deep passion, twisting and searching every spot.

She felt his need to have her. She was not going to deny him. She placed her arms around his neck and lifted her bottom up. He placed himself at her entrance and slowly slid her down onto his girth. She felt him deeper than he had ever been.

"We are going to take this slow and easy, baby. I want you to enjoy this," he said seductively.

He started moving in a slow circular motion with small thrusts. She followed his lead and moved in the same rhythm. It felt exquisite. She felt a sensational feeling building up in her that made her eyes roll to the back of her head. He had found that one magical spot. She gasped loudly.

"Look at me, baby, I want to watch you. I love you, baby," he said with a soft, sexier than hell voice.

Our bodies started to shake violently. We held each other for several minutes. Quinn rubbed my head gently. "You are made for my body, Annie. You. Are. Mine. I'm never giving you up!" he whispered.

I frowned and looked away from him.

"What's the matter, Annie?" he asked.

He took his finger and gently placed it on my chin, moving my face back to him. "What's wrong?"

"Quinn, I know you love me with all your heart, and I love you with all my heart, too. But... but, I'm worried."

"About?" he asked.

"I don't want your love for me to cloud your judgment while you are looking for Morgan. Promise me you will think with a clear head and not your heart. I don't want you hurt. Promise me that Quinn. I don't ever want to lose you!"

He put his arms around her. "I promise, Annie. I'll use my head," he kissed her gently on her shoulder. "But right now, we need to bathe." He put some soap into his hands and rubbed them together until he had a good lather. He started washing her with his hands. He started at her neck, then her arms, under her arms, then her breasts and tweaked her nipples. "Turn around," he demanded. When she turned around, he washed her back, and moved to her legs and feet.

Annie grabbed a clean washcloth and soaped it up. "If I let you wash the rest of me, we won't get out of this tub!"

He watched as she finished washing herself. She lathered her hands and started bathing Quinn. "You have the softest and tiniest hands I have ever seen," he said. She smiled.

When she finished washing him, she reached for a washcloth and lathered it up with soap. "Here, you can finish washing yourself."

"What? Why won't you finish washing me?" he asked with a sheepish grin.

"I just remembered I have some place I have to be. I have a date with a man!" she claimed as she was rinsing off her body, then started rinsing Quinn's body.

"Should I be jealous of this man you have a date with?" he asked.

"Oh, I hope so!" she said playfully. "He said I could fall asleep in his arms tonight. I am so looking forward to his arms," she said flirtatiously as she scrunched her nose at Quinn.

"He's a very lucky man," he said as he finished washing himself. "Okay, let's get you ready for your date."

Annie scooted down to the other end of the tub while Quinn stood up, then he helped her to stand. He wrapped a fluffy white towel around her. He toweled himself off and stepped out of the tub. He helped Annie out of the tub and helped her to towel dry. They walked out of the bathroom into the bedroom area. Instead of putting on one of Quinn's t-shirts, she chose a sexy nightgown.

"I have to look good for my date when I sleep in his arms!" she said as she climbed into bed.

"Wow, I hope you know your date will find you very irresistible. Are you sure you want to wear that?"

Annie just cocked her head and smiled. She watched Quinn as he slipped a pair of boxer shorts on, climbed into bed, and turned the light on the bedside table out. Annie laid her head on his left shoulder and he wrapped his arm around her. He kissed her softly on the lips. "I love you, baby. Sweet dreams," he whispered to her.

"Only of you, Quinn. I love you, too." She laid her arm across his chest and snuggled up against him until she was very comfortable. It wasn't long before she drifted off into a peaceful sleep.

As he held her in his arms, watching her sleep, he thought of the coming days. He must keep her safe from this maniac. He hoped the police could shed some light on this whole situation. What are the police not telling the general public? Morgan had raped so many girls and now he had killed one of them. He knew Annie was right about one thing; he must keep a clear head. Then he prayed silently as he closed his eyes. *"Thank you, dear Lord, for bringing Annie into my life. She has filled a void in my life I never thought could ever be filled. Please, Lord, show me how to protect the love of my life. She is everything to me. In Jesus name I pray, Amen."* He kissed her softly on top of her head and whispered, "I love you, Annie Taylor," and he fell asleep.

He awoke feeling refreshed at 7:30 a.m. He couldn't believe how much better he slept now that he was married to Annie. He hated to wake her, but he knew he must. "Annie, wake up honey, we have lots to do today." He kissed her gently on the lips, "wake up, baby," he said. "Come on, I'll help you wash your hair."

"Do I have to?" She asked as she sat up on the side of the bed, stretching and yawning.

"Yes, baby, you do. In addition to everything we must do today, we are going to get married again at City Hall." He kissed her gently on her lips. "Now get up, baby."

Quinn helped her wash her very long dark hair. While Annie used the hair dryer, he washed his hair. Her hair was naturally curly and she could style her hair by using a hairbrush. When she had finished, she brushed her teeth and put on some make-up.

"Annie, I have a small idea I want you to do." Annie turned her head to look at him.

"Okay," she said.

"I noticed there was a little gift shop in the lobby of the hotel when we checked in last night. They have some women's hats for sale. I would like for you to buy one today and a really big pair of sunglasses. Before we leave to go to the police station, I want you to put all of your hair into the hat and wear the sunglasses while we are in the police station."

"Okay," she said thinking she understood why for that request. She twisted her hair into a high ponytail and then wrapped her hair into a bun securing it with some pins. All she had to do now was put the hat overtop of her hairdo.

Once they had dressed and before they had left for breakfast, Quinn pulled his cell phone out to call Mrs. Davis. He told her he did not want her to come to work for the next few days. She said she would go visit her children in Alabama until he called her for a return date. Then he telephoned the Chief of Police.

"Hello, may I speak to Chief Hansen, please?" He paused to listen. "My name is Quinn Taylor," and he listened again. "Thank you."

"Chief Hansen speaking."

"Chief Hansen, my name is Quinn Taylor. I was

wondering if I could make an appointment for my wife and I and two other friends to meet with you regarding something of grave importance this morning."

"Are you Reggie's son?"

"Yes, I am. I didn't know you knew my father."

"I'm not a close friend of your father's, but we have met a few times at some social gatherings. Your father is a fine man. What is the nature of your request to meet with me?"

"It's regarding the serial rapist. We think we know who it is. We think we know what his motive is."

"All right. You know I really can't discuss this case with you, but if you think you know who it is, I'll listen. How soon can you get here?" asked Chief Hansen.

"We'll be there around 11 a.m." said Quinn.

It was 8:55 a.m. when they left the comfort of their hotel room, got on the elevator, and met Joe and Jax in the lobby. As they walked towards the hotel dining area for breakfast, Joe started sniffing the air and leaned in towards Quinn, laughing. "You smell nice, Quinn. Is that Jasmine?" and he took another sniff of the air. Quinn gave him a "mind your own business" glare. Jax laughed.

After breakfast was over, Quinn announced they would be making a stop at City Hall before their meeting with Chief Hansen.

"Annie and I are going to get married again."

"So, does that mean if she wants to divorce your ass, she has to divorce you twice?" asked Jax with a laugh.

"Would you cut it out with a divorce already! We've only been married a few days!" He punched Jax in the arm.

"I don't know the international laws on marriage and property. I just want to make sure that if anything happens to me that Annie can get all of my holdings without any trouble. She is mine in every way and I want her to have everything I own. We have an appointment to see our attorney right after we talk to Chief Hansen."

"Quinn, I don't want…"

"Annie, it's a legal thing. You must understand that. Everything I own is yours now and I want to make sure it is legal. Do you understand?"

"Yes, I understand."

When all the necessary paperwork had been filled out, Quinn and Annie stood before the Justice of the Peace. "Who is your Best Man, Mr. Taylor?"

"I am, sir," stated Joe.

"Do you have a maid of honor, ma'am?"

"I am her maid of honor, sir, err, man of honor, that is," stated Jax.

"How unconventional," said the Justice of the Peace. It was a simple wedding ceremony. Quinn was very happy.

"Are you sure we don't have to do this a third time?" giggled Annie.

"Well, maybe on our 50th anniversary we can renew our vows," he said smiling down at his new bride. "You really are mine now."

"Honey, I've been yours since I saw those dimples of yours!" She kissed her husband passionately. "Maybe we should get married a third time, after all, we met on the third. Maybe that is our lucky number!"

Quinn laughed. "Or we could have three kids!"

"Oh for crying out loud," said Jax. "Let's go see Chief Hansen. This is getting a little gooey."

"Did he just say gooey?" asked Quinn.

"Yes, I said gooey, you know, sickening?"

"We have got to get him married!" said Quinn.

CHAPTER 17

"GOOD MORNING, CHIEF HANSEN," Quinn said as they shook hands. "Thank you for seeing us on such short notice. I would like to introduce to you my wife, Mrs. Taylor, and my friends Joe Turner and Jackson Xavier. He prefers to be called Jax."

"Please, have a seat," pointing to a conference table in his office. "As I stated before, I am not at liberty to discuss this case with you, but if you have any proof at all, I really would like to hear it."

"First of all, I would like to say that I purposely had my wife come in here today with a hat and sunglasses on for a reason. Honey, would you take them off now please and shake you hair loose?"

Annie stood up and turned around so that her back faced everyone. She removed her hat and removed the pins in her hair that held her hair in place. She bent forward and shook her hair loose and brought her head up so that her hair cascaded across the front of her shoulders. She took her sunglasses off and turned around.

Chief Hansen let out a gasp. He stood up and

walked over to her. He looked at her hair, then at her eyes. "How tall are you?"

"I'm 5 feet 2 inches tall and I weigh 105 pounds," she said.

He kept studying her. He looked at Quinn, then back at her. "Your husband introduced you as Mrs. Taylor. What is you first name?"

"My name is Anna Marie Marshall Taylor. I... umm, Quinn and I just got married last Monday. My friends call me Annie."

Chief Hansen had a scowl on his face. "You may sit down, Annie," and he returned to his seat.

"Would you like to tell him or would you prefer I tell him what you told me?" asked Quinn.

"Annie, I would rather hear this from you if you are up to it," said the Chief.

"Yes, I'll tell you," said Annie.

"Would you like to do this in private?"

"No, sir. I would rather my husband and my friends stayed with me. I promise, I won't leave anything out."

"Would you care if I recorded your statement? I don't want to forget anything you tell me."

"That's fine."

"I'm going to ask a couple of other people to join us that has been involved with this case."

Chief Hansen walked over to his desk and telephoned his secretary, "Maggie, tell Detectives Evans and Brown to come to my office immediately. Tell them to bring a recorder with fresh batteries, and hold all my calls," he demanded and placed the phone down on the receiver. He walked over to the small refrigerator in his office and pulled out a bottle of water.

"This is for you, Mrs. Taylor, in case your mouth goes dry."

Just then the door to his office opened. Governor Marcovich walked in.

Everyone stood to greet the Governor. Chief Hansen shook his hand. "I'm sorry Governor Marcovich, did we have a meeting this morning that I had forgotten about?"

"No, Chief Hansen, we didn't. Reggie Taylor told me you would be meeting with the Taylors and their friends this morning. I wanted to attend this meeting as well."

"I heard congratulations are in order, Quinn," and he shook Quinn's hand. "Umm, is that Jasmine I smell?" Quinn frowned.

"And you must be Annie. Congratulations to you, too, my dear," he said as he shook her hand. "I just wish we could have met under better circumstances."

"Please have a seat, Governor Marcovich," instructed Chief Hansen as he pulled a seat out for him.

Detectives Evans and Brown walked into the room. Detective Evans sat the recorder on the table. When they saw Annie, they immediately looked at each other and then at the Chief.

Introductions were made to Detectives Evans and Brown. The recorder was turned on and placed directly in front of Annie.

Chief Hansen started speaking. "Today is Thursday, July 9, 2015. My name is Timothy Hansen. I am the Chief of Police of Columbus, Ohio. We are having a meeting today to discuss the rapes of several women in the Columbus area that have taken place over the past 18 months or so. One of these seven women has recently been found murdered."

"In this meeting, we have Governor Marcovich, Detective Jonathon Evans, Detective Billy Brown, Jackson Xavier, Joe Turner, and Quinn and Annie Taylor. The Taylors have requested this meeting. Mrs. Taylor believes she knows who the rapist is. She also believes this rapist is the murderer of one of the seven raped women. Annie, I'm going to turn this over to you. Take your time and let us know why you think you know whom this perpetrator is. I need for you to state your full name and what your friends call you."

Annie was nervous as she looked at everyone in the room. She decided she must be strong. Quinn scooted his chair as close to her as he could. She took his hand for comfort.

Her throat had suddenly gone dry. She reached for the bottle of water, removed the lid, and took a drink.

"My name is Anna Marie Marshall Taylor. My

friends call me Annie. Before I speak, I need to make something perfectly clear to everyone in this room," she stated as she looked at Quinn for support.

"I want this person caught as much as you do. Ever since we realized who this person was, Quinn has been trying to keep me in the dark about some things because he didn't want to frighten me. He was doing his best to protect me. I am here to tell you that I will no longer be left in the dark about anything related to this case."

"As I stated to you before, Mrs. Taylor, we are not at liberty to discuss this case with you," said Chief Hansen.

"I understand what you are telling me, Chief Hansen, but I am not just an ordinary citizen. I think in whatever perverted way, I am caught in the middle of this crime, and, I don't like it. If you refuse to tell me everything so that I can protect myself, then this meeting is over!" Annie emphatically said as she tapped her fingers on the table.

"But, Mrs. Taylor," Detective Evans said, "As a citizen, it is your duty to tell us what you know so that we can catch these creeps."

"Creeps, as in more than one?" Annie questioned as she looked at Chief Hansen.

"No comment," said Evans.

"I agree with you, Detective Evans. I came here today on my own accord to tell you what I know;

however, my first duty is to me. I need to protect myself first. Because if I don't, I could be the next one raped and murdered. And you still won't know who is committing this crime."

The room became very quiet. Suddenly, Annie stood. She knew she should stay and tell the police everything she knew, but she felt she must take a stand in order to protect herself. "Come on, Quinn, I'm leaving."

Just as she started to move away from the table with Quinn, Joe, and Jax at her side, the Governor spoke up.

"Young lady, please sit back down. Reggie said you were a spitfire," he paused. "I'll make you a deal. You tell us what you know. If we think everything you have told us is pertinent to this case, then we will tell you what we know. Is that fair enough?"

Annie looked at her husband, then at Joe and Jax. She sat back down in her seat.

"That's fair enough," Quinn, Joe, and Jax returned to their seats.

Before she began talking, she noticed Detective Brown was looking at her a little too closely for her own liking. Maybe he was comparing her to the other ladies. He was making her feel very uncomfortable. She looked away from him.

"This all started six years ago while I was a freshman in college at the Columbus Music Academy."

She told the police that someone has been

following her for the last six years. She told them about the only two dates she had with David Morgan and how Morgan had tried to rape her. She spoke of his scary apology, and how he spread horrible rumors all over campus about her. She told the police how she was afraid to leave her apartment, except for classes and grocery shopping. She told them how paranoid she had become.

"Well, to make a long story short, for the last six years, I have had the creepiest feelings that someone has been watching me from the shadows, always lurking around. I have always felt safe in my apartment. Then on July 3rd, I felt like someone was watching me inside my apartment."

Annie continued talking, telling the police and the Governor how she had gone to the store for groceries the night before, how she had found someone had made coffee in her apartment, had placed the new can of coffee in her refrigerator, and how the chain to her door was not attached to the door frame, and the door was unlocked. She told them she had gone to La Seals with her cousins that evening and how she had gone home with Quinn. While at Quinn's she had received a phone call from her neighbor, Tony, telling her someone had broken into her apartment.

"You should have a record of that on file because Tony called the police. He is the one who reported the break in."

"Did the police dust for fingerprints?" asked the Chief.

"I don't think so. When Tony couldn't find me, he told the officer I was missing. He said the officer said there wasn't much they could do for 48 hours and told him to call back if I didn't show up."

"I had my cell phone in my purse and I had left my purse downstairs at Quinn's house. That's why I didn't hear it ringing. When I finally answered my phone, Quinn and I drove back to my apartment. That's when Quinn noticed something strange outside of my apartment building. Quinn, I will let you take over now," said Annie as she took a sip of water.

"When we arrived at Annie's apartment and got out of my car, she told me she felt like someone was watching us. I started looking around. I didn't see a soul, but something caught my eye. He told the police that he suspected someone had set up some surveillance equipment to spy on Annie and how Jax brought in his Navy surveillance equipment and did a check on the area. Jax detected at least four audio and video bugs outside her apartment. He was able to scramble those bugs. We were able to go into her apartment. We did a thorough check inside."

"We found one in her bathroom, two in her bedroom, two in the living area, one in the kitchen, and two in the hallway. All in all, we found 12 bugs in the apartment, the hallway, and outside of the building."

"Jax was able to pick up a video and audio signal. With a few codes, we were able to see the person on the other end. It didn't tell us where his exact location was, but we can tell you with certainty, he is in the general vicinity of the academy."

Jax opened up his laptop and turned it on. When he accessed what he needed to show the police, he turned it around.

"This, gentlemen, is David Morgan. We believe he is the rapist."

Detective Brown spoke up, "is this all you have?"

"Yes," said Jax.

"We will need your computer to analyze the video for authenticity," said Brown. Annie noticed that he looked somewhat suspicious, but of what, she thought.

"I'm sorry, I can't do that," said Jax.

"Why not? That is obstruction of justice," yelled Detective Brown.

"I'm sorry sir. Here is a copy of the video. You should be able to get what you need from this copy," and Jax handed the copy to the police chief.

"Why can't you give us your computer?" asked Detective Brown.

"Because it's a government computer, sir," and Jax looked at Governor Marcovich for support.

"We could get a court order, you know."

"Back off, Brown," said the Governor. "You

would have to go all the way to the Supreme Court Justice to get that computer. It would take years to get it. I am certain that what he has given you will suffice."

"Let me get this straight," said Detective Evans. "The only proof brought to us today is a lady that looks like the other victims, and proof that a guy is stalking her."

Quinn's voice raised. "It is no wonder you haven't caught this guy. He is a hell of a lot smarter than you. Ask yourself when you look at her. Is she his next victim because she looks like the other ladies; or, are the other ladies a manifestation of Annie in his mind? Personally, I think he seeks out ladies who look like her so that he can have the next best thing in his eyes."

"Now, I ask you, gentlemen, what are you going to do about this? Because as far as I can tell, he is after my wife and I'm telling you right now, he's not going to get her! I will do everything and I mean everything in my power to protect her. Do I make myself clear?"

"I have a question for you, Mr. Taylor," said Detective Brown with a smirk. "How long have you and Mrs. Taylor been married?"

"What does the length of our marriage have to do with this case?" asked Quinn.

"Just answer the question, Taylor."

Quinn looked at the detective and gave him a scowl. "I don't think I like your tone, sir."

"You don't have to like—"

"Since Monday. Why do you want to know?" inquired Annie. "When we married, is none of your business and has nothing to do with this case."

"Oh, it may not have anything to do with this case, but how do you know Quinn isn't your stalker? How long have you known each other before you married? How do you know he isn't the rapist? After all, you look like all the other girls!" he said with a smirk.

"Stop this!" Annie screamed out as she stood. "Stop this right now! Quinn is not the stalker. He is not a rapist or murderer! What's wrong with you? I don't think I want to be here anymore. This was a mistake coming to you! Let's go, Quinn!"

Quinn was livid! He couldn't believe what Detective Brown just insinuated! He knew he was not a stalker. He knew he was not a rapist or a murderer either. Annie just took up for him, but what if she put more thought into that statement and suspected that he was?

"Annie," Quinn said with a scared look on his face. "I'm not a stalker or a rapist/murderer. I promise you, I'm not!"

"I know you're not, I know," and she caressed his cheeks with her hands.

Governor Marcovich stood up and slammed his hands on the table.

"Enough! Brown, stand down now or I will

throw you out of here on your ass myself! Sit down, young lady. We are not finished!"

Quinn stood ready to fight. One could see the fury building up around his neck and his blood pressure was rising. His face was beet red. No one talked to his wife like that.

Governor Marcovich pointed his finger at Quinn. "Back off, Quinn! Sit down and I mean now!"

Joe and Jax were on either side of Quinn, forcing him down in his seat.

"Now isn't the time, brother. Not now," pleaded Joe.

Everyone became very quiet. Evans got up from his chair and started pacing. Brown had a look of satisfaction on his face. The tension in the air was so thick you could cut it with a knife.

"First of all, Brown, I think you are out of line. Quinn is not the kind of man to stalk, rape, and kill women. This man is a fucking war hero, for crying out loud. He doesn't need to hear your bullshit, and quite frankly, neither do I! Do you understand what I am saying to you, Detective Brown?"

"Maybe you are too close to the Taylors, Governor," replied Brown very calmly.

"*What are you implying, Detective Brown? Before you answer, you'd better think before you speak!*" he yelled!

Detective Brown was at a loss for words. He glared at the Governor instead.

"Do you honestly think he would come in here on his own accord with his wife and friends and present us with evidence if he was the rapist?" He has had enough of Brown's bullshit.

"Tim, get him out of here, now! I've had about all I can stomach of this idiot!" screamed the Governor.

"Wait in the outer office, Detective Brown. I'll speak to you when this meeting is over."

Detective Brown's face turned red. He was quite tall when he stood. He threw his shoulders back and gave Quinn a snide laugh. He walked out of the door.

The Governor sat back down in his chair. He had a scowl on his face. He was pissed and was trying to calm himself down. He took a deep breath, and then another.

"Tim, I think you should tell them what you know about the other girls," said the Governor.

"Are you sure you want me to do that? What if it turns out this Morgan isn't the guy we're looking for?"

"Listen, Tim. This maniac has been raping our women for the last year and a half. This is the only lead you have had; and, they are the ones that found it. Quinn has the right to protect his wife. You have a duty to this city. Tell them everything you know," demanded the Governor.

Chief Hansen walked over to his refrigerator and pulled out seven bottles of water, handing one to each person in the room. He took a long drink. "Ugh!" he said as he wiped his mouth with the back of his hand. "I think I need a stiff drink!"

"Okay, what I am about to tell you can not leave this room," said Chief Hansen, taking a deep breath and letting it out.

"Each woman has been raped and beaten. That is all the public has been told. What the public does not know is that all of the girls were drugged and kidnapped. They did not go willingly with their abductors. The girls could not tell us where they were taken. When the girls came to, their mouths had been taped shut with duct tape and masking tape was put over their eyes. They were chained up all of the time. Sometimes they were chained to a wall with their arms and legs spread open and raped. Other times, they were chained to a bed in the same fashion and raped. They were even hung from the rafters with their hands tied together. That's when they were beaten. Each girl was beaten worse than the last. They were raped like nothing I have ever seen before. These men are savages of the worse kind! One girl said if there was an orifice on her body that could be screwed, then it was screwed repeatedly. They even found semen in her ear.

"They were beaten with canes, floggers, small chains, belts, whips, and even switches. The girl that died had been beaten with all of these things. One of the whips caught her jugular vein and ripped it open. Even her anus had been ripped to her vagina. She bled to death, caused from all of the beatings she had received. She didn't stand a chance of survival like the others."

Annie let out a gasp.

"Were any of the survivors able to give any kind of description?" asked Quinn.

"One of the victims said there were two guys. She thinks one was taller than the other and one might have been older. She wasn't sure. She said when the guys were raping her, one man's body felt firmer than the other. That is why she thinks one might have been older. Anyway, we do have two sets of DNA, but we don't know their identity."

Chief Hansen took a drink of water.

"That's not all. When they were done with each girl, they cut patches of long hair from their scalps. They used the long strands of hair to form letters and taped them to a white poster board. When they dumped the body of each girl on the side of the road, they would leave a sign taped to their stomachs."

"There have been a total of six signs and they are all different. She's not Annie; Annie is mine; I want Annie; Annie belongs to me; He can't have Annie. And the last message really bothered me. It said "I'll kill her before I let him have her!"

Annie gasped. She covered her mouth with her hands. "I'm not going to cry. I'm not going to cry. I'm not going to cry." Tears started flowing down her cheeks, but she did not make a whimper. Quinn handed her some tissues from a box that was on the table, then ran his hand through his dark hair. The neck muscles on all of the men in the room were tightly clinched. Their hands were making fists, opening and closing, opening and closing. If any of the men could get their hands on these two rapists and now murderers, there wouldn't be anything left of them.

"When the last girl was found dead, we didn't know if she was Annie or not. Everything was the same with the beatings and the way she was raped. The same two DNA's were found in her; but, there was no sign and her body wasn't found on the side of a rural road."

"We are waiting for her dental records to come back. We thought the dead girl was the Annie he was talking about killing to keep whomever from having her."

"Where was her body found?" asked Joe.

"Her body was found in a dumpster behind the Columbus Music Academy.

"Don't you think there are some red flags here? I mean David was a student at CMA and he owns a coffee shop right there on campus. Annie recognized him on the computer and now a girl is found dead in a dumpster behind the college! What more do you need gentlemen?" yelled Quinn.

"Hard Ass Proof! That's what we need!" shouted Detective Evans. "We need a sample of Morgan's

DNA to compare it to the DNA we retrieved from the girls. If it matches, he's going to prison."

"Calm down," said Governor Marcovich. "We are all on the same side here."

Quinn took a drink of his water to help calm his frayed nerves.

"Have you interviewed the President of the Academy yet?" he inquired.

"Yes, we did. He said the deceased was not a student of the Academy and he did not know her. He promised the academy would give us full cooperation. He also gave us permission to interview anyone on campus.

"Annie, do you know of anyone on campus that ran around with Morgan? Perhaps a friend or an associate that worked for him?" asked Quinn.

"No, I stayed to myself so much that I never knew his friends. I never went to his coffee shop after that night."

"Do you remember having pissed off someone enough that they would want to cause you bodily harm in anyway?"

"The only person I've had words with was Morgan. Oh, and the President of the Academy. You know, your Dad called him a weasel. I think he might be a friend to Paul Morgan. Could that be his accomplice?"

Just then there was a knock on the door. The Chief's secretary walked in. "Excuse me, sir, I don't mean to interrupt," she said as she walked towards the chief. "This just arrived. It's the girl's dental records you have been waiting on."

Chief Hansen started opening the envelope. "Thank you, Maggie," he said as she left the room. He read the contents of the report to himself and then looked at Annie, Quinn, and the Governor. "The young woman's name is Marsha Butler. She was a student at Capital. She was barely five feet tall and only weighed 96 pounds. She was just 19 years old." The room became very quiet for several minutes.

"I wonder," said Quinn. "Was she raped and killed somewhere on campus at CMA? Were they all raped somewhere on campus? Were they going to take her body to a rural road like all the others and dump her body? Did they see someone in the process as they were taking her to their car and to keep from getting caught, just dumped her body into the nearest dumpster? If that is what happened, surely, someone had to have witnessed something!"

"Chief Hansen," said Governor Marcovich. "I think you should set up a task force. I want Quinn Taylor to be in charge and I want Evans at his side. You can recruit anyone you want to help you Quinn. But, I DO NOT want Brown on it. And, I want 100% cooperation from the police department."

"Governor Marcovich," said Detective Evans, "they have not been trained by the police academy."

"No, son, they haven't. Are you a veteran, son?" asked the Governor.

"No sir, I'm not."

"No offense to you, Detective Evans. You have been an exemplary employee of this police force, but these men are US Navy Seals. They have more experience with weaponry. They have outsmarted the enemy on numerous occasions and their surveillance skills surpass anything I have ever heard of. The only thing they don't have is the full working knowledge of the law. That is why I want you on this task force. You can help them with that. I would appreciate it if you would work very hard with them and follow their lead. They are not here to take your job. When you have found these monsters, then the task force will be dissolved and they can go back to their lives and you can go on with your job."

"Thank you, Governor, for your vote of confidence," said Quinn, "but I don't want to be on a task force. I will not leave my wife's side for one moment so I don't know how well us being on a task force would work. And quite frankly, Joe should protect his wife as well; but, I do have an idea. Could we be sworn in as temporary detectives instead? That way, we can do our own investigation and let you know what we have discovered? We will be more than happy to work along side of Evans."

Governor Marcovich looked at Chief Hansen.

Both men sat back in their seats. Governor Marcovich nodded his head.

"As long as you keep us informed of everything and work with us, I don't see where that would be a problem," said Chief Hansen. "I can't make you a detective, but I can make you a Reserve Officer. This will afford you the right to investigate, but you must report your findings. Do I make myself clear?"

"Yes, sir. I think that will work for us," replied Quinn.

"Does each of you have a gun permit?" asked the Chief.

"Yes, sir, we do."

"I need to make a copy of your gun permits. We will need to take your fingerprints, too. This is just standard procedure when I hire any officer. We need to take your photo as well," explained the chief.

After all the official formalities had taken place, Quinn, Joe, and Jax were sworn in as temporary Reserve Officers of the Columbus Police Force. Badges were issued to each man with a photo ID. The men opted to use their own weapons and would furnish their own bullets.

"Quinn," asked Chief Hansen, "did you remove the surveillance equipment from Annie's apartment and her surroundings?"

"No, sir, we didn't. We left everything as is."

"I think it would be a good idea for my

department to go in and remove them and dust for fingerprints."

"Annie, I need for you to give me a list of names that have been in your apartment recently," requested Chief Hansen.

"That's easy, they are all in this room except for one other person and that's Tony O'Hara."

"And where is he?" asked Detective Evans.

"We felt he was in danger, so I flew him to Ireland," said Quinn.

"Tony O'Hara. Would that be Anthony O'Hara?"

"Possibly," said Annie. "Why do you ask?"

"Was that his car that blew up a few days ago near your hotel?" asked Evans.

"Yes, it was."

"How do you know that Tony isn't one of the rapists?" said Detective Evans.

"Not Tony. NO! I can't believe that. No, he has always been a good friend to me, you know, like a big brother! No, I refuse to believe that!"

"Annie, are you sure about that? He admitted to me that he was in love with you," Quinn said as he looked at his wife.

"When did he say that?"

"He admitted it to me on the plane trip to Ireland. He said he had asked you to go for coffee at the Coffee Campus House for about a year and," he paused, "you always refused to go with him."

Quinn's brain was going in too many directions. "Shit! If it's him, I'll kill him!"

"Quinn, why would he help us get married if he was in on it? That doesn't make any sense! He even gave me away at our wedding, Quinn. I refuse to believe that!"

"I know how we can prove he didn't do it," announced Annie. "I have a key to his apartment. He left all of his belongings here for safekeeping. I'm sure his toothbrush and dirty drinking cups are still in his apartment; plus, he plays the bagpipes. You can check for his DNA on one of those items. I am sure it will not match the two DNA's you already have."

———◆———

That very afternoon, Quinn and Annie met the Columbus Police Department and the Columbus Fire Department at her apartment building. Two fire trucks with buckets hoisted forensics experts into the trees to disconnect the bug devices. They found one at each entrance to the apartment building, one in a tree near the parking area, and one in a tree facing directly at Annie's picture window to her second floor apartment. Then the forensics experts went into her apartment building.

Quinn and Annie sat outdoors on a bench waiting for forensics to finish.

"Quinn, you're awfully quiet."

He didn't say anything. He leaned forward and

placed his elbows on his upper legs near his knees and put his face in his hands. He sat like this for a few minutes.

Annie got up from the bench, removed his hands from his face and straddled his lap. She took her hand and lifted his face to look at her.

"Quinn, I know you're not a stalker and I know you're not a rapist or murderer, either."

"How do you know, Annie? You haven't known me that long! How can you be so sure?"

She took one of his hands and placed it over her heart.

"Because I feel it here, in my heart, and the heart doesn't lie," she whispered softly as tears started to roll down her cheeks.

Quinn looked deep into her eyes.

"Oh, Annie, I love you so much!" He put his arms around her, pulling her tightly to his chest.

"I was so worried Brown put doubt in your mind about me. It's been killing me all afternoon!"

"No, Quinn. I could never think that about you!" and she placed her lips on his.

"What did I ever do to deserve you?" he asked as he held her tightly.

It took another couple of hours for the forensics department to gather all of the surveillance equipment, dust for fingerprints, and gather any other evidence they deemed necessary from both apartments. When they were finished, Quinn telephoned Joe and Jax for help in packing all of the personal belongings from both apartments. They moved all of the boxes to Quinn's penthouse for storage.

CHAPTER 18

WHEN THE LAST OF THE boxes had been stored away, they all went downstairs to the restaurant at Taylor Suites for dinner. None of them had eaten since breakfast. The waitress came and took their orders. The men ordered steaks, but Annie only wanted a pecan salad with cranberries and a glass of water.

"Are you going to stay here or at the Royal tonight?" asked Joe.

"I think we will stay at the Royal tonight. Tomorrow, I would like for us to start installing all of the surveillance equipment at my hotel and then at La Seals. If it was just me, I would stay here, at Taylor Suites tonight, but I need to keep Annie safe."

"Quinn, don't start spending all that money on equipment because of me. Surely they won't come here and try to kidnap me, not in this place of business. We can stay here tonight if you'd rather. You are just being over cautious," and she started rubbing the back of her neck and her forehead.

The food finally came and everyone ate heartily,

except for Annie. "Honey, you've hardly touched your food. Are you alright?"

"I think I'm getting a migraine," she replied. "Can we leave?"

"Of course we can," Quinn called for the waitress. "Put this on my expense account please," and he handed her a $50 tip.

"I'm sorry sir, I'm new. Can I have your name, please?"

"I'm Quinn Taylor, your boss, young lady," he smiled. "I sign your paychecks." Annie kicked him under the table.

"YYYes, sir, right away sir," said the intimidated waitress. "Thank you for the tip. Have a good evening, sir."

"Quinn, why did you say that? You scared that poor girl to death!" Annie scolded.

"Because it's fun!" he smirked.

"To you maybe, but not to her!" she continued scolding.

"Annie, you are looking bad in the eyes. Let's get you back to the Royal."

"Joe, have you turned your rental back in to the airport?" asked Quinn.

"No, I haven't," replied Joe.

"Can you meet us there in the morning at 10 a.m.?" asked Quinn.

"Yes, I can do that."

"Jax, would you drive my Hummer to the Royal Plaza Suites tonight? That way, you can follow me back to the airport to return the rental. We can all come home together," and he tossed Jax the keys.

"Yes sir, right away, sir, anything you say, sir. I'll even kiss your feet, sir," Jax said laughing as he punched Quinn in the arm.

"Ouch!" Quinn said as he rubbed his upper arm. Before he could say anything else, he noticed his wife's eyes were squinting rather tightly. He knew from experience that any kind of light and noise only made a migraine worse.

"Annie, do you have something to take for your migraine?"

"Yes, I have something in my purse." Quinn reached for her purse and pulled out an over the counter bottle of migraine medication.

"This stuff won't help you. Come on, we'll stay here tonight. I have some prescription migraine medication upstairs. You can take some of them."

"No, Quinn," Annie said, "it's not good to take someone else's medications."

"I'll call the doctor when we get upstairs. I'll ask him for his approval, if it makes you feel better. If he doesn't approve, I'll take you to the ER instead. Maybe we should stay here tonight."

"Jax, can you get your equipment from your van? I guess we are staying here tonight." He wanted to make sure Morgan or his accomplice hadn't installed any bugs in his penthouse.

Annie stood from the table where they had been sitting and she took Quinn's proffered hand.

As they walked towards the elevator, she put one hand over her eyes. When they stopped at the elevator, she leaned her face into his chest to shield her eyes. "Is the light bothering you, baby?" Then a soft ping sounded announcing the arrival of the elevator. She quickly placed her hands over her ears.

"Ah, fuck, this isn't good." He walked her into the elevator, inserted his key card to access the penthouse, and pushed the button for the 25th floor. He bent down and picked up his wife in his arms.

They sat in the formal living area, allowing time for Joe and Jax to search the penthouse for intruders and unwanted surveillance equipment. While they waited, Quinn called his doctor and got approval to give Annie one of his migraine medications. When the search was completed, Quinn carried her straight to their bedroom. "Honey, I'm going to help you undress." He whispered, knowing full well his voice would sound like he was screaming at her.

He picked up the remote and closed all of the curtains so the room would be very dark. He got one of his t-shirts from his dresser. Sitting her down on the side of the bed, he started very gently removing her socks, shoes, and all of her clothing. After he had put his t-shirt on her, he pulled the bed covers down.

"Don't get in bed yet. I have to get the medication

for you," he whispered. It didn't take him long to split a pill in half and get a glass of water. "Annie," he said softly, "the doctor said to only take half of the pill since you don't weigh very much. He said if you weren't feeling any relief in two hours, he wanted you to take the other half, okay?" Annie swallowed the pill with water, "Thank you, Quinn."

"I'll come back in shortly and lie down with you. I just want to talk to the guys. Try to get some rest, baby. I love you," and he kissed her gently on her lips.

Quinn turned all of the lights off in the bedroom. He turned the night light on in the bathroom and left the door slightly ajar, should she need to get up. When he left the bedroom, he left the door slightly opened.

Quinn walked into the kitchen and took a six-pack of beer from his refrigerator. Joe and Jax were sitting at a table near the patio doors.

They took the caps off their bottles and each took a long swig. "Umm, nice and cold!" said Jax. "Just the way I like it!"

"Is she alright?" asked Joe.

"She should be by morning," replied Quinn. "I'm hoping the medication I gave her knocks her out. Did you look in all of the rooms?"

"Yes, we looked in all of the rooms inside the penthouse, but we haven't gone onto the terrace yet," stated Jax. "We looked out through the windows, but there are a lot of big items setting out there that anyone could hide behind."

"Maybe I should have them removed from the rooftop for the time being."

"Quinn, I want to say that I like this new change in you," smiled Joe.

"What are you talking about? What change? I haven't changed," questioned Quinn.

"Yes, you have. Ever since Kayla left, you have been the meanest, most arrogant, son of a bitch I know. There have been some days, old friend, where I couldn't stand you."

"Trust me, there have been plenty of days when I couldn't stand myself," said Quinn as he took another drink of beer.

"If I hadn't seen it myself, I would have never believed that one tiny little woman weighing 100 pounds could have you wrapped around her finger so damn tight from the moment you laid eyes on her. It's nice to finally see you in love."

"You know something?" asked Quinn, "the feelings I have going through me for Annie aren't the same as I had for Kayla. What Annie and I have feels like love. It feels strong, and when she is in my arms I have never felt more at ease, more satisfied and more needed and wanted by anyone in my entire life. I feel whole with her. And trust me, if anyone, and I mean anyone, tries to hurt her in anyway, I'll kill the bastard!"

"CRASH!" "CRASH!" Again.

"What was that?" Jax said as they jumped to their feet. "Maybe one of your chairs just toppled over from the wind."

"No, everything I have out there is too heavy for the wind to move. There's someone out there!" said Quinn.

He quickly turned off the lights and ran to his bedroom to get Annie. Just as he started to push the door open, Annie appeared in the doorway.

"I heard something on the rooftop," she said sounding anxious.

"I know, we heard it, too," he said as he took her hand and walked her to his walk-in closet.

He grabbed a robe and helped Annie put it on. Behind his clothes was a wall that slid open, exposing a wall safe with a combination lock. He made a few turns, left, right, and left again and opened the safe. He took out three pistols and six clips with bullets. He locked the safe. "Let's go and be very quiet. I'll protect you."

When they arrived back into the kitchen area where they had been sitting, Quinn gave each man a gun and two clips of bullets.

"Is this door the only way to get on the rooftop?" asked Joe.

"There is a stairwell at the end of the hallway by the elevator. I keep it locked," replied Quinn.

"Is there any other way to get out there?" questioned Joe.

"Only by helicopter, unless you use a parachute," stated Quinn.

"I'm calling Detective Evans for back-up." He pulled out his cell phone and called Evans.

"Detective Evans, this is Quinn Taylor. We may have a breach at my hotel on the rooftop. Would you send several officers to surround my hotel to investigate?" He paused. "We heard a crash like something falling over on the rooftop. No, it isn't that, everything I have on the roof is too heavy to be blown over by the wind." He paused again. "Do me a favor, tell the officers to arrive without their lights and sirens on. Tell them to park in the parking garage. Text me when you get here. I will send the service elevator down to get you from the garage. I don't want to upset my guests. Turner and Xavier are on the scene. Annie is with me. Thanks."

Joe and Jax went outside to the rooftop with their guns in hand. They started looking all around very cautiously. They looked behind all of the heavy patio furniture and large ceramic flowerpots. They even looked in the corners of the swimming pool. Joe noticed that a smaller pot of flowers was turned over. There was no way it could have turned over with the wind. Someone had to have run into it. Then he saw someone.

He was dressed in black from his head to his feet. The man fired his gun at Joe. Joe shot back at him. He knew he shot him, but the man kept running towards the stairs to the hotel's helipad. By the time they reached the helipad, the man had climbed into a helicopter and had flown away.

The police arrived a minute later. "Detective Evans, Jax and I did a search right before you arrived. We had heard a crash out here earlier and we found a flowerpot right over there that had been knocked over. That's when I saw a man dressed in black. When he saw me, he fired his gun, but he missed. I fired back and I'm pretty sure I got him. He ran up the stairs to the helipad and before we could get to him, he climbed into a helicopter and flew away."

"Did you see if he was alone?" asked the Detective.

"No, I really couldn't tell. The chopper was painted all black and there were no markings on it either."

The detective, along with the police, did a thorough search of the rooftop. They went inside to talk to Quinn.

"We found a black duffle bag with a glasscutter, a folded white cloth, and enough ether to knock out a horse. There was even a syringe filled with some kind of medication. We will need to get this all analyzed. Joe shot the perpetrator. We found some blood splatters where he was going up the steps and found some droplets of blood on the floor to the helipad. We'll do a DNA on the blood. I will contact the area hospitals to see if any gunshot victims came in and I'll ask Chief Hansen to contact aviation control at the airport. If I were you, I think I would stay somewhere else tonight."

"I agree. Thank you, Detective, for your help tonight," he said as he shook his hand. "I think we'll get a room downstairs. Annie has a migraine and she needs to get to bed soon."

After all of the policemen had left, Quinn packed a few items including extra migraine medication for Annie and extra ammunition for his gun.

He had already telephoned the front desk for three rooms next to each other for the fifth floor under the fake names of Michael Conner, Thomas Marsden, and Frank Withers. Joe and Jax stayed with Annie while Quinn went to get the room keys.

———◆———

It was nearly 1 a.m. when they finally got into their rooms. Annie's head was still throbbing. She couldn't stand the lights or the noise. She was very tense with all that had happened tonight.

He gave her the second half of the pill and she downed it with water. After she had used the bathroom, she climbed into bed. He opened a little bit of the curtains to allow for some soft outdoor lighting to come into the room from the outside, took his clothes off, and climbed in next to her.

Annie laid her head on Quinn's chest. He kissed her gently on the forehead. She felt a little warm.

"Sleep, baby, I'll take care of you. I love you, baby."

She kissed Quinn gently on his chest. "I love you, too," she said and tried to go to sleep, but she was too wound up. It took another 45 minutes before her body finally succumbed to the medication and she drifted off to sleep.

Quinn laid in bed for the next hour trying to think. He had to find a way to keep her safe. This was ridiculous, he thought. I need to get her out of the country, but I know she won't go. Sending her home to stay with her parents wasn't a good idea either. They don't live that far away. If Morgan would figure that out, then her whole family would be in danger. He decided the only thing he could do was hide her in plain sight, but how?

Maybe I could build a panic room in the penthouse just in case he comes back.

Annie stirred. She moved herself off of Quinn's chest. She was wet with sweat from their body heat. She laid on her side facing Quinn. Some of her hair had fallen on her face.

He gently moved it to the back of her ear. "Maybe she could dye her hair blonde or red," he thought. She would look just as beautiful, but I would miss her dark hair. Maybe she could cut her hair short, but would that deter Morgan away from her? Would he still continue to look for other young women who look like her? Would he continue his assault on these poor unsuspecting women?

God, she was so beautiful. Why should she dye her hair or even cut her hair for that matter? Quinn wanted to catch the bastard and kill him. That was the only way to get their lives back on track.

A couple of days had passed when Detective Evans made a visit to see Quinn and Annie. "Good afternoon, Mr. Taylor, Mrs. Taylor. I just thought I would come by and give you a report on our findings from a few nights ago."

"Please, have a seat Detective Evans. Can I get you a cup of coffee?" asked Annie.

"No, thank you ma'am. I think I have had my quota for the day."

"So, what do you have for us Detective?" questioned Quinn.

"Well, I think the perpetrator meant to do some bodily harm, probably to you, Quinn. You know he had enough ether in the bag with him to knock out a horse. I think he was planning to use that on Mrs. Taylor. We had the substance analyzed in the syringe. Have you ever heard of Ketamine?"

"Isn't that a very strong pain medication?" asked Quinn. "I think I remember some soldiers receiving that at the field hospitals when I was serving in the Navy."

"No sir, it's not a pain medication. It is an anesthetic. When used properly, under the care of a physician, in most cases, it won't hurt you. He had enough ketamine in this syringe to kill a person."

Annie looked at Quinn and a chill went through her body. "Oh, Dear God! When is this going to end?" she said sharply.

"I also wanted to let you know, your friend Tony did not have anything to sample or swab for DNA in his apartment. His apartment was immaculate. There were no dirty dishes; no dirty utensils; no paper cups; no garbage; no toothbrush; and his bagpipes were missing. Even the sheets on his bed were clean. The only thing we found was his finger prints."

"Don't you think that is kind of odd?" asked Annie.

"Yes, Mrs. Taylor, I do."

"Now for your apartment. The only fingerprints they found in your apartment belonged to Joe, Jax, Tony, Quinn, and you. There were no fingerprints on any of the surveillance equipment. I can only assume that the perpetrator used gloves with everything he did in your apartment. There was nothing out of the ordinary."

"I don't think I need to tell you this, Quinn, but I'm going to anyway. I know you have top-of-the-line naval surveillance equipment. I also believe Morgan is watching Mrs. Taylor; but, we need more evidence than that to hold up in court. We have no evidence of him committing rape. We have no evidence of him committing murder, and we have no real evidence of him stalking Mrs. Taylor. We need irrefutable proof. If we were to arrest him on what we have, which is very little, a good attorney would get him off and he'd walk. I need real proof," said Detective Evans adamantly.

"What about the blood droplets you found after Joe shot the intruder?"

"We don't have anything in our database, but we will keep it on file. It could be anybody," reported Evans.

"Thank you for your time, Detective Evans. We really appreciate your help. Have a good day." They shook hands and Detective Evans left.

There hadn't been any more reports of rape or murder over the past week. Joe and Jax had installed motion detectors with bright lights all over the rooftop. They even installed more surveillance equipment all over the hotel, including the rooftop, conference room areas, ballroom areas, all of the elevators, all entrances and exits around the hotel, and the parking garage. Some were installed on the light poles in front of his hotel.

La Seals received the same treatment. It was

state-of-the-art equipment. Quinn hired other former Seals to watch the surveillance monitors around the clock at both places. They were sure no one would be able to penetrate his properties without being seen. He had non-uniformed security guards placed throughout his hotel. Next would be his home in Indian Creek.

CHAPTER 19

August 15, 2015

"WAKE UP SLEEPY HEAD, TIME to get up," said Quinn as he started to tickle her.

"No, stop, please stop! Quinn stop, please!" she yelled and she started grumbling with a giggle. "Why do I have to wake up?"

"Because, I've got a surprise for you. We're going somewhere special today."

"Where are we going?"

"Now, it wouldn't be a surprise if I told you, would it?" he said as he kissed her on her lips and threw the covers off of her. "Now get up. You've been in bed too long. It's already 9 a.m. and you still need to get into the shower. Oh, and pack your make-up bag. We are staying overnight."

"What do I wear today?" she asked looking confused.

"Anything you want is fine," he said as he left their bedroom so that Annie could take her shower.

As he walked into the kitchen to get another cup

of coffee, his cell phone rang. He got a concerned look on his face. It was Jason, with his security team. "Is there anything wrong Jason?"

"No sir. Just thought I would let you know that Jax is running a little late this morning. He said he overslept. He said he would be here in ten minutes. I'll stay until he gets here."

"Thank you, Jason. Mrs. Taylor and I will be leaving in about an hour or so. Please let Jax and Joe know that we will be going to Annie's parents today. We will be back sometime tomorrow afternoon. And, while we are gone, make sure you double check all security measures."

"Yes, sir," stated Jason.

Quinn poured his coffee and sat down on the Queen Anne chair in his formal living room to wait on Annie. He noticed a couple of magazines that she had purchased lying on the end table by the sofa and a pair of her shoes on the floor by the table. He took a drink of his coffee then stood to walk over to fetch the magazines. "Hmm, they're recipe magazines. I wonder if she is planning on making something," he thought as he flipped the pages, not really looking at anything in particular.

He looked around the room and he eyed her Android tablet setting on the coffee table. He picked it up and slid the bar to turn it on. It needed an access code to activate. "I wonder if she will let me have the code. I think she was reading a book on this a few nights ago."

What intrigued him the most was the white tablet and pencil lying on the baby grand piano. He picked up the tablet to look at it. He saw music notes. She was writing a song. "When has she done this?"

He smiled. "This is nice," he thought. Six weeks ago, there was no evidence of a female visiting in my penthouse, let alone living here. I can't believe the difference she has made in my life. He frowned. "While this feels more like a home to me, I'm sure it doesn't feel like her home. It's too manly. We need something that is our home. I wonder if she could make my home in Indian Creek our home? The house was nearly empty and just waiting to have the feminine touch added. Would she want me to sell it and rebuild something to suit her? I wouldn't care where we lived as long as she was there."

He sat back down in the chair and took a drink of his coffee. He continued thinking of Annie. These last few weeks have been nice. Everything seemed normal, except that she hasn't been able to go out on her own like she had always done. I'm sure she feels like a prisoner. I just wish we could catch the son of a bitch. Sooner or later he was bound to make a mistake.

Annie walked into the formal living room. She was wearing a pair of khaki dress slacks with a thin matching belt and a white camisole tucked into her pants. She had on an aqua colored loose-knit top over her camisole. Quinn really liked her in that color, as it accentuated her eyes. She had put her long dark hair into a bun at the base of her neck. She looked very sophisticated.

"Oh, that's where I left my shoes," she said softly.

She saw where Quinn had placed the magazines and her mini tablet on top of her music notes in a neat little pile on the baby grand piano.

"I'm sorry, Quinn. I left a little mess in here."

"Don't worry about it, baby. I like seeing that you live here." He picked her up and carried her into the kitchen and sat her down on the kitchen island.

"I think you like sitting me up here," Annie said with a giggle.

"That's because you are eye level with me," he smirked. "It's much easier to kiss you," and the corner of his lips curled up.

"Are you telling me I'm short, sir?"

He spread her legs apart, leaned in towards her and put his arms around her waist. "Well, you ARE short, but you are beautiful and smart and talented and sexy and you are all mine! I love you more than you will ever realize!" and he kissed her. "Are you hungry?"

"I'm starved!" answered Annie.

"Good, we'll stop for a late breakfast on the way. Are you completely ready to go?"

"I just need to grab my small travel bag and purse," Annie replied.

"Here, drink some orange juice," he said as he handed her a small glass of OJ. "This will tie you over until we get to the restaurant." After she drank her orange juice, Quinn helped her down from the kitchen island.

While Annie went back to the bedroom to get her travel bag and purse, Quinn slipped on his sport coat. He checked his gun and made sure he had his temporary Reserve Officer's badge. Annie saw him with his gun in hand. He pulled the clip from the gun to check for bullets.

"What kind of gun is that?" she asks.

"It's a Smith and Wesson 9mm," he stated as he reloaded the clip into his gun.

"Does it have a safety feature?" asked Annie.

"Are you worried I'll accidently shoot myself?" he inquired with a small laugh. She raised her eyebrow at him with disapproval of such a ridiculous question,

"Yes, dear, it has a safety," he smirked. "Come here." He grabbed her hand and pulled her to where he was standing with her back to his front.

"This is where the safety is located," and he demonstrated how to take the safety off. He put the safety back on. "I want you to take the gun with both hands and remove the safety." Quinn showed her how to hold the gun. Annie successfully unlocked the safety. His hands are still on her hands.

"If anything should ever happen and you need to use this gun, I want you to hold it like this and gently squeeze the trigger. Just make sure you are aiming exactly where you want to shoot. Do you understand what I have just shown you?"

"Yes, I understand, but I hate guns, Quinn. Are you expecting trouble?"

"No, just being cautious. I don't want to let my guard down until he's caught," he said. "I just have a feeling something is going to happen. It's been nagging at me all morning." He slipped the gun back into his holster. "I think when we get back, I'm going to take you to the shooting range and give you lessons. It wouldn't hurt for you to know how to use these things properly."

"Is that why we are leaving; even though, I told you I don't want to run anymore?"

"No. I have had this planned for a few days," he smiled a sheepish grin at her.

"Then tell me where we are going. Please?" She begged.

"Well, I thought we would drive to see your parents today." She put her arms around his waist and gave him a huge hug. "Thank you so much! Can we leave the gun in the car? I don't want to scare my parents."

He grabbed the handle to the small travel

suitcase and picked up her small travel bag. "What do you have in this thing?"

"Oh, you know, make-up, shampoo, hair brush, hair spray, hair dryer, deodorant, etc. Just all the stuff to make me look beautiful for you," and she smiled from ear to ear.

———◆———

They were on the elevator heading towards the sixth floor when Quinn received a "Code Red" text on his cell phone from Jax. "Code Red" meant something was going down in his hotel regarding the intruder and to be prepared. As soon as he read the text, he dropped his hold on the travel bags and pushed Annie into the corner of the elevator and stood in front of her. "Stay in the corner, behind me and don't move!" He demanded as the door to the elevator opened on the fifth floor and a very tall woman entered. Quinn sized this woman up.

As the woman entered the elevator, she pulled her hat down to hide most of her face. She was wearing a big yellow hat and sunglasses. Her hair didn't look natural—must be a wig and her legs looked like men's legs. She was wearing a dress and had a shoulder bag hanging on her right shoulder and her right hand was inside her purse. She pressed the door close button to the elevator and the elevator continued its descent to the first floor. "This doesn't look good!" thought Quinn.

Just as Quinn turned his head to his left to

make sure Annie was out of harms way, the woman pulled a syringe out of her purse and jabbed it into Quinn's neck. Quinn could feel himself going down, but he was able to put his strong hands on the attacker's wrist. He pushed the syringe out of his neck before all of the liquid substance was injected into him. He fell purposely into Annie as heavy as he could so that it would be more difficult for the attacker to get to her. Annie was screaming.

Annie reached underneath Quinn's jacket and quickly removed his gun from his holster. She pointed the gun at their attacker just as he was reaching towards her with the syringe still in his hand. He quickly reached into his purse and pulled out a wet rag.

"Back off, now or I'll shoot!" she yelled. She realized she still had the safety on. The attacker knew it, too, and continued his ascent on her. She quickly removed the safety and fired a shot. Her hands were shaking, but she managed to shoot him. He stilled.

"Drop everything, NOW!" she screamed at him! She was not shaking as bad and she aimed at his private parts. He dropped everything and raised his hands in the air. Just then, the door to the elevator opened up to the first floor and he quickly escaped. "HELP, HELP, SOMEONE PLEASE HELP!" she screamed.

Annie could hardly move with Quinn's body

partially laying on her. Jax arrived in seconds peering around the sides of the elevator with his gun in hand. "Annie, it's Jax. I'm here to help." He moved to where she could see him and he put his gun back into his side holster. Jax saw she had the gun in her hands. She was still aiming the gun. Very slowly he reached towards Annie from the side and placed both of his hands over Annie's, securing her hands and the gun.

"It's okay, Annie, I've got it now. You did well. Now, just let me have the gun. It's okay." She looked at Jax and released her fingers. Jax secured the gun and put the safety back on and stuffed it down the back of his jeans.

Joe had arrived along with Jason. They helped move Quinn's limp body so that Annie could be freed from underneath him. "Call 911. He injected something into Quinn's neck. He doesn't look like he is breathing! You gotta help him!" she cried and she grabbed his hand with one hand and rubbed his cheek with her other hand. "Stay with me, baby, please stay with me. I love you!"

Jason called 911 and requested an ambulance and then called Detective Evans. Jax leaned down to his old friend to check his pulse. "His breathing is very shallow. Hang on, buddy, hang on. We'll take care of you."

It felt like hours, but the ambulance arrived within five minutes. Two paramedics arrived on the scene. One immediately put an oxygen mask on Quinn while the other person started taking his vital signs. When the vital signs had been taken, they inserted an IV into his right arm. "My name is Tom. I'm a paramedic with Columbus Medi – Transport. Can you tell me his name and what happened?" Annie was still shaking.

Joe pulled the paramedic aside to answer their questions so Annie could stay with Quinn. "His name is Quinnten Taylor. A man dressed as a woman got onto the elevator and attacked him. He injected something into his neck."

"How did he inject it?" Tom asked.

"He used a syringe," answered Joe.

"What hospital do you want him to go to?"

"The closest one, please, and hurry!" Annie demanded. When they had received all the information they needed, Tom called the ER at Grant Medical Center.

"This is Columbus Medi-transport #2421, calling Grant Medical Center."

"Go ahead Columbus Medi-Transport #2421," said a voice over the portable radio.

"We have a 30-year-old, white male who was attacked in an elevator and was injected into the neck with an unknown substance by way of a syringe. His vital signs are as follows: Blood pressure is 70/50 and dropping, and his pulse rate is 65 and dropping. His respirations are shallow. Do you copy?"

There was a crowd of onlookers already in the

lobby trying to see what had happened. A distorted voice came over the airwaves. "Copy that. Do you have the syringe with the unknown substance?"

"Do you have the syringe with the unknown substance?" asked Tom.

"Yes," Joe answered as he handed it to him. "Tell the doctor it could be Ketamine. I'll explain at the hospital. You will need to let either Detective Evans or Chief Tim Hansen know what the contents of this syringe is asap," and Joe showed him his law enforcement badge and told the paramedic that Quinn was also with the police force.

"Grant Medical Center, this is Columbus Medi-Transport #2421. We have reason to believe the unknown substance could possibly be Ketamine. We have the syringe for further evaluation. Please advise the doctor on duty and tell the doc the victim is a detective."

The paramedics put Quinn onto a gurney and lifted him into the back of the ambulance. "Grant Medical Center, this is Columbus Medi-Transport #2421. Our ETA is six minutes."

"Copy that," replied the voice over the radio. They allowed Annie to ride with them.

"Jason, can you stay here and tell the police what happened. Give Detective Evans a copy of the video footage. Ask Detective Evans to do a thorough search of the hotel and follow his lead," demanded Jax. "Tell him we will be at Grant."

"Will do, sir," replied Jason.

The ambulance arrived at the hospital in five minutes with the lights and sirens blasting. Joe and Jax followed closely behind. The paramedics opened up the back door to the ambulance and hoisted the gurney onto the ground and ran inside with Quinn. Two nurses and two doctors ran to him.

"Take him into room four, yelled a nurse." One of the paramedics gave the syringe with the unknown substance to one of the doctors. The doctor handed the syringe to another nurse and yelled, "Take this to the lab. Tell the lab I want to know what it is stat! Tell them to check for Ketamine first. Tell them I need the answer yesterday, and, don't make me wait!"

Joe, Jax, and Annie followed them. Just as they started to enter the room, one nurse said, "I'm sorry ma'am. Are you family?"

"Yes ma'am. I'm his wife, Mrs. Annie Taylor and these two gentlemen are his brothers." She didn't want to tell the nurse they really weren't blood brothers. She knew Quinn loved them like they were his real siblings.

"Wait here, the Doctor will be out to see you shortly. He needs to do his preliminary work up on your husband, Mrs. Taylor," said the nurse in a stern tone.

Annie started pacing. She was really worried. "What is taking them so long?"

"Annie, it's only been five minutes," said Jax. "We need to give the doctors a little time to do what is best for Quinn. Why don't you come over here and sit down?" Jax grabbed Annie by the elbow and lead her to a chair in the hallway near his door.

"I'm sorry, Jax. I am a nervous wreck right now." Annie sat down. She crossed her right leg over her left leg and shook her right foot up and down. She crossed her arms. Then she changed the direction of her legs, putting the left leg over her right and shaking her left foot up and down. She couldn't stand the waiting. She needed to know how her husband was. She got up and started pacing the hall again. "What's taking so damn long?" she cried.

Joe's arms went around Annie to console her. "It's going to be all right Annie. Quinn has been in worse situations than this." He handed her a tissue. "You really do love him, don't you?"

"More than you know, Joe," she said with tears rolling down her cheeks. "I've never had anyone affect me like he has, from the first moment I laid eyes on him." She wiped the tears from her eyes. "I can't lose him, Joe."

"Try not to worry too much. I guarantee he is fighting like hell to come back to you," Joe said with concern.

"Thank you, Joe, but I can't help but worry."

Annie was very frustrated, and she started pacing again. A nurse finally came out of his room. "Excuse me, can we go in now?"

"In a few minutes, ma'am. The doctor will be out to talk with you shortly."

"You tell the doctor he has five minutes and then we are coming in. Five minutes!" and Annie held up one hand, spreading her fingers, indicating five minutes. The nurse started pointing her finger at Annie. "Don't be threatening anyone or I will call security."

Joe and Jax held out their law enforcement badges.

"That won't be necessary, ma'am. We are just worried about him. He's one of us; and, of course, he is her husband. They are newlyweds," informed Joe.

"Nurse?" said the kindly doctor. "I've got this. You may leave now," the nurse left giving Mrs. Taylor a sour look. "Mrs. Taylor, I'm Dr. Keith Michaels. Is your husband Reggie's son?"

"Yes, Dr. Michaels, he is."

"I thought I had recognized him, but it has been awhile. Mrs. Taylor, gentlemen, please come in."

Everyone walked into the room and surrounded the gurney Quinn was lying on.

"Mrs. Taylor, we need to move your husband to the Intensive Care Unit. Dr. Joseph Irwin and I are going on the assumption that your husband was given an overdose of Ketamine. He was very lucky he was able to pull it out of his neck when he did. Right now he is in a deep sleep and his body needs to let it wear off."

As soon as Annie walked into the emergency room cubicle, she saw Quinn lying on a gurney with his head propped up at a 45-degree angle. Attached on his left arm was a blood pressure cuff set to automatically take his blood pressure readings every 15 minutes. A pulse ox was on his left forefinger, and he still had the IV the paramedics had put into his right arm. He was wearing an oxygen mask and they had inserted a catheter. He looked so helpless.

She walked over to Quinn and took a hold of his hand. She kissed him gently and cradled his hand to her face. "Is he going to be all right?" asked Annie with tears in her eyes.

"Well," the doctor said softly, "anytime a person has been knocked out for any length of time, whether it is from a sedative or an anesthetic or whatever form, can be dangerous. My personal opinion is that he should be all right, but it is up to Quinn right now."

"Do you know how long he could be out?" asked Annie.

"It's anyone's guess. He could wake up in an hour or two, or it could be six hours or more. It is entirely up to Quinn's body. Quite frankly, we don't know what he was given or how much he was given. These next few hours are critical," said Dr. Michaels. "We will be taking him to ICU in just a few minutes. I am on my way to the lab now. I would like to find out what was in the syringe. While I am there, I will order some blood work."

"Dr. Michaels," said Joe. "We need to be very forthcoming about something. Quinn and Annie's lives are in danger. We think the man who did this to Quinn is the serial rapist plaguing Columbus."

"Why would he be after you and Quinn?" asked the doctor.

"Because all of the raped women look like me," and Annie took her hair down from her bun and shook her hair loose.

Dr. Michaels looked at Annie. "May God in Heaven, help us!" He walked around to check Quinn's vitals again. "Very well. I will assign one nurse, Dr. Irwin, myself and another nurse as his primary caregivers. We will work 12 hour shifts."

"Thank you. We will need to meet your other nurse. No one else comes in without our knowledge. Annie, Jax, and I will be in the room to offer protection at all times. Can you do the blood draws and any injections yourself?"

"Yes, I can," said the doctor.

"Good, we would much rather you do it. We can't trust anyone with this. The less people involved, the better."

"Of course," said Dr. Michaels. "Mrs. Taylor, would you like for me to contact Reggie?"

"No, sir, not yet. I'll agree that his parents do have the right to know about their son, but I would rather wait at least a little while. If they would return to the States right now, their lives could be at risk. I don't think Quinn would want that."

"I understand. I'm going to the lab," said Dr. Michaels. "Dr. Irwin will stay in here with you."

Jax brought a chair over to the gurney so that Annie could sit next to him. "Wake up, baby, please don't leave me, I love you," she said softly as she stroked his hand.

"Annie," Joe asked, "you got a good look of the guy in the elevator. Did you recognize him?"

"No, I didn't recognize him. He had on some sort of disguise, you know, like you would see in the movies? The kind you can peel off their face. And with the sunglasses and the wig, I didn't recognize him at all. He even had flesh colored gloves on."

"Did he say anything?"

"No, not a word! Who the hell is this guy, Joe?"

"Was there anything about him that would remind you of Morgan?"

"Joe, it happened so fast! I have no idea who he is!" she cried. "Oh, Quinn, wake up! Please wake up! Joe, he saved me! Quinn saved me!" and she continued crying.

"Annie, I think you saved him too," he said softly as he put his hand on her shoulder for comfort. "I just wish you had killed the son of a bitch when you shot him!"

"I was shaking so badly, I was just so scared Joe. When is this going to end?"

Just then two male nurses came in to transport Quinn to ICU. They followed. Quinn was given a corner room away from most of the other rooms. He was in room number 10. There were glass windows with blinds that had been closed and his door had a lock on it. Detective Evans arrived at the same time they had arrived in ICU.

"Dr. Irwin, do you suppose we could keep Quinn's identity quiet? I mean, if anyone should call in asking for his room number, could they just say no one was here under that name?"

"Certainly. I'll call admissions and tell them he has been discharged," said Dr. Irwin.

"Jason gave me the run down on what happened," stated Detective Evans. "He also gave us a copy of the video footage. I watched as Annie shot him and we found some blood. It is being analyzed as we speak."

"Yeah, I wish she had killed the son of a bitch!" Joe said emphatically.

"Yeah, she sure would have done Columbus a huge service if she had!" said Detective Evans. "I think crime in Franklin County is at an all time high!" He paused.

"How is she holding up?" asked Detective Evans.

"As well as can be expected, I guess," replied Joe. "Right now she's scared and when Quinn wakes and hears what she did, he is going to be very proud of her. I think she is a lot stronger than any of us realized."

"Annie," said Detective Evans. "I'm very sorry this has happened, but I need to ask you a few questions."

"Can't it wait until later today?" she asked.

"No, I wish it could, but I need to ask now while everything is fresh in your memory."

"Trust me, I'm never going to forget what happened today!" she said with such animosity.

He put his hand on her shoulder as he sat down in a chair next to her. "Can you start from the beginning?"

Annie patted Quinn's hand. "Today started out so nice," she began. "He was going to take me to see my parents today. We got on the elevator to leave at 10:30 a.m. We were almost to the sixth floor when he received a code red text from one of the guys. Quinn moved me into the corner of the elevator and stood directly in front of me and told me not to move."

"The elevator stopped on the fifth floor. A woman got on and I heard the doors shut. Quinn looked at me. That is when the woman injected something into Quinn's neck with a needle. Quinn didn't see it coming. I remember screaming. Quinn had grabbed the woman's arm and was able to pull her arm with the needle back away from his neck. Right after that, Quinn collapsed into me. Everything happened so fast. Quinn slumped to my left and when he did that, I was able to reach under his sport coat and I got his gun. I yelled at her to stop, but she started to come at me, so I shot her. I'm not sure, but I think the bullet may have gone straight through her. I aimed for her stomach, but I was shaking so badly, but I'm sure I shot her on her side. I yelled at her to drop everything. She did and that is when the elevator doors opened and she ran out."

"Which side did you shoot her on?"

"Her left side."

"Did she say anything to either of you?"

"No, she didn't; but, she looked stunned that I shot her."

"What did she look like?"

"She had on a big yellow floppy sun hat and big round black sunglasses, but her sunglasses fell off during her struggle with Quinn. She wore a yellow and green print dress with long sleeves and she had a big green cloth purse hanging off her shoulder. I remember she had big feet and had on white running shoes." She paused for a moment and then looked at Jax. "Oh My God, she was a man!"

"Why do you say that?"

"His legs! They were too muscular to be a female

and when he took off running, he didn't run like a girl! That was most definitely a man."

"What did his face look like?"

"You're going to find this weird, but it looked like rubber. You know, like in the movies when someone has put some kind of facial disguise on and you can peel it off. He looked weird! And he had on flesh colored rubber gloves."

"Now, I want you to think really hard. Was there anything about him that you recognized? Perhaps his eyes, the way his lips moved, or the way he stood? Anything?" Annie leaned back in her chair and closed her eyes. Her brow formed a "v". She was deep in thought.

"I don't know, but there was something about the eyes. It's almost like I have seen them before, but I can't place them. I don't know if it was the color of his eyes or the shape, or if it was that he looked so stunned that I shot him. I don't know. The facial mask was around his eyes and he had on fake eyelashes. There was something familiar, but I can't put my finger on it."

"Could it have been David Morgan?"

"I really don't know," shaking her head no, "I really don't know!"

"Did either of you see him in person?" Detective Evans asked of Joe and Jax.

"He was already gone by the time we got there."

Annie spoke as Detective Evans stood from his chair. "Detective Evans, Quinn saved me today.

Tell me what I can do to stop that bastard. I won't let him hurt my family anymore!"

"Annie, you really did good today." He paused. "I tell you what you can do. When Quinn wakes up and after he gets his strength back, let him take you to the shooting range. Let him teach you how to use a gun properly. Then, heaven forbid, if this should ever happen again, you aim to kill the bastard! In the mean time, you let us handle it, okay?" He patted her on her shoulder again.

"I'm going to check with all of the hospitals and urgent care centers for anyone coming in with a gun shot wound to the left side; but, if she did shoot him and it went plumb through, I'd say he will treat his own wound."

The door to Quinn's room opened. A man in a white lab coat walked in. "I'm Dr. Michaels," he said as he reached for Detective Evans hand.

"Very glad to meet you, sir. I'm Detective Evans."

"Then you are the man I need to talk with," Dr. Michaels said. "The liquid substance in the syringe is definitely ketamine. I don't know how much was in the syringe, nor do we know how much was injected into Mr. Taylor. The good news is, it was not poisonous, but it is an anesthetic. So, my guess is Mr. Taylor should be coming around in a couple of hours. He should be fine."

Dr. Michaels handed Detective Evans a plastic bag with the syringe in it. "I thought you might want this. It didn't have a plastic lid over the needle, so for safety reasons, I put one on it. Here is a written report of our findings."

"Thank you, Dr. Michaels. I'll get this to our lab." said Detective Evans as he left.

"Dr. Irwin, if you would like to take a break for a while, I'll stay." He picked up Quinn's chart and started looking at it.

"Thank you, Keith. I'll be back in a little while. Call me if there are any changes."

CHAPTER 20

I T WAS 3 P.M. AND Quinn had been asleep for four hours. Annie was still holding his hand with her thumb under his palm and her fingers lying on top of his fingers. All of a sudden, he made a fist grabbing her thumb.

"Did you see that? He grabbed my thumb!" said Annie. "Does that mean he is starting to wake up, Doctor?"

"Well, that is a good sign," and the doctor started checking his vital signs again.

"Quinn, baby, wake up. It's me, Annie." He didn't stir. "Doctor, I want to try something."

Annie immediately climbed onto the bed with Quinn, being careful not to touch any of the medical equipment attached to him. She leaned over and whispered into his ear.

"Quinn, it's Annie. I'm okay. I love you." She put her lips on his and gave him a kiss. His pulse rate went up a little on the monitor by his bed. "Try that again, Annie," said Dr. Michaels.

Annie leaned in and kissed Quinn again, but this time she started sucking on his lower lip.

Quinn's right arm moved and went around her left leg.

"Quinn, wake up, baby. I love you. You have been asleep too long." She kissed him again, sucking on his lower lip. "Come on, baby, open those beautiful eyes for me."

His eyes started to flutter, but he was having trouble getting them to open. Annie could tell he wasn't quite ready to open his eyes.

"It's okay, baby, I'm right here and I'm not leaving you. Jax and Joe are with me. You are safe and in the hospital. We aren't going anywhere." She kissed him again and then climbed off the bed.

"No," Quinn whispered. He wanted Annie to lay right beside him. She started holding his hand again. Her eyes started tearing up and she had a little smile on her face.

Jax leaned into Joe. "Now, that is what I want." Joe knew what he was referring to, but he wanted him to say it anyway.

"What?" Joe said with a half smile.

"I want a woman to love me like that," whispered Jax. Just then, Dr. Irwin reappeared.

"I never knew you wanted to fall in love," said Joe. "I always thought you just wanted to stay single."

"There is a lot you don't know about me. Maybe I just haven't met the right woman yet," he smirked.

"Well, I'll be damned," said Joe, and he smiled.

"Wait 'til Quinn hears about this," and he patted Jax on his shoulder.

Jax sat down in a chair near the door. He pulled his cell phone out and started checking his email. Joe excused himself to go out into the hallway. He wanted to telephone his wife.

Joe: "Hi, honey. How's my girl?"

Cindy: "Missing you."

Joe: "Yeah, I miss you, too."

Cindy: "How's thing going?"

Joe: "I'm at the hospital right now with Jax and Annie. Quinn was attacked in the hotel elevator. He's in ICU right now. His attacker put a needle to his neck and injected him with an anesthetic. He's out cold and has been for the last four hours."

Cindy: "Is he going to be all right?"

Joe: "I think so. He's trying to wake up."

Cindy: "How's Annie holding up?"

Joe: "Scared shitless." He paused.

Joe: "Cindy, I really miss you. Would you come home?"

Cindy: "Is it safe?"

Joe: "We have so much surveillance equipment and Seal brothers helping us, I'll keep you safe. I promise. I really need you, baby."

Cindy: "I'll get on the computer and see when I can fly out. I'll call you back in a few minutes. Love you."

Joe: "Love you too, baby."

Joe decided to take the elevator down to the

main lobby where the snack bar was located to get some coffee.

"May I help you, sir?"

"Yes, please. I would like three medium coffees with cream and a dozen chocolate chip cookies."

"That will be $12.00, sir," said the clerk behind the counter at the snack bar.

She handed him a small paper bag with a dozen chocolate chip cookies and placed the coffees into a cardboard cup holder.

"Thank you ma'am," Joe said as he picked the cardboard coffee holder up.

Cindy returned his call at 3:45 p.m. just as he was re-entering Quinn's room. Joe placed the coffee and cookies on a table.

Joe: "Hello, Cindy?"

Cindy: "I was able to get a flight out tonight."

Joe: "What time?"

Cindy: "My flight is at 8 p.m. I should be in Ohio no later than 1 a.m."

Joe: "Wonderful! I can't wait to see you! Call me when you get to the airport."

Cindy: "I'm going for now. I have to pack. I think I will leave for the airport at 6 or 6:30 p.m."

Joe: "Be careful, babe. Love you!"

Cindy: "Love you, too!"

Joe: "Bye."

Joe smiled as he put his cell phone away. He picked up a cup of coffee and offered it to Annie. "Thanks, Joe."

"Cindy is flying home tonight," he announced. " I can't wait to see her!"

"That's wonderful, Joe! I know how much you have missed her!"

He handed Jax a cup of coffee, too, and took a drink from the last cup. "I have some cookies." He offered Annie a cookie. "No, thanks. I'm really not hungry right now."

"I think you should eat one, Annie. I bet you haven't eaten all day," said Quinn in a soft voice, and sounding very groggy.

Annie quickly looked at him with a big smile! "Oh, Quinn, you're awake!" And she climbed back onto the bed and gave him a kiss.

"Easy now," said Quinn. "I don't want you to fall off the bed."

"How are you feeling?" asked Dr. Michaels.

"Well, my neck is sore."

"Do you remember what happened?"

"Yeah, some fucking lunatic put a needle into my neck. What did he give me?"

"You got a dose of Ketamine. We don't know how much he gave you, but you have been out for a while," said Dr. Irwin.

"How long have I been out?"

"Roughly five long, agonizing hours," said Annie.

"Annie, can you climb back down off the bed so that we can check him out again?" asked Dr. Irwin.

Dr. Michaels and Dr. Irwin did various checks. They checked his blood pressure again, looked into his eyes, checked all of his reflexes, listened to his heart, and asked him various questions. Then they took blood and emptied his catheter. "I'll take his blood samples to the lab," said Dr. Michaels. "Good to have you back, Mr. Taylor."

"Thank you," replied Quinn.

Quinn reached for Annie's hand. "Are you okay?"

"I am now," she declared.

"Were you able to catch him, Joe?" asked Quinn.

"No, he got away just seconds before we got to the elevator; but, you won't believe this. Annie shot him!" Quinn looked at Annie with a surprised look in his eyes. "You shot him?" He said as he looked at his wife.

"Yes," and she smiled.

"Did you kill him?"

"Unfortunately, no. I was shaking too much," she explained.

"She just grazed him on his side," said Jax. "You should be very proud of her."

"I am. That's twice you have saved me," Quinn said as he winked at her.

"So when can I go home?" he asked.

"We want you to stay here for tonight and if everything looks as good in the morning as it does right now, then you can go home," said Dr. Irwin.

"Oh, I feel really stiff. Can I get up and sit in a chair?" asked Quinn.

"I would prefer you stay in bed at this time. You might be a little weak from the anesthetic and from the fall," explained Dr. Irwin. "Are you hungry?"

"Yes, I am hungry, but not for hospital food. Would you care if I had some food delivered from the hotel for all of us?" asked Quinn.

"I think that would be all right," said Dr. Irwin.

"We can call Eula. She can bring us whatever she has from the hotel. Honey, where is my phone?" stated Quinn.

"No, I don't think that is a very good idea," said Joe. "We don't want anyone to know you are here. I'll just go down the street and get us all something to eat. We can save the cookies for later. Everyone good with Chinese take out?"

"Just get us a large wonton soup and a dinner portion of pork-fried rice. Quinn and I can share. I don't want him to have anything real heavy or too spicy right now," said Annie. "And two large iced teas."

Joe wrote down what everyone wanted, including the doctors and the two policemen guarding his door, and Quinn's security detail on duty at the hospital. He called the "Chinese House" and placed the order. When he left to pick up their orders, he took Jason with him to help carry them.

While they were gone, Dr. Irwin and Dr.

Michaels checked Quinn's vital signs. The nurse in charge of Quinn's care removed his catheter.

"We should get you up to walk in a little while, but we can wait until after you have eaten," said Dr. Michaels.

They arrived back at the hospital within 20 minutes. The food smelled heavenly as they walked into Quinn's room. Annie had raised the head of the bed to allow Quinn to eat without difficulty. She had also released the side bed rail down so that she could sit on the edge of the bed and she placed the bedside tray table next to her. She wanted to feed Quinn. She knew he was able to feed himself, but she liked feeding him. After all, she thought, "he is in the hospital and I just want to take care of him."

Joe started emptying out the sacks of food and brought Quinn and Annie's food to them first. Then he grabbed his food and sat in a chair. Everyone else can help themselves to their own food, he thought.

Annie started feeding Quinn some pork-fried rice. Then she fed him some wonton soup. Some of the broth spilled onto his chin. Quinn laughed.

"What are you laughing at, Mr. Taylor?" asks Annie.

"Oh nothing."

She fed him some more soup and again, broth spilled onto his chin. Quinn's lips curved into a big smile.

249

"Stop it," said Annie, "or you will be feeding yourself!"

She wiped his chin off with a napkin.

"In that case, I'll just go back to sleep and dream of French toast and syrup," he whispered. He leaned his head back against the pillow and closed his eyes with a smile.

"Hmm, a quiet husband." She took her finger, dipped it into the broth and rubbed it gently on his lips. He bit her finger with his teeth and let out a very low growl. He grabbed her hand. "If you don't feed me, I'll just have to eat your fingers," he said softly with a sexy grin.

Just then he raised his knee up. He was getting an erection and he didn't want anyone to see this happening. The thin sheet lying on top of him would not hide him. "Annie," he whispered, "I need a blanket."

"Why do you need a blanket?" She asked just a little too loudly. "Are you cold?"

Jax knew what had happened. He watched as Annie had rubbed Quinn's lips with the soup on her finger; and he watched as Quinn bit her finger. He saw Quinn move his knee up under the sheet, which only meant one thing.

Jax got up from his chair and looked in the small closet in his room. He found two folded blankets. He didn't want his friend embarrassed. "Here, Quinn," he said as he tossed the blankets to him. "This should warm you up quite well." He said with a wink and laughed out loud as he walked back to his chair. Quinn laid both blankets over his groin area and lowered his knee.

Annie caught on, but she didn't say anything. She smiled at her husband. "Open your mouth," she said with a giggle. "I think you need to eat your food and behave!"

"Give me that food. I'll feed myself," he growled. He removed the pulse ox from his finger and grabbed the pork-fried rice container and the fork from Annie's hand. He wasn't upset with her and he wasn't upset with Jax. He was upset with himself for acting like he was in high school.

Annie let him eat in peace. Too much had happened today and now wasn't the time to start anything. She handed him his iced tea. Once he had something cold to drink, she handed him some wonton soup to eat.

When everyone had finished eating, Dr. Irwin asked Quinn's charge nurse for a large garbage bag. Everyone helped in the clean up by throwing away all the food containers into the bag. After receiving directions to the hospital dumpster, Jason left to take the garbage out.

Just as Jason was leaving with the garbage, Dr. Michaels walked in. "Mr. Turner, remember when you asked Dr. Irwin if we could keep Quinn's identity a secret?"

"Yes," said Joe. "Is there a problem with that?"

"No, not really. I thought I would let you know

that a male called in just a little while ago to see if Quinn had been admitted. The receptionist told that person we did not have anyone by that name," informed the doctor.

"Quinn, you should probably call your dad on the outside chance someone from the hotel calls them. You really don't want them to come over here right now," suggested Annie.

"I think you are right. Can you give me my cell phone?"

Annie went fishing in her purse for Quinn's cell phone. "Looks like you have several missed calls."

Quinn looked at the phone numbers and listened to his messages. There were none from his dad. He decided he would call him anyway, on the outside chance that he may have heard of the elevator attack.

"Dad, how are you?"

"I'm good, son, how are you?"

"Are you in earshot of mom?"

"No, she isn't here at the moment. What's up?"

"Well, don't panic. I'm okay, but when Annie and I were riding down the elevator at the hotel this morning, we were attacked. Someone jabbed me in the neck with a syringe full of Ketamine. Annie shot him with my gun, but he got away."

"And you are sure you are okay, son?"

"Yes, I've slept for about five hours and Dr. Irwin told me I could go home in the morning if everything still looks as good as it does now."

He paused. "Dad, I need for you to do me a favor. I don't want anyone to know I am in the hospital. I don't want any information given out about what happened either. I just hope the press hasn't gotten ahold of this. And I really don't want mom to know because she will panic and then start running Annie down. I don't want that. If you have to tell her, make sure you tell her Annie shot him and that she saved me."

"What have you done regarding security for the hotel? You know you need to keep your guests safe."

"I have three men every eight hours watching the surveillance cameras and doing hall checks. I think I will add more security to ride the elevators now, too."

"That sounds like a good idea. Would you like for me to come and offer any assistance?"

"No Dad, please stay away until this maniac is caught. I don't want to have to worry about you and mom. You need to stay safe. Go anywhere you want, just don't come to Columbus. If I need you, I will call you. Okay?"

"If that is what you want. Just stay safe. I love you, son."

"Bye, Dad, love you, too."

"Quinn, how would you like to take a walk now? I know there isn't much room in here, but walk to and from the bathroom a couple of times and I want you to sit up in the recliner a bit, too," said Dr. Irwin.

Quinn threw his covers back and sat on the edge of the bed putting his feet on the floor. "Careful," said Dr. Irwin. "Stand up first to get your balance."

Quinn stood up. "Are you feeling dizzy?" asked the doctor as he held on to Quinn's arm.

"No, sir, I'm not." Quinn walked a few feet, stopped and smiled. "I can do this," and he started off walking normally to the bathroom. He walked around his room a few times and sat in the hospital recliner. "It feels good to get out of that bed."

"Quinn," said Joe, "Cindy is flying home tonight and I'm going to pick her up at the airport at 1 a.m. If you like, Annie can go home with us tonight so that she can rest."

"Thank you, Joe, but no. I wouldn't dream of going home with you tonight. You haven't seen Cindy in a very long time."

Jax grinned in a teasing fashion as he looked at Quinn. "I can take her to the Royal and get adjoining rooms to protect her if you like."

Quinn pointed his finger at Jax and started to speak, but Annie spoke out instead.

"Thank you guys, but I'm staying right here tonight." She sat down on Quinn's lap. "I made a promise to my husband, that we would not spend one night a part and I mean to keep my promise." She kissed him gently on the lips.

"Do we have security outside this door?" asked Quinn.

"Yes," Joe said. "Detective Evans has two cops outside the door. They will be changing shifts at midnight. Jason has offered to stay until Champ gets here after La Seals closes."

"Dr. Irwin, Dr. Michaels, with security outside my door tonight, why don't both of you go home and get some rest. I'm sure I will be okay. Just leave instructions for no one to enter my room tonight. If I should need a nurse, I can use the call button," suggested Quinn.

"If you are sure," said Dr. Irwin. "I would like to leave. I'm scheduled to be in surgery in the morning at 7 a.m."

"I'll stay at the hospital tonight. If anything should happen, they can page me. All of your vitals are great. We are very glad you came out of this okay. I'll do as you suggest and give instructions that no one is to enter this room," said Dr. Michaels.

"Thank you both," said Quinn and he reached out to shake their hands.

"Yes, thank you so much for saving my husband." Annie gave both doctors a hug before they left the room.

"Annie, what did you do with my gun?" asked Quinn.

Jax interrupted. "I took the gun away from Annie at the hotel and I put the safety back on. When the nurses took your clothes off, they gave

Annie your holster and all of your other personal belongings. I put it back into the holster and Annie slipped it into her purse."

"Well, since I have protection in this room, why don't you and Joe leave for tonight." said Quinn. "Get some rest, Joe, take the day off tomorrow so that you can spend some time with Cindy. Jax, I'll need you here in the morning. I want to leave this place asap. We will need to beef up security a little more. Can you be here at 0800 hours?"

"Sure thing, boss. I think I will stay at the hotel tonight. I want to check in with the rest of the team working tonight to make sure the perimeter is safe."

"Thank you, Jax. Stay in the penthouse if you like, or get a room, but make sure you rest."

On their way out, Joe and Jax gave Jason and the two police officers guarding his room, instructions that no one was to enter his room for any circumstances unless Annie or Quinn gave the okay.

Annie walked over and made sure the door to his room was locked. "Annie, why don't you sleep in the bed, I can rest in the chair."

"Oh no you're not. You are the patient and I am sure there is some kind of rule that states patients sleep in their beds. Go on, get into bed!"

"Boy, you are a bossy little thing, aren't you? I've never had a woman boss me before."

"Oh, you've probably just forgotten. I'm sure your ex bossed you plenty."

He stubbornly sat in his chair. "Please, Quinn, get into bed. You really scared me today. I thought I had lost you," Annie said as tears filled her eyes.

He reached for her hand and she helped him out of his chair. He pulled her close to him. "I love you so much, Annie. I'm sorry that I scared you," and he kissed her on top of her head. "Come on, maybe we can both sleep in this bed."

"Quinn honey, don't be sorry. It wasn't anything you could help. Now get into bed and don't get any ideas."

"And what do you mean by that?" he said with a half curled smile.

"I mean, I know what you are thinking, and I'm not having sex in a hospital bed! You can wait until we get home tomorrow!"

CHAPTER 21

QUINN WAS DISCHARGED BY 9 a.m. the following day. Jax did a thorough sweep of the penthouse and found nothing out of the ordinary. Quinn had contacted Detective Evans to come to the penthouse for a meeting. He wanted to know why David Morgan hadn't been arrested. Evans said he would be at his hotel no later than 11 a.m.

When they got home, Annie went straight to their bedroom. The clothes she was wearing were badly wrinkled and she wanted to change. But first, she took a quick shower. She put on a pair of shorts, a sleeveless top, and slipped on some sandals. She opted to not dry her hair. Instead, she pulled her hair into a high ponytail. When she was finished, she put on a pot of coffee.

Quinn had just put on his swimming trunks for his morning swim. Before he went out onto the rooftop, he received a call from his contractor in Atlanta regarding his new La Seals club being built. Quinn did not look happy, which meant there must be a problem. She didn't want to disturb him, so she picked up her cell phone, checked for any messages, and called her mother. When she was finished, she telephoned security to make sure it was all right to go out onto the rooftop. When she got the okay, she poured herself a cup of coffee, added cream, and headed outdoors.

She started to sit down to relax in the sun, but something caught her eye. It looked like an outdoor extension cord that she had not noticed before. She sat her coffee down, followed the cord with her eyes, and walked towards the pool. She noticed the cord was plugged into an electrical outlet with the other end hanging in the pool. Just then, Quinn came outside. He was going to do his usual 50 laps that he did most mornings. He started to jog towards the pool for a running dive.

Annie screamed, "NO!" She immediately started running towards him and crashed into his side with all her might, causing them both to fall onto the concrete floor.

"What the hell! Annie, why did you do that!" he said in a raised voice as he looked at his wife to see if she was all right.

"Look!" and she pointed to the pool. "Someone has the water electrified. You would have been killed if you had jumped into the water!"

Quinn was stunned when he saw the extension cord hanging in the water and plugged into an outlet several yards away.

"Shit!" Quinn picked Annie up off the ground.

"Are you okay?" He immediately started looking at her head, arms, and legs. He noticed a scrape to her knee, which was bleeding. "Do you feel all right? You haven't broken anything have you?"

"I'm fine, Quinn, it's just a scratch." Annie could see he was a little shaken. "Are you all right?"

"Let's go back inside. You need to get your knee cleaned and bandaged." He picked her up and carried her into the kitchen, and sat her down on the kitchen island. He was quiet, but he was livid.

Just as Quinn sat Annie down to clean her wound, Jax and Champ came rushing into the penthouse. "We saw Annie push you down and saw her pointing to something. What's going on?"

Quinn turned to face Jax and Champ. "Looks like someone wanted me dead. Someone put an extension cord into the pool. If it hadn't been for Annie, I would have been electrocuted when I jumped in." He paused, scratching his head, "When did this happen?"

"I'll look at the footage we have, but I suspect someone hacked into my system and looped the footage long enough to zap the water."

"Champ, let's go to the boiler room. I want to take a look at the circuit breakers."

"You know, now that I think about it, Quinn, the boiler room is the one place we didn't put surveillance cameras. I didn't even think about putting one down there," said Jax. "I'll be back in a minute." Champ and Jax left for the boiler room.

Quinn turned to the cabinet and pulled out his first aid kit. He took a clean rag and gently washed off her knee, patted it dry, and poured some hydrogen peroxide over the wound to clean it more thoroughly. After he had patted it dry again, he put some antibiotic ointment on the wound, then covered it with a large bandage. He put the first-aid kit back into the cabinet and walked back over to her.

Annie didn't like him taking care of her like this. It made her feel like a child, but she wasn't going to say anything to him about it... maybe later. "Pick and choose your battles," she told herself.

He moved her legs farther apart and leaned up against her, putting his forehead to hers. He could feel her trembling. She wrapped her arms around his neck. "Oh, my God, Quinn. You could have been killed!" She started to cry.

"It's all right, baby, I'm still here. I love you! It's okay." He hugged her tightly, rubbing her back.

He had a frown on his face. He had many thoughts going through his mind. Did Jax stay in the apartment last night? Did he hear anything on the rooftop? How could someone hack into my security system? Jax was a genius at this stuff. How could he not catch on to it? Quinn's cell phone received a text message. "It's from Champ."

"Perp in BR. Shots fired. Take cover!"

Quinn ran to the sliding glass doors leading to the rooftop and locked them. Then he slipped a metal bar down into the door track for extra security and pulled the curtains. He lifted Annie down from the kitchen island and they ran to their bedroom. "Is my gun still in your purse?"

"Yes, it is," and she grabbed her purse from the closet. Annie reached into her purse and pulled out the holster with the gun.

"Do you remember how to use it?" he asked as he turned the lock on his safe to get another gun and some ammunition.

"Yes, I think so."

"Stay behind me. Keep the safety on. Only use it if you have to. I don't want you getting nervous and shooting me in the back by mistake, baby." He turned off all the lights. The rooms were fairly dark with the room darkening curtains pulled. Very little daylight could be seen in the room.

"Well, thanks for all of your faith in me. Maybe I won't save your ass next time!" she smirked. Her hands were shaking. He bent down and kissed her. "Be quiet, baby. I need to listen."

It was killing Quinn not knowing what was going on,, but he knew he needed to protect his wife and himself. He wanted to call Jax, but that might put their lives in danger. They waited approximately 30 minutes before he received a call from Jax.

"Talk to me," demanded Quinn.

"Perpetrator got away. We found his point of entry. He came in through the sewer hole in the floor of the boiler room. We should probably weld it shut. Also, we found some clips attached to the rooftop circuit breakers and some electrical tape.

"Detective Evans is with us. He heard the gunshots just as he arrived. He has called for some officers to come in and dust for prints. I've shut the breakers off to the rooftop. We'll be up in a few."

"We should be okay now," Quinn said as he put his cell phone back in his pocket. He took the gun away from Annie and placed it on top of the shelf in his closet of their bedroom.

"I really want to take you to a shooting range. Maybe we can go this afternoon. I would feel better if you would learn how to use a gun properly."

"Quinn, sometimes I wish we had never met."

"Why do you say that? Don't you love me anymore?" his voice sounding worried.

"Quinn, I fell very hard for you, and very quickly. It is because I love you so much that I say this. If you had never met me, then you would not be in any danger. I don't ever want to lose you, but I feel like I need to do something!"

"Like what, Annie? What on earth do you think you could possibly do?" He put his arms around her and caressed her tightly.

"I don't know Quinn, but I need to do something!"

"Look at me, Annie," and he tilted her chin upwards so that she could look him in the eyes.

"Look at me and you listen to what I have to say." He gently put both of his hands on her cheeks. "I am never, and I mean never, going to let you go. I will never give you up. You will never belong to anyone but me. I would gladly give my life to save you. I love you!" and he pulled her into his body again in a tight hug. "Promise me you will never leave me."

Annie's voice cracked, "Oh Quinn, I don't ever want to leave you!"

"Quinn?" yelled Jax as he and the detective walked into the penthouse. Jax immediately unlocked the door to the rooftop, removed the extra bar, and walked to where the extension cord was plugged in. He telephoned Champ.

"Are you sure the breaker is off?" He paused. "Here goes." Jax safely unplugs the extension cord and pulled it out of the water. He shook his head. "Man, this could have been a totally different scenario if Annie hadn't seen this. We have got to catch this bastard soon!"

"I agree," said Quinn. "Thanks for coming, Jon. Annie, would you fix us some coffee, please. I think we all need to sit down and talk about what we should do."

"Certainly." Quinn leaned down and kissed her gently on the forehead before she walked back into the penthouse.

"Wow, that was a close call, old friend," said Jax.

"Yeah, too close for comfort. What the hell happened, Jax? How did you miss something like this? You are a damn genius with this stuff!"

"I'm sorry QT, but anyone who is well versed in surveillance technology can purchase radio frequency detection equipment. We use to be able to detect it when someone was hacking into your system by a small glitch in the picture. Now, it's next to impossible to detect, but I'll see what I can do." He paused. "Quinn, Annie looks very scared. What are you going to do now?"

"Yeah, I'm worried about her. I think she is just about at the end of her rope, if you know what I mean. I'd take her on a trip somewhere if she would let me, but I know she won't go."

"Do you think she would go now since this happened?" asked Jon.

"I doubt it. She has that look of a lioness trying to protect her cub. Mix that with fear and I think it is a deadly combination. She is really pissed."

They walked over to the seating area. Annie came out carrying a tray of cups, creamer, sugar, and a carafe of coffee. She poured four cups of coffee and instructed them to fix their own the way they liked it. "I have another pot brewing."

Joe walked out onto the rooftop.

"Quinn, are you all right?" asked Joe as he shook his hand. "Champ called and told me what happened. I thought you might need me."

"Thanks, Joe. My girl saved me, yet again. Can you believe that?" Quinn said as he smiled at Annie. "But, you should have stayed with Cindy."

"Do you honestly think I am going to let him out of my sight?" declared Cindy as she walked up to Quinn and gave him a hug. "I'm glad you are still with us."

"Thanks, Cindy."

She walked over to hug Annie.

"Welcome back, Cindy. Did you have a nice visit with your sister?"

"Yes, I did, thank you. Are you okay?" Cindy asked as they walked back inside to get more coffee.

Annie paused and took a deep breath. "Oh, Cindy. I don't know what to do!"

Cindy put her arms around Annie. "It'll be okay, Annie. Just remember, they all have your back; and, they are really good at what they do."

Annie pulled away from Cindy. "Don't you understand? We have had two very close calls in a matter of two days. Whoever this is won't stop until he has either captured me or killed Quinn or both of us. I need to do something, but I feel totally helpless. I just don't know what to do, damn it! I'd give myself up to these guys if I thought it would save Quinn, but I don't even know who they are!"

"Annie, please don't say that! Don't even think that!" scolded Cindy. "Sit down a minute. I want to tell you something."

Annie walked to the small table in the kitchen area and took a seat.

"Annie, I wasn't around when Quinn's ex dumped him, but I heard about it from Joe. Quinn was totally devastated. From what Joe has told me, Quinn has much deeper feelings for you than he ever had for Kayla. If something were to happen to you, Annie, well, let's just say Joe is really worried about him. So please, don't think about doing something really stupid. Quinn really loves you. Okay?"

Annie had tears in her eyes. "I can't let anything happen to Quinn," she whispered. "He's my life!"

The sliding doors to the rooftop opened. "Honey, is the coffee ready yet?"

Annie jumped up from her chair and wiped her eyes. "Yeah, just give me a minute."

Quinn gave Cindy a questioning look. "Honey, are you okay?"

"I'm fine," she stated as she handed him the carafe. She turned to walk towards their bedroom. Quinn looked very confused.

"What just happened, Cindy?"

"She's worried about you. She said she would let herself be kidnapped if she thought it would save you."

"Ah, shit! Here, take the coffee out. Tell them I'll be out in a few minutes," and he walked towards their bedroom. He opened the door slowly. "Annie?"

"What!"

Well, hell. She was really pissed. How do I get her to calm down? She may be small, but with the rage she is feeling right now, I bet she could kill those two fuckers with her bare hands. She had the right to feel angry.

"Annie, we need you outside. We want to devise a plan and we want your input." He held out his hand to her.

"I'm sorry, Quinn. I shouldn't have snapped at you," and she took his hand.

He pulled her close to him. "There's nothing to feel sorry for, baby. I love you." He kissed her on the top of her head. "Come, we need to get outside."

Annie poured herself and Quinn a cup of coffee and sat down in a chair next to him.

"Quinn," asked Detective Evans, "Do you have any enemies or have you pissed anyone off bad enough where someone would want to kill you or your wife?"

"Jon, I have pissed someone off on a daily basis for years. I didn't get where I am today by being Mr. Nice Guy; however, I don't recall anyone being that pissed at me."

"Okay, I have to ask this. I know you haven't been married long, but I have to look at all the angles so that I can rule things out."

"I know where this is headed, so don't even go there, Jon." He took Annie's hand. He knew this would probably piss her off like it did when they visited his parents.

"We have been married about six weeks and she still doesn't know my net worth. She offered to sign a pre-nup and I refused to allow her to do that. She knows where my checkbook is and she has a credit card with no limit on it. I've told her she can spend all of the money she wants. She can have it all if she wants it, so why would she want to kill me?"

Annie turned pale as a ghost. She remembered how her mother-in-law accused her of being a gold digger. This wasn't setting well with her at all.

"Why would I save Quinn twice if I wanted him dead!" and she gave everyone a scowl. "It would appear to me that you don't know exactly where to look, do you?"

"I'm not the criminal here. You have two rapists out there somewhere and they are after me! ME!" she screamed. "And now they are after Quinn."

She sat her coffee down on the table near her and pointed her finger at Detective Evans.

"I want to say something. I have watched and listened to you and your Chief over the past couple of weeks and you two are stumped. These two men have out-smarted you 100 to one. Why haven't you brought in David Morgan for questioning? He would have been the first person I would have brought in after we showed you what we had."

"And furthermore, I don't know a lot about David, but this much I do know. He was a music student and while he could play music, he wasn't that good. I think he was just there because he did not want to go to a traditional college to learn a trade. I would even bet he didn't want to go to college at all, but dear ole daddy probably told him he had to go somewhere."

"I can't see him being smart enough to be an electrician. Any idiot can plug a cord into a socket and throw the other end into a pool. You and I know it would throw a breaker, but do you know what to do to a circuit breaker to get it activated with the clips and such? I'd be scared to death to even try for fear of electrocution! I could be wrong, but I doubt if he is that smart. He might know his way around computers, but I think that is a little different than working with electrical current and stuff."

"Now as far as the Ketamine, he could have gotten a hold of that because his dad owns Morgan House Pharmaceuticals."

"We didn't know his dad owned Morgan House Pharmaceuticals," said Detective Evans.

Annie was on a roll now. "And what about the helicopter that was on top of our helipad? Did you ever follow up on that? What about the disguise the man wore in the elevator yesterday? Did you think to go around and check costume places to see if anyone had sold anything like what he had on?"

"You know, I resent what you are implying, Mrs. Taylor. We are doing the best be can right now." said Detective Evans.

"Are you? Are you really? Did you tell that to the rape victims? Did you tell that to the parents of the girl that died? How would you like it if it were your daughter? How would you like it if a police officer came to your house and said, "I'm sorry, we are doing the best we can? Well, that's not fucking good enough!"

"From the way I see it, you can go home to a safe house at night to your loved ones. You can sit and eat a nice meal with your families without worrying about someone coming through your door to kill or kidnap you. You can take your wife or your girlfriend to bed at night and make beautiful love to her and not worry if she will be alive tomorrow or if both of you will be alive the next day! Your wife or a family member can walk out of the damn door and you don't have to worry about them being kidnapped, raped and tortured!

When you go home at night, you can rest assured your friends lives are not in danger. Our friends should be with their families. So are you really doing the very best you can do? REALLY?"

Annie threw her hands in the air. "I HATE THIS!" she yelled. "AM I GETTING MY POINT ACROSS TO YOU! I WANT THESE

271

BASTARDS CAUGHT, NOW. I AM DAMN SICK AND TIRED OF THIS! DO I MAKE MYSELF CLEAR?"

Everyone sat there in silence looking at Annie, but she wasn't done.

"You should be out there trying to find the rapists of those poor seven young ladies and now one of them has died! But, instead, you are more worried about accusing me of being a fucking gold digger and me wanting to murder my husband so that I can get all of his money! You need to get your priorities straight with this case! In fact, if you don't get your shit together and start investigating better than you have been, then I'm going to do it for you!"

Everyone sat there very quietly. They didn't know what to think about Annie's outburst.

"Well," Quinn said as he stood from his chair. He didn't quite know what to say, but he figured Jon would rather take his leave about now. "I think that about says it all. Thank you for coming," and he shook Jon's hand. They walked back inside his penthouse and Quinn showed him to the door.

Everyone was quiet when Quinn reappeared on the rooftop. He sat down next to Annie, taking her hand.

"Well, do you feel better getting that off your chest now?"

She looked at Quinn with a scowl on her face. "And I suppose you think I was too hard on him!"

"Now, wait a minute, baby. On the contrary, I'm quite proud of you! This has gone on far too long. I think he had it coming. I might have been a little more diplomatic about it, but I would have said the same thing."

Man, I hope I never piss her off that bad, he thought. She has a temper!

"I think Champ and I will get back to work," said Jax.

"Come, Joe," as Cindy took his hand, "I think we should leave for now. We can come back later." Joe stood and so did everyone else.

"Annie, well done!" He wrapped his arms around her in a friendly hug. "You have a lot more spunk than I thought."

Annie smiled.

"Please, wait a minute. I have an idea I want to discuss with you," said Annie. "Quinn, is there somewhere we can go for lunch that doesn't have any surveillance equipment around them? I don't want anyone to hear us."

"All right, you have me intrigued. Where would you like to go?"

"I really don't care. Let's just get in the car and drive. We'll find a place."

"I should probably change my clothes. I don't think I should be seen going into a restaurant wearing my swimming trunks," laughed Quinn.

While Quinn was changing his clothes, Annie locked the sliding glass door to the rooftop.

"I'm sorry, everyone, for losing my temper. I should have acted more like a lady."

"Don't worry about it, Annie," said Jax. "You can lose your temper on us anytime you want. Besides, he had it coming."

"Yes, he did," said Quinn as he entered the room. "Are we ready?"

"Are we sure the Hummer isn't bugged?" asked Annie.

"I don't know, let me check before we get in."

Jax pulled his detector from his pocket and activated it with a few numbers. He opened the vehicle door and checked inside. He walked around the Hummer, checked under the vehicle and in the engine.

"We're clear," he said as he opened the front passenger door for Annie to climb in.

When they were on I-270, Quinn asked where she wanted to go for lunch.

"Can we go to Waverly? There is a nice pizza place there, off the road, and away from places that could have cameras."

"You want to go that far away?" asked Quinn.

"Please?" she begged.

He smiled at her. "I'll take you anywhere you want, baby."

She shook her head.

"What?" he asked.

"You have got to quit calling me baby in front of your friends!" she laughed. "It makes me feel... juvenile."

"Hmm," he said with a frown on his face, "I bet you didn't like me bandaging your knee either."

"Well, now that you brought it up," she giggled, "I felt like my father was taking care of me."

"Your father?" he yelled. "Oh, you wound my heart!" and he put his fist to his chest.

"Annie, I have never seen another woman who can keep up with Quinn's wit. You are wonderful!" said Joe.

CHAPTER 22

IT TOOK THEM ABOUT AN hour and twenty minutes to arrive in Waverly. They were able to find a quiet table away from the other customers.

"Are their pizza's good?" asked Champ.

"Everything tastes good, but I recommend their steak sandwiches and onion rings."

"I don't think I have ever had a steak sandwich before," said Joe. "I think I'll try it."

When the waitress came, they all agreed on steak sandwiches, onion rings, pizza and iced tea.

"Will this be on one check?"

"Yes, ma'am," replied Quinn.

"You should let me pay for it, Quinn, after all, it was my idea to go somewhere for lunch. I have the money to pay for this."

"Don't you think the point is moot? It's our money now, remember, we're married?" and he wiggled his wedding ring finger at her.

She rolled her eyes at him and giggled. "I've told you before, you are going to have to work on this."

He put one arm around her shoulder, and pulled

her in for a kiss. "What if I don't want to?" and he patted her nose with his finger.

She shook her head again. "What am I going to do with you?"

"I can think of a few things," he said with a curled lip.

"So, Annie, what is your idea you wanted to talk about?" inquired Joe.

She looked around the table to make sure no other people were within hearing distance.

"Now, what I am about to suggest, I don't want leaving this table. It must be strictly between us. Can I have your word?"

Everyone nodded in agreement.

"I want to hire a private detective, and I don't want one who works or lives in Columbus. I want the best detective money can hire from out of state. Maybe New York, California, anywhere, I don't care where he comes from as long as he is the best."

"What is your reasoning for hiring a PI?" asked Quinn.

"I'm getting bad vibes from the Police Department. It's been about twenty-one months since the first girl was raped. Wouldn't you think the police would have found something by now? It's like they are dragging their feet on this."

"I agree," said Jax. "What are your suspicions?"

"I can't put my finger on anything in particular, but something doesn't add up to me."

"In what way?" inquired Quinn.

"Well, I have had a stalker following me for the last six years. Then in the last 21 months, seven women were raped and one of them killed. We learned all of them look like me. Do these rapes have anything to do with my stalker?"

"Then I marry and all of a sudden, someone is trying to kill my husband. How does this tie in?

Are the rapists and the stalker two different crimes altogether?

Is the person or persons pissed at Quinn because we married and they are trying to get rid of him to get to me?

Is there a third crime going on here? Does someone want to kill Quinn for a different reason altogether?"

"Then it dawned on me this morning when I was so eloquently ripping Detective Evans ass. Who knew we were going to visit my parents yesterday? Who knew Quinn was being discharged from the hospital at a certain time that morning? Who else knew that Quinn liked to swim laps in the morning? Either this person is someone he doesn't know and has investigated him thoroughly; or it is someone he knows, that knows his routine."

"Do you have anyone in mind that you want the PI to investigate?" asked Cindy.

"Yes, I have a huge list of people in mind."

"I think you should put me on that list, Annie," stated Quinn.

"Don't start, Quinn. I don't think you or anyone else sitting at this table should be investigated."

"But, you would know for sure that I am not the stalker or rapist."

"Quinn, stop. I told you I know you aren't," Annie said as she took his hand.

He smiled at her. "Do you have an investigator in mind?"

"No. I thought maybe your Father might know someone."

"So, what do you all think about her idea?" asked Quinn.

"I think it is an excellent idea," replied Joe.

"I think you should be the one to call my Father. After all, it is your idea. Better yet, why don't we fly to England and you can ask him in person? Besides, I think it would give us a break from all of this."

"That means I would have to be around your mother," she said with distaste in her mouth.

"Please? You know you are going to have to see her at some point in time. May as well be now."

"I don't want to, but I do think we should leave. Can we leave this evening?"

"Wow, I never thought I would hear that from you. Of course, we can leave this evening." Quinn pulled his cell phone out and called Rocko.

"Rocko, can you have the helicopter at the hotel at 7:30 p.m? We are going to the airport. And, keep this quiet please. Thank you."

Next, he telephoned his pilot, Captain Henley.

"Mike, I need to fly to England this evening. Can you have her ready at 8 p.m.?"

"Would you contact the Whites? I don't think we will need Kathy. It's just going to be Annie and me. Thank you."

"Okay, we're all set. Would you like to call my Father and let him know we are coming?"

"No. Isn't it rather late in England right now? Why don't we just call them, when we land? It will be our surprise."

The food finally arrived.

"Would any of you like to go with us?" asked Quinn.

"I would love to go, but I have to work," said Champ.

"What about the rest of you?"

"Cindy, would you like to go to England?"

"Honey, would it be safe for them to go alone this time? You know, this could be a little honeymoon for them."

"I don't know. They would be going to another country and no one knows they're going, but us. What are your thoughts on this, Quinn?"

"Well, Annie has done an exemplary job at protecting me, so... I think we should be all right."

Annie rolled her eyes at him.

"Would you like to have a small honeymoon in England?"

"As long as we can have our own suite. I don't want to stay with your parents."

Quinn smiled from ear to ear. "I think that is an excellent idea, honey."

He leaned over and whispered in her ear. "Do you know what the Mile High Club is?"

She giggled as she jabbed him in his ribs, "Is that all you think about?"

"Well, we will be on our honeymoon!"

"Would anyone like to have a re-fill?" asked the waitress.

"No, ma'am, but I would like the check, please."

"Right away, sir."

CHAPTER 23

ANNIE WAS LOOKING OUT OF the window, as the jet climbed into the sky to 30,000 feet, leaving Port Columbus International Airport. The view was spectacular. The sky was decorated with beautiful shades of pinks, oranges and blues on the western horizon with only a few clouds in the sky. It would be getting dark soon and all of the colors would be disappearing. Never had she seen the sky look more beautiful.

The jet changed course and headed east towards New York. The pilot liked to stop at LaGuardia to top the fuel off. The jet had enough fuel to fly to England, but he didn't like to take chances.

The "Fasten Your Seat Belt" sign turned off and Quinn went to the galley. When he returned, he was carrying two drinks. He had a beer for himself and a Miami Vice for Annie. He handed her the drink and she took a sip.

"You know, for a packaged drink, these are pretty good. Can you get Long Island Iced Teas in a packaged drink?"

"I don't know. I'll have to check. I really don't like you drinking such a strong drink."

"Quinn, please don't start treating me like you are my father."

"It's only because I love you."

Annie grinned at Quinn and caressed his face with her hand. She laid her head on his shoulder.

"Quinn, do you really think we'll be safe in England?"

"Nothing in life is ever guaranteed, baby. If you start feeling like someone is watching us again, just say the word. I'm sure Dad has some bodyguards we can use, if we need them."

Annie was very quiet for the next hour.

"What were you thinking about?"

"My idea to hire a private eye. Do you think it will help?"

"I think it will, if we can find the right man for the job." He paused. I got the impression at the Pizza Shop you didn't want to say whom you wanted to investigate.

"I didn't."

"Is there a reason why?"

"Well, I think Jax, Joe, and Cindy would do anything in the world for you. I trust them, but I don't know Champ that well. How well do you know him?"

"I think he is a good man to have around."

"Remember, Quinn, one of my suspicions is that someone close to you knows what you are doing all the time; or, there is a bug that Jax hasn't picked up on yet."

"So, just who do you want investigated?"

"For obvious reasons, David Morgan is on the top of my list. I also want Dr. Charles Gilmore investigated, along with Jason, Champ and Danny, even if it is only to rule them out. I even want Tony investigated."

"Why Tony, I thought he was your best friend?"

"Something about his apartment being so damned clean is bugging me!"

"You want to investigate him because he is a clean freak?"

"That's just it, I've been in his apartment many times. He is not a clean freak."

"Okay, is there anyone else?"

"Yes, Detective Billy Brown and his side kick Jon Evans."

"They're the law, Annie. Why them?"

"Brown looks familiar, like I should know him. But how do I know him? Where have I seen him before? I don't know any Browns."

"Besides that, he was looking at me so strangely when we were in Chief Hansen's office. He was weird acting and he gave me the creeps."

"Quinn, do you suppose we can go see the Chief when we get back?"

"Why do you want to see him?"

"I would like to have permission to interview one or all of the rape victims. Maybe they would be willing to tell me something we don't know since we look alike."

"If that is what you want to do, I'll make an appointment with him when we return."

"On second thought, why don't we just show up at the police station? I don't want to give Brown or Evans a heads up on what I want to do."

"You really are suspicious of them."

"I just don't understand why the police are dragging their feet. Something isn't right with this case, and I want to know what it is. It shouldn't have taken this long to find who is raping these young women. To me, there are too many red flags and no one is doing anything about them."

"You know, Annie, I have been having those some feelings. I didn't want to say anything because I think you are worrying enough already."

"Quinn, someone is trying to kill you and I don't like it one bit! I'm just trying to figure out what to do!"

Annie leaned forward putting her elbows on the table in front of her and placed her head into her hands.

The "Fasten Your Seat Belt" sign came on indicating they were landing at LaGuardia International Airport to add fuel to the jet. They would probably be at the airport for about an hour.

"Sit back, Annie. We will be landing in a few minutes."

Annie sat back in her seat. Quinn wrapped his

right arm around her shoulder and grabbed her left hand with his left hand. He knew she hated take-offs and landings.

The jet landed safely and taxied to the refueling point. When the jet finally stopped, Quinn and Annie got off the jet to stretch their legs for a while and breathe fresh air. Quinn started texting on his cell phone.

"Who are you texting?"

"Jax. I have an idea about something and I want to know if he can do it."

"What's your idea?"

"I don't want to say just yet."

"Quinn?"

"Honey, will you please trust me for a little while? I promise to tell you as soon as I know if he can do it," he begged as he looked into her eyes.

She looked at him with questioning eyes and shook her head.

"Okay," she said with a frown. She hated being left in the dark about anything, but she did trust him with her life.

It was now 11 p.m. and the jet had finally taken off for England. They would arrive in approximately eight hours. Annie had been very quiet for the last 45 minutes. This concerned Quinn.

"Honey, I think we should try to sleep a while. This is going to be a long trip."

He helped her to unfasten her seatbelt and she stood. Quinn took her hand and led her to the bedroom quarters of the jet. She immediately walked into the bathroom.

He would love for her to join the Mile High Club, but he knew her mood was very subdued. So he wasn't going to suggest it.

When Annie came out of the bathroom, she was wearing her bikini underwear and a camisole to sleep in. Quinn was sitting up in the middle of the bed with nothing on, but his boxers.

Annie crawled over to the middle of the bed where he was sitting.

"What's wrong, Annie. You have been awfully quiet."

She looked at him with such a sad look in her eyes and lowered her head.

He placed one hand under her chin and raised her head to look at him. "What is it, Annie?"

"Why did you marry me?" she asked very softly. "I have been nothing but trouble for you since we married."

He pulled her onto his lap and hugged her tightly. "Oh baby, don't say that!"

"But Quinn," she said.

"No, no, no, no," he said as he placed two fingers on her lips. He didn't let her speak.

"I know we have had a rough start of things, but it won't last. You have to believe that, Annie.

We are going to get through this." He paused and looked deep into her eyes.

Annie looked at him with a worried look, not feeling as secure in that thought as he was.

"Baby, I married you because I fell head over heels in love with you that night! I have never known another woman like you in my life. You are different from every woman I have ever met."

"Different? How am I different?"

"Well, you are the only woman who has ever treated me like a normal guy. I liked that. You made me feel very relaxed."

"I made you feel relaxed? That's funny because I never felt relaxed at all. You know, Quinn, right after I paid for my drink that night, I almost left."

"Why?"

"I was so nervous!"

"Nervous? How? I didn't mean to make you nervous."

"I know. It's just, well, I've never really dated very much and I found you very hot looking. I thought you would find me boring."

"What made you stay?"

"I don't know really, but for some reason, I felt drawn to you."

Quinn kissed her softly. He placed his hands on her cheeks forcing her to look into his eyes.

"Annie, you turned my whole world upside down that night. No other woman has ever had that effect on me, ever!"

She gave him a shy smile.

"Annie, I will love you and only you for eternity."

"I will forever love you, too, Quinn."

Annie reached down and grabbed the bottom of her camisole, pulled it over her head, and threw it on the floor.

"Quinn, make love to me right now. Please?"

Quinn smiled showing his dimples as he laid her head down on the pillow. He slid her panties slowly down her legs and pulled them off over her feet. He stood up from the bed and took his boxer shorts off, turned the light in the cabin down and crawled back into bed.

He gently kissed and pulled her bottom lip into his mouth and sucked her lip. Then he sucked her top lip and she let out a sexy moan. Their tongues invaded each other's mouth while Quinn caressed her breasts. Then he kissed and sucked on each nipple.

One of Quinn's hands was cupping her sex. He inserted two fingers inside her. She writhed. He started a slow assault on her. In, out, in, out, over and over.

Suddenly, he was kissing her... there, sucking and thrusting his tongue into her as far as he could.

"Quinn," she yelled. "Please, Quinn, I need to feel you, please!" and her body writhed.

"Not yet, baby, don't come yet." He spread her legs with his and positioned himself at her entrance. Just as he pushed forward, the jet hit some air turbulence and it pushed him into her deeper.

Annie screamed out, wrapped her legs around Quinn's back, and threw her arms around his neck.

He stilled. He knew it had scared her. He smiled.

"Oh baby, gotta love that air turbulence about now!" and he thrust again and again and again. They experienced a couple more air pockets.

"Come for me, baby! Let me have it!"

He no sooner said it and she came, wildly in the throes of passion.

"Oh, Quinn!" she screamed. "Wow!"

Quinn was grinning from ear to ear. "Welcome to the Mile High Club, baby!"

He pulled her body next to his and wrapped a sheet around her.

"I love you, baby. Go to sleep now."

"I love you, too."

———◆———

They arrived at Taylor Suites Hotel in London, England at 7 a.m.

"Good Morning, Mr. Taylor. How can I help you?" said the clerk behind the check in counter.

"Good Morning. I would like to have one of the suites closest to my father."

"Certainly. How long will you be staying with us, sir?"

"I'm not sure yet."

He smiled at Annie knowing full well, the

length of their stay depended on how his mother treated her.

The clerk handed him two key cards to their room. "Do you need any help with your luggage, sir?"

"No, thank you. We can manage. Please don't tell my parents we are here. I want to surprise them."

"Of course, sir. Have a pleasant stay."

They arrived in suite 2425 on the 24th floor. The suite was quite large with three bedrooms, a formal living room with a baby grand piano, four bathrooms, a private dining area and fully equipped kitchen.

Unlike most of the other Taylor Suites Hotels, this hotel was built for the Heads of State from all over the world. His father knew many world leaders visited London from time to time and he wanted this hotel to be very exquisite, catering to their needs.

"Annie, I want to have breakfast with my parents this morning."

"Then, you go have breakfast with them and I'll stay here in our room. I'll call room service for something to eat."

"No. You are not staying here by yourself. I won't have it," he said sternly. "You are going to have to face my mother sooner or later. Her behavior towards you stops today or I am washing my hands of her forever."

"Quinn, don't say that. She's your mother! I don't want to come between you and your mother!"

"Annie, I will not let her put you down! Now, please, go get ready!"

Annie pursed her lips. She started to say something, but changed her mind. She walked into their bedroom and unpacked a nice pair of gray dress slacks, a pale pink blouse, and a pair of gray heels. She walked into the bathroom, washed her face, brushed her teeth, applied her make-up and styled her hair into a twist. Then she dressed. She decided to leave her purse in her suitcase, but grabbed the key card to their room and her cell phone just in case she needed to make a hasty exit. She walked into the living room and found Quinn sitting on an ottoman in front of one of the Queen Anne chairs.

"Annie, come here, baby. Please sit down a minute. I want to explain something to you."

Annie strolled over to the chair and sat down facing Quinn.

"I'm sorry I snapped at you earlier. I shouldn't have done that. It's just that my mother makes me very angry sometimes, with her controlling attitude towards me. In a sense, you signing a pre-nup, has nothing to do with you."

"Of course it has something to do with me. Your mother thinks I'm a gold digger! She wants me to sign a pre-nup to protect you, Quinn. Don't you see that? You wouldn't be going through this if you would let me sign one."

"You are not signing a pre-nup! END OF DISCUSSION! I DON'T WANT TO HEAR THAT ANYMORE!"

"Why Quinn? It's what your parents want!"

"No, Annie. It's what my mother wants." Quinn took a deep breath in order to calm down.

"I would rather give my dad back all of his holdings in the U.S. that he signed over to me than allow you to sign a pre-nup. Do you know why that is?"

Annie gave him a questioning look.

"No, Quinn, I don't."

"After Kayla left me, I became very hard towards others. It made me a damn good officer, but I was one mean bastard. Then after my injuries while serving in the Navy, I developed PTSD. I began drinking heavily. Mother never thought I was stable enough to take on all of the business holdings in the U.S that Dad wanted to give me. She tried to talk Dad out of it, but he had faith in me and signed it all over to me anyway. He said I needed something to focus on. I worked very hard to make Dad proud of me, but Mom has always had her doubts. Now, by me refusing to allow you to sign a pre-nup, she thinks I am on my way to squandering all of Dad's hard-earned money. It all boils down to trust. She does not trust me to make sound decisions."

"So, how does your Dad feel about all of this?"

"Dad trusts me, Annie, in all things. He even trusts my decision in marrying you, but he feels it would have been better if we had waited a month or two."

Quinn reached over and grasped her hands. "Annie, don't get me wrong. I love my mother very much, but I'm too old to let her run my love life or my business life. You are my life now and she must accept you no matter what. That is the only way I will have it. Do you understand that?"

Annie stood up from the chair and sat down on his lap and put her arms around his neck. "I love you, Quinn Taylor, but if you ever change your mind…"

"No Annie, I won't." He kissed her softly on her lips. "Now, let's go and get this over with. I'm hungry."

CHAPTER 24

INSTEAD OF WALKING THROUGH THE doorway, as any son would do, Quinn decided to knock on the door. "Annie, promise me you won't lose your cool," and he smiled at her.

"I'll try not to."

Quinn's Mother opened the door. She smiled a big welcoming smile at her son and reached to give him a hug, but she saw Annie and frowned.

Quinn walked Annie past his Mother.

"What's she doing here? She is not welcome in my home!"

"Dad, are you home, Dad!" Quinn yelled.

"Mother, if she isn't welcome, then I'm not welcome. If I turn around and walk out of here, I will never look upon your face again, ever!"

Reggie arrived in time to hear Mother and son having words. He grabbed Gloria by the arm.

"WOULD YOU SHUT THE FUCK UP, GLORIA? I HAVE HAD ABOUT ALL I CAN TAKE FROM YOU. THIS IS MY HOME, AND MY SON AND HIS WIFE ARE WELCOME ANYTIME THEY WANT TO COME HERE.

IF ANYBODY LEAVES, IT'S GOING TO BE YOU! I'M TIRED OF YOUR FUCKING BULLSHIT! DO YOU UNDERSTAND ME? NOW GET IN THERE AND ASK THE COOK TO FIX US SOME BREAKFAST!"

Gloria's face turned beet red. She hadn't heard her husband yell at her like this in years. She knew better than to say anything.

"AND AFTER YOU HAVE REQUESTED OUR BREAKFAST, I WANT YOUR ASS BACK IN HERE VISITING WITH YOUR FAMILY AND I WANT YOU TO TREAT THEM NICE AND WITH RESPECT." He paused. "GO, GLORIA, NOW!" he shouted.

Gloria straightened her shoulders and held her head up high. Before she left the room to order breakfast, she gave them all a very disgusting look.

Reggie walked over and took Annie's hand, placing a kiss on it. "I'm sorry you had to witness that my dear, but damn, that felt good. I should have put my foot down the last time you were here."

He walked over and gave his son a big bear hug. "It's really good to see you, son. I guess I have our Annie to thank for that."

He walked back to Annie and gave her a big hug.

"Thank you, Annie, for saving my son," and he had a little tear roll down his cheek. "Come, let's go into the dining room."

"Dad, we need to talk to you privately before we leave today."

"Sounds serious."

"It is, but I want Annie to do the talking. It's her idea."

"We'll talk right after breakfast."

They walked into the dining room and sat down at the table.

"Gloria, get us some coffee, now, please!" he demanded. It won't hurt her ass to do something once in a while he thought.

Gloria came into the dining area with a tray of cups, creamer, sugar, napkins, spoons and a carafe of coffee. She dropped the tray down on the table and toppled the cups.

"Shall I pour your coffee, too, your highness?" she said very arrogantly.

"Sit the fuck down, Gloria. I've had it with you!" Reggie reached over and picked up all of the coffee cups, and placed them in front of him. He reached for the carafe of coffee and poured coffee for each person. He smiled and handed Annie the first cup.

"Here you are, dear. Would you like some cream or sugar?"

"Thank you. I would like some cream, please."

"Son, this if for you."

"Thank you, Dad."

He placed a cup of coffee down on the table in

front of Gloria with a slight thud and frowned at her.

"You know, something just came to my mind that has been stored away in my brain for a long time. In fact, this happened so long ago, that I had totally forgotten about it. This will be important information for you to hear, son."

He winked at Annie. "You might even find this amusing, Annie."

He took a sip of his coffee.

"I started working for my father when I was 16 years old. He owned the first Taylor Suites Hotel in Columbus. It wasn't as big as the one that you have, but nonetheless, it was very profitable. I had graduated from high school when I was 17 years old and immediately began taking college classes. My goal was to graduate from college early. But, like you, son, I quit school when I turned 19 years old and joined the Navy and eventually became a Seal."

"While I was in the Navy, my Dad started building the Taylor Suites that you now own son. She was a beauty. About six months after it opened, Dad passed away. That was when I left the Navy and came home to take care of the family business. My mother didn't know the first thing about Dad's business and he had left it all to me with the promise that I would take care of my Mom. And I did. I have worked very hard all of these years and I think I have made my father proud. And, I am very proud of you, son for all of your accomplishments." He smiled at Quinn and Annie.

"When I met your mother, I thought she was the most beautiful, smartest, sweetest woman in the world. I still think you are beautiful Gloria, but having money has made you into a different person and sometimes, I don't like that."

"Don't, Reggie, don't say it," stated Gloria.

"What you don't know, Quinn, is before Gloria and I married, my Mother insisted on her signing a pre-nup. My mother said the same thing to her as Gloria said to you, Annie. She accused Gloria of being a gold digger. And, as I recall, it didn't sit well with Gloria either."

Annie's mouth dropped open. She was at a loss for words.

"The agreement she signed at the time stated if this marriage failed, she walked away with nothing whatsoever."

"That will never hold up in court, Reggie. We have been married too long!"

"That is where you are wrong, my dear. I have already checked it out. It is an iron clad contract."

"So, my dear, I have a proposition for you. I still love you, always have and I always will. You either accept Annie as your new daughter-in-law, and start treating your son better than you have been or I will honor that contract if you get my meaning."

"You wouldn't dare!"

"Oh, but I would, Gloria. Look at our son. He is very happy. He is happier now than I have ever seen him. That is important to me and it should be to you, too."

Gloria hung her head and started to cry.

"Mom," said Quinn. "Mom?"

Gloria looked at her son with tears in her eyes.

"There is something you don't know. Annie saved my life this week. Not once, but twice. Someone is trying to kill me."

Gloria's eyes got great big with fear. "How? Why?"

"We were going down the elevator at the hotel and a man got on and stabbed me in the neck with some medication, knocking me out. Annie got my gun and shot him, but he ran. Then after we came home from the hospital, someone put an electrical cord in my pool. I came out to swim and Annie pushed me to the ground to keep me from jumping in or I would have been electrocuted. Mom, she's not a gold digger. You need to give her a chance."

"She really did that? She really saved you?"

"Here's the scratches on my arm where she pushed me down with her body." And he raised his shirtsleeve so she could see the scratches.

Gloria stood from her chair and walked to where Annie was sitting. "I'm sorry, Annie. I should have remembered what it felt like for me when his mother accused me of being a gold digger. I didn't even know Reggie was wealthy until he asked me to sign that damn pre-nup that his mother insisted on. Will you forgive me?"

"Yes, I'll forgive you, but I want you to know something. I fell in love with Quinn, the man with a beautiful heart." And tears filled Annie's eyes.

Quinn got up from the table and put his arms around his Mother and his wife, giving them both a hug. This is the way it should have been from the very beginning, he thought. Now maybe we can be a real family.

CHAPTER 25

WHEN BREAKFAST WAS OVER, QUINN and Annie went back to their hotel suite. Annie had ordered coffee for three from room service and it arrived at the same time as Reggie. "That's perfect timing," said Quinn.

Reggie and Quinn walked to the dining area of the suite while Annie poured them coffee.

"So, Annie, Quinn tells me you have an idea. What is this all about?"

Annie looked at her husband, smiled and took a sip of her coffee. When she looked at her father-in-law, she had a very serious tone to her voice.

"Well, I want to hire a private investigator."

"Okay," he said, pausing to look at her. He took a drink of his coffee. "I take it you are not happy with the police force and their investigation."

"No, I'm not," she replied. "The police are getting nowhere in finding the two rapist in Columbus, and now someone is trying to kill my Quinn. I don't know if there are two different crimes going on here or if they are related. Are they trying to eliminate Quinn to get to me or is something else going on here that we are totally unaware of? I just don't know what is going on and I feel helpless."

"Have you talked to the police about this?"

"You should have heard her telling Detective Evans off a couple of days ago. He knows exactly how she feels," said Quinn.

"Have you discussed this with Chief Hansen?"

"Not yet, and I don't even know if I want to," said Annie.

"So, what can I do to help?"

"We were hoping you could recommend a good private investigator; one that can be very discreet," replied Annie.

"Who do you want him to investigate and why?"

"David Morgan for obvious reasons, my friend Tony, Charles Gilmore, and Detectives Brown and Evans, and three Seals."

Reggie didn't like the idea of investigating any of the Seals. "Why the Seals?"

"In all probability, they can be trusted. I just want to eliminate them for my own peace of mind. Someone knows Quinn and knows what his routine is. I think the only people that knew we were going to see my parents were the Seals and that was the day the guy jumped us in the elevator. There are just too many unanswered questions and I don't like it."

"Both of you take your cell phones out. I'm going to give you the name of a P.I. and his phone number as soon as I can find it. Oh, yes, here it is. I think this is the right man for the job. His name is Pete Sanford. S-a-n-f-o-r-d. His number is 555-873-4576. He has done some work for me before. Tell him that I recommended him. He might give you a good rate."

"Thanks, Dad. I figured you would know someone."

"So, do you have other plans?"

"Well, I need to get the addresses of the rape victims in hopes of interviewing them. Do you think Hansen would give me the addresses?

I'm hoping they can tell us something we don't know. Maybe something the police missed and I don't want Detective Brown or Evans knowing I want to interview them."

"Maybe Pete can find out where they live and then you can interview them without Hansen's knowledge."

"You know, Annie, that's not a bad idea."

"So, how long are you planning on staying in England?"

"I was hoping we would stay for the week, but that depends on what Annie wants to do. I know she is anxious about getting this over with."

"Reggie, I just want a normal life for Quinn and me. I'm tired of all of this! It scares me that someone is trying to kill Quinn and that someone is after me. It doesn't set well with me."

"You are a very smart woman, Annie. If you and

Quinn want me to come to the states to help you, just say the word. I want this to end as much as you do."

"Thanks, Dad, but I would prefer you stay right here. I don't want someone trying to get to you or Mom. It's bad enough someone is after us. I couldn't take it if someone got to either of you."

"I understand, son. Just don't forget, I was a damn good Seal long before you came along," and he gave his son a wink.

"Do you dance, Annie? I know Quinn does," asked Reggie.

"She thinks she can dance! She actually has two left feet," he said with a wink.

"I do not, Quinn Taylor! Don't you be telling lies on me!"

"I'm only kidding, baby," he said with a laugh.

"Good! Would you consider going out to dinner with your Mother and I this evening? I want to take your mother dancing. I was pretty harsh on her this morning and I want her to know I still love her. Plus, I want her to see how much you two love each other."

Quinn stood behind Annie, wrapped his arms around her waist and kissed her on top of her head.

"Sure, we'll go," he said. "What time do you want to leave?"

"The name of the place is called Sweet Williams. We'll leave at 6:30 p.m. That should give us enough time to have a nice dinner. Music starts at 8 p.m."

"I must leave now. I have a scheduled meeting downstairs with the staff."

Before he walked out of the door, he gave Annie a hug and kissed the top of her hand.

"You are such a charmer, Reggie," Annie stated with a big smile.

"Love you, son," he said as he hugged Quinn.

"Love you, too, Dad. We'll see you this evening."

Reggie walked out of the door.

"I can't believe we are going on a double date with your parents!"

"Come to think of it, Annie, I don't think I have ever gone on a date with my parents before. This could be a very interesting evening."

"Honey, I don't have anything to wear tonight."

"Come, there are a few dress shops down the street within walking distance. Let's go shopping." She took her purse from her suitcase and placed her hand in Quinn's hand.

The air outside was breezy, but warm. Traffic was moving at a steady pace. It felt very strange to Annie to see drivers on the right side of a car and driving on the opposite side of the street.

They found a quaint little dress shop a block from the hotel. It was very charming inside and the staff was very courteous and helpful. Quinn helped Annie pick out seven dresses and he wanted her to try each of them on. He wanted to choose the right dress for her.

"Doesn't my opinion count for anything Quinn? After all, I can tell how well if fits on my body."

"Of course, your opinion counts. Listen, a man knows what really looks sexy on a woman. I want everyone to know I have the sexiest woman alive and she belongs to me and me alone." He smiled a broad, sexy grin that showed those dimples she loved so much. "I'll make a deal with you, baby. You tell me which dresses you like the most and I'll pick from the ones you like. Is that okay with you?"

She ran her hands through her hair and placed her hand on her chin. What am I going to do with him, he is so exasperating! He really seemed to be enjoying this. Shopping with a man was a new experience for her.

After trying on a total of seven dresses, Annie decided she didn't want to try on anymore clothing. She decided she liked the pale blue dress with the full skirt. It looked more appropriate being as they are going on a date with her in-laws.

"Have you decided which of the dresses you like?" asked Quinn.

"Yes, I think I like the blue one."

The store clerk handed Quinn his credit card. "Thank you, sir."

"Quinn, what did you do?"

"Well, you looked so damn sexy in all of them and I couldn't make up my mind, so I bought all of them."

"No, Quinn, I only need one dress," she said, standing with her hands on her hips, watching as the clerk handed Quinn all seven dresses on the hangers with a bag wrapped around all of them.

He smiled again. "You'll have more opportunities to wear the other dresses." He kissed her on top of her head and took her hand and led her out of the shop.

They walked about a half a block and Annie stopped.

"Annie, please don't be mad at me. I just find you so beaut... What's wrong, Annie?"

Annie was looking all around, across the street, up the street, down the street, at all the cars, all the people, everywhere.

"Annie, what is it?"

"Someone's watching us."

"You're sure?"

"Yes, it feels just like at my apartment."

Quinn started looking around, but didn't see anything out of the ordinary. "Come, let's get back to the hotel."

He took Annie's hand and held on to her tightly. They walked very fast. When they entered their hotel room, they found their room had been ransacked. Everything in their suitcases was thrown everywhere. Some of the furniture was over-turned, and sofa and chair cushions were on the floor.

"Annie, stay behind me." He laid the dresses

across one of the chairs and took Annie back into the hallway. He called his Dad.

"Dad, are you and Mom all right?"

"Yes, what's going on?"

"Don't say anything to Mom, but call security and meet us in the hall by our room."

"Why? What's happened?"

"Someone has broken into our room." He immediately hung up.

Quinn looked down at Annie and saw she was scared to death. "Annie, don't worry. It will be okay, baby. I'll protect you."

Within two minutes, Reggie came running down the hallway.

"Slow down, Dad. You'll have a heart attack. I don't think anyone is in there, but I want to check. Stay here with Annie."

"No, Quinn, No. Please don't go in. Please," she begged.

"No, Quinn. Here comes security. Let them check. That's what I pay them for."

Annie put one arm around Quinn's elbow. "I'm not letting you go in!"

"Honey, I can take care of myself. I want to go in with these men."

"You are my hero and I know you can take care of yourself, but I couldn't stand it if something happened to you." Her thoughts reminded her of how someone tried to kill him two different times this week and this has set her nerves on end.

"What's going on, sir?" said one of the security guards.

"Someone has broken into my son's room and it needs to be thoroughly checked to make sure that no one is in there."

"I don't think there is right now, but make sure you check every closet, look behind all the drapes, under the bed, anywhere someone could hide. And be careful," stated Quinn.

The two security guards removed their guns from their holsters and walked cautiously into the suite. Five minutes later, one of the guards gave the all clear.

"Sir, there is a note on the kitchen counter addressed to you," said one of the guards.

Quinn walked to the kitchen and started to pick it up.

"Stop! Don't pick it up!" screamed Annie.

"What has gotten into you, Annie? It's just paper," and he started to reach for it again.

She slapped his hand away from it and pushed him away from the counter.

"Maybe I am one crazy female, but I would rather act on the side of caution than be sorry. Maybe I have watched too many mystery movies and maybe I have read too many mystery books, but someone could have laced the paper with some kind of chemical that would instantly kill you if you touched it."

"Annie, I kind of doubt that."

"Yes, and who would have thought someone would try to kill you by injecting Ketamine into your neck and then try to electrocute you the next day. Who, Quinn? We have to be careful with all things."

Quinn rolled his eyes. "You do have a point." He walked away from the counter. "If that is the case, then we shouldn't touch anything in here."

"I think she's right, son. I'm calling the police. We'll have this note checked out."

Minutes later, the London Police arrived. Reggie explained to them what was going on, especially with the note, and then they questioned Quinn and Annie.

The police decided to err on the side of caution and act on Annie's instinct. They called in a request for a small HAZMAT team.

"Do you have any idea who could have done this?" asked one of the policemen.

"No, sir. Not yet. I am involved in an ongoing investigation in Columbus, Ohio, where seven women who look like my wife have been raped and one of them has died. I am a Reserve Officer with the Columbus Police Department back home."

"Yes, and someone has tried to kill him two times this week, so we really aren't sure if they are trying to kill him to get to my daughter-in-law or if someone has a vendetta against him," said Reggie.

"We are going to dust for fingerprints. Can you

tell me who has been in your room?" asked the policeman.

"Well, we just arrived early this morning, so it has only been my father, my wife and myself and these two security guards. You will probably find the housekeepers prints, too."

The policeman looked at Reggie. "Could you let me know who the housekeeper was so that we may rule him or her out?"

"Certainly. I have fingerprints of all my staff, if you need them. With heads of state staying here frequently, it is one of my requirements of all staff."

"Yes, sir. That would be very helpful."

Reggie called downstairs to the office. "Susan, this is Mr. Taylor. I need for you to make copies of all the fingerprints we have on file and give to the police as soon a possible. Thank you, Susan."

"Mrs. Taylor, do you know if you are missing anything?" asked the policeman.

"I don't know what it would be. I'm wearing the only jewelry I brought. We only packed a few clothes and our toiletry items."

"I do have a gun, but they didn't take it," added Quinn.

"May I see it, please?"

Quinn handed the gun to the policeman.

"Hmm, a Smith and Wesson 9mm. Nice gun. The policeman smelled the tip of the gun to see if it had been fired. Do you have a gun permit?"

"Yes, sir," he stated as he was going through his

wallet for his gun permit. "As I have already told you, I work as a Reserve Officer for the Columbus, Ohio Police Department in the states. I carry it everywhere I go because I am trying to protect my wife."

The policeman handed the gun back to Quinn. "Try not to use this while you are here in London, sir. I need to see your passports, too, Mr. Taylor."

Quinn reached into his sport coat and pulled out his passport while Annie searched her purse. They both handed them to the policeman.

"Your passports seem to be in order, but I will need both of you to come down to the police station to give a statement. Right now, I want to inspect your room."

"We just gave you a statement," replied Quinn, looking very annoyed.

"Please come down in the morning. I should have the results of our findings on the note," he ordered. "Where will you be staying?"

"They will be staying with his Mother and I upstairs in the penthouse."

"I don't know about that, Dad. Maybe we should get another hotel. I don't want to put you and mother in any danger."

"I don't think that matters anymore, son. I'll just triple up on security."

CHAPTER 26

REGGIE YELLED FOR GLORIA WHEN they walked back into his penthouse. "She must not be here. I know she said she had some errands to run this morning. She evidently isn't back yet."

Reggie called his head of security for the hotel and told him to add six security guards on his garden rooftop and four in the hallways by his door, around the clock. He also ordered two security guards for his wife should she need to leave the penthouse, two for his son and daughter – in-law and two for himself.

"Son, I think we should cancel this evening. I don't want to take any chances."

"That's fine." Quinn ran his hands through his hair and started pacing the floor. "Maybe Annie is right. Maybe someone close to me knows my schedule. But who would it be? Who in the hell knows we are here? I know Joe, Cindy, Jax, and Champ does."

He shook his head trying to think. "I really hope it isn't any of them. Surely they wouldn't have said anything to anyone. I've told no one at the hotel. My two pilots know and, of course, Mr. White probably told his wife he was flying to London. The air traffic controllers would know due to the flight plan, but I can't see them as a threat. Annie, did you tell anyone we were leaving?"

"No, Quinn. I haven't said the first word to anyone, not even my mother. There has to be another explanation. I can't see Joe, Cindy or Jax doing this or even Champ. Do you suppose they could have told someone we were leaving?"

"We need to get back to Ohio as soon as possible. Dad, do you suppose you and Mother could go on a vacation somewhere and get out of London for a while? At least for a few weeks?"

"Well, I guess we could go to New York. Gloria has wanted to travel to New York for some time now to do some shopping, take in some plays and go to some of the art museums. We can fly there with you and Annie and you can just drop us off in New York. There is no sense in taking both jets."

"I couldn't talk you into traveling to the Mediterranean or France or somewhere else? I really don't want anything to happen to you and Mom."

"We'll be fine, Son. I don't want to be clear across the world if something were to happen to either of you. I would rather be as close to Columbus as possible. In fact, I've half a mind to go to Columbus anyway and stay in another hotel just so we can be near you. We can check in under another name."

"No, Dad. I don't want that!"

"I'll talk to Gloria when she gets back and see what she wants to do."

Just then, Gloria walked into the penthouse. "Talk to me about what; and, who are those men standing by our door?" asked Gloria as she came in the door and sat several packages down on the floor.

"Good, they're here already," said Reggie as he kissed his wife on the cheek. "Quinn and Annie did a little shopping this morning and while they were gone, someone broke into their suite. I've added some security."

"What do you mean someone broke into your suite? Did they take anything? What would they be looking for, Quinn? What is going on?" she said as she hugged her son.

"I don't know, Mom. We didn't bring anything important. Annie is wearing the only jewelry she brought. We didn't even bring our laptops. Just our cell phones and our passports, besides a few clothes, that is all we brought. I don't know what they would be looking for!"

"So what happens now?" Gloria asked.

"We must go to the police station in the morning to give a statement and to find out the results."

"What results?" asked Gloria.

"There was an envelop on the kitchen counter

with my name on it. Annie wouldn't let me pick it up. She said it was a gut feeling, but with everything that has happened, she didn't want me to take any chances."

"What do you mean, didn't want you to take any chances."?

"I'm sure it's nothing, Mrs. Taylor. I've just read too many mysteries and watched too many movies, but since someone has already tried to take Quinn's life twice this week, I wanted the police to check the envelop for any kind of chemical residue that could kill a person instantly when they touch the envelop. They are also checking all the toiletry items to make sure they are safe as well."

"In heaven's name, Quinn, who is doing this? Why are they doing this?"

"It's all right, Mom. Annie is probably over-reacting." Quinn sat down next to his Mother on the sofa and put his arms around her. He doesn't want to worry his Mother, but he was beginning to wonder if there was that possibility. Maybe David Morgan could get his hands on some kind of chemical through all of his Dad's contacts.

"Gloria," Reggie said. "Would you like to travel to New York for a while? You could visit with some of your friends and see all of the sights."

"And what are you planning to do?" she asked.

"I'm going to Columbus to be near Quinn and possibly help him."

"You are not going without me!"

"Mom, I don't want you to go. Hell, I don't want Dad to go either!"

"It's settled then. Pack your clothes Gloria. We leave tomorrow as soon as the police tell Quinn they can leave."

Quinn threw his hands up in the air. "I can't believe this fucking shit! It's not as though I don't have enough to worry about with Annie and myself. Now I have to worry about the two of you!"

He walked out onto the garden terrace and slammed the door. He paced back and forth, trying to figure out what to do.

Reggie started to follow him outside.

"Wait, Reggie," demanded Annie. "Don't go. Just give him some time to think. He needs to figure this out on his own."

Reggie ignored Annie's plea. He walked out onto the garden terrace and father and son started exchanging heated words.

"Well, this is a fine mess you've gotten our family into!" mouthed Gloria.

Annie was stunned at the accusation. Tears sprang to her eyes.

"Don't you dare use those tears on me. Tears don't work around me, you little bitch! I have half a mind to throw you out of here!"

"Don't bother! Tell Quinn I'll wait for him in the restaurant downstairs," Annie said through her tears. She grabbed her purse and ran out of the door.

"Good, damn little bitch!" Gloria walked into her kitchen and poured herself a scotch and water.

Fifteen minutes later, Quinn and Reggie walked back inside. He didn't see Annie so he started searching the penthouse. He saw his mother in the kitchen, pouring herself a drink. "Mother, where's Annie?"

"I don't know," his mother replied.

"What do you mean, you don't know?" asked her son very sternly. "WHERE'S ANNIE?"

"Like I said, I don't know. She left! And I'm glad she has gone! She is tearing this family apart!"

"How long ago did she leave, Mom?"

Gloria didn't answer.

"I SAID, HOW LONG AGO?"

Gloria took another sip of her scotch.

Reggie reached over and took her drink away from her. "Your son asked you a question. Answer him, NOW!"

Gloria looked at her husband with dread and rolled her eyes. "About 20 minutes ago."

"Shit, SHIT. WHAT DID YOU SAY TO HER?"

"MOTHER, IF ANYTHING HAPPENS TO HER..."

He reached for his sport coat and put it on. "Mother, I don't ever want to look upon your face ever again! Do you hear me? We are done!"

"Quinn, I..." cried Gloria.

Quinn ran out the door.

Reggie looked at his wife with hatred in his eyes. "Gloria, I want you to pack your bags and get out. I no longer want you to be my wife! You have no heart! You don't deserve to be a mother."

"Reggie, No! You don't mean that!" Gloria started to shake. "I'm sorry, I was just upset. I didn't mean it. How was I supposed to know she would leave?"

"If you are not gone by the time I get back, I will personally throw you out on your fucking ass so fast it will make your head spin! Now I said pack your clothes and get out!"

"I can't believe you are letting that little tramp ruin our marriage!"

"She had nothing to do with ruining our marriage, Gloria. You did that all by yourself. Now, I want you out of here within the hour."

"You can't make me leave! I'm not going anywhere. This is my home!"

Reggie opened the door and picked the biggest guard standing there. "Mr. Stevens, I have a job for you to do and you had better do it to the letter or I will fire you. Do you understand?"

"Yes, sir. What do you wish me to do?"

"Gloria Taylor is no longer welcome here. If she has not left here in 30 minutes, you are to escort her out of this building, even if you have to use bodily force. Do you understand me? And, she is not allowed back here ever!"

"Reggie, you gave me an hour! I can't pack everything up in an hour let alone 30 minutes!"

"You are absolutely right."

Reggie opened up Gloria's purse and took her keys out, credit cards, and her debit cards. He took the car key off and handed it to her. "This is the only key you will need. You can have the car. I will have the title changed to your name."

He took his cell phone out and called his bank. It is a direct number to the office of the President of the Bank of London.

"Jonathon, this is Reggie Taylor. I need for you to do something for me immediately."

"Yes, sir. What can I do for you?"

"I need for you to remove Gloria Taylor's name from all of my accounts immediately."

"Yes, sir."

"If you fail to do so immediately, I will transfer all of my holdings to your competitor. Do I make myself clear?"

"Absolutely, sir. Anything else, sir?"

"Yes, I want you to add my son's name in her place. His name is Quinnten R. Taylor. Quinnten is spelled Q-U-I-N-N-T-E-N. I will have Quinn come in and sign the necessary paperwork as soon as possible."

"Anything else, sir?"

"Yes, I would like to open up a new account in her name only. Transfer 640,000 pounds into this account."

"Are you aware that she just opened a new account today?"

"No, sir. I was not aware of that. How much is in it?"

"19,200,000 £."

"I see. Then cancel that last request. Thank you, Jonathon."

"Gloria, Gloria, Gloria." Reggie stated in wonderment. "Jonathon told me you have been to the bank today and transferred $30 million dollars into a new account in your name only. You have never done anything like that before. Were you planning on stockpiling up some of our money since I told you this morning about your pre-nup still being valid?"

"I've earned that money just as much as you have, Reggie!"

He looked at her in amazement. "You haven't earned anything, but my new hatred and distrust for you, Gloria. But, I'll tell you what I'm going to do. I will let you keep that $30,000,000. If I find out that you have been to any of the other banks and have taken anything else, I will have you arrested for theft and anything else I can come up with. After all, you did sign a pre-nup!"

Gloria laughed. "I found your precious pre-nup, Reggie. I burned it! I can take half of everything your own!"

"You know Gloria, you are not as smart as you think. That was a copy that you burned. The original is in a very safe place, far away from your deceptive little hands." He paused and looked at her with distaste. "Escort her out now, Mr. Stevens." Reggie demanded as he handed Gloria her purse.

Gloria's mouth flew open. She was shocked! "Well, I never!"

"That's right, Gloria. That's where the problems lie. You never think about anyone, but yourself. Just let me know where you will be staying and I will send your stuff to you. On second thought, you have enough money to start completely over. I'll not be sending you anything. It will be either donated to the poor or thrown out in the trash!"

He walked out of the door with her and Mr. Stevens. He looked at the other guards. "Gentlemen, this woman is not allowed in this building or this penthouse. If she returns, escort her out. If you need to, call the police. If all else fails, shoot her fucking ass!"

"Reggie!" she said.

"Get her out of here, now! Put her in her car and watch her leave. I can no longer stand the sight of her!"

Mr. Stevens grabbed her by the elbow, but she jerked away from him.

"Don't you dare touch me! I can leave on my own."

"Ma'am, get in the elevator or I will pick you up and throw you over my shoulder."

"You wouldn't dare!"

He walked towards her to throw her over his shoulder, but she walked into the elevator.

When the elevator doors closed, Reggie took a deep breath. He was at a loss at what took place that afternoon with Gloria, but he didn't have any more time to think about it. He must find Quinn and Annie.

"The girl that left here this afternoon, did anyone follow her?"

"Yes, sir. Paul Masters did, sir."

"Did anyone follow my son?"

"Yes, sir. Carl Smith followed him."

Reggie took the elevator down to the first floor. He walked outside into the evening air. The doorman was standing nearby. "Mr. Ames, did you see my son leave about an hour ago?"

"Yes, sir, I did. He looked to be in a bit of a rush, sir."

"Which way did he go?"

"East, sir."

"How long have you been standing here, Mr. Ames?"

"I've been here for the last hour and a half to two hours, sir."

"Did you happen to see a petite young woman wearing a pink blouse come running out of here? She could have been crying."

324

"No, sir. I haven't seen anyone fitting that description."

"Thank you, Mr. Ames."

Reggie looked back at the hotel. He wondered if she was inside, perhaps she never left. He walked into the restaurant of the hotel. It was dimly lit and there were only a few guests having dinner. There she was, sitting in the corner alone. Her head was in her hands and she had been crying. Where is her bodyguard? He saw him. Reggie took out his cell phone and called Quinn. He was very brief when Quinn answered. "She is in the restaurant of the hotel and she is safe."

Within 15 minutes, Quinn came running into the hotel restaurant. Reggie stopped him before he saw her. "Quinn, there is something you need to know before you talk to Annie." He paused. "I kicked your Mother out. Our marriage is over. I can't live with a woman who cannot treat my son and his wife with respect and love."

Quinn looked at his dad with sorrow and wrapped his arms around him. "I'm sorry, Dad."

"Me, too. I'll be expecting you both to stay with me tonight. I don't think I want to be alone."

"Okay." He hugged his Dad as tears filled his eyes. Why is his mother so hateful? Why can't she love her family the way she should? Why can't she trust him like his Dad does? Why can't she accept Annie?

"I'm going upstairs now. There are two bodyguards

sitting at the bar, watching over you. Their names are Carl and Paul. You should be safe. I love you, son."

"I love you, too, Dad."

CHAPTER 27

QUINN WALKED OVER TO THE corner booth were Annie was sitting. She immediately put her arms around him and started crying. "It's okay, baby. Not here. We are going upstairs."

"No, Quinn," she said through gritted teeth. "I will not be in the same room as your Mother!"

"You won't be. Dad kicked her out after you left."

"What do you mean, he kicked her out?"

"Just what I said. We'll talk when we get upstairs." He reached into his wallet and threw some money onto the table. He grabbed Annie's hand and walked towards the bar.

"Can I help you, Mr. Taylor?"

"Yes, sir. Give these two gentlemen anything they want to eat and drink and put it on my tab."

"Thank you, sir."

"Thank you for keeping an eye on us today. We won't need your services for the rest of the evening. Enjoy your dinner."

Quinn hung onto Annie's hand for dear life. He had so many mixed emotions going through his head right now. How long was he going to be able to hang on to his sanity? He felt he was just about at the end of his rope.

"Quinn, I'm sorry your..."

He stopped her from talking in mid-sentence. "Please, Annie, I need some space."

She pulled her hand away from his. She walked toward the front of the elevator waiting for the doors to open. She didn't want him to see new tears filling her eyes.

"Why did you pull your hand away?"

"I'm just giving you some space. I know what that means," she spoke very softly.

"Good evening, gentlemen," Quinn said as he unlocked the penthouse door. When they walked inside, he yelled for his Dad.

"I'm in the kitchen. Would you like for me to fix you a drink?"

"No." He walked into the utility room and found a pair of swimming trunks. He needed to swim and burn off some energy. He felt too wound up inside. He walked past Annie, took all of his clothes off and slipped on his swimming trunks. He grabbed a towel and walked past her again. She followed him to the garden terrace where she watched him go into a running dive into the pool.

"He should have been an Olympic swimmer." Reggie said as he handed Annie a glass of iced tea. "I've seen him like this before. He just needs to think. He thought he lost you today."

"I'm sorry for your loss, Reggie."

"It's been going to happen for a while." He paused and took a sip of his ice tea. "If I were you, I would go into the utility room and get one of the swimming suits located in the dresser. When Quinn gets like this, he likes to swim for about two hours. After he swims for about an hour, start swimming with him. I'm sure he will simmer down. I'll be in my office if you need anything. I have much work to do."

Annie changed her clothes into the red bikini suit she found in the utility room. She found a white and red checked beach towel and wrapped it around her and headed out to the pool.

She sat in a lounge chair and watched him swim. He moved through the water with such grace and speed. He was an amazing swimmer. He was born to be on the water and in the water. After watching him for nearly an hour, she decided she was going to join him.

She waited until he made it back to the end of the pool where she was standing and dove in. She knew she wouldn't even come close to beating him to the other end. His strength plus his body length alone would guarantee that, but she didn't care.

Quinn noticed Annie was swimming in the lane next to him. What the hell was she doing? He slowed his swimming strokes down some so that she could keep up with him. She was swimming as fast as her little arms and legs could go. At this rate, she would only be able to complete two laps, if she were lucky.

Annie made it to the end of the pool and was able to turn around and push off. Quinn decided he was going to swim ahead of her to the other end. He was going to stop her.

When Annie finally made it to the end of the pool, Quinn moved in front of her forcing her to grab onto his shoulders. She wrapped her legs around his waist.

"What are you doing, Annie?" he asked softly.

"I'm swimming with my husband." She smiled.

He wiped some of the water from her eyes and forehead. He frowned.

"But you left me this afternoon," he said softly.

Annie placed both of her hands on his cheeks. "I left your mother. I waited for you. I knew you would find me."

She looked deep into his eyes. "Quinn, I could never leave you." She kissed his lower lip, sucking it into her mouth. "I love you!" She assaulted his mouth with her tongue.

He groaned. He pulled her face away from his. "Why didn't you come out here and get me?"

"You were having a heated conversation with your Dad. You didn't need for me to add any more drama. You have had way too much added on to you since we married."

"I was so scared when I couldn't find you, Annie.

I didn't know if you had left me for good or if someone had taken you. I was ready to go out of my mind when I couldn't find you."

"Quinn, I told your Mother to tell you I would be in the restaurant downstairs. Didn't she tell you?"

"No, she didn't. She said you left and she didn't know where you had gone."

"Why didn't you look in the restaurant?"

"Baby, I couldn't think. I thought you wanted to get away from this family as far as you could. I even thought someone had grabbed you." He laid his forehead against her forehead. "Baby, I was a hell of a soldier and I had excellent tracking skills, but when it comes to you, I don't know what it is. I just turn to shit! I can't think straight."

Annie laid her head into his neck.

"What did Mother say to you to make you want to leave?"

"When you and your father where out here having what looked like a heated discussion, she accused me of making a fine mess again of this family. When I started to cry, she told me she had no use for tears, called me a bitch and said she had half a mind to throw me out on my ass. I told her not to bother and asked her to tell you that I would be in the restaurant; and, left. Honestly Quinn, I didn't say anything out of line to her. Honest!"

"I believe you, baby. Promise me you will never let anyone come between us ever again!"

"I promise, Quinn. But promise me I won't ever have to be around your Mother ever again. Promise me, Quinn!"

"I promise. I don't even want to be around her."

"Quinn?" yelled Reggie as he came out onto the terrace carrying a couple of terry robes. "Detective Blackwell is here to see you with the results of their investigation this morning."

Reggie extended his hand to Annie to help her get out of the pool as Quinn jumped out. He gave them towels and they quickly dried themselves. When they were finished drying, Reggie handed them each a robe.

"Can you ask him to join us on the terrace?"

Reggie escorted the detective to the terrace.

"Mr. Blackwell, this is my son, Quinn Taylor, and his lovely wife, Annie Taylor."

Quinn extended his hand to Detective Blackwell. "Glad to meet you, sir. Father told me you have the results of your investigation already. Please have a seat."

"Yes, sir. I do." Mr. Blackwell stated as he sat down. "The police officer that was here this morning said you would really like to know as soon as possible as you needed to return to America."

"That is correct, sir. We are involved in trying to solve a case where seven women have been raped and one of them killed."

"Yes, I read up on that today, and please forgive me for saying this, but those young ladies do resemble you, Mrs. Taylor."

"So, Mr. Blackwell, what are your conclusions, sir?" asked Annie.

"Well, there were no chemical residues on the envelop, but there was a message inside the envelop for you, Mr. Taylor. I thought you might want to read it."

Mr. Blackwell handed the note to Quinn. It was wrapped in a heavy see through plastic so that no fingerprints touched the note. He read the words to himself and then he read it out loud.

"You are dead. She's mine."

"Do you have any idea who could have written this note and wants to see you dead, Mr. Taylor?"

"No, sir, we don't."

"May I ask you a few questions?" asked Detective Blackwell.

"Of course," replied Quinn.

"How long have you two been married?"

"Since July 6th of this year."

"Did you have a long standing relationship before you married?"

"Only four days," replied Quinn, as he squeezed Annie's hand. "We first met each other on the evening of July 3rd of this year."

"I see. Very interesting. Mrs. Taylor, I'm quite curious. Had you been seeing anyone prior to meeting your husband?"

"No, sir."

"Hmm. Do you remember when your last date was and with whom?"

"Yes, sir. It was in September, six years ago."

"Please forgive me ma'am, but as pretty as you are, you're telling me you haven't been out with anyone for six years prior to meeting your husband?"

"Yes, sir. That is correct."

"I find that very hard to believe."

"It's quite complicated, sir."

"Oh? How so?"

"Six years ago, while I was in my first year of college, I met someone. We went out on one date, and the next time I met up with him, he tried to rape me. I refused to go out with him and he has been stalking me ever since. To make a long story short, sir, I chose not to date anyone as long as I was in school."

"Very interesting. Could this person be the author of this note?"

"He is at the top of our list of suspects, sir," replied Quinn. "That's why we need to get back to Ohio."

"Of course. Would you be willing to travel back to London, should we need you regarding this case?"

"Yes, of course. We live at the Taylor Suites in Columbus. It shouldn't be difficult for you to track us down."

"Well then, I'll take my leave. Oh, before I forget, I've brought all your clothing and toiletries with me. I have left them by the door. Have a safe trip back to Ohio. Good evening, Mr. and Mrs. Taylor, Mr. Taylor."

"Thank you for coming. I'll show you out," replied Reggie, very politely.

Reggie walked back out onto the terrace. "I need to speak to the both of you. Now would be a good time to talk to you about your Mother, Quinn."

"I should leave and let you talk alone," stated Annie.

"No, young lady. You are a big part of this family," Reggie stated as he looked at Annie. "Please, sit down."

Annie did as he asked and sat down very close to Quinn

"Your Mother done something this morning that was very underhanded. I am going to take the blame for it because I feel it was partially my fault. Not only did she betray you as a mother, she betrayed me as my wife. I don't know if I can ever forgive her for that."

"What did she do, Dad?"

"Remember this morning when I reminded her of her pre-nup that she had signed 34 years ago when we married? Well, she went to the bank this morning, found a copy of the pre-nup, burned it and then withdrew $30 million dollars and put it into an savings account in her name only. I have since learned, she has tried to do the same thing in other banks across the world. She didn't succeed, of course, but nonetheless, she betrayed me."

"I'm sorry, Dad."

"Quinn, we have been having some marital problems for about four years and I have suspected she only wanted me for my money as of late."

Quinn looked at his Dad very confused. "I hate to ask this Dad, but has she been having an affair with someone?"

Reggie threw his head back against the chair he was sitting in and took a deep breath. "I don't think so, son. But then, what is it they say? The spouse is always the last to know." He paused. "She's changed a great deal over the past years. I don't know what happened for her to change so much. She used to be such a loving mother, always doting on you, and she was a wonderful wife." He frowned and wiped a stray tear from his eye.

"Anyway, the reason I am out here. I have contacted all of my banks and my attorneys and I have taken Gloria's name off of everything and I have added both of your names on all of my accounts. I will need for you both to sign all of the necessary paperwork."

"Now, wait a minute," spoke Annie. "I don't want my name on anything!"

"You must, Annie," said Reggie. "Quinn is my only legal heir. If something were to happen to me, everything I own goes to Quinn. Should something happen to Quinn after my passing, I want everything to go to you. I have no one else to leave it to. I don't want everything I have worked so hard for all of my life to go to the state. Do you understand?"

Annie looked at Reggie and Quinn. "Look, I come from very humble beginnings, watching my parents working hard to make ends meet from payday to payday. Having this kind of money and responsibility scares the living shit out of me!"

Reggie walked over to the loveseat Annie was sitting on. He stooped down and took both of Annie's hands.

"Annie, in the short amount of time that I have known you, you have proven to me beyond a shadow of doubt that you are more than worthy of being in this family. You are very smart and I believe with my whole heart that you really are in love with my son. I want you to be one of the executors of my estate, along with my son. I trust no one else but the two of you. One day, hopefully, you will give me some grandchildren and you and Quinn can leave everything to them. My wish is for my business to remain in our family for generations. Will you do this for me?"

Annie was completely overwhelmed. She didn't know exactly what to say. How on earth did she fall in love with a rich man? She looked at her husband for guidance. He smiled a little smile, showing his dimples. A tear started to travel down her cheek.

"Reggie, if I ever have a daughter, the very first thing I am going to teach her is to beware of men with dimples. They are very hard to resist."

"Then you will sign?" asked Reggie.

"I don't want to, but yes, I'll sign."

"How soon will the paperwork be ready for us to sign, Dad?"

"I have most of it ready. My attorney will be here shortly with his secretary. He has a lot for us to sign. He will take care of all the legal aspects for all my holdings in other countries. We need to go to the bank in the morning and sign some papers there as well. Thank you, son. I am really glad the both of you are here."

"Baby, I think we should go take a shower and get dressed before the attorney arrives."

CHAPTER 28

THE TAYLOR SUITES HOTEL JET left Heathrow International Airport at 2 p.m. the next day. Reggie insisted on flying back to Ohio with Quinn and Annie. He wanted to help capture the persons who were threatening the two most important people in the world to him. This had gone on long enough.

Quinn and Annie were sitting across the table from Reggie. Quinn and his father were having an in-depth conversation about finances. As Annie listened to their conversation, she found that she was in awe of the two Taylor men.

She had decided Quinn was so much like his father in so many ways. They were both extremely handsome. Quinn had very dark brown hair, while Reggie had dark hair with gray streaks, especially at his sideburns. Reggie was very distinguished looking. She could only imagine Quinn would age exactly like his father. She guessed that Reggie must have looked exactly like Quinn when he was his age.

They were each 6 foot 6 inches tall and they

have deep blue eyes. They even have the same hands, the same facial features, the same dimples and they are built the same; although, Reggie isn't as toned at his son. They laughed the same and their voices even sounded the same. If it wasn't for the age difference, one could almost swear they were twins.

She could listen to them talk to each other all day. They were so intelligent and were knowledgeable in so many subjects. Quinn adored his father; and anyone could tell that Reggie was very proud of his son.

There hadn't been any mention of Gloria since they left the bank that morning. How sad she thought. How could a beautiful woman become so bitter and betray a beautiful husband and her beautiful son? She had everything a woman could ever want. Did she have a craving for his money all along? Is that the reason she only had one child? Reggie said she was a good wife and mother. What really happened in her life? Surely, she didn't think I was a threat. Didn't she want to see Quinn happy? I don't think I will ever understand.

"You are awfully quiet, Annie," said her husband. "Are you okay?"

She smiled a big broad smile. "Yes, I'm okay. I've just been sitting here, listening to the two of you."

"I'm sorry," said Reggie. "We must be boring you to tears."

"On the contrary. I think I could listen to the two of you all day. I've actually decided that Quinn is an exact clone of his father."

"Is that a bad thing?" asked Reggie.

"Not from where I am sitting." Tears started to fill her eyes. "I love your son more than you will ever know! He is such an amazing man. I see where he gets it."

Quinn put his arm around her and pulled her in for a kiss. "Now, Dad, you see why I wanted to marry her so fast. Baby, it is I who is in awe of you! I love you, too, baby."

Reggie grabbed Annie and Quinn's hands and held them in his. "I want you both to promise me that you will love each other forever, as much as you do right now. No matter what life throws at you, never lose sight of what you really mean to one another. And above all, always be honest with each other. Promise me."

Annie nodded her head 'yes' as she looked at her husband.

"We promise, Dad."

"Good." He released their hands.

"Son, I wish I knew where I went wrong with your mother. She had been acting strange for about the last four or five years. Nothing ever seemed to be good enough for her. Seemed like I was always doing something wrong in her book. I really don't know what happened. I love your mom. I think a part of me always will."

341

"Are you sure she hasn't had an affair, Dad?"

"I don't think so. Maybe. I don't know." He paused. "I think... I think maybe," he stated as he started to choke on his words, "I could forgive her if she had, but what she did yesterday... she betrayed me, son. I don't think I could ever forgive her for betraying me. And what galls me more than anything is, she betrayed you, too."

"Yes, she did betray us, Dad, and I wish I knew why."

Reggie stood up and walked to the bathroom.

Quinn's jaw clenched. "I wish I knew what to do to help Dad through this."

"Right now, I think time is the best healer. Why don't you fix all of us a drink? It may settle his nerves a bit."

When Reggie returned to his seat, a Jack and coke was waiting for him. "Thanks, son. That's just what I needed."

"So, Annie, what do you think of England?"

"Well, I really haven't seen that much of it to form an opinion."

"We were going to have a little bit of a honeymoon while we were there, but it didn't work out that way. I'm sorry, honey."

"That's all right, baby. As long as we are together, I can wait on our honeymoon."

"When all of this is over, I'll take you someplace really special, okay?"

"Sounds good," and she smiled, laying her head on his shoulder.

"Have you called Pete Sanford, your private investigator yet?"

"No, Dad, not yet. When you gave us his number, we didn't know what date we would be back in Ohio, so we thought it best to wait."

"What about Chief Hansen?"

"I don't think I want to see him just yet, Reggie. I like your idea of letting Mr. Sanford find the information that I need."

"Dad, I haven't been able to devote as much time to the hotels since all of this shit started. Would you look after it for me for a while? I'm sure we are going to be busy with the private investigator and our own investigations, too. It would be a big help to me?" He figured this would keep his Dad safer and away from danger.

"Certainly, son. I'll do what I can, although I can't help but feel you are trying your best to derail me away from everything!"

"You know me well, Dad. I promise to keep you informed. If I need your help, I will let you know. But right now, I do need some help with the family business."

It was approximately 5 p.m. when they arrived in New York's LaGuardia International Airport. They got off the jet to stretch their legs and breathe in some of the warm August air while the jet was being refueled. Quinn telephoned Joe.

"Good evening, Joe. How's everything in Ohio?"

"Everything is fine. How's the honeymoon going?"

"It didn't happen. Someone broke into our room and ransacked it. We should be in Ohio in a couple of hours. I'll tell you all about it. I'd like to have a meeting this evening with you and Jax at the penthouse. Can you make it about 8 p.m.?"

"Sure. Have a safe trip. See you when you get here."

"Yeah, later."

Quinn ended his call with Joe and called Jax.

"Hey, man. Anything happening on the rooftop?"

"QT, how are you?"

"We're fine. Just thought I would check in with you. We'll be home in a couple of hours. Dad is with us. I want to have a meeting with you and Joe when we return about 8 p.m. Can you make it?"

"Yes, I'll be there. You sound very tired."

"I am. Can you get six more bodyguards for Dad? I want two following him everywhere he goes, every eight hours. I want them to start first thing in the morning."

"I'll get right on it. See you soon."

"Thanks, Jax."

The jet finally took off from LaGuardia International Airport at 6 p.m. They should be arriving at Port Columbus International Airport in approximately 1 hour and 20 minutes.

"Dad, Joe and Jax will be meeting with us

this evening at 8 p.m. at the penthouse. You are welcome to stay for the meeting, but I know you are very tired. I don't want you to leave the penthouse tonight. I have some security guards guarding the place tonight, but I have asked Jax to hire some bodyguards for you. They won't be able to start until sometime tomorrow or even the next day."

"You mean I'm not safe to walk around the hotel?"

"Reggie, we don't want anything to happen to you. Will you do as Quinn asked? Please?"

Reggie ran his fingers through his hair. When did I become the child? He shook his head. "All right, I'll do as you ask."

They all were very tired and the remainder of the flight was very quiet. Reggie fell asleep in his seat with his legs propped up, while Annie slept with her head resting on Quinn's shoulder. Quinn couldn't sleep at all.

His mind was racing, with a million things going through it. He couldn't seem to get the nagging question out of his head. Who knew they had gone to London? He'd bet his life that none of the Seals were responsible. There has to be another explanation.

Think, Quinn, think! We haven't found anymore listening devices or video bugs since we found them in and around Annie's apartment. Then it dawned on him. What about a tracking device? But, where would it be hidden? I know we don't have anything on our bodies, and it can't be on my cars, or on the jet. They knew exactly what room we were in at the hotel. It had to be the cell phones, but how can that be? I bought new ones when we were in Dublin.

He took his cell phone out of his pocket and removed the back. He removed the sim card and started looking underneath and all over the phone.

His Dad woke up. "What are you doing?"

"I'm checking my phone for some sort of tracking device."

"Here, you might want to use my pen light."

He took the penlight and examined the phone everywhere. "There's nothing there." He put his phone back together. "Annie, wake up, baby. I need your cell phone."

Annie yawned and reached down to get her purse and pulled out her cell phone and handed it to Quinn. He immediately started tearing it apart.

"What are you looking for?"

He didn't say anything as he was concentrating. He pulled the sim card out and looked underneath where it went. He took the penlight and looked closely at everything. Then he started smiling from ear to ear.

"I found it! It's a tracking device. Someone has been tracking our every move!" It looked like a small filament wire with a very small piece of clear tape holding it in place. It was taped to the inside back of the phone near the bottom.

He took his pocketknife and very gently peeled it from the phone. Next he cut it in half and then cut it in half again.

"Annie, have you loaned your phone to anyone since I purchased it for you?"

"Not that I can think… wait, I loaned it to Tony the night we married in Dublin. He said he left his phone at the hotel."

Quinn rested his head back on the seat. "If it's him, I swear I'll kill him with my bare hands!"

"What made you think to look for a tracking device?" asked Annie.

Just then the 'Fasten Your Seat Belt' sign came on. They would be landing in Port Columbus in just a matter of minutes.

"I'll tell you when we get back at the penthouse when we meet with Joe and Jax." He smiled. "Maybe this is the break we've needed. I feel more hopeful now that we will catch those bastards!"

Joe and Jax arrive at the penthouse at exactly 8 p.m.

"Quinn, I'm too tired to sit in on your meeting. I think I am going to take a shower and then go to bed. You can fill me in later."

"Okay, baby." He kissed her goodnight. "I shouldn't be too long."

"Dad, you remember Joe and Jax."

Reggie shook hands with them. "Of course, I

do. Quinn told me you have been very helpful. I personally want to thank you."

"You're quite welcome, Mr. Taylor. We would do anything to help Quinn," said Joe.

"Please, call me Reggie."

Quinn grabbed some beers from the refrigerator for himself and each of the men as they sat down at the dining room table. He proceeded to tell them about the break in at his hotel room in London and about the note.

"I think we have enough security guards and surveillance in the hotel for now. Were you able to hire some bodyguards for my father?"

"Yes, Quinn. Two bodyguards will be assigned to your father starting at 6 a.m. They will change shifts every eight hours.

"They will be waiting for you in the hallway. They have been instructed to follow you everywhere, sir."

"Now, for the good news," said Quinn. He took a small plastic bag from his pocket and placed it in front of Jax. "Do you know what this is?"

Jax took the bag and studied it carefully. "Yes, I think it is a tracking filament. I've been researching these since you called me a week ago with your idea. Where did you get this?"

"Annie's cell phone."

"Isn't that a new phone?" asked Joe.

"Yes. I bought one for her and one for Tony when we were in Dublin. And you will never guess who she loaned her phone to!" he said with amazement.

Everyone looked at Quinn.

"Tony O'Hara. He said he left his cell phone at the hotel that night when we went to Mac's Pub."

"That's odd," said Jax. "I'm almost certain I saw him use his cell phone right after you left to go back to your hotel."

"Now, we don't want to jump to conclusions just yet, but if I find out he's one of the two guys that's been raping women who look like Annie; and if I find out he is the one who wrote me that threatening note, I'm going to fucking kill him!"

"I thought he was Annie's friend," said Jax.

"I thought so, too. That's what is so hard for me to grasp. According to Annie, he had always been good to her. That's why it had been hard for me to believe he would do anything like this."

They took another drink of their beers.

"Listen up, everyone. Don't use your cell phones. I want to replace them. Check for any tracking devices, and then destroy your phones. Write down all your contact numbers. I think we should have new phone numbers. This request also includes you, Dad, and I want to buy one for Cindy, too. I will purchase new phones for all of us first thing in the morning. I think I am going to switch cell phone carriers for the time being. I want to be ahead of these fuckers for a change."

"I think that is a good idea, son. So when are you calling Pete?"

"We'll call him right after we get our new phones."

"Well gentlemen, it has been a very long day. I think I'm going to bed," announced Reggie.

"If there is nothing else, I need to get back to the club."

After Joe and Jax left, Quinn made sure all of the doors were locked tightly. turned out the lights, and walked into their bedroom.

He took a fast five-minute shower, toweled off and laid down next to his wife, naked. She was sound asleep. He spooned his body next to her back, but she quickly turned over and laid her head on his shoulder. Annie draped one arm over Quinn's chest. He kissed her lightly on her forehead. *"God, I love this woman so much! Lord in heaven, I thank you everyday for making her my wife. Please help me Lord to keep her safe. In Jesus name I pray, Amen,"* he prayed softly.

As tired as he was, he was having trouble sleeping. He was so stoked that he found the tracking device, but it weighed heavily on his mind. It was in Annie's phone. That worried him. He would not leave her side now for anything. What if it was Tony? What if Tony managed to kill him and got to her. No, he wouldn't let that happen! Not now, not ever! He told himself to go to sleep. He needed to be refreshed and alert at all times, especially now that his Dad was staying with him, too.

He awoke the next morning at 6 a.m. His wife was not in bed with him. That scared him. He walked to the bathroom to see if she was in there, but she wasn't. He ran into the living room and then into the kitchen. Annie and his dad were seated at the small kitchen table.

"Are you in the habit of running around naked, son?" He took another drink of his coffee and giggled. "I didn't know you were such an exhibitionist. This is a new side of you I didn't know existed."

"Maybe this is how I like to drink my morning coffee!" Quinn smirked as he sat down at the table and crossed his legs.

"Reggie, I'm sure he was just checking on me. Quinn, baby, please go put some pants on."

"Wife, are you embarrassed?" he said laughing.

"Err, no, but your father might be."

Quinn looked at his father who immediately looked back down at the newspaper he was reading. "All right," he said as he rolled his eyes.

Annie smacked her husband's behind as he walked back to their bedroom to dress. She laughed out loud as she walked to the stove to fix him some breakfast. Reggie looked at her.

"Life with Quinn is definitely going to be interesting."

CHAPTER 29

LATER THAT MORNING, QUINN PURCHASED six new cell phones. After her cell phone had been fully charged, Annie called Pete Sanford, the private investigator. She made an appointment to meet with him at 4 p.m. that day. He told her he didn't have an office, but would meet her at "The Village Café" on West Broad near the new casino. He said he would be wearing a tropical shirt.

Feeling confident they would not be tracked, Quinn and Annie drove to meet Mr. Sanford, alone.

She spotted Mr. Sanford sitting at a table in the far corner of the establishment.

"Mr. Sanford, I presume?"

"Who wants to know?"

"My name is Annie Taylor. We spoke this morning."

He stood and extended his hand out to shake.

"Mr. Sanford, this is my husband, Quinn Taylor."

"Glad to meet you, Mr. Sanford. You come highly recommended."

"You know, this is very unusual. I normally get cases where a spouse is investigating the other spouse. I don't usually have a meeting with both spouses at the same time." He eyed them very suspiciously. "You said I came highly recommended. I would be curious to know who made that recommendation."

"That would be my father, Reginald Taylor."

"Hmm, I thought you looked familiar. And I'm sorry to say, Mrs. Taylor, you look very much like those young ladies…"

"I know, sir," Annie said, cutting him off mid-sentence. "That is why we are here. I would like to hire you for your investigative skills. I would appreciate it very much if you would be very discreet about it."

"Hmm, I see. Before I accept this case, would you mind telling me whom you want investigated and why?"

Annie hands him a list. "First of all, I would like for you to track down the addresses of the six raped women on that list. Please don't approach these ladies. I am sure they are very fragile right now. I would rather talk with them alone. Maybe they could tell me something they forgot to tell the police, since I look so much like them."

She handed him another list of names. "Next, I would like for you to investigate these people. See if there are any connections to this case or each other."

"You want me to investigate two cops?"

"Yes, sir. That is why I need for you to be very discreet." She told him her reasons why.

"Mr. Sanford, I have very strong reasons for wanting these people investigated. Our lives are in danger, and someone has already tried to kill my husband. They are trying to kidnap me. We really need your help, sir."

"Will you help us?" asks Quinn.

"Do you think any of those men on your list are the rapists of those poor girls?"

"It is a very strong possibility, sir."

Mr. Sanford looked down at the two lists of names and programmed them into his cell phone.

Annie and Quinn looked at each other, wondering why he was doing that.

Looking over the top of his glasses, Mr. Sanford handed them back the list of names that Annie had given him. "Yes, I'll take your case. I don't like a paper trail. That's why I don't have an office. That way no one can break in and steal your information."

"Here are our phone numbers. You can contact my husband or me when you have something to report. If something happens and you can't get in touch with either of us, contact those last three cell numbers. They are my husband's best friends and his father. They will know what to do."

"Do you need a retainer fee?" asked Quinn.

"$15,000, upfront."

"$15,000?"

"Yes, sir. I'm expensive, but I am the best there is. I use the best equipment, work fast, and I can guarantee results."

"Will you accept a check?"

"Being as you are a Taylor, I'll accept it."

Quinn took his checkbook from his sport coat, wrote out a check in the amount of $15,000 and handed Mr. Sanford the check.

"I'll let you know if I need anymore expenses."

"Just make sure you have results, Mr. Sanford," said Annie.

"Yes, ma'am."

"One more thing, Mr. Sanford," added Quinn. "We needed this information yesterday. Do you understand what I am saying?"

"Yes, sir, I do."

"Call us day or night, Mr. Sanford. Thank you for seeing us."

By 11 a.m. the next day, Annie received a phone call from Pete Sanford, informing her that he had the addresses of the six rape victims. Three ladies lived in and around Columbus. One lady lived on Fishinger Road in Upper Arlington, one lived on Trabue Road, and another lived on Hayden Road. The other three ladies were from out of state and went back home to live with their parents. They lived in Florida, Arizona, and Kentucky.

Quinn was in a meeting with his father and a hotel manager in his penthouse office. Annie would have to wait to tell him the news.

She decided to sit down and think about what she would ask of these unfortunate women. She realized they might not want to talk to her. If they refused, she would understand why. If they agreed to talk to her, where does she begin? Then realization hit her. What if these women realize they were all raped because they looked like her? Shit, she thought. This could really get ugly. She didn't want that for these women. They had been through enough. She would introduce herself using her middle name, Marie Taylor, or she could just call herself Mrs. Taylor.

Now that she knew how she would introduce herself, what questions should she ask? Not realizing it, she spoke out loud. "Where do I start?"

"Where do you start with what, baby?" and Quinn leaned over and kissed Annie on the cheek. He grabbed a bottle of water from the refrigerator.

"Is your meeting over?" she asked.

"Yes, and I'm all yours for the rest of the day."

"Sit down, honey. We need to talk," she demanded.

Quinn took a drink of his water and sat down at the table next to her. "What's going on?"

"Pete Sanford just called. He gave me the addresses of the women."

"That's fast. Where do they live?"

"Three live in Columbus and three live across the country."

"So, do you want to talk with all six ladies or what?"

"Why don't we just visit the ones that live here and see how much info we can get, then make our decision on whether to travel to Florida, Arizona and Kentucky."

"If that is what you want."

"Quinn, I'm scared."

"Why?"

"What if they realize I am the reason they were raped?"

He squeezed her hand as he leaned forward and kissed her tenderly. "Baby, it's not your fault they were raped."

"I know that, Quinn, but these women are very fragile right now. I don't want to upset them. My interviewing them could produce a negative outcome for them."

"Yes, Annie, it could. But it could produce a positive outcome for us."

Annie frowned and looked down at her hands.

Quinn grabbed her hands in his. "Why don't we visit one of the ladies this afternoon and play it by ear. If you see it is going to upset her, we can leave. If that happens, maybe you could leave your phone number with her. She could change her mind and call you at a later time. Sometimes, just acting on your own instinct is the best way to go. Just do it and see where it takes you."

"You really think that is the best way to do it?"

"Yes, I do."

She looked at Quinn and wondered how she was so lucky to have met up with him. She moved herself over to his lap and put her arms around his neck. "I thank God everyday for deciding to go out with my cousins on July 3rd. You are the most amazing and wonderful man I have ever known."

"Hmm, I thought I was the only man you've ever known." His lips curled up a little and he gave her a panty-busting smile that only he could give.

"Well, you are the only man I've known-known. But you aren't the only man I have ever met."

"Oh, and what do you mean by that?"

She brushed his lips with hers and sucks on his lower lip. Tears started to fill her eyes. "You have been and always will be the only man in the world for me. I have never loved anyone before you and will never love anyone after you. You are it for me, baby, from here on out, through eternity, Quinnten Taylor."

Quinn put both of his hands on her face and gently wiped the tears from her eyes with his thumbs. "Oh, baby, I love you," he said as he looked into her eyes. "I've never felt or known love like this before. I know in my heart I will never love anyone but you."

They kissed, inserting their tongues into each

other's mouth and encircling them with a gentle force. When they had finished kissing, she kept her arms embraced around his strong shoulders and cried softly into his neck.

"Oh, baby, don't cry. Is there something else wrong, baby?"

"No," she said softly. "These are happy tears. I don't understand how I became so lucky to have you for my husband."

"Oh, baby, I'm the lucky one. God gave me you. And I'm not giving you away for anything in this world!"

He kissed her gently on the lips again. "Why don't you go fix your make-up and we'll go see one of the girls on your list. I want to get this whole investigation over with so that we can go on our honeymoon!"

CHAPTER 30

ANNIE DIDN'T WANT TO TAKE any bodyguards with them when they visited any of the ladies. She didn't want them to feel like they were in any danger. They chose to travel to Hayden Road in the Dublin district to visit with victim number three, Beatrice "Beatie" Smith. She was the oldest of the seven ladies at 20 years of age when the attack happened. She was probably going on 22 years of age now.

Quinn was feeling a little more relaxed in going out without an extra bodyguard. After all, they had gone to see Pete Sanford, the private investigator, and nothing happened. He would be extra cautious today and drive around to make sure they weren't being followed. He didn't want to lead the rapists back to any of the girls' homes in case they didn't know where they lived.

Annie was very nervous when she knocked on Miss Smith's door.

The door opened a tiny little bit and Annie heard a voice say, "Can I help you?"

"Miss Smith, Miss Beatrice Smith?"

The door opened wider and Miss Smith's eyes became very large. "You look like I use to look a year ago. Who are you? What do you want?" She started to shut the door.

"Please, Miss Smith. They're after me, too. Please, I need your help." Annie begged softly.

Miss Smith looked at them closely. "Who's the man?"

"He's may husband, Quinn Taylor. He's also my bodyguard everywhere I go. And my name is Anna Marie Taylor. I just want to ask you some questions."

"I've told everything to the police already. There's nothing else to tell."

"Please, Miss Smith. I've been following this case since we look so much alike. I'm very afraid. May we please come in? I promise we won't stay long. I just have a few questions, please?"

Reluctantly, she opened the door and allowed them to enter. "I'm keeping the door open. Please make it fast."

When they walked into the living room, the first thing Annie noticed was an 11 x 14 inch picture of Miss Smith with her long dark hair. She has much shorter hair now. "Forgive me, I can't believe how much we look alike."

Miss Smith was very guarded. "So what questions do you want to ask?"

"May we sit down, please?"

"Yes."

"I, we that is, don't want to talk to you about the rape itself. We are more interested in what you can tell us about what you saw. We've read everything in the newspaper and it hasn't been very revealing. I've even gone to the police and they won't talk to us about it. They've told me to hire a bodyguard.

"I know you know what it feels like to be petrified all of the time. Someone has been stalking me and I fear it's your attacker, I fear he is after me now.

"You should be afraid. There are two attackers."

"Two attackers?"

"Yes, two."

Annie knew this, but she didn't want Miss Smith to know she knew. "Did you see what they looked like?"

"My eyes had masking tape on them. I remember crying so much that the tape wasn't sticking very well to my cheeks. I remember it coming loose on one eye and I saw a tattoo on the upper left shoulder of one of the men."

"Could you tell me what the tattoo looked like?"

"It looked like a coat of arms, like a family crest or something."

"Were there any family names or designs— like a bird or a snake of some kind on it?"

"I really couldn't tell. My eyes were very fuzzy. I think I was drugged."

"Do you know where they took you?"

"No."

"Ma'am," asked Quinn, "May I ask you a few questions?"

"Okay."

"I was in the military for several years and I can remember many things about the undesirable places I had to go. Would you close your eyes and think back to how the building you were in smelled or felt. Do you remember anything?"

Miss Smith closed her eyes and her body tensed. "I remember it was very hot and smelly during the day and cold and breezy in the evening. It smelled like animals, old hay, and tobacco."

"That's interesting," said Quinn.

"Could you tell what kind of animals it smelled like?"

"I'm a city girl, sir, but if I had to guess, I would say horses, maybe cows, I don't know."

"Do you remember the floor?"

"It felt like dirt and straw."

"Do you remember hearing doors open?"

"No. Come to think of it, I think I heard the doors sliding open."

"Do you remember hearing any kind of noises when they weren't there?"

"No, except for maybe a nearby creek, and I think I heard a far away train."

"No cars, kids playing, dogs barking, anything?"

"There was nothing. Just total quiet."

"These men, did they, for lack of a better word, did they visit you together or separately?"

"Both, and quite often, too."

"Do you remember anything about these men, perhaps the way they smelled, the way they talked, chewed gum, laughed, anything ma'am?"

She closed her eyes again. "Oh, yes. I remember like it was yesterday. The one with the tattoo might have been a little taller. He was cleaner smelling. Always had on cologne, but he often smelled of beer. He was gentler than the other one. He said he wanted to give me pleasure in all ways. He was always humming.

The other one wasn't as nice. He liked to beat me during and after sex. I thought he was going to kill me. I was very afraid of him. He was clean, but he smelled of cigarettes and whiskey. And he had bad breathe."

"Did either of them have an accent?"

"Come to think of it, the gentler one had a bit of an accent. I think he tried to disguise his voice."

"Do you know what country he sounded like he came from?"

"I don't know. Could be British or Irish. It could have been Australian, for all I know."

"Do you remember anything else?" asked Annie.

"The mean one had on some kind of watch that kept dinging every hour."

"Like a Maritime watch?" asked Quinn.

"Yes, like a Maritime watch," she said.

"Miss Smith," said Annie, "we want to thank you for talking with us. If you could do us one more favor. Please don't tell the police we were here, and please don't tell the police anything that you think you may have forgotten that you told us. We have our reasons. We want to do our own investigation and see if we can't get these monsters off the street where they can't hurt anyone anymore." She reached into her purse and pulled out a piece of paper and an ink pen. "Here is my phone number. If you think of anything else, please call me day or night. Okay?"

"Thank you, ma'am."

"You are welcome, Mr. Taylor. You and your wife may come anytime. I won't speak to anyone. I hope you catch the bastards."

As they walked out onto the porch, Quinn took his time and assessed the area, looking at everything. Nothing looked out of the ordinary so they proceeded to their car.

"So, Quinn, what do you think?"

"I think you were magnificent with her." He started the engine and pulled out into traffic.

"About the maritime watch. Do you think it could be a Seal?"

"No, Annie. I don't think this person is a Seal."

"Oh?"

"Anyone can purchase a maritime watch, from a person in the military to the average Joe. Fishermen even purchase them. You can buy them online." He paused. "And besides that, I don't remember ever seeing a tat on any of the Seal's back described like she described and none of the Seals that I know smoke. So, I really don't think either of the men were Seals."

"That's good to know," she said.

"Do you suppose one of them could have been David Morgan? I know he smokes."

Both were very quiet for a while. "Have you ever seen a tat on Tony's back before?"

"That's what I have been trying to remember. I've seen him in a sleeveless t-shirt, but I don't think I have ever seen him without a shirt."

Quinn's cell phone rang. He took the phone out of his shirt pocket and answered it.

"Taylor."

"QT, it's Jax. Where are you?"

"We are on our way back to the hotel. Why?"

"I think I have developed a way of tracking Annie. I want to test it out."

"We'll be there in 15 minutes." He ended the call.

Quinn was smiling.

"What was that all about?"

"Remember when we were in New York and I called Jax with an idea?"

"Yes, I remember."

"Well, I asked Jax if he could develop a way of tracking you without using any kind of injectable device. I didn't think you would allow me to inject you with anything like that."

"Good thinking, Quinn, because I wouldn't ever do that."

"He has developed something and he wants to check it out."

"Did he say what it is?"

"No, but we will find out what it is when we get home."

CHAPTER 31

J AX WAS WAITING FOR THEM with Reggie in the kitchen when they arrived. He was looking very pleased with himself. There was a small box on the table setting in front of him.

They sat down at the table looking very intrigued. "So, Jax, this must be pretty damn special. You look very pleased with yourself."

"You bet your sweet ass, boss." He grinned from ear to ear.

"Okay, what have you got for us?"

"I have four items I think would be useful in locating Annie, when she decides she has had enough of you, boss and you can't let go." He winked at Annie as he started taking the items from the box.

He took out a brown ponytail holder with very small golden streaks running through it, a four by 5/8 inch brown hair barrette, a silver chain, and a small box. When he opened it up, there was an antique filigree ring.

"This one is my favorite. Annie, I took a guess,

but I figured you might wear a size 5. Would you put this on your right hand."

"So, how does all of this work?" asked Quinn.

"I bought the ponytail holder and the hair barrettes from the gift shop downstairs. I wrapped gold metallic thread around some tracking filament and I weaved it through the elastic band of the ponytail holder. I cut the ponytail holder in half and attached a clasp because filament doesn't stretch." He showed Annie how to unclasp and clasp it. "I was able to remove the top of the barrette and I wove the filament in a wavy design and glued it back on."

"The chain on the necklace is actually the tracking device. I would suggest you use one of your own pendants on this necklace."

Annie was wearing an 18-inch white gold chain with a small heart. The letter *A* was engraved in the middle of the heart. It was a gift to her from her grandmother when she graduated from high school. "Will this work?"

"That's perfect. If the rapist knows you, he will recognize the necklace and not suspect anything."

She unclasped her necklace, slid the pendant onto the tracking necklace, and fastened it around her neck.

"As I said, the ring is my favorite. This ring is antique white-gold filigree from the antique store down the street. I melted the band on the ring and was able to fuse the filament to the gold and make a new band. Quinn, you said money was no object and I thought this would be the best way."

"If it works, I won't care how much it costs."

"So now, I need your help in testing the signals range." He opened his laptop. "Do you see these two cartoon characters? One is Quinn and one is Annie. The moment you put any of those items on, it will show me where on your body it is, even if you put it in your pocket or your purse, as long as it is with you. Now watch this."

Jax keyed in another code on his computer and a GPS system displayed in the background. "Those items will show me where you are." Jax smiled. "I'm hoping the range will exceed my expectations, but I'm not really sure. That's why I need for you to help me test it."

"Wow, Jax, this is amazing! How far do you want us to drive?"

"I don't know. Fifty miles in all directions?"

"How many miles is it to where those girls were found on the rural roads?" asked Annie.

"That's a very good question." Jax started looking at the map and did a calculation from the hotel to the specific road where they were found. "From here, it looks to be about 25-30 miles."

"Jax, I have a question.

"I'm assuming these are all activated. Can they be turned off and reactivated at a later time?"

"That's another good question, Annie. Yes, these items are currently activated. I have given all of these items the same code sequence and the only way they can be turned off is through Quinn's computer. I can observe it on my computer in the surveillance room and I can hide it from view, but I cannot turn it off. Only QT can do that."

"Well, Annie, are you ready to go? We'll stop and get something to eat too."

"Quinn, I'll call you every 30 minutes and will let you know where you are. You can let me know if I am correct," Jax said.

"See you all tonight."

As they climbed into his Porsche, Annie asked, "Are you thinking what I am thinking?"

"Yes, that is if you are thinking of traveling to the rural roads where the girls were found."

"Do you have your gun with you?"

He smacked his right side under his sport coat. "I have it right here. But first, I want to run by Indian Creek and put this baby in the garage. I want to take my truck instead."

They arrived at Indian Creek 20 minutes later, parked the Porsche in the garage and walked over towards a chocolate brown dual cab Silverado 4x4 truck.

"You know, Quinn, we haven't been back here since that first night. I'd really like to take a tour of your house."

"You are right. We haven't been back, and it is OUR house now."

He lifted Annie into the front seat as the truck

stood a little too tall for her to climb into. He smiled at her showing his dimples.

"We'll come back soon, and when we do, I want more French toast with syrup. Then I want you on every surface of our house. We will initiate every corner and space because I want us to make our own memories. I want you to remember everywhere we have been, baby."

He fastened her seatbelt and leaned in for a soft kiss on her lips. He didn't stop there. He invaded her mouth with his tongue and swirled it around in her mouth. "Damn, I wish we could do it now." He ran his hands through her long dark hair. "You are so beautiful; and you are all mine!"

He climbed into the truck, opened the garage door, started the engine, backed out of the garage and closed the garage door.

It took about 40 minutes to get to Route 37. Quinn pulled his truck to the side of the road and took out a map.

"The girls were found on this road, but it runs for a few miles. I don't know where on this road the girls were found. But something Miss Smith said has me baffled. She said she smelled tobacco. No one has grown tobacco in these parts in a lot of years. It's mostly corn, soy or pumpkins."

"Are there any connecting roads to Rt. 37?" asked Annie.

"Yes, there are several. Seems to me, there was an old farm around here years ago. If memory serves me correctly, the farm had two huge barns. Someone was killed in one of the barns when it caught fire and burned to the ground. The owner was an old man and he died shortly thereafter. There were no living relatives, so the property went to the state."

His cell phone rang. "Taylor."

"You are on Rt. 37," said Jax.

"You are totally awesome, man! Are all of the items showing up on display?"

"They sure are!" replied Jax.

"Jax, I'm heading south on Rt. 37 to see just how long this road is and to see what roads veer off of it. We might need that information later. Something is telling my gut that the rapists took the girls to an old barn located near here. I just don't know where the barn is located." His gut was also telling him that danger might be ahead.

"Quinn, can we go back now? All of a sudden, I don't like this place. I want to leave, now. Please?"

Quinn pulled his truck over as far to the right of the road as he could and turned around. After all, his wife's instincts have not been wrong when she thought someone was watching her. He wasn't going to doubt her instincts now.

They headed north on Rt. 37, but, instead of turning west on Interstate 70, Quinn turned towards the east. They would be near Buckeye Lake. He was hungry and wanted to find a nice restaurant for dinner before heading back to the hotel.

They drove past pizza places, ice cream shops, burger joints, and a chicken and rib place. Nothing seemed to appeal to either one of them, so they decided to head back to Columbus. Quinn had decided he wanted a big, thick, juicy steak and he wanted it to moo at him.

Just as they were passing the junction for Rt. 37 on I-70, Annie let out a gasp.

"Quinn, I think I just saw Detective Brown turning onto Rt. 37."

"Did he see you?"

"No, I don't think so."

"Good. I know he knows we have the Lexus and the Porsche, but I don't think he knows I have this truck. I bought this right before we met and I haven't really driven it anywhere."

To be safe, he took the exit onto Swamps Rd and turned west onto Rt. 40.

"I'm glad you know where you are going. I don't know where we are."

"I've traveled these roads many times over the years. Don't worry, I know how to get us home." He squeezed her knee. "I'll keep you safe, baby."

"I don't doubt that one bit," she said smiling as she laid her hand on his.

He kept his hand on her knee for several minutes.

"You know Quinn, you should always drive

with both hands on the steering wheel. After all, you are always saying you will keep me safe. Well, I want the same thing for you. I want you to be safe, too."

He smiled a wide toothy grin and showed his dimples.

"I would love to kiss you all over your face when you smile with those big dimples of yours. You just don't know what you do to me when you smile like that!"

"Really? Maybe I should pull over somewhere so that we can make-out in the car."

She let out a giggle. "You just keep on driving. I want to go home. I'm hungry!"

"What are you hungry for, baby?" he teased with a very husky voice.

"Why, food! What else is there?" she admonished.

"You are so bad, Mrs. Taylor. So bad!"

She scrunched her nose up at him with another grin.

"You know, Annie, I can't believe how much better I feel with you in my life. I feel like I am at home with you, like you are where I belong. I hope you are in this for the long haul because there is no way I will ever let you go."

"I feel the same way about you, too. If you ever left me, I think I would curl up into a little ball and just die. The thought of losing you scares the hell out of me, Quinn."

"You know you really shocked me that first evening we spent together."

"Shocked you? Really? I know you shocked me!" she said with a giggle.

"I know, again, I'm sorry. But, up until that time, I had never had a virgin before and no woman, and I mean no woman, has ever run out on me before, either. You really threw me for a loop that night! I mean I know us guys can do stupid things sometimes, but how was I supposed to act?"

"Like a grown-up, I would think!" she said laughing.

"Maybe, but you stole my car!" he said in a matter of fact tone.

"I did not steal your car, Quinn Taylor. I borrowed it. And besides, nothing happened to your precious car and I returned it to your hotel within 15-20 minutes. Besides, I wanted to get as far away from you as I could."

He frowned. "You know, I wasn't very grown up when that happened. You made me feel like a major prick and no other woman has ever made me feel like that."

"I'm sorry, Quinn. After that happened, I thought I had done something wrong. I felt humiliated. I didn't think you liked me."

Quinn pulled over into an empty parking lot.

"Annie, I've never wanted another woman as much as I wanted you that night. And strange as it may seem, I knew that very evening, I wanted you to be mine forever."

He unbuckled her seat belt and pulled her as close to him as he could. "I love you, baby, more than life." He kissed her lips, invading her mouth with more emotion than he had ever kissed her.

She moaned. "I'm going to love you forever!" and she started kissing his dimples, his lips, and his chin.

"Oh, baby, I have got to get you home!"

They arrived at the hotel at 7:30 p.m. Quinn scooped Annie up in his arms to carry her back to the penthouse.

"Quinn please put me down! I want to go to the restaurant to eat. I thought you were hungry and wanted a steak!"

"We can eat later, baby. Right now I want you!"

Annie's stomach started to growl loudly. "I'm starving. I haven't eaten anything since this morning and I'm starting to feel a little weak. Please take me to the restaurant. Please?" and she batted her eyelashes at him.

"Okay. I would feel terrible if you passed out on me." He kissed her on her nose and placed her feet back on the floor.

"Thank you."

"What would you like to have, baby?" he asked as he sat down next to her at a table.

"Are you still ordering a steak?"

"Yes."

"Could you order the big 22 ounce steak and share it with me? The smaller steak is too big for me."

"Do you want the usual then?"

"Yes."

Just then the waitress arrived at their table.

"Good evening. My name is Jolene and I will be your server this evening." She handed them each a menu. "What would you like to drink?"

"Good evening, Jolene. We would like to have two glasses of iced tea please."

"Would you like to have an appetizer?"

"No, thank you, Jolene, but we do know what we want to order."

"Yes, sir. What would you like?"

"My lady would like to have a small cranberry pecan salad with ranch dressing on the side and a small baked potato with butter and sour cream. I would like to have the 22-ounce steak, rare with a baked potato and the house salad with red dressing. And please bring us an extra plate."

"I'm sorry, sir, but the cranberry pecan salad comes in one size and it is quite large."

"You obviously don't know who I am, do you?" he said very angrily.

"I'm sorry, sir. Would you like to speak to my superior?"

"Yes, I would," he said emphatically.

Oh goodness, Annie thought. Is he really angry or is he in one of those moods where he liked to give his staff a hard time just because he thought he could for the fun of it.

As Jolene turned to walk back into the kitchen, Quinn got up to follow her. Annie followed to make sure he didn't go off the deep end with the waitress.

"Sir, you can't go into the kitchen with me. It is against health code regulations."

He walked into the kitchen and eyed Eula Stewart, his favorite employee, cooking at the stove.

"Jolene, is it?" he shouted. "I'll have you know I can go anyplace I want in this hotel. I pay lots of money to stay here and that means I can go anywhere I want!" He pointed his finger at her, trying his best to stifle a grin.

"Jolene, he ain't no paying customer!" and she swatted his behind with a towel.

"Would you like me to call the police, ma'am?"

She looked at Quinn with a glare in her eyes. "I don't think I would, Jolene. He's your boss. He owns this hotel and the restaurant and lives in the penthouse on the top floor of this hotel."

"Eula, how's my favorite girl?" Quinn asked as he picked her up and swung her around.

"Put me down, you over-grown boy! Why do you always try to scare my staff?" she scolded. "I ought to turn you over my knee!" she giggled.

"I'd pay good money to see that!" replied Annie with a laugh!

Quinn grinned from ear to ear showing his double dimples. "Because I know how it riles you!"

"Jolene," said Quinn. "Please accept my apology. You did everything correctly. You passed the test."

"Ump!" She glared at him for a few seconds with a frown. "Don't do that to me ever again! I don't appreciate arrogant bosses!" she said as she shook her finger at him and then walked away.

"Well," Eula laughed, "I guess she's got your number now, doesn't she!"

CHAPTER 32

ITWAS 11 A.M. AND Annie had just finished taking a shower when she received a phone call from the private investigator that she and Quinn had hired.

"Hello."

"Mrs. Taylor, this is Pete Sanford. I have some very important news for you." He said in a very business like tone.

"Very good, sounds like you have been very busy. What is your news, Mr. Sanford?"

"It's too important to tell over the phone. Can you come to the Village Café right away? I'm afraid it is of grave importance. I would come to you, but I have another appointment in an hour and I must prepare for it."

"Certainly. I'm on my way," and she hung up her cell phone.

"Shit, I need to tell Quinn, but he is in an important meeting and I hate to disturb him," she said out loud. "What should I do?"

She hurried to her closet and picked out a pair of jeans and a shirt to wear. She slipped on a pair of bikini panties, her bra, and a pair of ankle socks. She scurried back to the bathroom and brushed her teeth, quickly applied some make-up and dried her hair. She threw her shirt on over her head and put the tracking necklace that Jax had made for her around her neck, using the letter *A* pendant her grandmother had given to her. Next she brushed her hair.

She decided to let her hair hang long, but pulled the sides of the hair to the back of her head near the top and secured it with the hair barrette that Jax had made.

When she had put her jeans and her shoes on, she put the ponytail holder in the front pocket of her jeans and slipped the antique ring with the tracking device on her ring finger of her right hand. She was not going to leave anything to chance, in case one of the devices failed to work.

She was reasonably sure she would be safe. Nothing had happened over the past week when she and Quinn had been out alone in Columbus and the surrounding areas. Anyway, with the tracking devices, she felt safer.

She started pacing the floor having second thoughts about leaving. What if this was a bad idea? This would really piss Quinn off if I go, even if nothing happened to me, but we need this information. Mr. Sanford said it was of grave importance and wouldn't give the information out over the phone. Maybe I should call Quinn.

She reached for her cell phone and called Quinn's number. It went straight to voice mail. "Shit!" she yelled. She decided to leave him a message.

"Quinn, it's me. It is 11:25 a.m. I just got a call from Pete Sanford. He said he has some information that is extremely important that we should know about. He has to leave in an hour and asked if we could come right away. I've tried calling you, but since I can't get ahold of you, I'm going on my own. I have all of the tracking devices turned on, just in case. I'm going to the Village Café. I will just go there and come straight back. Please don't be mad. I love you with all my heart!"

Her gut was telling her to turn around, but on the other hand, she was feeling liberated in not letting those rapists dictate what she did each day. She was tired of not having the control to be able to go anywhere she wanted at anytime during the day without a bodyguard. She wanted her life back the way it used to be!

In the back of her mind, she felt that maybe that was the only way she could get her life back. Maybe she should put herself out there to get caught. But what price would she pay? Would Quinn be able to find her with the new tracking devices she was wearing? Would he be able to save her? Would Quinn be killed in the process? A shiver went through her body at that thought. *"Please God, No! Please keep him safe!"* she pleaded.

Would she be killed? *"Oh Dear God, Please keep us both safe!"*

Another thought popped into her head. Would Quinn be so pissed at her for going that he would want to end their marriage, claiming he would not be able to trust her anymore? After all, Reggie booted Gloria to the curb because he couldn't trust her. But, then, this situation is completely different. A cold chill ran through her to the bone. I'll just have to take my chances. I am tired of all this shit! Oh, Annie, what the hell are you doing this for?

In a moment of strong determination, she grabbed her purse and her car keys and headed out of the door towards the elevator.

There were two guards standing in the hallway guarding their penthouse. "Mrs. Taylor, are you leaving?"

"Yes sir, I am. There is no need to follow. I'm not going to be gone that long. My husband knows I am leaving."

"Yes ma'am."

Before starting the engine to her car, she took her cell phone from her purse and placed it over the sun visor. She wanted to be able to answer her phone quickly, should he call.

She arrived at the Village Café in fifteen minutes. Before she got out of her car, she looked around to make sure she hadn't been followed. Everything looked all right, so she put on a face of confidence and walked inside to meet with Mr. Sanford.

As before, Mr. Sanford was sitting in the corner in the back of the café. He stood to greet her, and offered his hand for her to shake. "Good afternoon, Mrs. Taylor. Thank you for coming so quickly."

"You are very welcome."

"Can I get you a cup of coffee."?

"No, thank you, sir. We need to do this quickly."

"Very well," he said as they both sat down. "In my investigations, of all of the people you wanted me to check into, I found a link between three of the persons on your list. I found it to be quite strange."

"Oh, how so?"

"It would appear that Dr. Charles Gilmore has two sons, but neither of the boys go by their father's last name. Charles Gilmore was married to Nancy Brown Gilmore in 1982. They lived in Portsmouth, Ohio. They had one son in 1983. His name is William Gilmore. William or Willie, as he was called, did not have a good relationship with his father."

Annie's eyes suddenly become very large and she let out a gasp and covered her mouth.

"Now this is where it gets interesting. William and Nancy Gilmore divorced right after he graduated from high school in 2001. When the couple divorced, Willie took on his mother's maiden name and changed his name legally to

William Brown. You know him as Detective Billy Brown."

"Oh My God! That's why I didn't recognize him. His hair is darker and longer and he looked so much older. And with his name change, I can't believe I didn't recognize him! That's why the police can't find who the rapists are! He must be one of the rapists, and he is doing something to all of the evidence!"

"Now, I'm not finished. I said he has two sons. The other son is Tony O'Hara. Somewhere around 1990, Charles Gilmore had an affair with Sarah O'Hara while married to Nancy. He refused to leave Nancy after finding out Sarah was pregnant. Sarah went back to her hometown in Dublin, Ireland, to have her baby. Right after she went back to Ireland, Nancy found out and left Charles, but they didn't divorce until little Willie had graduated from high school."

"Oh my God! It's all making sense to me now. What about the other names on my list?"

"The three Seals are good men, but I'm not so sure about David Morgan. Several women have claimed he got them pregnant; although, they won't say he raped them. Some of my sources have told me that his father has paid these girls handsomely to not file charges against him. In my opinion, he is nothing but a slime ball." He paused. He noticed Annie's face looked very distressed. "Are you all right, ma'am?"

Annie was starting to have that odd feeling come over her again, just like when they were on old Rt. 37 and she asked Quinn to turn his truck around. A cold chill ran up her arm as she looked around the room. Tears started to stream down her face. She was very scared.

"I-I must leave now. I need to get back to my husband right away." She reached for her purse. "Thank you for the information. You have been most helpful, Mr. Sanford." She ran out of the door before he could stand up from the table.

⬥

Quinn was in a meeting in one of the boardrooms of the hotel when he received an urgent text from Jax:

> Come quickly. David Morgan is
> in the lobby of the hotel.

Quinn grabbed his cell phone. "Excuse me, gentlemen, I have an emergency. Father will you take over?" and he dashed out of the door like a bolt of lightening.

Jax, Champ, and Joe arrived at the same time as Quinn. They encircled Morgan.

Not wanting to make a scene in the middle of a somewhat crowded lobby, Quinn ordered David Morgan to follow them.

Quinn led the way to the ground floor where the

boiler room was located. There was a vacant room there that would enable them to talk privately.

"Sit down!" Quinn yelled. "I ought to kill your fucking ass right now for what you've done to Annie and those girls! Where the hell have you been hiding?" Just as Quinn slammed his hands down hard on the table, his cell phone pinged indicating a voice message. Quinn didn't hear the ping.

"I'm sorry for what I did to Annie. I truly am, but I can explain. I can help you. I know who the rapist is."

"I don't trust you, Morgan. You would rat out your own father if you thought it would save your sorry ass!"

"I promise, I have proof, here, in my back pac! I want to help save Annie!"

"Why would you want to help her? You tried to rape her in her freshman year of college! What decent guy does that to a woman? Huh, Morgan? You are a first class prick!"

"I'll admit, I was wrong, but I was crazy drunk when I tried that! I wanted her to me mine! She was just so beautiful!"

"Careful now, you are talking about my wife!"

"You're married? When?"

"Doesn't matter! Why were you stalking her?"

"I-I wanted her to me mine in the beginning, but then I was trying to protect her."

"Why would you need to protect her?"

"There was a guy on campus following her around. He looked kind of shady."

"How do you know he was watching her? There must me hundreds of kids on campus every day!"

"He had binoculars and he was always looking her way."

"Did you report it to anyone?"

"Yes, I reported it to Dr. Charles Gilmore."

"I didn't see him as much after that, but he still came around once in a while."

"Why should I believe you? You had fucking video feeds in her apartment watching her getting dressed, taking showers, you pervert! You broke into her apartment, Morgan. Why did you do that?"

Quinn made a fist and slugged him hard in the jaw. "Why would you do that?" he yelled. "You are nothing but a perverted little weasel!" And he slugged him in the jaw again. "Tie his fucking ass up. I don't trust this son of a bitch!"

CHAPTER 33

As soon as Annie walked out of the Village Café, she looked around to see if anyone she knew was there, particularly Willie Gilmore aka Billy Brown and/or Tony O'Hara. She had a feeling that someone was watching her. She was very scared and she knew she must get into her car and take off. She must go home and tell Quinn the news.

Seeing no one familiar, she punched her key sensor for her car to unlock and ran to the driver's side of the car. She opened the door and just as she started to climb into the car, someone grabbed her from behind and put a wet cloth over her mouth and nose. Her purse dropped to the ground.

She fought with all of her might to get loose from her attacker, but he had such a strong hold on her. She felt she was losing ground and succumbed to the anesthesia, known as Ether. When she had completely passed out, her kidnapper put her into the passenger seat of his car.

Quinn heard his cell phone ring. It was Pete Sanford. He listened to what Pete was telling him and it knocked the breath out of his lungs. "Would you lock her car and secure her purse? I'll be there when I can." He hung up.

He noticed he had a voice mail from Annie. He listened. "FUCK!" he yelled. "Champ, stay with Morgan. Don't let him out of your sight and keep a gun on him. If he tries to escape, shoot him in his balls! Jax, grab your laptop and meet us in the garage. We need to track Annie. She's been kidnapped. Joe, come with me!"

All three men took off running towards the elevator. Jax went to the surveillance room to get his laptop and Quinn and Joe went into the penthouse. They quickly changed into camouflage pants, shirts, and boots.

Quinn opened up his gun safe and took out three Smith and Wesson 9 mm pistols with several 17 round clips and three long-range rifles with scopes and extra bullets.

Joe helped himself to three long hunting knives; three camouflage hats, a pair of pants, a shirt, and a pair of boots for Jax. It was a good thing they all wore the same size clothing. Jax could change in the truck.

Quinn grabbed his keys and the holster he had been wearing with another gun. He and Joe got on the service elevator and went to the garage floor. Jax was already waiting on them with his laptop.

Joe handed Jax some clothes to change into. He gently placed some weapons on the floor of the truck, behind the front driver's seat.

<hr />

They climbed into Quinn's truck. It was a 4x4 with a stick shift and a V-8 engine. It was capable of going up to 160 miles an hour.

Quinn started the engine and peeled out of the garage as fast as he could.

"Please tell me the tracking device is working!" Quinn barked.

"Yeah, it's working. They are on the move. It looks like they are headed to the place you were last night, on Rt. 37."

He pulled his cell phone out and dialed 911. "This is Reserve Officer Taylor. This is an emergency. Patch me through to Chief Hansen!" he ordered. He handed the phone to Joe. "Tell him what is going on. Ask him to cut me some slack with my driving and to have him and Detective Evans meet us on Rt. 37 as soon as possible. Tell them to not use their sirens or lights. And don't send anyone else."

"Chief Hansen's office."

"Maggie, this is Reserve Officer Joe Turner. This is an emergency. I need to speak with Chief Hansen."

"Right away, sir." She transferred his call to Chief Hansen's office.

"This is Chief Hansen."

"Chief, this is Reserve Officer Joe Turner. Annie Taylor has been kidnapped. We know who the kidnappers are and we know where they are hiding. We are on our way there now."

"Are you telling me the Columbus Rapists have kidnapped her and you know where they have taken her?"

"Yes sir," he paused, "Chief Hansen, Detective Billy Brown is one of the rapists."

"Say that again. I thought I heard you say Detective Billy Brown is one of the rapists."

"Yes sir, that is correct. Billy Brown is one of the rapists. Can you put a bulletin out to all law enforcement to NOT follow us? We don't want any sirens or lights or any grand standers."

"If Billy has a radio with him, he'll hear it and take off before you get to him. He could even kill Mrs. Taylor in the process, if he thinks he is being cornered."

"Chief, we just passed a state trooper and he is in full pursuit of us. Can you contact him and ask him to lead the way to I-70 and then to the park and ride on old Rt. 37?"

"Yeah, hang on a minute."

The phone was silent for approximately three or four minutes. "Joe, are you still there?"

"Yes sir, I am," responded Joe.

"I have contacted the Ohio State Patrol. Slow down enough to allow him to get in front of you.

I have explained the situation. He will lead you to the park and ride. I'm on my way."

"Good," replied Joe. "We'll fill you in there. Come in an unmarked car. We don't want to scare off anyone. If you are not there within five minutes of our arrival, we are going on without you."

Quinn slowed his truck down enough so the Ohio State Trooper could move in front of him. The patrol car had his lights and sirens going, while Quinn had his truck flashers following the trooper. They were traveling at speeds in excess of 120 miles an hour.

It didn't take as long as they thought to arrive at the park and ride. When they pulled into the parking area, the State Trooper walked over to speak with Quinn to offer assistance. He noticed that Quinn and his two friends were dressed in Navy fatigues. "Are you military police?" the trooper asked.

"No sir, we are not, but we are working with the Columbus PD on this case." He flashed his reserve officer's badge. Quinn briefly explained that his wife has been kidnapped and was being held in an old barn off Rt. 37. He told him the kidnappers were the two men who raped seven young women and that all of the women looked like his wife. He asked the trooper to wait for Chief Hansen and fill him in.

"Joe, there are a box of flares in the side compartment of the truck. Can you get them out please and put them in the front seat?" asked Quinn.

"Sure thing, QT."

Quinn turned to look at the trooper. "When the Chief gets here, head south on Rt. 37. We'll leave a flare in the road to show you where to turn. One flare, turn left, two flares turn right. Make sure your lights and your sirens are off. Don't drive up to the barn, park a distance away and keep all communications off. I want the element of total surprise. I have got to keep my wife safe. Understand?"

"Oh, one more thing, tell Chief Hansen to send an officer to Taylor Suites. We have David Morgan tied up in the boiler room of the hotel. I'm sure my wife will want to file charges on him for stalking her and invading her privacy."

"Jax, do you know how far we need to travel?"

"I'd say two, maybe three miles. They are on the right side of the road."

"My gut tells me Annie is in real danger."

Quinn felt like he had aged 100 years since he had received Pete Sanford's phone call. Why didn't she just wait for me? Why didn't she just interrupt me in my meeting? If anything happened to her, I will kill the fucker! He was getting nervous and started to shake. Then he remembered something Annie said to him recently. "I need for you to think with your head and not your heart. I don't want anything to happen to you because of me, Quinn. I don't want to lose you. I love you too much!"

For some unknown reason, that soothed him. He closed his eyes for a moment. He said a little prayer. *"Dear Lord, help us save Annie. Help me to think with my head and not my heart. Please, Lord, help me and my friends stay safe. In the Lord's name I pray, Amen."*

He hadn't realized he had said this prayer out loud, until he heard Jax and Joe say Amen in unison.

He looked at his friends. "Are we ready?" And just like when they were on a mission in the Navy, all three bumped their fists together and yelled, "Hell, yeah!"

Quinn started the engine and headed south on Rt. 37. They drove about two miles and Jax instructed Quinn to turn right at the next road. He stopped before he turned right so that Joe could get out and ignite two flares. He placed them in the middle of the road to alert Chief Hansen where to turn.

———◆———

Annie was starting to wake. She tried to move her arms, but she couldn't. She was handcuffed to a chair. Her shirt and pants had been removed, but she still had her bra and panties on. She heard voices. Two men were arguing about her. She tried to open her eyes, but they had been taped shut. Tears started flowing from her eyes. She let out a whimper.

"Tony?" she said softly. "To-Tony, is that you?"

"To-Tony, I know it's you. I recognize your voice."

He walked over to where she was sitting and pulled the tape from her eyes.

"Don't do that!" said Billy. "She'll see who we are!"

"I don't think it matters much now, Billy. I think she already knows."

Annie blinked rapidly to get the tears from her eyes. Tony wiped them with his thumbs.

"Why are you doing this, Tony? I thought you were my friend! You were my best and only friend in the world, Tony. Why, please tell me why would you do this!" she begged softly. Her heart was broken at the friendship she had lost.

"It's... complicated Annie. I had to do this to protect you from him! I've been in love with you from the moment I helped you pick up your books outside our apartments two years ago."

"Get away from her!" yelled Billy.

"I'm going to help save you and then we can run away and marry!" he whispered.

"No, Tony, I can't marry you! I love Quinn!"

"I said, get away from her, NOW!" yelled Billy as he cracked a whip over Tony's back.

He used the whip on Tony a few more times.

397

"She's Mine!" he yelled in a terrible growl that sent chills down Annie's body.

Tony was able to grab the whip and pull it from him. He tossed the whip to the side of the barn. He circled Billy a couple of times, sizing him up. "You are a sadistic son of a bitch, Billy. I won't let you hurt her!"

"And what pray tell made you think you are any better than me, O'Hara?" He growled. "You are just as guilty as I am. You raped those other girls as much as I did and you enjoyed it! You are a bigger piece of shit than I am!"

Annie kept squirming in her seat, trying to escape. She didn't want to be here and she didn't want to watch them eviscerate each other.

Tony lunged at Billy, hitting him in the stomach with his fist and again in the mouth.

Billy staggered. Blood was streaming down his chin. He laughed, loudly. "Yea, I'll admit it. I get off on beating women. It puts them in their place where they belong! But you, you like to shave their heads to make crazy messages. You, O'Hara are the sick son of bitch!"

Billy threw a one-two punch at Tony and hit him first in the eye and then in the jaw.

He nearly fell, but caught his balance. He took off running after Billy and crashed into him, pushing him on the ground. Tony sat on top of him and beat him with his fists over and over.

Billy managed to flip Tony over and put him

into a scissor lock around his neck with his legs, chocking him.

Tony managed to grab ahold of Billy's arm and head and was able to get away from his deathly grip.

Tony knocked him in the side of his head with his fist.

Billy lay motionless, trying to catch his breath.

Tony yelled at him. "I told you, she's mine!" He pulled an extra set of handcuff keys from his pocket and started to walk towards Annie to set her free.

Billy stood up and drew his gun. "TONY, I WOULD RATHER KILL HER AS TO LET YOU HAVE HER!" He aimed the gun at Annie.

"NO!" Tony yelled and jumped in front of Annie as Billy fired a shot.

CHAPTER 34

"QUINN, PULL OVER HERE," SAID Jax. "The barn is about 100 yards away."

The weeds in the fields beside the road were very tall. No one had taken care of this property in years. Quinn pulled his truck off the road into the weeds. He gathered some sticks and make an arrow on the road pointing to his truck and an arrow pointing up ahead.

They grabbed all of their weapons and cautiously ran in the direction of the barn. They were about 40 yards away when they heard a gunshot and a blood-curdling scream. It sounded like Annie's voice.

They ran as fast as they could and within seconds, they saw the drive area leading up to the barn. There were two vehicles. One was an old Ford Bronco, and the other was an unmarked cop car. Quinn could only assume the cop car was driven there by Billy Brown, so the other car must belong to Tony O'Hara.

He heard another scream. Quinn motioned for Jax to move to the right, and he motioned for Joe to go to the left. He was going to go straight up the middle.

He noticed the door to the barn was slightly opened. He sidled himself beside the door and peeked in. The only thing he could see were stalls on both sides of the barn, probably for livestock of some kind. Many of the doors to the stalls were just barely hanging onto the hinges, as the wood was very rotten. Above the stalls was a loft, probably where hay was stored. There were many holes in the loft, as well as on the roof. The barn hadn't been used in decades. He could hear a male voice, but could not make out what he was saying.

Quinn, with gun in hand, quietly eased his way into the barn, walking in the dark shadows to hide himself. He didn't want to be seen. As he crept closer to where Annie was being held, he saw a male body lying on the ground near her with a gunshot to his back. Annie was in a chair, with just her underwear on and her hands cuffed behind her back.

His jaw clenched. He wanted to kill him. He noticed on the left side of the barn, there was an old mattress with blood splattered on it and a couple of dirty looking blankets. On the wall above the mattress were some chains, ropes and cuffs. This must be where the girls were raped. To the right of the bed was an old table. On the table lay scissors, white poster board, tape, and an assortment of sadistic sex tools, which were for torture and torture only.

There was an assortment of switches, whips, canes, floggers, belts, chains, a spreader bar and other items. To the right of the table, he noticed a large amount of dried blood on the ground. When Quinn looked up, he could see where someone had been hanging as some of the wood on the beam had split. This must be were Brown had beaten each of the girls. This was one sick bastard.

He closed his eyes for a quick second, telling himself to save Annie first and then kill the son of a bitch next. He looked around to see where Jax and Joe were located. He told himself to stay calm. Treat Brown like he was a Taliban like he encountered while actively serving as a US Navy Seal. Brown may be an American, but today, he is the fucking enemy and the enemy needs to be killed. The military taught him to kill or be killed. Today, Brown dies!

He positioned himself in a spot where he didn't think he could be seen, although his friends knew exactly where he was. He aimed his gun at Brown, telling himself he would rather kill him with his bare hands. He waited for Brown's next move.

"Now, look what you made me do. You made me kill my baby brother!" Billy said with a wicked sneer, showing no remorse. He walked slowly towards Annie.

"Get away from me, you sick piece of shit!" and she screamed once more.

He walked very slowly around her. "Hmm, now, what am I going to do with you?" he said very calmly. He looked her over very closely and licked his lips. "Hmm, I have dreamed about this day since you were 12 years old, my little sex kitten," he stated very slowly.

Annie had chills go through her body just thinking about what he just called her. "You are a sick, perverted creep!" she yelled out. "You make my skin crawl!"

He holstered his gun and took his gun belt off, laying it down on the ground. He slowly unbuttoned his shirt, but didn't remove it. He flexed his muscles and removed the belt from his pants. He folded the belt together and then made it smack a loud slapping sound. He did it again, and then again. The sound of his belt smacking together scared her.

"Its just you and me now," he said as he smacked the belt together. "I could kill you first and then have my way with you, but somehow I don't think it would be nearly as fun as watching you squirm against my body." He smacked the belt together one more time, smacking it very hard.

"Don't you dare come anywhere near me! You are nothing but an animal! A vicious, ugly animal!"

She stated through gritted teeth. "I'm warning you, if you so much as lay one finger on me, my husband with kill you!"

He slapped her hard across the face with his hand. "You lying little bitch! You aren't married! I'll teach you to lie to me!"

Just as Billy raises his hand to slap her again, Quinn took his gun and pressed it hard into the back of Billy's head.

"I wouldn't do that if I were you," Quinn said very calmly. "Now, very slowly, move away from her. NOW!"

Billy started to lower his arms to his side, but instead of slowing moving away from her, he quickly moved in back of her, brandishing a knife he had hidden in his long sleeves. He very quickly pulled her head up by her hair and placed the knife at her neck.

"Drop the gun, Taylor, or I'll kill her."

Brown felt another gun at the base of his neck.

"Drop the knife or I'll kill you," said Chief Hansen.

"I know what kind of gun you have boss. I can slice her to the bone before you can cock the trigger, so I think you need to drop the gun," he threatened.

"That may be," said the Chief. "But what about the two high powered rifles aimed at your heart and your head."

Billy looked down at his chest and saw a small

red dot shining on his chest. He moved his hand with the knife away from her neck and dropped it to the ground. Quinn kicked the knife away.

"You want a piece of me before you die, Billy?" asked Quinn. "Cause I sure want a piece of you!"

"Can I boss? Let me show him how a real man fights! I've been wanting to kick your ass ever since you have entered the picture!"

Quinn backed himself up to the middle of the barn floor. He gave Joe his rifle and his two Smith and Wesson 9 mm guns and took his shirt off. Billy was standing in the middle of the barn floor and had removed his shirt as well. They started circling each other.

"NO, QUINN, DON'T DO IT, HE ISN'T WORTH IT! PLEASE!" Annie yelled.

Jax saw Annie's clothes and shoes lying near the makeshift bed in the barn. He grabbed them and handed them to Annie as Chief Hansen unlocked the handcuffs. She threw her pants and shirt on in just a few seconds. After she slipped her shoes on, she started to run towards Quinn.

Jax grabbed her arm. "Trust your husband, Annie. He doesn't need distracted right now. He needs to do this."

When Annie looked up at Jax, she knew with such clarity that he was right.

Quinn was about four inches taller than his opponent and he looked far more muscular. Even

Quinn's hands were huge. His fists alone could be used as a weapon of destruction!

Both men had their fists in the air ready to strike each other. Billy struck at Quinn but missed; however, Quinn planted his fist square on Billy's nose causing him to stagger back.

"You broke my nose, asshole! I'm going to kill you!" and he lunged at Quinn. He had his hands around Quinn's neck, choking him.

Quinn brought both of his arms under Billy's and stretched his arms away from his neck. Then he hit him in the side of the head with one fist and in the eye with his other fist. Quinn made another fist and hit him in his nose again.

Copious amounts of blood were bleeding from Billy's nose. "I'll kill you, Taylor!"

"Yeah, you keep saying that!"

Billy pulled up his pants leg and pulled out a large knife. He started waving it from side to side. "I'm going to carve you up real good!" he growled with wicked intent.

"Quinn!" yelled Joe as he threw him an even bigger knife.

"Now, lets see who carves who!" Quinn sneered.

Billy lunged at Quinn again forcing him to fall near the ground where Annie was standing.

"GET HER OUTTA HERE, JAX!"

Jax grabbed her by the arm to lead her out, but she pulled away from him. "I'M NOT LEAVING MY HUSBAND!" Jax leaned down and picked her up. "PUT ME DOWN, JAX! PUT ME DOWN!" she screamed as she hit him with her fists.

"Quit fighting me, Annie!" He ordered as he tightened his grip on her. "I'll put you down, but if you move an inch, we will wait in the truck until it's over! Do I make myself clear?"

"But he is my husband, Jax," she said with tears in her eyes.

"Yes he is, but he is my best friend and he wants you safe." He has a very stern look on his face. "We've seen first hand what losing a woman did to him before with Kayla. We aren't letting him go through that again. He loves you, Annie. Do we have a deal?"

After she nodded her head in agreement, he put her feet back down on the ground. She put her head into his chest and sobbed hard. They wait outside the barn for five minutes, then it's ten minutes and they hear two gunshots. She pushed away from Jax so hard and so fast that she nearly knocked him off balance. She ran into the barn screaming Quinn's name with Jax right behind her.

When they got to the middle of the barn where they had been fighting, they saw Chief Hansen holding a gun pointed at Billy Brown with a gunshot to his forehead, lying motionless on the ground. Joe was still pointing his gun after shooting the knife from Billy's hand. Quinn was standing next to Chief Hansen, holding his right side. He had been stabbed during the fight.

Jax exited the barn quickly. He had noticed Quinn had a knife wound to his lower right side so, he ran back to get Quinn's truck. If the stab wound was as bad as he thought it could be, he wanted to get him to the hospital as quickly as possible.

"Quinn!" Annie yelled as she ran to him and jumped up into his arms. She immediately started kissing him. She kissed his eyes, his forehead, his nose, his cheeks, on his mouth, in his mouth. He wrapped his arms around her waist and he dropped to his knees, rolling onto the ground. "Oh, Quinn, I thought I had lost you!"

"Oh, baby, are you all right?" he said as he held her face with his bloody hands.

"I'm fine, baby, but you're hurt. You're bleeding."

Joe came running over to Quinn. "Annie, let me see his wound."

Joe examined his wound. "Well, old buddy, I think we need to get you to the hospital. I think this one is going to need some stitches."

"Don't worry, baby, it's nothing serious." He didn't want Annie to worry.

"Annie, would you get me Quinn's shirt? I need to make a bandage."

Annie ran for his shirt and brought it back to Joe. He cut his shirt into several pieces with his knife, folded them, and placed them on his side. "Hold this on your wound, Quinn and apply pressure as hard as you can," ordered Joe.

Just then, Jax pulled Quinn's 4x4 truck into the barn. He grabbed the blanket he had seen on the makeshift bed and quickly laid it across the back seat of the cab in his truck.

"Come, we need to get you to the hospital."

"Chief, can you do without us now?"

"Is it bad?" he asked.

"I don't know. He's losing a lot of blood."

"I've called for an a ambulance. You sure you don't want to wait?"

"No, we aren't waiting. He needs to get to the hospital now!" shouted Annie.

Chief Hansen saw the state trooper that helped escort Quinn and his friends to the barn. "This man needs to get to the hospital fast. They don't want to wait for the paramedics. Would you lead them again?"

"Which hospital, sir?"

"Grant Medical Center." Annie shouted.

Joe and Annie helped Quinn to his feet. The state trooper walked over and spoke with Jax and then ran to his cruiser.

Jax and Joe lifted Quinn into the back seat of his truck.

"Joe, how serious is this?" questioned Annie in a fearful tone.

"Well, he needs to have as much pressure applied to his wound as possible. I don't think you are strong enough. I think you should ride in the front seat, while I ride in the back."

"Okay," she said, "but you will have to lift me into the truck."

"Quinn has always liked big trucks," he said with a smirk. He opened up the door, then picked her up and sat her down on the seat. "Buckle up and close your eyes," he ordered. "This will be a very fast ride."

Jax climbed into the drivers seat and started the engine. He turned the emergency flashers on and backed out of the barn. He had to drive a little slower on the old dirt road leading to Rt. 37. Once he and the trooper he was following turned onto Rt. 37, they floored it.

Annie noticed Quinn was having pain and was starting to look a little pale. She asked for Joe's cell phone and called Grant Hospital and asked for Dr. Keith Michaels. He had treated Quinn when he had been stabbed in the neck with a syringe filled with Ketamine. She wondered if Billy or Tony was responsible for that incident.

"Hello, Dr. Michaels, this is Annie Taylor, Quinn's wife. We have an emergency. Quinn has been stabbed in his lower right side and he is bleeding badly. We are about 20-25 minutes away. Can you treat him?"

"Yes, but why haven't we received an ambulance call on him?"

"We are in our truck. It would have taken too long to get an ambulance."

"Where are you now?" asked the concerned doctor.

"We are on Rt. 37 heading towards I-70."

"Are you applying pressure to his wound?"

"Yes, sir."

"Good, I'll have everything ready."

"Thank you, Dr. Michaels," she said and she hung up the phone.

Annie couldn't hold his hand like she so desperately wanted to, so she reached between the front seats and grabbed his leg. She said a prayer out loud. *"Dear Lord in Heaven, Please be with Quinn today. Please keep him alive so that we can have a beautiful married life together. Please keep him alive so that his best friends can continue to harass him and love him as I do. Please bless all drivers right now and keep them out of harms way. In the Lord's name I pray, Amen."*

She heard Joe and Jax say "Amen." Quinn whispered an Amen and then said, as he looked at his wife, "I Love You." Tears streamed down her face. She was so worried about her husband. She used Joe's cell phone again and called his Dad.

"Hello, this is Reginald Taylor."

"Reggie, it's Annie. Can you meet us at Grant Medical Center right away? Quinn has been stabbed."

"How? When?"

"We are about ten minutes out. I'll explain when we get there."

CHAPTER 35

JAX LEFT THE TRUCK RUNNING in front of the emergency room entrance while he ran in to get the nurses. They lifted Quinn down onto the gurney and ran back into the hospital. Jax jumped back into the truck to park the vehicle.

"Take him to Trauma Room 2," yelled a nurse. "Is this Quinn Taylor?" the nurse asked.

"Yes, ma'am. He is my husband. This is Joe, his brother. He has another brother coming in a minute. We are expecting his father, Reggie, anytime."

"Wait out here, please. The doctor needs to do their initial work up."

Reginald Taylor ran into the emergency room and asked for directions to his son. He was directed down the hall and to the left towards the trauma unit.

"Annie?" he yelled and ran towards his daughter-in-law.

"Oh, Reggie!" and she started crying as she gave him a hug.

"How's my son?" he asked, taking a deep breathe.

"We just got here. They just took him into room 2 and asked us to wait while the doctors do their examination."

"What happened?"

"While you and Quinn where in your meeting today, I got a call from Pete Sanford telling me he had important information for us. So, I went to get it. When I went back to my car, Detective Billy Brown kidnapped me and took me to an old barn somewhere off Rt. 37."

"Were you wearing your tracking devices?"

"Yes, that's how they found me. Reggie," she paused, "Detective Brown, and my friend, Tony O'Hara, were the two men who raped all of those girls that looked like me. I think they were going to do that to me today."

Dr. Michaels stepped out of the trauma room that Quinn was in. "Reggie," said Dr. Michaels as he grabbed his hand for a firm handshake. "Mrs. Taylor, we need to move Quinn to the operating room. It's nothing to serious, but when he was stabbed, we think the knife cut into his appendix area. We won't know until we get in there and take a look."

"It looks like when he was stabbed, his attacker also twisted the knife. That is why he is bleeding a little heavier."

Annie covered her mouth with her hand and tears rolled down her cheeks. The thought of him being hurt like that was unbearable to think about.

"He's going to be all right, Mrs. Taylor. This is a relatively simple procedure. It shouldn't take too long. He will need to stay a day or two."

"I'm sure he isn't going to like that!" said his father.

"Do we need to provide him with security like last time?" Dr. Michaels asked.

"Not unless it is to keep the paparazzi out," replied Jax.

"Oh?" said the doctor.

"Let's just say the two rapists plaguing Columbus are permanently off the streets forever!" replied Joe with a grin.

Dr. Michaels pulled his cell phone out of his pocket and called ICU. "This is Dr. Michaels. Please make a room ready for Quinn Taylor. I'll send the family up shortly." He looked at Quinn's family and smiled. "We can keep the paparazzi out of ICU!"

A nurse walked over to Annie with a clipboard in her hand.

"Mrs. Taylor, I need for you to sign this, giving us permission for the doctors to operate." Annie signed the necessary paperwork.

"Can we see him?"

"Just for a moment, Mrs. Taylor. They are here, ready to transport him to OR. We have given him something for pain so he may not respond."

They walked into the room to see him. Before he was transferred to the OR, Reggie planted a kiss on his son's forehead. Joe and Jax touched his arms and Annie kissed him on his lips. "I love you, baby. I'll be waiting right here for you."

"Mrs. Taylor, do you know where the waiting room is for surgery?"

"I know where it is," said Reggie.

"Good," replied the nurse. "You can wait there. When the surgery is over, the doctor will come out and talk to all of you."

"Thank you, ma'am."

Two male nurses dressed in green scrubs wheeled Quinn down the hallway towards the operating room doors.

When they arrived in the waiting room area, several people were already in there waiting on reports on their friends or family member who was having surgery at that time. There was a television on the wall with the name of the person having surgery. It gave a report on their status whether it was pre-op, in surgery, or post op recovery room. Quinn's name popped up on the screen for pre-op.

Joe and Annie went to the restrooms to wash the dried blood from their hands, while Reggie found them a table. Being the coffee drinker that Jax was, he saw the coffeemaker, poured four cups of coffee and took them back to the table.

"So, what happened next, Jax?"

"Right after we got to the barn, we heard a gun shot and Annie screaming. We thought he had killed Annie. I was afraid Quinn was going to lose it, but he remained very calm."

Joe and Annie have returned from the restrooms and sat down at the table.

"Detective Brown had shot Tony O'Hara in the back."

"Actually, Reggie," Annie informed, "the detective shot at me intending on killing me, and Tony stepped into the path of the bullet, saving me. I still can't believe he did that."

"So, did Quinn kill Brown?" asked Reggie?

"No," replied Joe. "Quinn wanted a piece of him badly and Chief Hansen knew it. The Chief let Brown fight Quinn. Our boy was beating the living shit out of Brown. Then Brown lunged forward. That's when he stabbed Quinn."

"Quinn wrestled him to the ground, sat down on top of him, and began beating him about the face with his fists. When Brown appeared to be out cold, Quinn got off of him and was walking towards Chief Hansen. That's when Brown got his second wind, grabbed his knife and was about to throw it into Quinn's back. I shot my gun into Brown's hand knocking the knife out, and the Chief fired at the same time, putting one in his forehead."

"Thank God, you guys were there today and thank you for being his best friends. You are my best friend, too, you know!" and she squeezed both their hands.

When Quinn was taken to recovery, Dr. Michaels came to give the family a report on his progress.

"Mrs. Taylor, Reggie, gentlemen. It went as I expected it would. The stabbing had damaged his appendix; so, we removed it, but there was no other real damage. We repaired the muscle area where his attacker twisted the knife, but other than that, everything looks good. He's going to be sore for a while."

"When will we be able to see him?" inquired Annie.

"He is in the recovery room right now. When he comes to, we'll transport him to ICU. He will be in room 14. You are more than welcome to wait for him there. I'm sure the nurses will have questions to ask you for his admission."

"Thank you, Dr. Michaels," said Reggie.

Annie gave him a hug. "Thank you, again, Dr. Michaels."

Two nurses brought Quinn to his room an hour later. He was still groggy, but that was to be expected. His father was the first person he saw in the room.

"Where am I?" he asked.

"You are in the Intensive Care Unit at Grant Medical Center. How are you feeling, son?"

"Like someone stabbed me again a second time," Quinn said with a smirk. "Where's Annie?"

"One of the nurses brought her in some scrubs so that she could get out of her bloody clothes. She's in the restroom changing right now."

"Am I so bad that they had to put me in ICU?"

"No, we figured the paparazzi would be wanting to take pictures of you and plaster them all over the newspaper. We didn't figure you would be up for that," replied Joe. He smiled and shook his hand. "Glad to see you're still with us, QT."

"Me, too," he said softly as he closed his eyes and drifted back to sleep.

Annie walked back into his room looking better than she did before. She walked over to Quinn's bed and kissed him gently on his cheek and interlocked her fingers with his. His fingers immediately tightened around hers. He woke up for a moment and smiled at her. "I love you, baby," she told him as she ran her other hand through his lush dark hair, "I'm right here."

He mouthed the words "I love you," and he closed his eyes again, drifting back to sleep.

A nurse walked in to check his vital signs and explained everything to Mrs. Taylor. He was hooked up to a monitor that automatically takes his blood pressure every 15 minutes. There is a pulse ox on his left forefinger. Hanging from an IV pole, were four bags. There was a bag of plasma to help restore the blood he lost, a bag of saline to prevent dehydration, an antibiotic of some kind to prevent infection and a small bag of pain medication that was being dispersed through a pain pump. Annie asked her to remove the pain pump.

"For God's sake, Annie, why don't you want my son to have pain meds after what he has done for you?" asked Reggie. He ran his hands through his hair, looking very bewildered and pissed at her.

"Reggie, I want him to have pain meds, too, but I also want to honor my husband's wishes. You know he is very anti-pain meds unless it is for a migraine. In my opinion, the pain pump is not what he needs. I know he won't use it. What I am suggesting is the nurse give him a pain shot now through his IV while he is out of it. I would much rather he rest and be comfortable and as pain free as possible. When he awakens, he can be the judge on whether or not he needs something for pain, but until then, I want him to have the full effect of a pain shot."

"All right, I'll agree with that," said Reggie. He wrapped his arms around her shoulders. "I'm sorry I snapped at you. I just want what is best for my son."

"So do I, Reggie, so do I," she said as tears filled her eyes. "You know he is going to be very pissed at me for wanting him to have pain medication."

"Yes, he probably will be."

She gave a little giggle and stated, "Well, he

will just have to add it to a long list of things that I am sure he is mad at me for."

They watched as the nurse removed his pain pump and finished checking all of his vital signs and his catheter bag. When she had finished, she left.

"I wonder if I should call Gloria," the elder Taylor said out loud.

"Do you think Quinn would object to her being here?" asked Annie.

"I don't know. Probably." He started pacing the floor, walking back and forth.

"You could wait until he wakes up and ask him," she suggested.

"Would it bother you if she came?"

"Yes, it would, but only because Quinn would be a little tense knowing that she and I can't seem to get along. If he were well, it would be different. And, if she found out that she is no longer on any of your accounts and I am, I think she would be coming after me. Quinn is not up for that right now."

He grabbed his chin with his thumb and forefinger and studied Annie. "Hmm. I think you're right. Quinn doesn't need that right now. He's not in any immediate danger, so I don't think I will call her."

"Thank you, Reggie."

Just then his nurse entered his room. She was carrying two syringes. "Mrs. Taylor, since Mr.

Taylor doesn't seem to be experiencing pain at the moment, Dr. Michaels has ordered him a sedative and a mild pain medication. He said if he needs something stronger and was willing to take it; he would prescribe it for him. This should make him sleep through the night, if you want to go home and get some rest." She injected it into his IV.

"No thank you, ma'am, I'll be staying here tonight with my husband."

"Very well, ma'am. Just let us know if you need anything," and she left the room.

Moments later, there was a soft knock on the door. Chief Hansen opened the door. "May I come in?" he asked.

Annie very carefully removed her hand from Quinn's. She walked over and gave him a big hug. "Thank you so much for saving Quinn today."

"Glad I could help. How is he doing?"

"He's going to be all right, I think. When Brown stabbed him, he cut into his appendix, so the surgeons took it out and patched him up. By the way, Chief Hansen, this is my father-in-law, Reginald Taylor. Reggie, this is Chief Hansen. He shot and killed Billy Brown."

"Yes, I remember you, Tim. I can't thank you enough for saving Quinn today," he said as they shook hands.

"I need to ask you and Quinn some questions," said the Police Chief.

"Well, if you want to ask Quinn, you'll have

to wait until tomorrow, but I can probably answer most of the questions you have. Please have a seat."

"First of all, I would like to know how you figured out it was Billy Brown. I mean, we have been working on this case for a couple of years and couldn't find the first piece of evidence," asked the Chief.

"We hired a private investigator and I asked him to investigate several people, including Brown and Evans. Brown gave me the creeps and he looked so familiar and yet I could not place him," she said.

Annie told him everything Pete Sanford had found out: how she had gone to the same school as Brown and his infatuation with her as a seventh grader. She told him of their trip to London and how their room had been broken into, and how Quinn found a tracking device in her cell phone. She told him she interviewed one of the rape victims and relayed what Beatrice Smith had told them. Then she told him that Jax had developed a tracking device for her at Quinn's request and the events that took place when she was kidnapped.

"You know, Mrs. Taylor, Columbus, Ohio, owes you, Quinn, and your friends a huge debt of gratitude for figuring out who the rapists were. I'm just sorry your husband was hurt in the process."

"Me, too, but I'm glad you were there to save him. I'm just sorry it was one of your men."

"Don't worry about that. I didn't like the bastard anyway. He got what he deserved." He paused.

"Mrs. Taylor, I need to know if you want to file charges on David Morgan. I can't hold him much longer without a reason."

"Do you have him in custody?" she asked.

"Yes, we do. Quinn said he appeared at your hotel yesterday. He has a broken jaw and a black eye from your husband. Morgan wants to file charges against Quinn for brute force. The way I see it, he fell. I doubt we can prove attempted rape, so would you like to file charges for excessive stalking?"

She took her time and looked at Reggie and then at Chief Hansen. She walked over to Quinn, who was lying peacefully in his bed. She held his hand. Not only was Quinn her hero, he was everything to her.

"Yes, I would like to file charges against David Morgan. I am sick of all of this shit. I want to put it all behind me. I want to put him and everything else behind me so that I can live a beautiful life with this man. From what the investigator has told me, I am reasonably sure Morgan is guilty of rape and his father is just as guilty by trying to bale him out of everything. This time it isn't going to happen. Throw the book at him, Chief!"

"Good, do you know when Quinn will be discharged?" he asked.

"I'm sure they will want to get him up to walk in the morning. I don't see him leaving until the day after tomorrow, maybe late tomorrow evening at the earliest."

"I am going to give a press conference tomorrow afternoon. If he leaves after my announcement, call me and we will give him safe passage back to your hotel. You know the press will be all over the place after this."

"Is there anyway of keeping their names out of it?" asked Reggie.

"I can, but you know the paparazzi can find things out a lot faster than us at times."

"Thank you, Chief Hansen," and she gave him another hug.

"I'll be in touch with you soon, Mrs. Taylor, Reggie."

"Reggie, it's getting late. Why don't you go back to the hotel and get some rest."

"I don't know. Do you really think it would be okay if I leave?"

"You're less than ten minutes away. I promise I will call you if there is a problem, which, I don't think there will be. Why don't you go home, get a couple of hours of sleep, and come back early in the morning." She walked to the door and opened it. "Champ, would you drive Mr. Taylor back to the hotel, please. He is really tired."

"Yes, Mrs. Taylor. I'd be happy to."

"Don't let anything happen to our boy, Annie," and he kissed her on the cheek.

"I won't. Just get some rest," and she kissed him on his cheek.

Just as Reggie was leaving, a nurse came in to get Quinn's vital signs. "Everything is looking good and he looks like he is resting good. Can I get you anything, Mrs. Taylor?"

"No, thank you. I think I'm going to try to get some sleep."

Now that she was alone with Quinn, she took three blankets from the small closet in his room. She placed one on Quinn, kissed him gently on his lips and scooted a chair as close to his bed as possible. She threw one blanket over her legs, and then placed the other blanket around her shoulders. She laid her head on the side of his bed, grabbed ahold of his hand and fell asleep.

———◆———

Something had awakened her. Quinn's hand was rubbing her head very gently. She raised her head to look at him.

"I didn't mean to wake you, baby."

"I'm glad you did. How are you feeling?"

"Like I have slept for a week."

"Are you in any pain?"

"No, no pain," and he smiled at her. "You know, I'm very mad at you," he said softly.

"Yeah, I figured you would be, but I'm very mad at you, too," she replied very softly.

He looked at her with sad eyes. "Get in bed with me, Annie."

"I can't this time, baby. You've had surgery. I don't want to hurt you."

"Baby, you're my medicine. I need to hold you. Get in bed with me," he ordered. He threw back the covers on the left side of his hospital bed.

Tears were filling her eyes. She knew she shouldn't, but she wanted to hold her husband as much as he wanted to hold her. She very gently eased herself onto his bed. She laid her head on his shoulder and he wrapped his arms around her as tight as he could. She felt a tear fall from his cheek onto her forehead.

"Oh God... baby, it feels... it feels so good to hold you!" he declared with his voice cracking. "I didn't know what to think after Pete Sanford called me and said you were missing. He said your car door was open and your purse was lying on the ground by the car, but you were nowhere to be found. That's when he told me about Brown and O'Hara and how you figured they were the rapists. I thought... I thought... I was so worried. I remembered the words you told me... think with your head and not your heart... those words grounded me, baby. You grounded me. When we heard you scream, I knew right then I wanted to kill them both with my bare hands. When I saw Tony lying on the ground dead, and you tied up and in nothing but your underwear, I almost shot

Brown in the head right then. I didn't want you to see that ugly part of me. Oh God, Annie, I just love you so much!"

Annie started crying. "Oh, Quinn, there is nothing ugly about you! You came for me! You saved me! I will always, always love you, baby. I am so glad you are my husband. I am never going to let you go!" She scooted up into the bed a little further so she could reach his lips.

"Careful, baby. My lip is swollen."

"Yes, and your eye is swollen some and turning black now."

"See, I told you I was ugly."

She placed her hand on his cheek. "You will always be beautiful to me, Quinn, and you will always have my heart."

He reached for Annie's left hand and rubbed her wedding rings, over and over. "Annie, will you marry me, again?"

"But, we're already married, baby. Why do you want to do this again?"

"Well, I'm not sure, but I have a feeling the preacher that Tony got for me was not a real preacher and the second marriage wasn't very romantic, even though, we know it was legit. I would like to see you walk down the isle for real in a big wedding gown like you deserve. I would like to do it properly and take you on a long honeymoon like I promised. We can get married in a church in your hometown or here in Columbus, or we can get married at our home in Indian Creek. I want to buy you a new set of rings, too."

"Why do you want to do all of this, Quinn?"

"Because I want to put all of this behind us. I don't want us to start our new lives with all of these bad memories. It's time to make new ones. So, will you marry me again?"

She reached up to kiss him again. "Yes, I'll marry you!"

CHAPTER 36

Two months later...

ANNIE HAD BEEN WORKING VERY hard on making arrangements for a third wedding. This wedding would take place in less than two weeks in one of the giant ballrooms of the hotel. Quinn had made arrangements for them to honeymoon in Italy, but asked Annie if they could start their honeymoon at their home in Indian Creek.

The house in Indian Creek had very little furnishings. They had done some furniture shopping for their living room and dining room and were waiting for the furniture to arrive. While waiting for the furniture, Annie went into the kitchen to pour two glasses of iced tea. Quinn received a call from his father.

"Hello, Dad," said Quinn.

"Hello, son. We may have a problem at the bank," said his Father.

"Oh? What's going on?" asked Quinn.

"The bank President just called me. Someone

tried to withdraw $100,000,000 from our account. I'm on my way over there right now. The signature on the slip reads Ann Taylor. Would you tell Annie what is going on?"

"Did the bank give her the money?" asked Quinn.

"No, they didn't. They told her there was no way they could get that much cash together on such short notice; but, they would have it ready for her first thing in the morning," replied Reggie.

"Are they sure it was Annie?" asked Quinn. His face was turning red and he started pacing the floor. He was livid!

"Now, son, I know what you are doing. I really and truly don't think our Annie would do this. Just tell her what happened and gage her reaction. Don't jump to conclusions just yet. Be calm, Quinn," ordered his Father. "I'm on my way to the bank now and I am going to look at the video tapes of this woman." Quinn disconnected his call from his father.

Annie walked into the living area where Quinn was standing. She reached her hand out to give him his glass of iced tea. He looked at her with a scowl on his face and dialed a number into his cell phone.

"Hello, this is Quinn Taylor. My wife and I purchased some furniture yesterday and I would like to cancel the order. Please see if you can track down your deliverymen and tell them not to deliver. Thank you." Quinn put his cell phone in his pocket and started pacing the floor.

"Quinn, what just happened? What's wrong?" asked Annie.

Quinn just glared at her. He knows his father told him not to jump to conclusions just yet, but he couldn't help it. They had a signed receipt with her signature on it. It read Ann Taylor.

"Honey, you're scaring me. What's wrong?" she asked again.

Quinn walked over to the entrance door and set the alarm. "Come on, we are leaving. NOW!" he spoke harshly.

Annie ran to the kitchen and poured the ice tea into the sink, grabbed her purse and followed Quinn to their car.

"Quinn, please tell me why you are so upset!" she demanded. He still wouldn't say anything to her.

When they got onto I-270 W, he stepped down onto the gas and started speeding, going at speeds of 80 to 100 mph.

"Quinn, you're scaring me! What do you think I have done? Please, Quinn, slow down!" she screamed. "I haven't done anything!"

Quinn stared straight ahead, refusing to look at his wife, refusing to speak to his wife.

After he pulled the car into the hotel garage, Quinn got out of his car, walked to the driver's side, opened the door and pulled Annie out by her arm.

"Quinn, stop! You're hurting me!" she cried. "What on earth do you think I have done?"

"Just be thankful that is all I am doing to you!" he growled. "I want you to go upstairs and pack all of your belongings. I want your ass out of here and out of my life!"

Annie's mouth flew open. She couldn't believe what she was hearing. Tears started flowing down her cheeks.

Quinn started walking away from her, then stopped, turned around and walked back. "I really thought you were different from all the other women I had ever met. My mother had it right. She saw the signs and she was the only one who recognized them! I should have listened to her!"

"Quinn, I promise, I haven't done anything!" she cried.

"Don't you dare cry in front of me!" he started to walk away, but stopped. He turned around. "Why, Annie? Why would you steal from me? I would have given you everything I owned if you had just asked me for the money! I love you. Hell, Annie, I will love you until the day I die, but I will not stay married to someone I can't trust. I want you gone within the hour. Leave me an address where you can be reached. I will have my attorney get in touch with you. You can keep the money you asked for at the bank. It will be ready for you in the morning, but you will not get another dime!" he choked out with gritted teeth as he walked out of the garage.

"Quinn, please!" she cried! "Oh my God! Oh my God!" and she started crying harder. She walked to their private elevator and punched the key code for their penthouse.

"I can't believe this is happening!" She laid down on her bed and screamed deep, cathartic cries. She cried so hard, her chest hurt and she felt her blood pressure rising. She felt like her head was about to explode. This must be what it feels like to have a broken heart, she thought. "Oh, Quinn, why are you doing this!"

She went into the kitchen to get a drink of water. "What should I do?" she said out loud. "What made him think I stole his money? Think Annie, think!" she told herself. "I know. I'll call Reggie. Maybe he knows something." She called Reggie, but there was no answer. She left him a voice mail to call her as soon as possible.

"That's odd, he always answers his phone. Maybe Reggie thinks I'm guilty, too. Maybe that is why he didn't answer my call." She cried.

Annie went into their bedroom and grabbed a suitcase. She filled it only with the clothes that she had purchased out of her own money. She left behind all of the clothes, jewelry, (including the tracking jewelry), shoes, and trinkets that Quinn had bought her.

She went into his study and opened his safe. She removed the title to her car, her college diplomas, her birth certificate, insurance information, her banking books, bankcards, and credit cards, anything that pertained to only her before she married Quinn. She also took the keys to her safe deposit box where she kept all of the songs she had written over the past six years. Next, she grabbed a sheet of copy paper and a pen and took it into the kitchen to write a note.

> *"My Dearest Quinn,*
> *I can't believe this is happening. I can't believe you would not listen to me, which says volumes about your trust in me. I would never take your money. I DID NOT TAKE YOUR MONEY, NOR DID I GO TO THE BANK! In fact, I have yet to spend the first dime of our, NO, your money. I thought you knew me better than that! I am only taking the clothes and jewelry that I personally paid for before I met you. Here are my wedding rings and my cell phone. Get your divorce. I will not fight you on it. You have made it very clear you don't want to see me again, so please don't come looking for me. You will never find me. Quinn, I will always love you with all my heart. Annie"*

She left the note on the kitchen counter and placed her keys and cell phone next to the note for Quinn to find. She got into her purse and removed a savings account book; check book, debit card, and credit cards that Quinn had set up for her using the Taylor name. She placed them by her cell phone. She cried as she removed her wedding rings. She kissed her rings and laid them on the note under her signature.

Fortunately for Annie, she had saved her own money wisely. She had written and sold several songs over the past 3 years and it netted her just over $200,000. If she watched what she spends, she could get by until she could find her a good paying job. She also had her own car. It was a 2015 four-wheel drive Chevy Blazer, a graduation present from her parents after graduating from Columbus Music Academy, and receiving two masters and a PhD in Music Education. They were very proud of their daughter. She was grateful her car tags would not need to be renewed for another seven months, as she did not want Quinn to find her. She knew that as soon as he realized he had jumped to the wrong conclusion, he would have Jax looking for her. If he could not trust her now, there was no sense in staying married to him. She grabbed her purse, an 8 x 10 framed picture of her and Quinn, her overnight bag with all of her toiletries, her suitcase, her violin case, and a coat. Tears filled her eyes as she looked around the penthouse one last time. She left.

CHAPTER 37

I T WAS 4 P.M. WHEN Reggie arrived at the penthouse. It was very quiet when he walked in. The curtains had been shut and the lights were off.

"Quinn, Annie?" he yelled. "Are you here?" When no one answered him, he turned some lights on and started looking around. When he walked into the kitchen, he found the note with Annie's wedding rings and her cell phone lying on the kitchen counter. He began to read it.

"Well, fuck! What has that boy done?" When Quinn didn't answer his cell phone, Reggie called Joe at La Seals.

"Hello," said Joe as he walked away from Quinn.

"Joe, is that idiot son of mine there?" asked Reggie.

"Yes, he is, Reggie, and he isn't in a good way right now. Jax and I have been watching over him. I've been trying to reach Annie, but she isn't answering her phone. Can you tell me what is going on?"

"Is there anyway you and Jax can get his ass

back to the penthouse? If you can't, then I will be showing my ass in your establishment," stated Reggie. "I'll tell you all about it when you get here."

"We'll do the best we can," said Joe.

It took approximately 15 minutes for Joe and Jax to walk Quinn across the street to his hotel and ride up the elevator to the penthouse. Quinn looked like he was ready to pass out from too much booze.

When they walked into the penthouse, his dad was standing near the door. He walked over to his son and glared at him with deep, penetrating pissed eyes! "Of all the stupid, stupid things you have done in your life, this is, without a doubt, the most idiotic thing you have ever done, Quinnten Taylor! I can't believe you kicked out the best woman you have ever had in your life!"

"No, Daddd, Mommmm was rrright!" Quinn's words were slurring. "Mommm rec-recognizzzed it firssst, and I-I-I refused to see it! AnAnAnnie couldn't beee trusssted, Daddd. She is a go-goold digger just like Mommm said!"

Reggie was so pissed at his son. He was only supposed to tell Annie what was going on, not accuse her of trying to take their money. All of a sudden, Reggie made a tight fist and hit his son in the jaw as hard as he could. Quinn had a stunned look on his face and fell flat, face first onto the floor. He was out cold!

"Trust me son, that hurt me more than it did you!" Reggie said as he shook his hand in the air.

Joe and Jax looked at one another and made a move to go over to their friend.

"Stop right where you are boys! Let him be. He deserves this and a lot more!" said the elder Taylor.

"Can you tell us what happened?" asked Joe.

"You mean, he didn't tell you?" questioned Reggie.

"No, he didn't. We knew it was something bad, probably related to Annie, but he refused to speak to us," replied Joe.

"Yeah, he just came into the club, grabbed two bottles of Crown and four glasses. We knew it was bad when he filled the glasses and started downing them, one after the other. We got him to slow down, but he wouldn't tell us what was going on," stated Jax.

"So, what happened?" asked Joe.

Reggie stooped down and placed a couple of fingers on Quinn's jugular to make sure he was still alive. As pissed off as he was at his son, he didn't want him dead. When he felt the pulse in his neck was still beating, Reggie became more relaxed and stood up. "Have a seat boys," Reggie demanded, "this is going to be a long night."

After they all sat down, Reggie started talking. "Someone came into the bank this morning and tried to withdraw $100 million from our account. They signed Annie's name. I told Quinn to tell

Annie about it, while I went to the bank to look at the bank videos. Instead, my dear son, accused his wife of trying to take the money and he kicked her out."

"Oh, shit, not again!" said Jax. "So, did you find out who it was?"

"Yes, I most certainly did. Let's just say, boys, I will definitely need your help. He isn't going to like what I have to tell him when he is sober enough to listen."

"So, who was it?" asked Jax.

Reggie hung his head. He was ashamed of what he had to tell them. "It was his mother."

"What???" Joe and Jax said together. "Are you sure?" asked Joe.

"Oh, I'm positive, all right. It was most definitely Gloria."

"Oh my God!" Joe said as he pulled out his cell phone. "Champ, this is Joe. I won't be back this evening. I need for you to be in charge of closing La Seals tonight. Can you do that for me?" Joe paused. "Thanks, Champ." Next, Joe called his wife.

"Cindy, have you heard anything from Annie today?" inquired Joe.

"No, I haven't spoken to Annie for a couple of days. Why?" she asked.

"Quinn kicked Annie to the curb. It's a long story. I'll tell you about it when I get home, but for now, I'm going to stay at the penthouse with Quinn, his father and Jax."

"Would you like for me to come over, too?" she asked.

"No, that's not necessary, but if she should happen to call, would you tell her to call me?"

"Certainly."

"Call me if you need anything. I love you, baby," said Joe.

"Love you, too! Tell Quinn I'll be thinking of him," replied Cindy. "Bye."

About two hours or so later, Quinn started coming around. He slowly got up onto his knees and grabbed his head. "Dad, did you hit me?"

"Yes, I most certainly did and if you don't watch your mouth, I'll kick your teeth down your throat!" his father said very harshly.

"Why? I didn't do anything!"

"Here, drink this and then I want you to drink some coffee. You're going to need it with what your Dad has to tell you," demanded Joe as he handed Quinn a bottle of water.

Quinn downed the bottle of water and sat down at the kitchen table with the other men. Reggie placed a large cup of black coffee down in front of Quinn and demanded he drink it. Reggie sat down next to his son.

"Are you feeling better?" asked his father.

"I'm still a little fuzzy," replied Quinn as he took a drink of his coffee.

"Why did you accuse Annie of trying to take our money?" asked his father.

"Well, you said to talk to her and…"

"Did you talk to her or did you accuse her?" interrupted Reggie.

"What are you telling me, Dad? Annie didn't try to take our money?" asked Quinn.

"No, Quinn. She didn't."

Quinn made a fist and hit it hard on the table. "Fuck! Why did I do that? Damn it to hell!" He ran his hands through his hair and placed his head into his hands. He took a deep breath. "Then, who was it?" asked Quinn.

Reggie didn't have the heart to tell him that once again his mother had betrayed them. When Reggie didn't respond right away, Quinn looked at his father and asked, "Was it Mom?"

Reggie hung his head. "I'm sorry, son."

"Are you sure?"

"Yes, I'm positive," replied Reggie.

"Well, fuck. Why does she hate us so damn much and why does she hate Annie so much?" He paused. "Is Annie still here? I've got to find her. I've got to make this right! I got to apologize to her!" He started to get up from the table to look for her.

Reggie grabbed his son's arm. "No, son. It's too late. She left this for you." Reggie laid before Quinn all of her credit cards, savings account book, check book, and debit card that Quinn had set up for her in the Taylor name. Then he laid down the keys to their house in Indian Creek, keys to her car that Quinn had bought her, and her cell phone. "She also left these, Quinn." He gently laid down her wedding rings and the note she had written.

Quinn gasped. He picked her rings up and kissed them, then read her note. "Oh, God in Heaven, what have I done?" he choked up and tears immediately started filling his eyes. "I've got to find her!" He started to get up from his chair.

Joe and Jax both jumped to their feet and placed their hands on Quinn's shoulders. "You are not driving anywhere tonight, old friend. Not until you are sober!" stated Joe.

"Well, then, you drive, but one way or the other, I am going out of that door to find my wife!" shouted Quinn as he pointed towards the door.

"Well, if you want to find her, we will need to devise a plan," said Jax. "You never go into anything blind. You should know that!"

"Jax, I've got to find my wife!" shouted Quinn.

"I understand that, Quinn, but where is she going to go? We are her only friends! Searching for her in Columbus would be like us trying to find a needle in a haystack!"

All of a sudden, Quinn remembered something Annie had said to him. "Think with your head, not with your heart, Quinn. I don't want anything to happen to you." He remembered just how much her comment had grounded him once before. "I have an idea. I'll be right back," Quinn said, taking Annie's rings, and all the other items she had left behind.

Quinn walked into his study and opened up his safe. He had given Annie the combination because he had trusted her with everything he owned. How sad, he thought, he trusted her with all of this and yet he didn't trust her today. He opened up his safe to see if Annie had taken her old bank books, credit and debit cards that were in her maiden name. He smiled when he realized she had taken only those items. Now, he would have a way of tracking her. He placed her rings and the other items in the safe. Annie was such an honest person and she had never lied to him that he knew of, so why had he doubted her?

What Annie didn't know was he had a notebook in his safe with all of her account numbers written down, in case any of them came up missing. Now he would have a way of tracking her if she tried to use any of these accounts.

He placed the pages of the notebook on his printer and copied them. The last time he had looked at Annie's saving account book, she had somewhere over $200,000. "I hope that is enough for her to live on. I'll keep tabs on this and add more money if I see she is getting low, if we can't find her right away," he thought. When he had finished copying the information he needed, he returned the notebook to the safe and locked it.

"Jax, I just looked in my safe. Annie took all of her old banking books, bankcards and the like with her maiden name on them. Her maiden name was Marshall. Here are all of the account numbers. Her banking was done at CCNB (Columbus City National Bank). She also had a Visa credit card. Can you track her whereabouts using this information?" asked Quinn.

"You know, Quinn, what you are asking me to do is very illegal," stated Jax.

"Yes, I know it is, but I'm desperate!" said Quinn.

Jax placed his hand on Quinn's shoulder. "I'll do it as long as you don't go off half crazed when we find her."

"Thanks, Jax, I owe you," replied Quinn.

Quinn excused himself, went into his bedroom and shut the door. The first thing he noticed was their bed. He immediately started thinking about all the times he had made love to her. He walked over to the bed and touched the pillow where she laid her head at night; then he touched his shoulder. He could feel her head lying on his shoulder. Tears started rolling down his cheeks and he fell to his knees beside the bed. He folded his hands together, closed his eyes and lowered his head. He began to pray.

"Dear Heavenly Father,
Please forgive me, Lord, I have never been a man who prays. In fact, I don't feel much like a man right

now. I really don't know how to pray, Lord, so I don't know if I'm doing this right. I don't think I have ever prayed until Annie came into my life. I have you to thank for that, God. I never thought you would ever send anyone my way that was as loving, beautiful, kind, smart, sweet and special as she is to me, but Lord, I blew it. I threw it all away, because of my stupidity. I am so flawed, Lord. I know I am a sinner and I know I really and truly don't deserve her, but I really, really need her. Please, Lord, forgive me for not being the proper husband she so deserves. I hate myself so much right now. Please, God, please help me make this right. Please help me find Annie. Please find it in your heart to give me a small miracle in finding my wife. I know I will have a lot of making up to do, but that's okay, as long as I can win her heart back. Lord, I love her so much and really need her. Please, please, help me, Lord, and above all, please watch over her and keep her safe. In the Lord's name I pray," he cried. "Amen."

A SPECIAL THANK YOU

I would like to give you a very special "Thank You" for purchasing and reading my book. This has been a life long dream to write a book and I hope you have enjoyed reading about Quinn and Annie. If you have enjoyed my book, please recommend it to others. You may send me an email at shesmineseries@yahoo.com; or you may follow me on Facebook at www.facebook.com/shesmineseries.

May 2016 be a great year for us all, and I look forward to writing you another book about Quinn and Annie.

Made in the USA
Charleston, SC
16 April 2016